Thirty-Three
and a
Half Shenanigans

A ROSE GARDNER MYSTERY

Other books by Denise Grover Swank:

Rose Gardner Mysteries
(Humorous Southern mysteries)
TWENTY-EIGHT AND A HALF WISHES
TWENTY-NINE AND A HALF REASONS
THIRTY AND A HALF EXCUSES
FALLING TO PIECES (novella)
THIRTY-ONE AND A HALF REGRETS
THIRTY-TWO AND A HALF COMPLICATIONS
PICKING UP THE PIECES (novella)
THIRTY-THREE AND A HALF SHENANIGANS

Chosen Series
(Urban fantasy)
CHOSEN
HUNTED
SACRIFICE
REDEMPTION

On the Otherside Series
(Young adult science fiction/romance)
HERE
THERE

Curse Keepers
(Adult urban fantasy)
THE CURSE KEEPERS
THE CURSE BREAKERS
THE CURSE DEFIERS

New Adult Contemporary Romance
AFTER MATH
REDESIGNED
BUSINESS AS USUAL

Thirty-Three
and a
Half Shenanigans

A ROSE GARDNER MYSTERY

Denise Grover Swank

Copyright 2014 by Denise Grover Swank

Cover art and design: Nathlia Suellen
Developmental Editor: Angela Polidoro
Copy editor: Shannon Page
Proofreaders: Carolina Valedez-Miller and Cynthia L. Moyer
All rights reserved.
ISBN- 978-1500714383

Chapter One

One rule I'd learned was that when things were going well, trouble was bound to roll in and upend the apple barrel.

Bruce Wayne and I stood in the brand spanking new office of RBW Landscaping staring at a dead computer monitor.

"Neither one of them is working," I groaned. "I got duped."

He shook his head with a smirk. "I warned you not buy used computers from Roger Ditmore. His deals are too good to be true for a reason."

I shot him a scowl. "'I told you so's' won't help right now, Bruce Wayne. It might be nearly lunch time, but it's too early in the day for nonsense."

He crawled under one of the two desks in our tiny office. We didn't have a lot of money for splurging, so we'd found one of the wooden desks in a thrift store and made the other from a couple of saw horses and an old door I'd found in the barn behind my house. After jiggling the monitor plug with no luck, he plugged a lamp into the outlet. It didn't turn on either.

"See there," I said smugly, my hands on my hips. "It's not the computers after all."

Just then my head tingled, and my peripheral vision began to fade. I would have groaned in frustration, but I couldn't. I couldn't do anything. I've been plagued with visions since I was a little girl. I always see something in the future of a person who's physically close to me through his or her eyes. They can't be stopped or controlled. They just burst out of nowhere, and once one takes hold, I can only ride it out.

Our office suddenly disappeared, and I was in Henryetta's Piggly Wiggly, looking at the cheap Christmas stockings they had for sale in the seasonal aisle. I grabbed two off a hook and stuck them in my cart. Then, just as quickly, I was back in our office, staring at Bruce Wayne. "You're gonna buy Christmas stockings at Piggly Wiggly."

He scooted out from under the desk, his eyes slightly wider than normal. He was the only person who'd ever guessed my secret without being told. He said I get a strange, vacant look in my eyes when I'm having a vision, and besides, I always seem to know things I shouldn't. But while he was one of a handful of people who knew about my talent, I was sure he'd never get used to me blurting out what I'd seen. Especially when it was about him.

He scratched his head with an embarrassed grimace. "I've been thinkin' about getting some for David and me. We've never decorated before, but this year feels different."

"Don't get them at the Piggly Wiggly. Those things look nasty. I'm pretty sure Violet has some that didn't get destroyed when the store was vandalized. Let me check first."

"Okay," he mumbled, his face turning pink, although I wasn't sure if he was embarrassed by the offer, or because I knew he wanted to decorate for Christmas. "Let me check the fuse box in the back," he said, starting to get up, but my little dog Muffy scampered over to see what the fuss was about and jumped on his chest. He rubbed her head and set her on the floor. "It's an old building, Rose. The wiring's probably bad."

I glared down at him. "Is that supposed to make me feel better?"

He chuckled as he got to his feet. "At least your landlord will be responsible for fixin' it."

"Hmm." I pressed my lips together. "What's worse? Getting ripped off by the guy who sold me the computers or our office burning down?"

"Is that a trick question?" my boyfriend, Mason, asked from behind me. I hadn't even heard the door open.

"Mason!" I shouted as I spun around in surprise, my crankiness slipping away. "What are you doin' here?"

"Well . . ." he drawled as he waved to his leg. "I wanted to show you my good news." He stood in the doorway on his own two feet, without the cane he'd been toting around for two months.

"You're not wearing your leg brace!"

His grin spread. "I'm a free man."

I launched myself at him, wrapping my arms around his neck and planting my mouth on his.

He stumbled backward into the doorframe, then slid his arm around my back and pulled me close. "Be careful, or you're going to re-break my leg," he chuckled.

"God forbid," I murmured against his lips. "I have plans for you later."

His hold tightened as he grinned down at me.

Muffy barked at my feet. "Not now, Muffy."

Bruce Wayne released a fake cough. "I'm gonna go check on that fuse. Come on, Muff." My little dog took off after him without a backward glance, as if she was just as embarrassed as my business partner.

"You do that," I said, staring up into Mason's beaming face. I tugged on his hand and shut the door, just then realizing how cold it was outside. "I'm surprised to see you," I said. "I thought you had a busy schedule today."

"I do." He interlaced his fingers with mine and walked to the center of the room. "But the beauty of having your new office on the same square as the courthouse is that I can drop by when I leave my own office."

I gave him a sly grin. "I confess that might have had something to do with my decision to rent the space."

Bruce Wayne emerged from the back room, Muffy trailing behind him like he was the Pied Piper. "The cheap rent didn't hurt either. Which is why half of our fuse box is dead. Rose, I'm sorry to say it, but this place is falling apart."

"I'm having to cover two locations with the same amount of income," I said, a knot growing in the pit of my stomach. "We couldn't afford anything fancy."

Our new office was anything *but* fancy. The space had gone unused for a couple of years because it was too small to be an effective retail space, but mostly because Mr. Darby was a notoriously bad landlord. But we'd gotten it dirt-cheap, and it was tiny enough for the utilities to be affordable on our miniscule budget. It just needed a little TLC.

We'd painted the walls a soft off-white and scrubbed the dark wood floors. They were still a disaster, but the rustic desks made the old floors work, especially with the wool rug I'd found in the attic at my farmhouse. My other attic finds included a couple of stuffed chairs and an end table that we'd placed in front of the window. In the back of the room, we'd arranged a thrift-store-purchased small wooden kitchen table and four chairs, creating a designated space for client meetings. Photos of our landscaping jobs were framed on the wall. The end result was homey, and it felt comfortable.

"I wasn't complaining," Bruce Wayne said. "You know I don't do fancy. I'm only pointing out that sometimes you get what you pay for. We'll make it work."

I sighed. "I guess we'll have to call Mr. Darby. Again."

"Which means the electricity will get fixed next week," Bruce Wayne grumbled.

"Do you want me to call him?" Mason asked. "Nothing like a call from the Assistant DA to light a fire under someone's ass."

It would have made my life easier, but I was determined to stand on my own two feet when it came to the business. "No."

"Yes!" Bruce Wayne countered. "Sorry, Rose, but I'm outvotin' you on this one. He's a lot more likely to respond to a county official capable of bringin' charges against him for flakin' out."

"We don't even know he's goin' to flake out," I grumbled. "We don't want to tick off our landlord before we even open up shop."

"How about this," Mason said in a good-natured tone. "Why don't you call him now, and if he doesn't have an electrician here by tomorrow to fix it, I'll follow up?"

"Sounds great," Bruce Wayne said before I could say anything.

I shot him a scowl, but he just laughed. What happened to the meek guy I'd hired? He'd become a different man since our meeting with Skeeter Malcolm three weeks ago. No, he'd become a different man since I'd offered to make him my partner.

"I *do* have an official reason for being here," Mason said, lifting the leather satchel off his shoulder and moving to the table in the back. "Your business papers are ready for you to sign."

I glanced at Bruce Wayne, and his smile fell, a serious look taking over his expression.

Mason pulled some papers out of his bag and laid them out on the table. "It's all pretty cut and dry. You are both equal owners of the landscaping business, but Bruce Wayne's ownership doesn't extend to the nursery." He glanced up at me. "As we've discussed, the ownership of the nursery is more complicated now." He didn't sound happy about that, not that I blamed him. The main complication was my ex-boyfriend Joe, who had managed to insinuate himself into a part-ownership. "But basically, there are three entities: an overseer corporation and two sub businesses—the landscaping business and the nursery. Right now, we're dealing with just RBW Landscaping. The overseer corporation will be owned solely by Rose, but all profits will be returned to the two businesses."

Bruce Wayne grabbed a pen off his desk and joined Mason at the table.

"Bruce Wayne." Mason leveled his gaze with my new co-owner. "I know we've already discussed this, but I feel it necessary to reiterate that you have the option to have this contract reviewed by your own attorney before you sign it."

"Mason," Bruce Wayne said slowly, "I didn't put nothing down on this place. I don't have a right to any of this. It's only because of Rose that I'm here at all."

"You have to stop saying that, Bruce Wayne," I protested. "We've been over this a half dozen times."

"I trust you and Mason," he continued. "The day I can't trust either of you is the day I run off and join the militia group livin' in the backwoods. Because if you two cook up some way to trick me, then the world is surely comin' to an end." He swallowed. "And anything I get from this business is way more than expected."

Mason stepped to the side. "Okay. Then let's sit down and have a look." We all sat down around the table, and he went through the contract, explaining everything and telling Bruce Wayne and me where to initial and sign. When we were done, Mason turned to both of us with a grin. "Congratulations. RBW Landscaping is now official. I'll have my secretary get the DBA paperwork sent to the state, and you should be ready for your new grand opening after the first of the year when you have your re-opening open house."

Bruce Wayne stood and turned to me with a solemn expression and held out his hand.

I got up and looked him in the eyes. When I shook his hand, his grip was stronger than expected—another sign that this Bruce Wayne was a new man. "I can't think of anyone else I'd rather have as a business partner, Bruce Wayne. Here's to a great beginning."

His eyes twinkled. "If nothing else, it's bound to be an adventure."

Mason tucked the papers in his bag. "I need to get back to the office, Rose. Tonight we'll talk about signing the paperwork for the nursery."

That dampened my elation. "Okay."

He leaned over and gave me a gentle kiss. "Mom will probably show up around six. Will you be home by then?"

"It shouldn't be a problem. Will *you* be there?"

"That's my goal. The sooner I get back to the office, the sooner I get home."

I gave him a slight push. "Then what are you doing malingering in my office? Get going."

He laughed and stole another kiss. "I love you, Rose Gardner."

"I love you, too. Now get." I gave him another push.

But the front door opened before he could get to it, sending a gust of cold air blowing in from outside. Neely Kate stood in the doorway, her cheeks pink.

"Neely Kate!" I called out in surprise. "How was your doctor's appointment?" My best friend was in the first trimester of her pregnancy and had been fighting terrible morning sickness. She'd promised to call me after her doctor's appointment, but I wasn't all that surprised to see her at my doorstep instead. Bruce Wayne and I had only been in our new office for a week, and I swore she spent just as much time here as she did at the Personal Property Tax department. She hated her job.

"I'm stalling goin' back to work."

Mason grinned at her. "There seems to be a bit of that going around. How are you feeling?"

"A little better. The doctor seems happy."

"Good. You take care of yourself. Rose and I have been worried about you." He started to move past her. "Now I've really gotta go." He glanced back toward me. "I'll see you in a few hours."

He walked out the door, and I watched him through one of the big picture windows as he walked down the sidewalk toward the courthouse. Then I turned my attention to my best friend as she took several steps into the office. "What did the doctor really say?"

Bruce Wayne cringed, blushing again. "I'm gonna go call the landlord about the fuse box." Then he shot into the back room with his phone in his hand, not that I was surprised. Any time Neely Kate brought up her pregnancy, Bruce Wayne disappeared soon after. It was a wonder he hadn't changed his mind about becoming my partner, given how much Neely Kate had come over to talk about her nausea this past week. Muffy, apparently tired of the back and forth, hopped into her dog bed by my desk.

Neely Kate beamed with happiness, even if her face was thinner and paler than usual. "I had an ultrasound today, and now I have an official due date: July 1st. And my grandmother's tea leaves were wrong. I'm not having twins, thank heavens." She scowled at me. "No thanks to you. I've been completely stressed out about it. All you had to do was have a vision, and I would have known."

"I know," I said, sighing. "But you have to admit, the last few times I forced a vision, the results were terrible. I almost had to watch Samantha Jo and Moose have sex, not to mention that I saw Skeeter Malcolm die half a dozen times. What if I saw something bad about you? I wouldn't want to be the one to tell you." We'd had this conversation several times over the last week since her grandmother had seen twins in her tea leaves. "Besides, I'm not sure why you were so worried. You said your granny's tea leaves are wrong more often than they're right."

She gave me an indignant glare. "Technically, Carla Sue's leaves weren't wrong. Her husband *was* having an affair."

"I wouldn't exactly call relations with a sheep an *affair*."

She waved her hand. "Po-tay-to, po-tah-to. He was still sleepin' around on her."

"While he might have been meetin' the sheep at three a.m., I suspect they weren't *sleepin'*."

She made a face. "For someone who has the world by the tail, you seem mighty contradictory." Her lips turned up into a smug grin. "As punishment, I might not tell you who I saw at the doctor's office."

I knew I should ignore her dangled carrot. I had no doubt she was trying to torment me. Still, I couldn't help myself. "Who?"

She waggled her eyebrows in an exaggerated manner. "Maybe you should have a vision and find out."

I put my hands on my hips. "Neely Kate."

Neely Kate unbuttoned her coat and pivoted to take in the small space. "You and Bruce Wayne sure have been busy. This place was a disaster when you got the keys last week."

I gave her a smug grin. "Mason helped too."

"*Mason?*"

I knew why she was surprised. Mason was clueless when it came to anything DIY. "He painted."

"You got your computers, I see."

I waved my hand toward Bruce Wayne's desk. "But they don't work too well without electricity."

Neely Kate scowled. "I warned you about Old Man Darby."

"Well, if he doesn't send an electrician to fix it by tomorrow afternoon, Mason's gonna give him a call. I need electricity by then to get the phone and Wi-Fi installed."

"What's the hurry? You're not even opening for another month."

"You know I'm not one to sit around doin' nothing. And Bruce Wayne says if he's getting paid, he might as well be working." I shrugged. "So here we are."

I sat in one the chairs by the window, and she sat in the brown chair beside me, tucking her feet underneath her. "You're sure making it nice. How much time are you planning on spending in here?"

"I dunno yet. Since we don't have any jobs to work on right now, I splurged and got us professional landscaping software. Bruce Wayne and I can spend our time learning how to use it." I shifted in my chair, getting antsy. "So, are you gonna tell me who you saw at the doctor's office or not?"

Her eyes lit up. "Lucky for you, I don't hold a grudge."

I could have argued that point, but wisely held my tongue.

"Hilary."

"*Joe's* Hilary?"

"Do we know any other?" she asked, incredulous.

"What was she doing there? She has a doctor in Little Rock. In fact, what's she doin' in Henryetta period?"

"She's moved here."

I bolted upright like someone had held a lit candle to my butt. "*What?*"

"I heard she rented one of those restored older homes off the square."

"Why?"

She scrunched her nose. "You know why. She needs to be close to Joe to get him back. Have you talked to him?"

I shook my head. "Not since we had the argument over him going behind my back and hiring a company to clean up the nursery after it was vandalized." It had been more than a week, now that I stopped to think about it.

"Are you still planning to make him an official partner?"

Joe had bailed out the nursery after my sister Violet overextended us financially. She'd missed multiple loan payments, putting us in danger of a foreclosure. It didn't help that a bunch of cash had been stolen from me in the lobby of the Henryetta Bank before I could make a deposit. In any case, we'd been in trouble up to our eyeballs. Violet had gone behind my back to ask Joe—whose family was probably rich enough to own half the state of Arkansas—to loan us the missing payments. Instead, he'd paid off the entire loan. All one hundred thirty-six thousand dollars of it. Everyone kept reminding me that I hadn't entered into any type of legal agreement with him, which meant essentially his money was a gift. But what he really wanted was to be a partner. He'd put so much work into the nursery since the very beginning, I couldn't help but think that getting me back wasn't his only motivation.

"Yes."

Neely Kate groaned, then leaned her head back on the seat. "Rose."

The disappointment in her voice hurt more than I cared to admit. "Mason's fine with it," I said. "Why can't you be?"

She gripped the arms of the chair and leaned forward. "If you think Mason is fine with this, then you're even more deluded than I thought you were." She stood, putting her hands on her hips. "Mason's toleratin' it because he loves you and doesn't want to make waves." She pointed her finger in my face. "You better think long and hard before you give that man any legal rights to the business, Rose Gardner. You can't go undoin' it once it's done. You'll be stuck with him indefinitely."

I paused. "I know."

She shook her head once for emphasis, then gave me a soft smile. "You have a good heart, Rose. But sooner or later, it's gonna bite you in the behind."

I grinned. "Then let's hope it bites me later."

My cell phone started ringing, so I hopped out of my chair to retrieve it off the desk, nearly passing out when I saw the caller's name on the screen.

Skeeter Malcolm.

Chapter Two

Neely Kate stood and took several steps toward me. "Rose, you look as pale as a ghost. Who is it?" She grabbed the phone out of my hand and glanced at the screen. "SM." She gave me an ornery grin. "I didn't know you and Mason were into that. Is he trying to give you some secret code?"

I stared at her for a second until I realized what she was saying. "What? *No!* It stands for Skeeter Malcolm!"

"What's with the initials?"

"I can't very well have the new king of the Fenton County crime world's name on my phone, now can I? Not with an Assistant DA for a boyfriend and a chief deputy sheriff ex."

"Are you gonna answer it?"

I looked at the still-ringing phone. "I'm thinking. . ."

Bruce Wayne emerged from the tiny back room. "Darby promises to have someone here first thing tomorrow morning, but I wouldn't hold my breath." He took one look at the two of us staring at my ringing cell phone and stopped in his tracks. Fear crawled into his eyes. "It's him, isn't it?"

"What should I do, Bruce Wayne?"

He took a deep breath and straightened his shoulders, shrugging off his fear as he moved forward a few steps. "Don't answer it. I'll call his brother Scooter to see if I can find out what he wants."

I nodded, my heart racing. "Okay." Whatever Skeeter wanted couldn't be good. He was never going to leave me alone now that I'd used my visions to save his life . . . even though I'd spent the past couple of weeks pretending otherwise.

The phone stopped ringing, but the three of us continued to stare at it, as if we expected it to sprout legs and attack us.

"Don't you be gettin' mixed up with him again," Neely Kate finally said. "You got off lucky last time. The next time . . ." She didn't finish her sentence. She didn't need to. There were a whole host of scenarios that could play out, not a single one of them good.

After Daniel Crocker, the previous crime lord, had died—at my own hands—his business had been put up for auction by his second-in-command. Before Crocker's death, Skeeter had been the second most powerful criminal in the county, but he didn't like playing second fiddle to anyone. So it wasn't hard to figure out that he wanted Crocker's business something fierce, which is why I'd gone to him with information about the guys who'd been robbing businesses around town—my bank deposit included—to collect money in an effort to outbid him. I'd hoped we would part ways permanently after he returned my money to me. I'd been naïve. Not that Bruce Wayne hadn't warned me.

"Don't worry, Rose," Bruce Wayne said. "We'll figure something out. You're not alone in this."

Neely Kate grabbed my hand and squeezed. "I'm sorry I was so hard on you. But Skeeter Malcolm is bad news."

"I know. I'm trying to get out of it."

Neely Kate's newest ringtone—"Wildflower" by The JaneDear Girls—broke the silence. She dug into her rhinestone-covered purse and pulled out her phone. "Huh. It's my aunt. She never calls." She answered the phone. "Hey, Aunt Thelma."

Bruce Wayne grabbed his coat off the back of his chair. "Rose, I'm gonna run by the hardware store to get more hangers so we can put up the other two pictures."

"Good idea. Thanks, Bruce Wayne."

I caught part of Neely Kate's conversation as he went out the door.

"Nope, I haven't seen her," she said. "Did you check with Billy Jack? Last I heard, she was kinda living with him . . . What about her work?" She frowned. "Huh. Okay, let me know if you hear anything."

She stuffed her phone into her coat pocket and plopped down in my office chair. I grabbed Bruce Wayne's and rolled it next to her.

"Everything okay?" I asked, sitting down.

"My aunt's worried because she hasn't talked to my cousin in a couple of days." Her teeth tugged on her lower lip. "Dolly usually checks in with her momma every day, but she's been known to disappear for a day or two when she hooks up with a new guy. Still, this is a long time, even for her."

I sucked in a breath. "Do you think something happened to her?"

Neely Kate shook her head. "Naw. She's probably okay. Aunt Thelma's branch of the family tree is a bit shaky." Her mouth tipped up into a grin. "My aunt married a mucker."

"*Excuse me?*"

"He mucks out pig pens. It's dirty, stinky work."

"And that makes her family tree branch shaky?"

"Heck no. There's no shame in being a mucker, but it's all he talks about. He's a few cans shy of a six pack."

"Oh."

"Anyway." She flipped her long blond hair over her shoulder. "Aunt Thelma married Melvin the Mucker—"

I held up my hands. "Wait. That's what you call him?"

Neely Kate gave me a blank stare. "Well . . . yeah."

"Okay, go on."

"And they had three kids—Alan Jackson, Dolly Parton, and Tommy Lee."

My mouth dropped. "Oh, no."

Her grin spread across her face. "Oh, *yes*."

"Why didn't I meet them at your wedding?"

She hesitated. "They couldn't go. Uncle Melvin had a family reunion in Louisiana they had to attend. Dolly was supposed to be a bridesmaid, but her grandma on her dad's side threatened to disown her if she didn't show up for the forty-sixth annual Muston Family Fish Fry. Her granny's half-owner of a shrimp boat, so you can see Dolly's dilemma."

I didn't see the dilemma, but I wasn't about to ask. Instead, I shook my head, still stuck on their names. "I get the country singers, but Tommy Lee . . . ?"

She shrugged. "Granny says Aunt Thelma went through a rebellious hard rock stage." She lowered her voice and leaned forward. "We don't like to talk about it."

"Okay . . ." I wanted to point out that his name made it pretty hard to keep something like that under wraps, but I let it drop.

"And would you know, Tommy Lee is this meek little thing in his late teens, and Alan Jackson is in his mid-twenties and hell on wheels."

"And Dolly Parton?"

"She's the middle child and a blend of both of the boys. A little wild sometimes, but she always runs home. Still, Aunt Thelma's worried."

"What's she gonna do?"

"She's gonna wait a day or so for her to turn up before doin' anything."

I shook my head. I had enough troubles of my own. I didn't need to get mixed up in someone else's. "Say, you don't happen to know a bookkeeper, do you? Violet kept the books, and I don't have the time to do 'em myself even if I *did* understand them."

"My Aunt Wilma would have been great, but she's in prison now, so she can't be of any help."

"You'd recommend your imprisoned aunt? Seriously?"

Her forehead wrinkled in confusion. "Why not? She was the best bookkeeper in northern Fenton County, although her reign at best was short-lived." Her eyes lit up. "*Oh!* You think she embezzled money or something."

I gave her a sheepish half-shrug. "It crossed my mind."

Neely Kate shook her head. "Aunt Wilma might be a lot of things, but she ain't no thief."

"Then what's she in prison for?"

"There was an . . . *unfortunate* incident involving the first best bookkeeper. Which is how she took the crown for a time."

I was afraid to ask how she'd advanced her position, let alone who was responsible for ranking the county's bookkeepers. Some things about Neely Kate's family were best left to the unknown.

"Yeah, it was a real shame when she got locked up. Totally changed my career path."

That caught my attention. "How so?"

"I was studying accounting at the community college in Magnolia so I could go into business with Aunt Wilma. I was already working for her around my class schedule." She sighed. "I needed a job when she got locked up." Her lips pursed. "And that's the sad story of how I ended up working in the Fenton County Personal Property Tax department."

"You know bookkeeping?" I asked in surprise.

"Yeah. I was one semester shy of graduating with my associate's degree. I'm a bit rusty, but I do most of my family's taxes."

"Perfect! Do you think you can look at my accounting? Well, I mean the nursery's."

"Is it on QuickBooks?"

"No. Violet gave me a ledger." I slid my chair over to a file cabinet and opened a drawer, pulling out the blue book.

After I handed it to Neely Kate, she opened the cover and scanned a couple of pages before closing her eyes and groaning. "No wonder your money was a cotton-picking mess." She sat up, pinning me with her gaze. "Not to mention that using a ledger rather than a spreadsheet would make it about ten times easier for your sister to skim money out of the company."

"So, can you look at it for me?"

Neely Kate scowled.

"Please? Just help me out until I find someone else since your Aunt Thelma's incarcerated." I paused. "Say, when's she gettin' out?"

She turned a few more pages. "From the looks of *this* mess, it won't be nearly soon enough."

"But you'll do it? I'll do anything you want."

"Anything?" she asked with an evil gleam.

Any other person would take advantage of my offer, but Neely Kate wasn't like most people. I wasn't worried.

"You have to go to bingo night with me and my grandma next week."

Neely Kate had been trying to coerce me to go for ages. "Fine. But I'm not putting out any lucky charms." According to Neely Kate, her grandmother brought so many tiny stuffed

22

animals and knick-knacks for good luck, it took her ten minutes to set them up around her bingo cards.

She shook her head. "No can do. Granny'll have a conniption. You know how superstitious she is."

"Fine," I groaned. "Deal."

Neely Kate closed the cover. "No promises. I might not be throwing up as much anymore, but I'm still fast asleep by nine o'clock most nights. I'll try to sneak a look while I'm at work tomorrow."

"Well, don't get into any trouble over it."

My friend groaned as she stood. "Speaking of trouble, I need to get back. I've got a new manager, and she watches me closer than an aardvark studies an ant hill."

I got to my feet and followed her to the door. "But I thought you were the boss now?"

"I am—of my department. But there's a new supervisor in charge of all the departments, and she's got it out for me."

"*You?*" Everybody loved Neely Kate. "Why?"

An ornery grin lit up her face. "She didn't appreciate my assessment of her friendliness."

I gave her a blank stare.

"I might have mentioned she'd get along better with the courthouse employees if she took the hickory stick out of her behind."

"You didn't!"

"Well . . . not to her face. She overheard me telling someone in probate. And she's been gunning to get me fired ever since."

"Oh no! Don't you need the insurance for the baby?"

"No, thank goodness. I went on Ronnie's insurance. After all the county budget cuts, his is better than mine. Can you believe that? Besides, I'm hoping to quit when Ronnie Junior is born, so it wouldn't be the end of the world. But I still need my income to buy all the baby things."

"Then I guess you better get back to work, huh?"

"Yeah," she sighed as she got up, tucking the ledger in her purse. "I don't want a confrontation with Stella the Hun."

I hopped up and gave her a hug. "Hang in there. Just think, if you're due on July 1st, you have less than seven months left."

She made a face. "Seven months? *That's* supposed to make me feel better?" She shook her head, but she couldn't shake the grin off her face. "Bye, Rose."

"See you later."

I watched her walk out the door as my phone dinged with a text. My stomach tightened when I glanced at the message from SM.

We need to talk.

Not if I could help it.

Chapter Three

I was worried Skeeter might come looking for me, so I left a note for Bruce Wayne, telling him I was leaving for the day. I loaded Muffy into the truck and drove to the nursery, pulling into the parking lot with the intent to check in on the progress of the cleanup and reconstruction of the store. I sure wasn't expecting to find Violet's car in the parking lot. There wasn't much to do in the store until the construction guys finished their patch-up work, and they weren't scheduled to come in until later in the week.

She was sitting outside on a stool next to the live Christmas trees the nursery was selling, bundled up in the tan wool coat I'd given her for Christmas two years ago. The teen boy she'd hired to man the lot was nowhere to be found.

I got out of my truck, Muffy tagging along behind me, and walked toward her. I wondered which Violet I would face today. For the past three weeks I'd only seen my repentant sister, but I couldn't help expecting the bossy version to resurface at any time.

"Vi, what are you doing out here in the cold?" I asked.

She hopped off the stool when she saw me. Her collar was turned up to partially cover her ears, and her hands were stuffed in her pockets. "Rose, I thought you were working on your new office."

"I took a break to check on the store. And you didn't answer my question. Why are you outside?"

"The kid I hired to sell the trees had to take the afternoon off. And since the store's still closed, customers won't realize the trees are for sale if we don't have someone outside. You and I both know we need the money."

"We don't need it bad enough for you to get pneumonia." I grabbed her arm and tugged. "Let's go inside, and you can show me around."

Violet resisted. "You can take a look on your own. There's not much to see."

"Vi, please," I pleaded. "Come inside, and I'll tell you what I've been up to with the landscaping office."

Indecision flickered in her eyes, so I gave one more pull. Her shoulders sank. "Okay. But only for a few minutes."

With Muffy in tow, we walked past a huge Dumpster overflowing with debris from the vandalism the Gardner Sisters Nursery had suffered right before Thanksgiving, nearly three weeks ago. Joe had hired a company to clean the place and repair it, but I'd refused to hire anyone to reassemble the shelves and handle the restock. We'd done it all ourselves last time, and I wasn't about to let him pour even more money into the business. If we needed help, I knew Bruce Wayne and Mason would be more than willing. If there was ever a time it worked in our favor to shut down, December was it. Besides Christmas trees, there weren't too many plants that had their heyday at this time of year.

I walked through the doors and gasped. The walls were freshly painted, and new shelves had been put together. The place was spotless. A few boxes were stacked in the corner, and Violet noticed when my gaze landed on them.

"We're just starting to get new shipments," Violet said. "Since everything was almost a total loss, we had to reorder almost everything. But I think it will all be here by the end of the week, and we'll be ready to start putting the store back together."

Muffy ran to the back room, probably checking to see if her bed was still there.

"I thought the repairs weren't getting done for another few days."

"Joe decided to do them himself instead."

I wasn't all that surprised. Joe had always loved doing repairs on my house when we were together, both because he enjoyed it, and it saved me money.

"Mike helped too."

That one *did* surprise me. I whipped my head around to gape at her. "Mike?"

She shrugged. "He offered, plus he and Joe have been friends since you guys dated. I think he likes hanging out with him."

I nodded, trying to decipher the uneasy feeling in the pit of my stomach. I wasn't sure it was jealousy, but it certainly wasn't pleasant. Still, I was glad that Joe had someone, even if it was Violet's estranged husband. "I suppose if Joe ever needed a friend, it's now. Did you know Hilary has moved to Henryetta?"

Violet's eyes darkened. "No, but I'm not surprised. Joe says she's like a leech. She pestered him mercilessly to marry her next weekend, but she finally had to cancel it. He swears he's done with her now."

I narrowed my eyes. "He's said that before. It's gonna take more than a few weeks of holding firm to convince me otherwise." I took several steps into the shop and walked around a display case. "Besides, it's not technically my problem anymore."

"Joe still needs you as a friend, Rose. He needs all of us."

"And I plan to be one, but I have to consider Mason's feelings."

"Why?" She took a step toward me. "When you and Mason were hanging out as friends, you never really took Joe's feelings into consideration."

Anger filled my chest, but she held up her hands in surrender.

"I'm not trying to be belligerent, Rose, I promise. I'm just pointing out the truth, and you know it."

I released a frustrated sigh. "That was different."

"You didn't worry about Joe because you knew he could handle your friendship with Mason, but you don't think the opposite is true."

My jaw clenched. "Violet—"

She rushed toward me and pulled me into a hug. "I'll stop. I just want you to be happy. And safe."

I broke loose, groaning. "Not that again."

Violet grabbed my upper arms and stared into my eyes. "I've spent nearly twenty-five of my twenty-seven years worrying about you, Rose Anne Gardner. Don't think I can just stop now. It's not fair of you to ask." Tears glistened in her eyes.

"Violet." My voice softened, and I gave her a tiny smile. "I promise you that I'm completely safe with Mason. He would sooner die than hurt me. Look what he did to protect me from Daniel Crocker." I wiped a tear from her cheek. "I know it's not easy for you, but you've got to stop worryin'."

Violet started to cry in earnest. "You must think I'm a big baby."

"No, I think you're my overprotective big sister," I offered, but part of me held back. I loved Violet with all my heart, but we'd been through a lot over the last several months. Just like it was going to take time for Joe to convince me he was done with Hilary, it would take more than a few tears to convince me that Violet was done with all the backbiting she'd stooped to recently.

She wiped her face. "Ashley misses you. Do you think you can stop by and see her this week?"

"Mason's mom is moving into her new house tomorrow."

Violet cringed. "I'm sorry. I shouldn't have asked—"

"Violet," I interrupted. "What I was going to say is that I'm going to help her unpack some boxes in the afternoon. I can pick Ashley up after school and bring her over to work with us. I know how much she likes to organize things." I winked. "Just like someone else we know."

To my surprise, my sister burst into sobs.

"Violet?" I pulled her into a hug. "Why are you still crying?"

"I was so scared I lost you," she pushed through her tears. "I was so awful to you. I wouldn't blame you if you turned your back on me. After all, we're not real sisters—"

I pulled away, and my eyes narrowed in anger. "Don't you ever say that again. We couldn't be truer sisters than if we were identical twins. Even if we didn't share a father—or heck, even a single drop of blood—everything we've been through together would make us sisters." I grabbed her hand and clasped it tight. "I owe you more than I could ever repay, Vi. A few months of fighting isn't gonna make me forget that."

"Thank you," she said through tears.

"Oh, Vi. I love you. You could never lose me, no matter what. I couldn't have survived without you when we were kids. And that's something I will never forget."

"But I know how terrible I've been." She searched my face. "How can you forgive me?"

"I'm not going to lie. It's not easy. But we're off to a good start, don't you think? Let's just take it a day at a time."

She nodded. "Okay."

My phone dinged with a text, and I dug it out of my pocket, trying not to cringe when I read it.

If you don't come see me, I'll find you.

Crappy doodles.

I stuffed my phone into my coat pocket. "Vi, I have to go. I'll call you tomorrow about picking up Ashley."

Her gaze landed on my pocket, then rose to my face. "Is everything okay?"

I forced a smile. "Of course. I just remembered that I need to stop by the store to pick up something for dinner. Maeve's spending the night. She did all the cooking last time she stayed with us, so I want to make sure she takes it easy."

Violet looked suspicious. "I thought you were still banned from the Piggly Wiggly."

I scowled at the reminder. "Mason's working that out."

"Then how are you going to shop there today? And what about Muffy?"

At the sound of her name, Muffy came running out from the back room and sat at Violet's feet.

I bent down and scooped her up. "Maybe I'll order take-out from that new Mexican restaurant. Jonah took his secretary there a couple of days ago."

"Jonah Pruitt's dating his secretary?"

I shook my head. "You're slipping, Vi. I told you that days ago." I gave her a quick hug and moved toward the door, Muffy following. She'd eagerly sniffed every last corner of the store. "Now I really have to go."

"Be careful, Rose."

I was sure gonna try.

Chapter Four

Skeeter Malcolm was not a patient man. I wasn't sure why that irritated me so much. It wasn't like it came as a surprise. He couldn't expect me to drop everything and come running, but after his last text, I couldn't very well continue to ignore him. I wouldn't put it past him to show up at my front door during dinner, asking me to set an extra plate.

I started my truck and drove out of the parking lot while I called him back.

He answered on the first ring and laughed. "I figured that would get your attention."

"What do you want, Skeeter?"

"I need your help."

"I already gave you my help and almost got caught!"

"But you didn't. I made damn sure of that."

"I helped you before because I needed my money back. I don't need anything from you this time."

He paused. "Are you sure about that?"

Something in his voice gave me pause. What was he talking about?

"What do you want, Skeeter?" I repeated, not feeling as cocky as before.

"I need you to read someone."

"*Excuse me?*" I pulled up to a stop sign. "What does that mean?"

"You know," he fumbled. "I need you to tell me if somebody did something."

"I'm not a living lie detector, Skeeter Malcolm. I see visions of the future, not the past. I have no idea how I'd go about doing something like that, even if I wanted to. Which I don't."

"Well, I need you anyway, so figure something out."

"I can't. I have to get home to make dinner."

"What is it with you and making dinner?" he asked in disbelief. "What are you? Julia Crocker or something?"

I groaned. "It's Julia *Child* and *Betty* Crocker. And no, I'm just a normal person going home to make dinner like most normal people do."

"Baby, there's nothin' normal about you. Get over to the pool hall in ten minutes."

"Skeeter!" I protested, but he hung up. *Damn him.*

A car behind me honked, and I realized I was still at the stop sign. I drove through the intersection and pulled into the parking lot of the Burger Shack, going over my options.

First, I could ignore him, but I was certain he'd send someone for me or even come himself. How would I explain that? Which of course was what he was hoping would drive me to my second option: go to him and do as he asked. But if I jumped as soon as he called, I'd be setting a bad precedent. Maybe we could figure out some sort of compromise. I had Muffy with me right now, and I really didn't want to expose my poor dog to the seedy underbelly of Henryetta. She'd already endured enough.

Instead, I sent a text. *I'll meet you tomorrow morning. But not at the pool hall. I can't be seen there after what happened on Thanksgiving. Pick a place where no one will know me or my truck.*

He took so long to answer, I was sure I was gonna turn up dead in a ditch, just like Mr. Sullivan from the bank. Instead, he texted me back five minutes later as I was pulling into the Mexican restaurant's parking lot.

Fine. I'll let you know when and where.

My mouth stretched into a smug grin. Round one: Rose 1, Skeeter 0.

But my smile fell just as quickly. I was a fool if I thought I could best Skeeter Malcolm. Not that I had any desire to. I just wanted to stay off his radar, but I suspected that was a pipe dream.

Maeve hadn't arrived yet, so I took the aluminum pan of enchiladas into the kitchen and put them into the oven to keep warm. Then I went back outside with Muffy, shivering in the cold northern wind, thinking about Violet. Could I trust her? Over the past several months, she'd manipulated me and turned on me time and again . . . Part of me yearned to have my sister back in my life, but I knew I had to be careful.

Mason's car turned down my gravel drive, catching me by surprise. It was barely five o'clock. Butterflies took flight in my stomach, and I wondered if that feeling would ever go away. I sure hoped not.

He got out of his car, and I walked toward him, surprised when he swept me into his arms and kissed me with abandon.

"What are you doin' home so early?" I asked when I regained my senses.

"I wanted to celebrate getting the leg brace off before my mother showed up." He kissed me again before lifting his mouth inches from mine.

"You're definitely off to a good start."

Without another word, he bent down and scooped me into his arms.

"Mason! What are you doin'?" I shrieked as he took a step forward.

"Now that I officially live here, I'm carrying you across the threshold. Something I couldn't do with that damn leg brace on."

Muffy heard my cry and came running over, then stood barking at Mason's feet.

"I don't think Muffy approves," Mason said.

I giggled as he climbed the porch steps, still holding me fast. "She's worried that you're going to ravish me."

"Then Muffy has cause to worry." His mouth lowered to mine, and he kissed me again. Muffy's bark changed, though, and it was accompanied by the sound of a car crunching on gravel. Mason stiffened and looked over his shoulder before setting me down on the porch.

I glanced around him to see a sheriff car coming down the drive. "That can't be good," I murmured.

"No. I suspect it's not."

The car pulled to a stop, and a female deputy I didn't recognize got out of it. She was short and a bit stocky, with unruly red hair that she'd tried to tame with a messy bun. "Mr. Deveraux," she said. "There's been a development you should know about."

Mason gave her a quick nod, then turned back to me. "I'm sorry, Rose. I have to go deal with this."

"What's it about?" I asked, anxiety churning in my stomach.

"Official business. Nothing for you to worry about."

Only he looked so serious I couldn't help but be anxious. He started toward the steps, and I grabbed his arm to stop him. "Mason?"

He pulled me to him for a gentle kiss. "Sweetheart, don't look so worried. Everything's fine. Why don't you take Muffy inside? I'll be there in a minute."

Muffy was yipping at the woman who didn't appear to appreciate her watchdog behavior. Maybe Muffy had an aversion to redheads after all of Hilary's nonsense.

The deputy turned to look at me, making me uncomfortable with her piercing stare.

"Muffy. Come on," I hollered toward her.

She stopped barking and sulked as she crawled up the steps.

"That's got to be one of the mangiest dogs I've ever seen," the deputy said in a disgusted tone. "Are you sure she's caught up on her shots?"

Mason's back stiffened. "Deputy Hoffstetter, do you have a purpose for being here other than to insult our family pet?" He sounded furious, and I felt like cheering.

The deputy's face reddened, and she shot me a glare before muttering something too low for me to hear. If it was an apology, it was a poor one.

Mason nodded, then shot me a sympathetic look. "Rose, this should only take a minute."

"Okay," I grumbled, irritated that Deputy Crankypants had successfully ruined my quality time with Mason. I took Muffy inside and peered through the curtains. I watched them for several moments, although there wasn't much to see. Mason leaned with his forearm across the top of the open car door, and the deputy stood next to him talking. Finally, the deputy nodded at something Mason said and moved to get into the car.

I dropped the edge of the curtain and ran into the kitchen to grab a bowl for the tortilla chips the restaurant had given me. Muffy stopped next to her dog bowl and started crunching her dry dog food.

Moments later, Mason came up behind me and grabbed my hips as his mouth lowered to my earlobe. "Have you added lip reading to your list of skills?"

I froze, my hand in mid-air, before I recovered and pulled the bowl down from the shelf. "I don't know what you're talking about."

He turned me around, a sly grin lighting up his eyes. "I know you better than you think I do, Rose Gardner."

With everything I'd been up to lately, I sure hoped not.

"We could save a lot of time and effort if you would just tell me what you were talking about." I lifted my eyebrows as encouragement.

He laughed. "Sorry, sweetheart. Not this time."

"But you tell me everything."

He gave me a kiss. "Not this time."

I wasn't sure what to think about that. I knew that Mason dealt with official, confidential Fenton County business all the time, and usually I didn't care. But I had a gut feeling that this mystery news somehow involved me. Or rather the Lady in Black. "Is it about that big auction on Thanksgiving Day?"

He cocked his head with an ornery grin. "Good try." He slid his hand around my back and pulled me to his chest. "Where were we when we got interrupted?"

Mason was doing a good job of reminding me when Muffy started barking again.

"Hello!" Maeve called out from the living room. "Is anyone home?"

"Your momma's here," I said, breathless as I pushed him away and straightened my shirt. "She's early."

Mason groaned. "The universe is conspiring against me."

It was conspiring against both of us.

We found Maeve in the living room squatted down next to her overnight bag so she could pet Muffy. She smiled at us. "I wondered where you two were hidden." Picking up on the teasing tone in her voice, I blushed.

"You're here early, Mom," Mason said, putting his arm around my back.

"The movers finished a couple hours ahead of schedule."

"Well, we're so glad you're here!" I said. "You must be exhausted." I pulled her into a hug, then steered her toward the sofa in the living room so she could take a seat. "You don't have to worry about a thing. I have dinner taken care of."

Maeve's eyes lit up. "You can go back to the Piggly Wiggly now?"

I heaved out a sigh of frustration. "No. Mason's still working on that."

Mason laughed. "It's taken some impressive negotiating on my part, but I think we're close to an agreement." His face lit up with a mischievous gleam. "Did you get Neely Kate to go shopping for you?"

I put my hands on my hips and scowled. "No. I picked up enchiladas from the new Mexican restaurant—Buenaza Zarigüeya—on the way home."

His eyes widened. "I'm having a hard time trusting food from a restaurant whose name means Kind Opossum. I hope you got the *vegetarian* enchiladas."

"Fine, mister," I said in a haughty tone. "Suit yourself. I'll give your share to Muffy."

Hearing her name, Muffy shot toward me, shaking her tail so hard her back end swayed.

"See?" I said. "Muffy's not so particular."

A stench filled the room, and I gagged, waving my hand in front of my face. *Traitor.*

Mason burst out laughing. "I suspect Muffy's already had my share, and she's taken a bullet for me." He bent down to pet her head, then stood up, choking. "That dog deserves a medal of honor."

I stomped off to the kitchen, and Mason followed on my heels.

"Rose, I was teasing. I'm sorry if I hurt your feelings."

"You didn't," I sighed, pulling the pan out of the oven and setting it down on the stove top with a plop. "I'm just frustrated that I can't go grocery shopping." I shut the oven door and put my hands on my hips, still wearing the oven mitt. "It's embarrassing, Mason."

"I'm sorry. I'll put more effort into getting your Piggly Wiggly privileges reinstated. In the meantime, why don't you go to Peach Orchard Grocery?"

My mouth hung open. "Are you serious? That place fails the health department inspection on a regular basis. At least Buenaza Zarigüeya rated a ninety-two on their inspection." I lifted my eyebrows in an *I-told-you-so* look. "Yes, I checked."

He wrapped his arms around my back and tugged me to his chest. "God, I love you."

"Why?" I asked, my voice muffled from being buried in his shirt. "Because I'm serving you food that may or may not contain road kill?"

He chuckled, his chest rumbling against my cheek. "No, because I would never in a million years have expected to have this conversation with anyone, and I love every minute of it."

I leaned my head back to look up at him with narrowed eyes. "Don't think you can sweet talk your way into getting some enchiladas."

"You're a harsh woman, Rose Gardner."

"Yeah," I teased. "Remember that the next time you insult a woman's dinner, whether she cooks it or not."

"I have so much to learn."

"You've got that right."

Mason helped me set the kitchen table. We sat down to eat, and Maeve and Mason told me stories about their family home, which had played a part in many of their beloved memories. Maeve got a little teary-eyed, but took one look at my worried face and shook her head. "Nothing stays the same, Rose. Sometimes you have to recognize when it's time to move on. I'm good with selling the house. These are happy tears."

I kept a close eye on Mason. He seemed impartial to his mother selling his childhood home, but I knew it had to affect him in some way. Later, Maeve went up to take a shower, and while Mason and I cleaned up the kitchen, I asked him about it.

"I'm fine with it."

I studied him, and he gave me a soft smile.

"Believe it or not, I am. I think I said goodbye to that house after my father died. I came home for the summer after my junior year at Duke, and I didn't feel like I belonged there anymore. That's why I got my own apartment when I came back to Little Rock for law school instead of moving in with Mom to save money."

I thought about my own childhood home. I'd lived there until a couple of months ago. Now I could hardly stand to walk through the door when I went there to visit Violet. But Mason had grown up in a totally different environment.

He noticed my struggle to understand. "With Dad gone, everything changed. The three of us no longer knew our parts. Mom and Savannah figured theirs out while I was at school. When I got home, I didn't feel a sense of belonging anymore. It was like there wasn't a place for me there." He looked down at the bowl he was drying. "It wasn't intentional, and they were the ones stuck there with the memories. I understood."

"So what *did* feel like home?"

He didn't answer for several seconds. Finally, he set the bowl, which had to be drier than dust at this point, on the counter and turned toward me. "Honestly, I've never felt truly at home since before my father died. Not until I moved in with you."

I closed the distance between us and softly grabbed his face, pulling him down to give him a gentle kiss. "I love you."

He straightened and grinned. "I love you too." Then he glanced at the clock on the wall, and his smile faltered. "I have to go out in a bit."

Part of my elation faded. "Why?"

Something I didn't recognize flickered in his eyes. "It's work-related."

It was close to seven-thirty. I knew nothing was going on at the courthouse, and he'd started to bring work home so he wouldn't be gone so much.

"Are you going to see Joe again?" The last time he took off after dinner, he'd returned with a busted lip after confronting Joe about paying off the nursery's debt.

"No, it's nothing like that. I swear."

"Does it have to do with that deputy that showed up earlier?"

"Partially."

I waited for him to elaborate, and he sighed.

"Rose, I can't tell you what it's about. Ask me anything you want to know about my personal life, and I'll be an open book. But most of what I do at work is confidential. It's not that I don't want to tell you. I just can't."

"I know." I tried to keep the disappointment out of my voice.

He tugged me against his chest and rested his chin on my head. "I might be gone for a while, so don't worry about waiting up."

I couldn't imagine what he could be up to, but it was pointless to ask. I couldn't help wondering about the deputy's visit, but part of me didn't want to know. The person who had first uttered "ignorance is bliss" knew a thing or two about life.

Mason left shortly after we finished, giving me a long kiss goodbye on the front porch. "I love you, Rose. No matter what happens, remember that." Then he left before I could answer.

As I watched the taillights of his car disappear down my drive to the road, I couldn't ignore the feeling in my gut that Mason was involved in something dangerous.

***

Mason didn't get home until after midnight. Muffy and I were already in bed when Mason stripped and climbed under the covers, pulling me close.

When we got up the next morning, he seemed reserved, but was more like himself after he showered and dressed.

The moving men planned to show up at Maeve's by nine, so she left by eight-thirty. I offered to come with her and help, but she insisted she'd be fine until the movers left, telling me I should come by later in the afternoon like we'd originally planned.

I walked out with her when she left and let Muffy romp in the yard. When I went back inside, I found Mason in his office staring intently at something on his laptop.

I stood in the doorway, watching him. "Don't you need to get to the courthouse?"

"Not this morning," he said without looking up as he continued to type. "I was supposed to be in court at nine, but the judge called a recess, so I decided to do some work at home."

"What's got your rapt attention?" I asked, moving closer to his desk.

He looked up and tilted the screen away from me. "Dealing with the usual Fenton County mayhem."

I crossed my arms. "Uh-huh," I said. "Does this have anything to do with last night?"

Mason closed his laptop lid and scooted back his chair. "What do you have planned for this morning?"

I considered calling him out on changing the subject, but I knew it would be pointless. Instead, I gave him a saucy grin. "Oh, you know. *Creating* the usual Fenton County mayhem."

"Why am I not surprised?" He laughed and stood up. "How about I take you out to breakfast if you don't have to get to the office right away? We'll make it date."

"Really?" I asked, sounding more hopeful than I'd intended.

His smile fell slightly. "I'm doing a poor job as your boyfriend if you're this excited over eating at the Big Biscuit."

"Are you kidding? Have you *had* their blueberry pancakes?"

"I've had yours, and they're delicious." He stuffed his laptop into a satchel. "They'll be hard to beat."

I laughed. "You're a quick learner, Mason Deveraux."

He placed a hand at the small of my back and guided me to the coat tree by the front door. "I have a teacher who motivated me last night by making me beg for my dinner. And it doesn't hurt that it's true." He glanced down at Muffy, who pranced excitedly at my feet. "You're going to have to leave her here today?"

"I know she's used to coming with me now, but she'll be okay by herself."

I let her loose, and we locked the front door.

"Do you want to ride into town together?" Mason asked.

"No, I'm helping your momma this afternoon, so we need to take separate cars," I said. "Plus, I told Violet I'd pick up Ashley so she could help. She's been missing me."

Mason opened my truck door and smiled down at me. "Mom will love having Ashley there."

I climbed up into the driver's seat. "In hindsight, I suppose I should have asked her first."

"I'm sure she'll be happy about it. I'll see you at the restaurant."

I checked my phone a half dozen times on the fifteen-minute drive, surprised I hadn't heard from Skeeter yet. But no news was good news.

We ordered breakfast and were waiting for our food when Mason leaned his forearm on the table. "I know we didn't have time to talk about this last night, but the papers for the nursery are ready to be signed." He paused, searching my face. "I know your mind's made up, but as your attorney, I feel the need to reiterate that you do not have to include Joe Simmons or Violet in the ownership."

I sighed. "Thank you for understanding."

"It's your business, Rose, but once you sign these papers, it's going to be a whole hell of a lot harder to dissolve."

"Kind of like getting married." I smiled at him. "It's easy to say I do, but ten times harder to say I don't."

He hesitated. "Yes. Exactly."

"I'm not gonna change my mind, Mason. Especially after you added the clauses stating that Joe can't sell his share to anyone but me or Violet, and I can buy him out by paying off the money he put in after a year if I decide it's not working."

He took a deep breath and slowly released it. "Yesterday afternoon I emailed Joe and told him the papers would be ready today. I offered to send them to the sheriff's department so he could sign and return them at his leisure, but he insisted

that he wouldn't sign them unless you were there with him."
He didn't look too happy about it.

"Well, we are going to be partners," I said. "There are some things we need to discuss about restocking the nursery."

"When are you going to see him?" he asked.

"I have a light schedule today. I guess I'll call him after breakfast and see when he has time."

The waitress brought our food, and I poured syrup over my pancakes. "Neely Kate told me that Hilary's moved to Henryetta. She saw her at the doctor's office."

Mason's mouth pursed. "Did she move in with Joe?"

"No. Neely Kate said she's renting a house close to the town square. And Violet said Joe found a new place outside of city limits."

"I know."

I glanced up in surprise.

He shrugged. "He's moving into the farmhouse on the property south of ours."

It took me a moment to recover. "The farm where they found poor Mr. Sullivan's body? I didn't know it was for sale."

"It's not." He cut up a piece of his French toast, his gaze fixed on the plate. "The owners were renting out the farmhouse, but after the loan manager's body was found there, no one wanted it. So Joe got it for a steal."

"How did you know?" I asked, incredulous.

"The Fenton County Courthouse. It's one of the most gossipy places I've ever worked." His eyes lifted to mine. "The real question is how *you* didn't know. If something like that escaped Neely Kate, the world has turned upside down."

I scowled. I suspected it was a matter of Neely Kate not sharing what she knew, rather than her actually not knowing it. I wasn't sure I liked the thought of Joe being so close to me, and I wouldn't have been surprised to find out Violet had helped instigate it. Especially since she'd been pretty direct in telling me she'd rather see me with Joe than with Mason. "I didn't know, Mason. I swear."

"I know." He offered me a soft smile before returning his attention to his food. "The last time I checked, people can live wherever they want in Fenton County. He's within his legal rights."

"When did you find out?"

"Yesterday."

I lifted my eyebrows. "And you're sure that you didn't pay him a visit last night to discuss the matter?"

He shook his head. "No. I swore to you I wouldn't," he said without defensiveness. "I confess it crossed my mind, but I restrained myself. Joe and I cleared the air the last time I paid him a visit a few weeks ago. We may not be on the friendliest of terms, but we both know where the other stands."

"Well, thank you for making the effort to get along. Especially since he's my business partner now."

"Fenton County's not that large, so it's in our best interest to get along. In fact, we're actually working on something together." He took a sip of his coffee. "So, see? I'm making an effort."

"You're working on something together?" I asked in surprise. Could it be the Lady in Black? The couple of times I'd seen Joe since running into him at Maeve's new house I hadn't brought it up. He didn't seem to have any idea that I had a new alias, and I intended for it to stay that way. "Is the case you're working on together the reason that deputy came by yesterday? Does it have anything to do with where you went last night?"

He laughed. "Good try. I'm not spilling."

I decided to let it drop. I could try to pry it out of him later that night.

Mason was telling me about the quick sale of Maeve's house in Little Rock when he stopped speaking mid-sentence. His face hardened as he studied something over my shoulder.

"Mason?" I asked, glancing behind me, half-expecting to see Joe.

Instead, I caught Skeeter Malcolm's gaze.

My stomach dropped to my toes.

Skeeter was sitting at a table with one of his minions, Jed, both of them holding a menu.

I spun back around and started chopping off a piece of pancake.

Mason's hand tightened around his fork. "Rose, why do you look so nervous?"

I wasn't sure how to answer.

"Has Malcolm bothered you since I collected you from the pool hall last July?"

I shook my head. "No. Of course not. Why would he?"

"I don't know. But I don't like the way he looked at you." Mason shook his head. "I would have suspected he was looking at me, except his expression wasn't full of loathing."

My stomach squeezed around the pancakes I'd just eaten. "Does he really hate you that much?"

"Let's just say that since our first meeting on that hot July night, we've shared a healthy disdain for one another."

"Why?"

"Because I threatened to shut down his business." He pushed his French toast around on his plate, shooting pointed glances at the table behind me. "Skeeter Malcolm may look like a womanizing drinker, but don't let his performance fool you. He's all about business, which is why we're so worried about the results of that auction. Daniel Crocker thought of himself as forward-thinking, but he had nothing on Malcolm. Honestly, most of the sheriff's department was surprised it took him this long to make a bid for the top rung of the ladder."

My gaze narrowed on him. "But not you?"

"Malcolm's a lot more cunning than Crocker ever hoped to be. If he really took over like we think he did, he was smart to bide his time. Crocker was batshit crazy, and his crash-and-burn was inevitable. Waiting meant Malcolm avoided a turf war that would have produced casualties and a whole lot of bad blood. It gave him the opportunity to acquire a mostly intact drug cartel without the animosity a skirmish would have brought."

"So he's clever?"

Mason's eyebrows lifted as he dug into his egg. "More than most people give him credit for."

Myself included. "You said he hates you. Are you in danger, Mason?"

Mason's face lifted. "Rose, no. I'm fine. Don't worry. Malcolm's not stupid enough to come after me. At least not right now, anyway. He's been trying to keep a low profile since Thanksgiving."

"But after he threatened me this past summer, you told me that he's capable of killing the people who get in his way." Crappy doodles, I'd been so stupid. I'd helped a man who was after my boyfriend.

Mason's expression softened. "Are you worried he'll come after you to get to me?" He shook his head and took my hand. "Rose, if I thought that was even a possibility, I'd insist the sheriff's department place you under protection." He paused. "And you know that Joe would agree to it."

"I'm not worried about me, Mason." No, I was far too valuable to Skeeter for him to kill me. "Promise me you'll be careful."

"I promise." He gave me a soft smile. "Don't worry. He's not the first high-profile criminal I've gone after, and he won't be the last."

"So you're going after him?"

He narrowed his eyes and shot a quick glance in Skeeter's direction. "You bet your pretty little ass I am."

I swallowed a bite of bacon, but it didn't sit well in my stomach. Especially when my phone vibrated in my pocket with a text. I didn't eat much after that, and Mason seemed to have lost his appetite as well, so before too long he asked the waitress for our check.

When we got up to leave, we had no choice but to walk by Skeeter on the way to the door. I prayed he wouldn't say anything.

Of course, that was too much to hope for.

"Mr. Prosecutor," Skeeter said with a smirk, dipping his chin slightly.

"Mr. Malcolm," Mason returned in a low voice.

"I like your new accessory."

It took me a millisecond to realize he was talking about *me*.

Mason took half a step to put himself partially between us. "Are you threatening my girlfriend, Mr. Malcolm?"

Skeeter laughed. "Threatening a pretty little thing like that? God no. She's safer than you realize." He picked up his butter knife. "And why would you assume it was a threat? If you don't mind me saying so, you seem a little paranoid."

Mason didn't answer him. Instead, he ushered me out the door and into the parking lot, his breath coming in short bursts. "I don't want you to be alone today."

"Why?"

He stared into my face. "He mentioned you for a reason, Rose. Malcolm does *everything* for a reason. I'm worried that you're not safe."

Little did he know how safe I actually was. "Mason, you yourself said he's trying to keep a low profile. He's not going to do anything stupid. He's just tryin' to rile you up." I put my hand on his arm. "And look. It's working. I'm fine."

He walked me to my truck. "Call or text me today. Multiple times. I mean it. I'll be crazy with worry most of the day."

I placed my hands on his shoulders and kissed him, standing on my tiptoes. "I love how protective you are of me, but I'm fine."

"Maybe you should have a vision."

"Of how many times I'll call you today?" I teased.

"No, to make sure you're gonna be safe."

My heels dropped to the pavement, and my smile fell. "You're serious."

"Yes."

"Mason, you know it doesn't work like that. What you're wanting to know is so general—"

"Then try to have a vision of Christmas. That's far enough away to make sure Malcolm doesn't go after you soon."

I gave a tiny shake of my head. "Mason . . ."

"If our positions were reversed, would you be willing to wait and see?"

"That's not fair." But he was right. I *would* want to know. It was just that there were so many peculiarities in my life, I had no idea what would pop out of my mouth. Things I didn't want him to know. Yet, there was no denying he was worried for my safety, and the guilt of it was settling on my shoulders like a stack of bricks. "Okay. But if I spoil my Christmas present from you, you better get me something else. Despite my visions, I actually *like* surprises."

He kissed me, then took my hands. "Do you want to sit down on the truck seat?"

"Sure." I opened the door and climbed onto the driver's seat, turning so my legs hung over the side.

Mason moved closer, pressing his stomach into my legs and taking my hands again. "What do you need me to do?"

I realized I'd never purposely had a vision with him before. "Just keep holding my hands." I paused. "And promise you'll still love me no matter what comes out of my mouth."

Shock widened his eyes. "What could you possibly say that would change my feelings for you?"

I had a whole list, but I wasn't about to pull it out and dust it off. "Nothing. I just hate doing this." Indecision flickered in his eyes, making me feel guilty. I was more worried about his safety than my own, but I couldn't very well tell him why. Who knew, maybe my vision would reassure *me*. I reached up and kissed him again. "It's okay, really. Maybe I'll see something wonderful."

He looked so serious. "I hope so."

I took a deep breath and closed my eyes, concentrating on Christmas Day. It took longer than I expected—maybe because it was still a couple of weeks away—but the blackness gave way to my living room. A giant real Christmas tree filled the corner with decorations I didn't recognize. Presents were scattered underneath, and someone's back was pressed against my chest.

"I think this is the best Christmas I've ever had, Mason," my voice said wistfully.

"Me too," Mason said.

The vision faded, and I opened my eyes as I blurted out, "It's gonna be the best Christmas we ever had."

His face flooded with relief, and he pulled me to his chest. "Thank God."

I wrapped my arms around his neck. "I didn't know you were so worried about Christmas," I teased. "I better be certain to get you the best present ever."

He pulled back, smiling. "You're the best present I could ever hope to get. Everything else would pale in comparison."

"So you're saying you don't want a present . . ." I cocked my head to the side with a grin.

"Now I wouldn't go that far," he chuckled. "I like presents, no matter how small."

That was good to know.

"Well, I like presents too, so I'm glad I didn't see mine."

A ringing filled the silence. Mason groaned and pulled his phone out of his pocket to check the screen. "Duty calls. I've got to get to work." He lifted his eyes to my face. "What are you up to now?"

"I'm going to check on Bruce Wayne and the office before I pick up Ashley to help your mom. I suppose I should call Joe about the papers." *And meet with your current archnemesis.*

"Well, I emailed the papers to him this morning from home, so he'll have them. Hopefully, you'll just have to show up and sign them."

We both knew that was unlikely.

He gave me another kiss, then grabbed the side of the truck door. "Despite your vision, be careful, and if you feel unsafe for any reason, call me or the sheriff. Okay?"

"Mason, I'll be fine."

"Skeeter Malcolm is not a man to mess around with, Rose. He specifically mentioned you. That wasn't for nothing."

"Okay, and do I have a curfew too?" Mason's forehead furrowed, and I laughed. "I'm teasing."

"Well, I'm not. Be careful."

"I'll be as careful as I can be."

"Try to be with someone all day if you can."

I gave him a slight push. "Mason, go already. I'll be safe. I promise."

He grinned. "Why are you trying to get rid of me?"

"So you can get to work and come home to me sooner. Go."

He gave me another kiss and shut my door. I watched him get into his car as I pulled out my phone. Cringing, I glanced at the screen.

You're off the hook. For now.

I looked back at the restaurant. The text had been sent while I was sitting in the Big Biscuit with Skeeter watching my back. Had he changed his mind after seeing me with Mason? Maybe he was worried I'd tell his secrets to Mason. In any case, I'd earned a reprieve. With any luck at all, there wouldn't be a next time.

And if I believed that, then Santa was going to bring me a pony.

Buying a saddle wasn't a safe bet.

Chapter Five

I decided to suck it up and call Joe on the way to the landscaping office.

"Hey, beautiful," he answered.

"Joe, you can't call me that anymore."

"Why not? It's true."

I groaned. "Mason said he sent you the papers for the nursery, but you want me there when you sign them."

"I thought it would be good to go over all of it together."

"Well, we still need to discuss some things about the business, so I guess that works. Do you want me to come by the sheriff's office?"

"How about we meet at the nursery? I want to tell you a few ideas I have while we're there in the space."

"Is Violet gonna be there so you can both ambush me again?" I asked dryly.

"Rose, look." He released a heavy sigh. "I admit that we handled that badly."

"Oh, *really?* You think so?"

"I wish I had handled it differently." He paused. "I wish I'd handled a lot of things differently."

I wasn't going down that road again. "If you feel so badly, then let me buy you out."

He chuckled. "I don't feel *that* badly."

I bit my tongue to keep from cursing. "Then when do you want to meet?"

"How about mid-afternoon? I'm working on something, but I can be free by then."

"Fine," I grumbled. "Two o'clock?"

"That works for me." He hesitated. "And Rose, if you don't mind, I'd rather Violet not be there."

I couldn't help wondering what he had up his sleeve, but I had to admit that I didn't want the two of them together. The last time they'd met me at the nursery had turned into a disaster. "Okay. I won't tell her we're meeting."

"See you this afternoon."

Bruce Wayne was already at the office, sitting in his chair, when I arrived. The look on his face told me he was frustrated. He looked behind me, surprised. "Where's Muffy?"

"I had too many errands to run to bring her," I said, unbuttoning my coat. "Did the electrician not show?"

"Oh, he showed. It's what he didn't do that has me perturbed. Or rather what he wanted."

I shook my head. "What are you talking about?"

"He said it was going to cost eight-hundred dollars to fix the mess, and I had to pay up front."

"What? But Mr. Darby is supposed to pay for that."

"I know, and I told him that, but he said Darby ain't forking over a dime."

I put my hand on my hip and let out a loud huff. "Now what are we gonna do?"

"Oh, I already done something." He got up out of his chair. "I called Mason and told him. He's gonna make an official call to our landlord."

I groaned.

"You got the Assistant DA in your back pocket, Rose. Why ain't you usin' 'im?"

"You know very well why I'm not using him!"

"Rose." He took a wary step toward me. "That man would pull the stars from the sky and put 'em on a chain around your neck if you wanted 'em. Why won't you let him help you with this?"

"Because I spent twenty-four years lettin' other people make every single decision for me, telling me what I could and couldn't do. I was incapable of relying on myself, Bruce Wayne. I'm tired of being weak. I never want to be that girl again. I thought you of all people would understand."

"There's a difference between being weak and lettin' people who love and care for you help you from time to time, Rose. You made me partial owner of this business when I didn't put up a dime. Hell's bells, you gave me a job when no one else would. You saw I was down on my luck and gave me a hand. Was I weak to accept that?"

"No!" I protested. "That was different."

"No, it wasn't. Not really." A grin stretched his lips. "Besides, it's a done deal. Like I said, I took care of it."

I sat in my chair, perturbed. He was right, as hard as it was to admit.

"Nelly Kate dropped in earlier looking for you."

I checked my phone. "She didn't call me."

"She was on her way to work. She said to tell you that she'd looked at the books last night."

I sat up in excitement. "She did?"

"She also said she'd tried a new recipe, so she's bringin' some over for lunch. Said she'd tell you all about it then."

That drew a less enthusiastic response. "Oh."

He chuckled. "I suddenly remembered I've got somewhere I need to be for lunch. Sorry I'm gonna miss it."

Neely Kate had experienced a recent burst of domestication. Ronnie had put his foot down—a rare instance—and told her that she couldn't decorate the baby's room until she found out if it was a boy or a girl. Instead, she'd poured her energy into watching cooking shows and trying out new recipes. Only Ronnie rarely liked what she cooked, so she'd been forcing it on me and Bruce Wayne . . . when she could actually catch him. It had only taken two meals for us to figure out Neely Kate's gourmet adventure was akin to taking a joy ride on the *Titanic*. Mason seemed to have a sixth sense for when she was about to show up with leftovers. She'd stopped by his office with a stack of suspicious Tupperware a few times while I was over at the courthouse for a quick visit. He'd always claim he had a prior engagement or say he'd already eaten. I hadn't been so lucky.

"Did she mention what she brought today?"

"Something about tofu burgers and Brussels sprouts muffins."

I shuddered. "If she doesn't find a new hobby soon, I'm gonna beg Ronnie to let her decorate that baby's room."

"Good luck with *that*."

"Yeah, I know. Did she say what time she was coming?"

"She really wanted to talk to you, so she said she was coming early. Around eleven-thirty."

I glanced at the clock on the wall—10:40. What could she have found in the books? Dread knotted my shoulders. I knew Violet had been irresponsible, but surely she hadn't skimmed money off the business as Neely Kate had suggested was possible.

I looked around at what needed to be done. "Until we get the electricity situation sorted, we're sunk on getting the computers and Internet set up."

Bruce Wayne winked. "I got it covered."

"How?"

"I borrowed my cousin's generator."

"He let you?" I regretted the words as soon as I said them. Bruce Wayne's family had practically disowned him after he was arrested for murder last year. And they hadn't welcomed him back into the fold after he was acquitted, either. Violet and I had our differences, but we'd never turn our backs on each other like that.

Bruce Wayne shrugged. "He's on my biological dad's side. I didn't have much to do with them before . . . everything. But I've been thinking about my dad lately, so I called my cousin after Thanksgiving." He grimaced as though he was wading deeper into cold water than he'd planned. "He said we could borrow it until our electricity gets fixed. Or until there's a snow storm in the forecast, whichever comes first."

We spent the next forty minutes getting the computers situated and had just started installing software when the front door burst open. Neely Kate stood in the threshold, holding a plastic tub of food. "Who's hungry?"

Bruce Wayne's eyes bugged out like she was pointing a loaded gun at him. He jumped to his feet and grabbed his coat off the back of his office chair. "I just remembered that I've got to go do that . . . thing."

Neely Kate shot him a glare. "What thing?"

"Um . . . the electricity's out, and I need to run to the hardware store to get some supplies for the generator." Then he shot past her, faster than I'd ever seen him move.

Neely Kate shut the door, watching him beat it down the sidewalk. "He's not goin' after any parts, is he?"

"Um . . ." I didn't want to tell her the truth, but a white lie wasn't hurrying its way off my tongue.

She spun around and gave me an amused, disapproving look. "Rose, if you don't want to share my tofu and chipotle burgers with Bruce Wayne, you don't have to send him off. I'll just make double next time."

"Oh, Neely Kate. You really don't have to."

A smile lit up her face. "I don't mind at all." She grabbed Bruce Wayne's chair and dragged it over to me, setting the Tupperware on my desk. "Eat up while it's still warm. I heated it up in the microwave before I came over." She popped off the lid and handed me a plastic fork. "I don't have any plates today, so we'll just have to share."

"Okay . . ." I said as I looked down at the green goo-covered patty. Surely it couldn't taste as bad as it looked.

"Bruce Wayne said you had time to look over the books."

"Oh, yeah." She opened her big purse and dug out the ledger.

"I didn't think you were going to get to it 'til today."

"Neither did I, but I had a major case of indigestion and couldn't sleep."

"How bad was it?"

"My indigestion? Pretty bad."

I laughed. "Not your indigestion, although I sympathize. The books. How were the books?"

"Way better than I expected."

"So Violet didn't try to cheat me?"

"With the nursery's money? No. With everything else in your life . . . well, that's another story. I still think you should switch over to accounting software, though."

I let out a sigh of relief, feeling better until she glanced down at the food and up at my empty fork. "You better eat up while it's still warm." I noticed she wasn't exactly pulling out any utensils of her own, but there was no polite way to say so.

Holding my breath, I took a bite and nearly gagged. I was wrong. It was worse than it looked.

"What do you think? I made it last night when I couldn't sleep. I saw it on *Chopped*."

"Uh . . . Neely Kate, isn't that the show where they make dishes out of weird food combinations? They don't have actual recipes."

Her eyes lit up. "That's the challenge! To make something so unique without a recipe. When I saw this, I decided to try it. I made it while I was going over the ledger last night."

"Did Ronnie like it?"

She waved her hand, and I noticed her nails were painted green with red polka dots. "Please. That man wouldn't know fine food if it jumped out of the lake and into his fishing boat on a gold plate. I made it for *you*."

I tried another bite and began to choke. "Me?"

Neely Kate pulled a bottle of water out of her purse and handed it to me. "You're the only one who appreciates my cooking." She pursed her lips together. "I was sure Mason would, but he never seems to be around when I have gourmet meals with me."

I took a drink, trying to figure a way out of eating the glop in front of me. I decided to use Mason's trick. "This is delicious, but Mason and I had a late breakfast at the Big Biscuit." Then I told her about Skeeter's comment to Mason and the vision I'd forced of Christmas.

"Aw . . ." she gushed. "You two are so cute."

A smile spread across my face.

"Do you really think you're done with Skeeter?"

"If I was him, *I* wouldn't trust the girlfriend of the Assistant DA. I just hope he won't go after Mason."

"I suspect Mason's right. Skeeter's a pretty smart guy, and it would look suspicious if something happened to the Assistant DA right after he got his big promo in the world of crime." She put her fork down. "Speakin' of questionable characters, I've got a favor to ask you."

My eyebrows rose in surprise. "What is it?"

"You know how I was telling you about my missing cousin?"

"Dolly Parton?"

"Yeah." She shifted on the seat. "She still hasn't called my aunt, so she asked me to go out to her boyfriend Billy Jack's trailer to check on her."

I frowned. "So what's the favor?"

"I was hopin' you'd take me. My car's been acting up, and her boyfriend lives down by Pickle Junction. I'm afraid I'll break down. Do you have time?"

I looked at the gourmet mess on my desk. "Sure. I'm supposed to meet Joe at two at the nursery." I glanced up at the clock. "That's plenty of time to drive down to the Pickle Junction area and come back."

Neely Kate threw her arms around me and pulled me into a hug. "You're the best."

Something was up. "Why are you gettin' so excited over this?"

She gave me a perturbed look. "Because my aunt keeps calling, and she's gonna get me into trouble at work."

"So why don't you turn your phone to silent?"

"And miss her calls? I'd get into even more trouble. I snuck away early and figured I could take a long lunch break so we could drive down there, find her in his trailer while they're on some love fest, and tell her to call her momma."

I hopped up and grabbed my coat. I suspected there was more to this story than she was telling me, but if it got me out of eating tofu chipotle burgers, I was game.

As I headed for the door, she called after me. "Wait! You didn't try the peppermint Brussels sprouts muffins!"

I hurried out the door, pretending I didn't hear her.

Chapter Six

So why doesn't your aunt go out to Billy Jack's herself to see if Dolly Parton is out there?" We were almost to Pickle Junction, and I couldn't help thinking we were about to hop into a hornet's nest.

"Well . . . she can't on account of the squirrel jerky incident." Neely Kate tried to hide her cringe, but she wasn't fooling me.

I blinked. "Do I want to know about the squirrel jerky incident?"

"No." She pointed up ahead. "See that mailbox shaped like an armadillo? Turn there."

I slowed down and cast a suspicious glance at her. "Why did you really invite me along on this mission?"

"I already told you."

The road next to the battered metal armadillo had seen better days, but it was less beat up than the faded metal box. The once-red paint had faded to a pale pink, and someone had tried to attach what looked like plastic tusks to its face. There were two dents on its back—one on the front and the other on the back—that made the raised middle part look like a camel's hump.

"What in tarnation happened to that armadillo?" I asked as I turned down the dirt lane pocked with patches of gravel.

"Billy Jack's a big Arkansas Razorback fan. Rumor has it that he was drunk enough to think it was a razorback one night. He got pretty ticked off when he found out his mistake, which explains the dents in its back. He fixed it in another drunken stupor."

"I take it Billy Jack gets drunk a lot?"

"Define a lot . . ."

I slammed on the brakes, which didn't exactly have the effect I was going for, since we were only traveling ten miles per hour. "Neely Kate, what exactly are you draggin' me into?"

Her face scrunched in indignation. "Nothing! We're checking on my cousin. It's perfectly harmless." She gave a half shrug. "Probably."

I reached for my phone. "I'm calling Joe."

"No!" she shouted, grabbing my phone out of my hand and holding it out of my reach. "Don't! Billy Jack hates the sheriff's department. We'll never find her if you do that."

"Neely Kate, if you think she's in actual danger, let Joe come check on her. He's better equipped to deal with something like this than we are."

Before I could register what she was doing, Neely Kate opened the passenger door and hopped out, taking my phone with her and leaving the door gaping wide open.

I opened my own door. "Neely Kate! Come back here."

"You can wait there if you want," she called over her shoulder. "I'll be back in a minute."

"I'm gonna kill you, pregnant or not," I grumbled as I climbed down and started after her.

She'd already disappeared around a bend in the road, and when I found her, she was standing in front of a rusted trailer surrounded by rusted cars, a pile of assorted home furnishings, and knee-deep weeds. A giant "Keep Out" sign, written in spray paint, was nailed to a tilting post.

"Your cousin lives *here?*" I couldn't imagine anyone willingly living in those conditions.

"No. But she's spent a lot of time here with Billy Jack. The last time Aunt Thelma heard from her, Dolly was hanging out here."

I was glad she hadn't made a move toward the front door. I had a sneaking suspicion that Billy Jack's sign wasn't just for show. "Is her boyfriend violent?"

"Not usually."

"Tell me again why we can't call Joe?" I hissed.

"Because Joe won't give two figs."

My eyes narrowed. "What are you talking about?"

She turned toward me, disgust painted all over her face. "I didn't just ask you not to call him on account of Billy Jack. My aunt called the sheriff's department last night to file a missing persons report. They won't do anything."

"Why not?"

"They say she has a history of taking off. Aunt Thelma tried to tell them that it's different this time, that she's never disappeared for three days before, but they wouldn't listen. So it's up to me to find her."

"Neely Kate," I groaned. "Why didn't you just tell me? I would have helped you."

"After the whole thing with the bank robbers and Skeeter . . ." She gave me an apologetic smile. "Well, you got so deep last time that I wasn't sure you'd be open to it."

"We're best friends, Neely Kate. Where you go, I go."

"Thank you." She gave me a quick hug. "Now all you need to do is stay back on the other side of the road. I'll go knock on the door to see if she's here."

"If you think I'm gonna do that, you're as crazy as Billy Jack on a bender." I looped my arm through hers. "Though I suspect your story about your car breaking down was a crock of crap, and you want me here for more than a getaway driver."

She squeezed my arm. "You're the best friend a girl could ever hope to have."

"I'm gonna wait until we're on our way home to decide if I'm gonna return the sentiment." I winked. "So what's your plan?"

"Billy Jack and I have never had bad blood, so I'm not worried about him. As long as he's semi-sober."

"And if he's drunk as a skunk?"

"Run."

I supposed it was as good of a plan as any, given the circumstances. "At least he doesn't have any dogs," I muttered as we followed the trampled path to the trailer through a forest of weeds.

"Oh, he does. They're just in the house."

So much for that pipe dream. I glanced around. "Do you see your cousin's car anywhere?"

She frowned. "No. But that doesn't mean anything. I think it got repossessed."

"But you don't know?"

"No. I was hoping Billy Jack could tell us."

We stopped on the six-foot-by-six-foot porch, which appeared fairly new and was covered by a roof. The whole structure was in better shape than the rest of the trailer combined, even though empty beer cans had been shoved into a corner.

Neely Kate knocked on the front door and stood back, ready to make a getaway if necessary.

A bunch of yipping broke loose inside, and I cast a sideways glance at her while still trying to watch the door. "What is that?"

"Billy Jack's dogs. He breeds Chihuahuas."

"You're kidding."

Her nose scrunched up. "Why would I be kidding?"

The door started to open, and I tensed as a guy's face poked around the corner. "Whaddaya want?"

My best friend lifted her chin. "Billy Jack? It's Neely Kate, Dolly Parton's cousin."

The door opened wider, and five white Chihuahuas rushed out the crack and started jumping up on our legs.

He stood in the space, wearing a white wife-beater T-shirt and a pair of jeans, holding a can of Pabst Blue Ribbon in his hand. Several days' growth of beard covered his face, and his eyes were bloodshot. "Whaddaya want?" he repeated.

"I want to talk to Dolly. Where is she?"

One of the Chihuahuas pressed against my leg and started humping. Horrified, I gave my leg a tiny shake, but he just wrapped his front legs around my shin. The other four ran around Neely Kate and me like Indians circling a wagon train in an old Western.

Billy Jack looked at Neely Kate as though she was a horde of ants eating his chocolate cake. "How would I know where she is?"

Anger filled Neely Kate's voice. "Because the last time anyone talked to her was when she was with you."

The dog on my leg was still going to town, so I gave a harder shake, but he hung on for dear life.

He laughed, but it was a humorless sound. "Well, she ain't here."

She moved to the door. "Then you won't mind me comin' in and lookin' around." She shoved it open with the palm of her hand, and Billy Jack stumbled out of the way.

I stomped my foot hard, finally managing to dislodge the dog before I hurried inside after Neely Kate.

"Well come on in, then," he sneered, downing the beer as we walked past him.

"Don't mind if we do," she said, her voice syrupy sweet.

I sent up a little prayer that the dogs would stay outside, but they all came in, the last one barely making it through the crack before Billy Jack slammed the door shut.

Standing in the middle of the living room, Neely Kate waved her hand in front of her face. I couldn't blame her. It smelled like a rat had crawled up inside the tattered sofa and died. "What in tarnation are you cooking in this trailer, Billy Jack?" she asked.

He crushed the beer can with his hand, then tossed it over his shoulder into the kitchen, where it landed on the floor. "I'm working on my super-secret muskrat jerky recipe."

She shook her head in irritation. "Everybody and his brother knows the only reason you started seeing Dolly Parton was to get at Aunt Thelma's jerky recipes."

"That right there's a bunch of bullshit! I was making jerky for years before Dolly started hangin' around."

She put her hands on her hips and glared. "So where is she now?"

"I done told you. I. Don't. Know."

"When was the last time you saw her?"

"Two days ago. We got into a big-ass fight and she took off with some guy."

"What guy?"

"How the hell would I know?"

She turned her head and gave him a sideways glare. "You're standin' there tellin' me that you let Dolly Parton go out that door—" she pointed at the front door, "and get into a car with *some guy* you didn't know nothin' about?" Her eyebrows rose high on her forehead at his silence. "*Huh?*"

"All right." He opened a baby gate separating the kitchen from the living room, and the dogs immediately followed him. He moved over to the sink and opened a window, then reached through the opening and grabbed a can of beer.

The dogs ran deeper into the room and began snarling.

Billy Jack cast a backward glance at the dogs as he popped the beer open. "Go on now. *Git.*" He shooed them out of the kitchen and sauntered into the living room while taking a big gulp of his beverage.

The dogs skidded to a halt next to a nasty leather recliner, still snarling, and piled in a heap.

I felt a vision coming, and I nearly groaned out loud. Talk about poor timing. The nasty trailer faded away, and suddenly I was in a tiny room covered in cheap paneling. An old metal desk sat in the corner. A pretty brunette wearing something that looked like a two-piece swimsuit covered in sequins leaned against it, and she looked ticked off.

"I've done my part, and I want my money," I said in Billy Jack's voice.

She put her hands on her hips. "Well, you didn't really deliver in the end, did you?" Her face softened, but her mouth puckered into a pout. "Besides, I thought you did it for me, sugar."

"I did," I grunted. "But I still got bills to pay."

She sighed, gliding toward me, trailing her fingertips down the side of my face. "Don't you worry. I'll take care of you." The vision quickly faded.

"You did it for her," I blurted out as Billy Jack's living room came back into focus.

"What are you on about?" he hollered. "If she wanted to leave, I couldn't do much to stop her."

Neely Kate shot me a weird look, then turned back to him. "Cut the stalling, Billy Jack." She tapped her foot. "I ain't got all day. I got a boss nosier than a cat sniffing out a ball of catnip, wondering where in Sam Hill I am. Who'd Dolly Parton leave with?"

"Some guy from her work."

Neely Kate's back stiffened. "*What* guy?"

"I don't know. I think he's a bartender. He came out here lookin' for her, and she left with him. That's all I know."

She put her hand on her hips. "And you just let him take her?"

"It weren't like that." He waved his foot at the dogs in front of the recliner, and they scattered, one of them dragging the fur of something that looked alarmingly like a raccoon. Billy Jack flopped down in his chair without spilling a drop of beer—an amazing feat. "I done told you we had a fight. She locked herself in the bedroom, then she came barreling out and hopped in his car. She must have called him."

"Where'd she go?"

"Damn, woman, yer like a broken record. My answer's the same as the other first half-dozen times you asked. *I don't know.*"

Neely Kate considered his answer before asking. "What were you fightin' about?"

He stopped mid-sip, mumbling, "I forget." Then took a drink.

"You forget?" Neely Kate's tone was dry.

"That was two days ago—" he snorted his disgust, "you can't expect me to remember everything."

She crossed her arms over her chest. "Try again, Billy Jack."

They had a staring contest for several seconds before he looked away, squirming. "She thought I was messin' around on 'er."

"Were you?"

He looked defiant. "Even if I was, it still don't make it right that she smashed my TV on her way out." He gestured to a flat screen TV with a shattered screen. "I traded that for a hundred pounds of jerky to Big G at the pawn shop." His eyes widened. "Do you know how hard it is to make a hundred pounds of jerky?"

"Where's Dolly's car?" Neely Kate asked.

He shrugged. "The repo man came and took it two weeks ago." He downed more beer.

"If you see her, have her call me. I can't get her on her cell, and her momma's worried."

Fear filled his eyes at the mention of Neely Kate's aunt. "That woman's the devil."

"And you're lucky she didn't come out here and tan your hide." Neely Kate glanced at me. "Give me one of your cards."

My mouth parted. "What?"

"Your business card. Give me one."

Did she really think Billy Jack was gonna hire me to landscape his *yard?* "I don't think—"

She held her hand out to me. "*Give me one.*"

I dug into my purse and pulled out one of my new business cards. I gave it to her, and she handed it to Billy Jack.

"If you remember anything or hear from her, call this number."

"I ain't gonna hear from her. I told her not to bother comin' back."

Neely Kate headed for the front door, apparently done with him.

"Take that box with you," he called out.

"What box?" she asked.

He pointed to a cardboard box on an end table on the other side of the wall. "That's Dolly's stuff. Take it with ya."

Neely Kate looked torn with indecision, so I hefted the box on my hip. She gave me a grateful smile, then opened the front door. Just then, one of the dogs shot across the floor with the raccoon skin in his mouth and raced outside, the other four dogs following.

"You let my dogs out with that skin! Now I'll never get them back!" Billy Jack hollered, fumbling with the lever on his chair as he tried to put it down. "Fluffy! Carmen!" he shouted.

Neely Kate's eyes widened. "Run!"

We hurried out the door, trying to take advantage of our lead time and our sobriety. The dogs were shooting toward the woods, the dog with the raccoon hide in the lead.

We'd made it to the dirt road when Billy Jack finally appeared in the doorway. "Carmen! Poncho! *Mr. Wiggles!*" His gaze landed on us as we halted in horror, both of us staring at him. "I'm gonna get you for this!"

Neely Kate took off running again, and I struggled to keep up while juggling the heavy box. Thankfully Billy Jack was drunk enough that his coordination was off, and he missed the top step, landing flat on his face. He fell hard enough that I worried for a moment that he was really hurt, but as he struggled to his feet, it soon became apparent that Neely Kate and I were the ones in real danger.

We made it to the truck, and I swung open the driver's door and jumped in, heaving the box into the backseat as Billy Jack came staggering around the corner, moving faster than a drunk man had any right to.

"Hurry!" Neely Kate hollered as she leaped into the passenger side and shut the door behind her.

I dug the keys out of my pocket, shutting the door seconds before Billy Jack reached the truck. He slammed the palms of his hands on the truck hood.

"You lost my babies!"

"His babies?" I asked in disbelief as I fumbled to get the key into the ignition.

"Don't ask. Just go!"

She didn't have to tell me twice. I started the engine and jerked the truck into reverse. I floored the gas so hard that the truck shot backward, leaving Billy Jack off-balance with a stunned expression on his face.

I made it to the end of the lane and backed onto the highway, thankful there wasn't any traffic to hamper our escape.

"I'm gonna kill you, Neely Kate," I muttered as I checked the rearview mirror. I wouldn't have been surprised to see Billy Jack running down the road after us.

"You can kill me later. You had a vision, didn't you?"

I scowled. She was trying to change the subject. "I think Billy Jack was foolin' around on Dolly."

"Tell me what you saw."

I told her about my vision, then glanced over at her. "Wait, maybe I saw Dolly. What does she look like?"

"She's blond. About my height. Big blue eyes."

"So a lot like you?"

She grinned. "We spent a lot of time together when we were little. People used to think we were sisters."

"The girl in my vision definitely wasn't her. She had long brown hair."

"That only confirms that he *was* cheating on her. That lying snake in the grass."

"Looks like it."

"It's a good thing the sheriff didn't get involved." She shook her head. "Billy Jack wouldn't have told him a thing. Especially not what he told us."

"And what exactly did he tell us? That she left with the bartender?" I shook my head. "That's nothing special. Unless the vision means something."

"Only that he's cheating scum."

I cast a quick glance at her before returning my attention to the road. "So what are you gonna do? Tell your aunt?"

"Yeah . . ." She sat back in her seat, lost in thought. "But I've got a bad feeling about all of this. If she left Billy Jack's, why didn't she call Aunt Thelma? She always tells her when she has a breakup." She shook her head. "Something's not right."

"Well, like I said, I'm meeting Joe this afternoon. Maybe he can help."

"He's with the sheriff's department. You're wasting your time and your breath if you tell him about this."

Chapter Seven

After I dropped Neely Kate off at the courthouse at one forty-five, I had little time to spare before my meeting with Joe. And after trying to eat Neely Kate's tofu mess, I was starving. I decided to stop by the Burger Shack to pick up something to eat.

I wasn't all that surprised to see Eric Davidson behind the counter when I walked in. He was one of the five guys responsible for a string of robberies before Thanksgiving, including the bank robbery in which my deposit bag was stolen. He'd been at the auction, and while I'd been there, too, he had no idea I was the Lady in Black. Still, I hesitated at the counter long enough to get his attention.

"Hey, you're that woman from church."

My eyes widened in mock innocence. "What?"

"I thought I recognized you when you came in a couple of weeks ago, but your friend did all the talking." He looked worried. "You're the woman who said that . . . strange thing."

I shrugged, then shook my head. "I don't know what you're talking about." I hoped I was convincing enough to get him to let it lie. I'd had a vision and blurted out to a group of four malcontents from Jonah's support group that they were gonna rob another place. Things could have gotten ugly if Joe hadn't intervened.

His eyes narrowed. "Yeah . . . I think you do."

I considered turning around and running, but two things stopped me. One, I'd look guilty if I ran. And two, I was hungry.

I rubbed my forehead. "I wasn't myself that day." I leaned closer. "I hadn't taken my medication."

He took a step back, wariness on his face.

I straightened. "I want a hamburger with fries." I shifted my eyes back and forth a couple of times. "And could you hurry? I'm late in taking my medication today, and I feel kind of strange, if you know what I mean."

He quickly rang up my order, staying back from the counter. As he started to bag my food, I suddenly wondered what had happened to Mick Gentry, the large-animal vet who'd killed Norman Sullivan, the Henryetta Bank loan manager who'd been one of their co-conspirators, but had decided to rat them out. Mick had made the news when he disappeared the weekend after Thanksgiving. Had Skeeter disposed of him, or had he really run off as the police suspected?

Eric handed me the bag, still keeping his distance.

And that's when I felt another vision slam me with more force than usual.

I was sitting in the front seat of an old car. The passenger door opened, but I stared out of the windshield instead of turning toward it.

"Is it set?" the guy next to me said.

"Yeah."

"Let me know if you have any problems."

"Yeah."

The vision faded, and I was suddenly back in the Burger Shack. "Everything is set," I gushed out.

"What?" he asked.

Usually a vision came and went, but a fuzziness had lingered in my head this time, and I stumbled backward. "See? I better go take my medication."

I hurried out to the truck and set the forgotten food next to me, then drove the short distance to the nursery, anxious, though for the life of me, I couldn't figure out why. I was more upset over my vision than Eric was over me having it.

Joe's car wasn't in the lot, and neither was Violet's, and no one was manning the few Christmas trees we had left in the lot. I could have gone inside, but I found myself staring out the windshield at the building instead. What had I seen, and why was it so ominous? Lost in thought, I didn't pay any mind to my surroundings, so I shrieked when someone banged on my window.

When I turned, Joe's alarmed face was staring back at me. He immediately opened the truck door. "Rose, are you okay?"

I considered lying to him, but this felt important enough to share. "No."

He grabbed my elbow and helped me slide out of the truck. "What happened?"

My feet hit the pavement, and a frigid breeze blew my hair around my face. I suddenly felt foolish. I shook my head. "It was probably nothing."

"Don't tell me it was nothing. Something has you shook up, which automatically makes it something. You're not the sort of woman to react this way over nothing."

I took a deep breath.

Still holding my arm, he tugged me away from the truck and shut the door. "Let's go inside, okay?"

"Okay."

Joe unlocked the door with his own set of keys that Violet had given him and pushed the door open. He led me to the back room, where my potting bench and stool still remained in their proper places. After gently pushing me onto the stool, he squatted in front of me. "Tell me what happened."

"I had a vision."

His eyes widened. "Was it something bad?"

I shook my head. "I don't know. It didn't seem bad, but I just don't feel right about it. I guess it left me with the notion that something bad is about to happen."

"Tell me what you saw."

I relayed everything, which made me feel even more foolish, since it was, on the surface, one of my tamer visions.

"Don't dismiss it, Rose," Joe said, standing. "It might be nothing, sure, but it could be *something*. Who was the person associated with the vision?"

"Eric Davidson, the assistant manager of the Burger Shack."

His eyebrows lifted. "You know his name? You make it sound like you know him."

I held his gaze. If I wanted his advice, I needed to tell him a bit about the mess I was in. The question was where to draw the line. "It's not how it sounds. You know when you saw me with those guys at church? He's one of them."

Irritation clouded his eyes. "So you *were* talking to them?"

"Not intentionally. I really did want to talk to Samantha Jo about the bank robbery. But I had a vision and told them they were getting ready to rob something."

His eyes flew open. "Why didn't you tell me?"

I shrugged. I couldn't very well confirm his suspicion that Neely Kate and I had been trying to track down the bank robbers ourselves. "You were angry with me."

"Rose." His voice was heavy with disappointment. "Tell me that you at least shared this with Mason."

I remained silent.

"Why would you keep something like that to yourself?"

"It was a vision, Joe. Neither of you would have been able to use the information."

"Rose," he said, exasperated. "You told a group of men, some of whom had a criminal history, that you knew they were gonna rob something. You could have been in serious danger."

"But nothing happened," I insisted.

"It was a huge risk." He sounded so disappointed that it stole my breath. "You were lucky."

He had no idea. "There's something else I need to tell you."

He waited, his face expressionless.

"I think I know who killed Mr. Sullivan."

"What? How?"

How was I gonna explain this one? "I figured it out from my vision." Which was partially true. The killer had confessed his crimes in one of my visions, but it wasn't until the auction on Thanksgiving that I'd pieced together his identity. Ever since, I'd been trying to think of how to tell Joe or Mason the truth about him without giving everything else away. "He's the large-animal vet. Mick Gentry."

"Did you at least tell Mason about *that?*"

"No," I said, ashamed that it had taken me so long to pursue justice for poor Mr. Sullivan. "I only just put it together. Besides, he disappeared." I felt bad about lying to him, but I couldn't help wondering if justice had already been served vigilante-style by Skeeter Malcolm.

Joe's gaze pierced mine. "Does he have any way of knowing that you know?"

"No. I'm certain he doesn't." I sighed. "But it doesn't matter, Joe. It's like all the rest of my visions . . . it's not exactly admissible in court."

"We can try to link him to it. The fact that he ran off and disappeared doesn't speak of innocence either." His gaze softened. "It's more helpful than you know."

"You're not gonna yell at me?"

"Why would I yell at you?" He paused. "I'm just thankful you finally shared your vision with me. Are you feeling better?"

"No. But I'll be okay." I hopped off the stool, feeling guilty. "Maybe all this got stirred up because of Neely Kate's cousin."

He stilled. "What about her cousin?"

"Her momma tried to file a missing persons report on her last night, and the deputy she talked to wouldn't file it."

He stared at me for a moment. "Dolly Parton Parker is Neely Kate's cousin?" He shook his head, wearing an exasperated grimace. "Why am I not surprised?"

I grew indignant on my friend's behalf. "What on earth does that mean?"

"She has some colorful characters in her family is all."

"If you know her name, then why don't you tell me why the deputy wouldn't file the report?"

Joe held his hands up in defense. "Darlin', this isn't the first time her mother's filed a report on her, and it's not even the third. I looked over the previous instances with the deputy who took her call. She always turns up."

"Oh."

"She's also got a bit of a criminal record, nothing dangerous. Shoplifting. Solicitation."

"Solicitation?"

"She was arrested this summer and again a month ago, but the charges were dropped." He rubbed my arm. "Still, I understand you wanting to help your friend. It's one of the things I love about you."

I worried that Joe was about to venture into dangerous territory, so I took a step back. "Thanks for the clarification. Now don't we have some business to take care of?"

He looked relieved that I was going to let the whole Dolly Parton thing drop. "You wait here, and I'll go get the paperwork. I was worried about you when I saw you sitting in your truck like that, so I left it in the car."

I wandered into the retail space. There were more boxes than before. I found myself wondering what ideas Joe had cooked up.

After a moment, he came back inside and set a file on the shop counter. "I looked over all the paperwork. Everything looks to be in order. But since you wanted several specific clauses included, I thought we should be together when we signed it so there are no hurt feelings later."

"Okay." I moved next to him. "But are you sure you don't want to let an attorney—" I stopped as I realized what I was saying. "Sorry. I keep forgetting you went to law school yourself."

"I never fit the attorney mold. I found it too suffocating." He cringed when I stiffened. "Rose, I wasn't trying to insult Mason. Honest, that's just how I always envisioned it."

I relaxed. "Yeah, I have trouble seeing you as a lawyer."

"I told you before that I only went to law school to appease my father." He clicked his pen, getting ready to sign. "I've always wondered how different my life would have been if I'd stood up to him even then."

The thought made me sad—not just for him, but for me. "When's he gonna make you run for office again?" I asked softly. We both knew it wasn't a matter of if, but when.

"I don't know."

He sounded wary, and I decided not to push it. We both knew he didn't want to run, but he couldn't turn his father down. J.R. Simmons would make me pay if he tried.

"I heard Hilary moved to Henryetta." I still had a hard time picturing her living in such a small town, especially one as backward as ours.

He released a heavy sigh. "I didn't ask her to do it, but it might make things easier in the long run."

"But she's not living with you out at the house next to my farm?" I asked, sounding more defensive than I'd intended.

He held up his hands in protest. "I know how it looks—"

Tears burned my eyes. "I don't want to fight with you anymore, Joe. Every time we're ugly to each other, it takes what we had together and makes it seem pointless." I looked up at him. "But it wasn't pointless. What we had was wonderful. You gave me so much to be grateful for. Even so, our relationship is over now."

He studied me for several seconds, then swallowed. "I'm not moving out by you to start anything. The house is older and needs some work. Add onto that the fact that the banker's body was found on the property, and no one else wants to live there now. The owner's letting me rent the house for next to nothing in exchange for fixing it up."

"Why would you do that?" I asked, incredulous. "You can afford anything you want."

He shrugged. "Believe it or not, I like to fix up old things. It's a solid house that needs some attention, and it's something to fill my time."

I didn't respond.

"Look, it's taken a while for me to accept that you're really not mine. And while I'm not happy about it, I have to respect your decision." His face softened. "I don't want to fight with you either. You're the best thing that ever happened to me, and I don't want to live without you. If I can only have you as a friend, then so be it. It's better than not having you in my life at all."

I smiled up at him, resisting the urge to hug him. "I'm happy to hear that."

He studied my face for several seconds before giving his attention to the stack of papers on the counter. "And what's more, our effort to get along will be advantageous to the business."

We started to go through the papers, Joe reading all of it aloud, asking me if I had any questions when we hit a section containing a lot of legalese.

"Mason's already gone over most of this with me, Joe. If you need to get back to work . . ."

"No," he insisted. "This is important."

After we read the entire document and signed and initialed everything, Joe broke out into a smile, looking happier than I'd seen him in months.

"Joe Simmons, business partner." His grin broadened. "I like it."

"Well, Joe Simmons, business partner," I nudged his arm with mine, "tell me about your grand plans."

For the next ten minutes, he told me about his ideas for the expansion and inventory, most of which had serious potential. I told him so, but then said, "I don't want to sink more money into the nursery until it gets going in the spring. We don't know what kind of fallout Violet's indiscretion will have on the business, not to mention other things . . . The fact that the whole lot of us are steeped in controversy and scandal won't help matters."

He studied my face. "Are you really worried?"

"No . . . yes. But not enough that I'd change anything." I brushed loose hairs from my cheek. "Still, the reason we almost lost it all is because Violet tried to build us too big, too fast."

"Rose, I won't let that happen again."

"Maybe, maybe not, but there's no reason to put everything at risk. Let's just wait and see how it goes."

"Sometimes great risk means great reward."

He wasn't telling me anything I hadn't read in my business books. "Maybe next spring I'll be willing to bet it all and let it ride, but right now I could use a little safe and easy."

He grinned. "Since when do you do safe and easy?"

"I'd like to give it a chance."

He studied me again, and a war waged in his eyes before he nodded. "Safe and easy it is, Rose. But when you're willing to start gambling again, let me know." As he gathered up the paperwork, I couldn't help thinking that safe and easy was a pipe dream.

Chapter Eight

I left the nursery later than planned, so I texted Mason to let him know I'd signed the papers with Joe, and then called Bruce Wayne to check on the situation at the office.

"The phones and Wi-Fi have been set up without a problem. Now all we need is a working fuse box."

"I'm going to go help Mason's mom unpack. Let me know if you need anything."

"I might need medical attention after breathing in the fumes from that mess in the plastic tub on your desk. The place stank to high heaven when I walked in after you left. I spent five minutes searching for Muffy, 'cause she's the only thing I know that stinks that much."

"Oh dear. Neely Kate left the gourmet food there, didn't she?"

"It's gone now. I tried to feed it to a stray dog out back, but he got close enough to sniff it and took off running. You know something's bad when even starving dogs won't eat it." He laughed. "You're gonna have to tell 'er, Rose. That or risk food poisoning."

"I know," I grumbled. "I'll figure something out."

I got to Violet's house at right about the time Ashley came home from school. Violet had spent more time at home than at work over the last couple of weeks, and she genuinely did seem happier. She greeted me at the door with a bright smile. "Hi, Rose."

"Hi," I said, still wary.

"Ashley is so excited to spend the afternoon with you. Thank you so much for thinking of it."

"Of course. I love her." I paused. "I thought you should know that Joe and I signed the business papers today." I handed her the folder tucked under my arm. "I brought them for you to sign too."

"Oh." She looked surprised.

I lowered my voice so Ashley wouldn't hear. "I know you're upset that you only have ten percent ownership now, but you still have a say in things, Violet."

Tears filled her eyes. "It was *my* dream, Rose."

A lump filled my throat, but I couldn't back down. "I know, Vi, and I'm sorry."

She nodded and turned, her face breaking out into a bright smile when Ashley emerged from her room. "All ready to go with Aunt Rose?"

Ashley nodded and gave us a wide grin.

Violet dropped to her knees and pulled Ashley into a hug, stroking the back of her head for several seconds before pulling back to stare into her daughter's face. "Now you be a good girl for Aunt Rose and mind your manners with Miss Maeve."

"Yes, ma'am." Ashley's head bobbed.

Violet gave her a kiss on the cheek. "You have fun now."

"Do you want me to go over the papers with you?" I asked as Violet stood.

She shook her head, tears shining in her eyes. "No. I know what's in there."

"Okay." But I felt bad that I was just dumping them off after Joe and I had signed them together. I didn't want her to think she was some kind of afterthought. "I can pick them up after I bring Ashley home."

She nodded and disappeared into the kids' room without another word.

As I drove Ashley to Maeve's new house, I couldn't shake the thought that something was going on with my sister.

The moving men had come and gone by the time Ashley and I arrived. We spent the next two hours helping Maeve unpack the kitchen. Maeve asked Ashley her opinion on where to store everything from her bakeware to her spices. Thankfully the little girl had inherited her mother's organizational skills, so she was a help rather than a hindrance.

The sun set, and we turned on the lamps we'd unpacked, filling the small house with a cozy glow, even though we were surrounded by boxes and piles of bubble wrap and packing peanuts. Mason showed up at around six with two pizza boxes. "Who's hungry?" he called out as he made his way through the maze of empty boxes.

"Me!" Ashley shouted.

We cleared off the dining room table, and Maeve disappeared into the kitchen to look for a roll of paper towels for us to use as plates while Ashley washed her hands in the bathroom.

Mason pulled me into a hug and gave me a kiss. "I was worried about you today," he murmured in my ear. "Did you have any problems?"

"I had a weird vision, but I'm not sure what to make of it."

He leaned back, worry in his eyes.

"I'm ready to eat, Aunt Rose," Ashley said as she came down the hall. "I washed my hands really good."

I started to break loose, but Mason's arm stayed behind my back. "Did it have something to do with our run-in with Malcolm this morning?"

"No." I patted Mason's chest. "It was probably nothing, but I'll tell you all about it later. I told the chief deputy sheriff when I saw him earlier."

He tensed. "It must have been *something* if you told Joe. Was he concerned?"

"No," I prevaricated.

"Not even after our run-in with Malcolm this morning?"

"Mason," I sighed, hoping he didn't realize I was glossing over the fact that I hadn't told Joe about Skeeter. "That was nothing. I'm fine."

He didn't look convinced.

I looked over my shoulder. "Maeve, I need to talk to Mason in private. It will only take a few minutes."

"Take your time."

I smiled at Ashley. "You go ahead and start eating, and we'll be back inside in a minute."

Her head bobbed. "Okay, Aunt Rose."

I led him out to the front porch and pulled him close to help keep both of us warm. I told him pretty much exactly what I'd told Joe—about the vision today, recognizing Eric from church a few weeks ago, and the fact that Mick was responsible for Mr. Sullivan's death. As I'd done with Joe, I led Mason to believe that today's recent vision had jogged that particular realization loose.

I could see the disappointment in his eyes. "Why didn't you tell me weeks ago?" Hurt filled his voice.

"I'm sorry, Mason. Truly, I am."

He was silent.

"What do you think my vision meant? Before now, I've never felt bad after one before, and the sensation hung on for several minutes."

"I don't know, but I think you need to stay away from the Burger Shack."

"Okay."

"I'm going to talk to Joe about checking up on that manager to be on the safe side, as well as digging more into the vet."

"But that's just it, Mason. Nothing bad happened in my vision."

"Maybe not, but it's affected you all the same, and that has to mean something." His voice hardened. "In the meantime, promise me you'll stay away."

"I promise."

He hugged me and held me tight. "You scare me to death, the things you get into. Maybe I should quit my job so I can follow you around all day and keep you out of trouble."

"You're presuming I'm in the market for a bodyguard."

He nibbled my ear. "It would come with perks."

"I thought, as your potential employer, it was my job to offer the perks."

"I am definitely open to negotiation. What kind of benefits package are you offering?"

Laughing, I broke free and grabbed his hand. "We'll save the negotiations for later."

After we ate, we helped Maeve for another hour, making a lot of progress between the four of us. Around eight, I realized I needed to get Ashley home, since it was a school night. As I bundled her up in her coat, my phone rang. I breathed a sigh of relief that it was my best friend and not the largest current thorn in my side.

"Hey, Neely Kate," I answered in surprise. She typically took her grandma to bingo on Tuesday nights. "What's up?"

"Dolly Parton's still missing."

"Oh," I said, standing up and grabbing my own jacket.

"I was wondering how your day looked tomorrow. Do you think you can go with me on my lunch break to talk to her best friend?"

"Can't you just call her?" I asked as Mason picked up his coat and gave me an inquisitive look.

"Tabitha and I don't get along lately," she said with a tight edge to her voice. "She wouldn't answer my call. Trust me."

"Do you think she'll talk to you in person?"

"I'm hopin' she'll talk to *you* in person." She paused. "Will you help?"

"Of course, I will. What time do you want to go?"

"She tends to sleep late, so I'm thinking around noon. Lunchtime will work. Can we take your truck? She'll know my car."

Whatever had happened between the two women must have been fairly recent. Neely Kate had replaced her beat-up clunker with a used Toyota in August, right after her wedding to Ronnie. "Sure. Just come over to my office, and we'll leave from there," I said before I hung up, hoping this meant I could get out of eating more of Neely Kate's gourmet messes.

"What's going on?" Mason asked, concern in his voice as he helped me with my coat while Maeve said goodbye to Ashley.

I knew how disappointed Mason was about everything I'd been keeping from him—not to mention the whole Lady in Black secret, which he still didn't know . . . and hopefully never would—so I wanted to be on the up-and-up with him.

But now I was worried about what he'd think of our mission to find Dolly Parton.

"Neely Kate's cousin is missing." His eyes widened in alarm, but before he could say anything, I added, "It's not the first time. According to Joe, this is apparently a common thing with her. She takes off for a few days, her momma files a missing persons report, and then she turns up again. Neely Kate's aunt called to file the latest report last night, but the sheriff's office isn't going to follow up on it just yet."

Mason nodded. "It makes sense, but I take it Neely Kate's not content to sit and wait for her to come back?"

"No. She wants to go ask Dolly Parton's best friend if she knows anything."

Surprise washed over his face. "Did you say, 'Dolly Parton'? As in the singer?"

"It's a family thing." I waved my hand in dismissal. "Her brothers are Alan Jackson and Tommy Lee."

Mason watched me for a second, as though deciding what to say. He gave a little shake of his head. "Does Neely Kate have any idea where she is?"

"She had me drive her to see Dolly's boyfriend—ex-boyfriend, I guess. He said they had a fight, and Dolly drove off with a bartender from where she works."

"Sounds like maybe she's pissed at her boyfriend and took off."

"I think that's what Joe thinks."

"Talk to her friend, but just be careful, okay?"

I gave him a smile. "Okay."

We decided to ride home together and loaded a sleepy Ashley into my truck. After we dropped her off and I picked up the paperwork from Violet, I confessed to Mason how guilty I felt about only giving my sister ten percent of the business.

"You're well within your rights, Rose. She's put nothing down."

"But it was her dream, Mason. I feel like I'm stealing it from her."

"It may have been her dream in the beginning, but she wouldn't have gotten anywhere if you hadn't financed it. And she nearly lost the business for both of you after making decisions she had no right to make without you." He took my hand and squeezed it. "I think it's more than generous of you to give her anything at all."

"I gave Bruce Wayne fifty percent ownership of RBW, and he didn't put anything down."

"Sweetheart, if it'll make you feel better to give her more control of the shop, then do it. But just remember, Joe already owns thirty-five percent. How much more of your fifty-five percent are you willing to give up?" He paused. "I know you didn't ask, but I'm going to give you my opinion anyway. Keep at least fifty-one percent. That way you'll still control the business, no matter what happens."

I hadn't considered that. "Okay. Thank you."

"Who knows?" He gave me a grin. "Maybe Joe will sell his shares to Violet one day."

At this point, I wasn't sure what to hope for.

Chapter Nine

The next morning Mason and I sat at the kitchen table eating breakfast before he left for the courthouse.

"There's less than two weeks until Christmas," Mason said while buttering a piece of toast. "When do you want to put up a Christmas tree?"

I took a sip of my coffee. "I guess we need to *get* a tree first."

"Lucky for you, you've still got a bunch outside the store." Mason winked.

"Those Christmas trees were so much trouble, I'm not sure I want one in my house," I grumbled.

"Do you have an artificial tree you put up with your mother?" he asked, then stopped with his fork mid-air, his smile falling. "I'm sure your memories of Christmas with your mother weren't all that pleasant. I'm sorry, Rose. I wasn't thinking."

I grabbed his hand. "You didn't do anything wrong. It's a perfectly normal question. It's not your fault that my family was dysfunctional."

He squeezed my hand and grinned. "*Everybody's* family is dysfunctional to some degree. Yours was just a touch more so."

"A touch more so." I laughed. "That's like calling the pope a little Catholic." I leaned forward. "I want to wipe the slate clean of all my past Christmases. Are there any traditions you have that you'd like to do? Like put up stockings or bake cookies?"

He lifted his eyebrows mischievously. "I can assure you that you do *not* want me baking you cookies."

"We could make them together."

"Do *you* want to bake cookies?" he asked, sounding surprised.

I released a wistful sigh. "Ever since I was a little girl, I've always dreamed of decorating sugar cookies with my family. I'm not sure why. It just feels homey." I shrugged, feeling embarrassed. "What about you? What do you like to do for Christmas?"

"My father used to read *The Night Before Christmas* to Savannah and me on Christmas Eve before we hung our stockings and left cookies and milk out for Santa. I'd like to do that with my own kids someday."

I leaned over the table and kissed him. "I love you, Mason."

"I love you too." He gave me another kiss and pushed his chair back, pulling me to my feet. "I have to go to work now. I'd love to finish this conversation tonight, but I have a very important question for you before I leave." His eyes twinkled.

"And what question could that be?" I asked, giving him a sly grin.

"Turkey or ham for Christmas dinner?" I started to answer, but he put his finger on my lips. "Think carefully before you answer. The future of our entire relationship could hinge on this very moment."

I kissed the tip of his finger and pulled it down, laughing. "You're putting far too much pressure on me for this early in the day. But I already know my answer: neither."

His eyebrows lifted in amusement. "Neither?"

"Momma always made one or the other. I want to start my own tradition by having something else. With you."

His eyes softened. "I'll make sure this is the best Christmas you've ever had, Rose. I promise."

I stood on my tiptoes and kissed him. "It already is."

"One more question," he said as he grabbed his coat off the hall tree. "Real or artificial tree?"

"Real, of course," I said. "I love the smell of Christmas trees."

Mason left for work, and I started some laundry and cleaned up the kitchen, Muffy fast on my heels all the while. I needed to leave her at home while I was out with Neely Kate, and she could clearly sense it and followed me around, as if to complain about her impending abandonment.

Since I had nothing pressing to do at the office, I called Bruce Wayne to tell him I was going to stay home with Muffy for a while and take her for a long walk.

"Take your time, Rose. There's nothing to hurry in for. There's still no word from Mr. Darby."

"What about from Skeeter's brother?"

"He says Skeeter's under a lot of pressure right now, but he doesn't know any details other than that Skeeter's dealing with some new people in his organization. But he insisted it wasn't a big problem. Just some smoothing over. I didn't bring up your name. I figured the less there is to tie you to him, the better."

I released a sigh. He was right. "Thanks, Bruce Wayne."

After I took Muffy out the front door, I considered heading south on my farmland, but the last time I'd gone that way, I'd found a dead body on my neighbor's property. The fact that Joe was about to move in there was an even bigger deterrent. Instead, we headed north, following the road that bordered the fields. Muffy chased several squirrels and romped around for a half hour. My cell phone rang when we were on our way home, and I pulled it out and answered it without checking the number.

"Hello?"

"Hello, Lady," Skeeter said, sounding amused. "I need you to meet me in thirty minutes."

"Remember what I said. I can't be seen talking to you, Skeeter. Especially after yesterday with Mason." I took a quick breath. "What on earth was *that* about?"

He laughed. "I was just messin' with him. It's easier to push his buttons now that you're in the picture."

"Do you really think threatening me in front of my Assistant DA boyfriend is going to make me more compelled to help you out?" I shook my head even if he couldn't see me. "Even if I felt inclined to help you—and I don't—I can't risk being seen with you."

"No offense, Lady, but I have no intention of being seen with you either. Meet me at the old abandoned Sinclair gas station on County Road 110. The one with the giant dinosaur statue next to the building. You know which one I'm talking about?"

"Everybody knows that one." But even though everyone knew the spot, most people didn't pay much attention to it now. It had been closed for years.

"Then you won't have any trouble finding it. See you in thirty minutes." Of course, he hung up before I had the chance to respond.

I figured it would take me fifteen minutes to get there, and I was still a good five minutes from home. Stupid Skeeter.

94

I considered not going. What was the worst that could happen if I didn't show?

I wasn't sure I was willing to risk it.

Thirty-three minutes later, I pulled into the parking lot. A black sedan with tinted windows was already idling behind the run-down station. The car Skeeter and I had taken to the auction.

The driver's door opened, and Jed got out. The move would have been more effective if he'd been wearing a chauffeur's suit instead of jeans and a light brown canvas work jacket.

I reluctantly climbed out of the truck. "Good morning, Jed."

He grinned. "Lady."

I gritted my teeth. I hated that name. "I thought I was meeting Skeeter."

He opened the back door without saying a word. When Skeeter didn't emerge, I realized he wanted me to climb inside.

Skeeter sat in the back wearing a black thermal shirt, jeans, and a shit-eating grin. "Lady."

I slid in next to him. "Make this quick, Skeeter. I have things I need to do."

"It's only ten-thirty. You can't be rushing home to cook one of your dinners." His eyes lit up in amusement.

I grimaced. "Very funny. What do you want?"

His smile faded. "I've got competition."

"What does that mean?"

"I won the auction fair and square, but the way it ended left a bad taste in some people's mouths."

"You mean the bust?"

He shifted in his seat. "The fact that we won the bid and then the sheriff showed up immediately afterward—not to mention we got away . . . Well, some people think I set up it all up."

I shook my head in confusion. "Why would you do that?"

"Although the auction itself wasn't illegal—they had no proof of what was being auctioned—some of the people in that barn had outstanding warrants. It would be a great way for me to get rid of some of my enemies."

"Did you set it up?"

He laughed. "What do you think?"

I studied him for a moment while thinking about what Mason had told me about Skeeter. "No. I think you're smarter than that."

He chuckled, crossing his arms as he eyed me. "Really? Why's that?"

"You could have challenged Daniel Crocker long before he died—"

"Before you killed him," he added, putting his hand on my knee.

He was right. Before I killed him. A fact I was trying my best to forget, despite Jonah and Mason's insistence that I had to deal with it. I hadn't wanted to kill Daniel Crocker, but he'd certainly deserved it.

"That's right. And don't forget it." I gave his hand a hard shove.

Skeeter laughed. "Go on. What makes you think I'm smarter than my enemies realize?"

"You waited, bided your time until you could get Crocker's business peacefully—well, as peacefully as is possible for you people. You won—fair and square, as you said—so why would you want anyone else to get arrested? It would only cause bad blood."

"Aw . . ." he said, with a knowing tone. "And who would benefit from bad blood?"

I rubbed my forehead. "Is that why I'm here? To help you strategize? Do you really think that's wise? After all, I'm going home to cook one of my dinners for the man who's vowed to bring you down." I gasped as I realized what I'd just admitted.

He laughed. Skeeter Malcolm was awfully jovial for a guy with so many people out to get him. "You haven't told me anything I didn't already know. Deveraux's been after me for months."

"Then why are you talking to me?" I asked in disbelief. "How do you know I'm not going to run to his office and tell him everything?"

A menacing gleam filled his eyes, making him look even more predatory than usual. His hand reached for my throat, and he rested it there, his thumb putting light pressure on my carotid artery. "Because I trust you, Lady."

"What you're doing now doesn't suggest you find me trustworthy."

"Habit," he uttered in a low growl, but his hand stayed where it was.

Anger burned in my chest, overriding my fear. "Do you think threatening my life is goin' to make me want to work with you, Skeeter Malcolm?" I shoved his hand down. "I thought we'd already established that wouldn't work. I'm done here." I reached for the door handle.

He grabbed my upper arm. "We are *far* from done here."

And just like that the car faded, and I was in Skeeter's office. I sat behind his desk, while Jed was sitting in the chair across from me.

"It's not looking good. Rogers is turning," Jed said, looking grim.

My fist slammed down on the desk. "Teach him a lesson."

The vision ended, and I was back in the car. "Rogers is turning, and you're gonna teach him a lesson."

"What?" Skeeter's grip on my wrist loosened, and his free hand turned my face to look at him. "Did you just have a vision?"

Still dazed, I nodded.

"What did you see?"

I was getting my wits back, and I jerked my arm from his grip. "Get your hands off me, Skeeter!"

"Tell me what you saw."

"What happens if I don't? Are you going to threaten me again? That's a terrible way to do business."

"I'm not messing around, Rose," he spat through gritted teeth. "What did you see?"

"We need some rules before I tell you one more cotton-picking thing."

He grabbed my arm again and pulled me closer. "Let's not forget who has all the power here."

I stared into his eyes, getting angrier by the minute. "Yes, let's not."

His grip tightened momentarily, then he released his hold and burst out laughing.

I rubbed my arm. "You are in serious need of some mood-altering drugs, Skeeter."

He continued to laugh. "I like you, Rose."

I scowled. "Too bad the feeling's not mutual."

He only laughed harder.

"I don't have time for this nonsense." I reached for the door handle again.

"Rose, wait." His voice was softer, and his hand was gentler as he reached for me. "I keep forgetting that you're not like everyone else I know."

I sat with my back to the seat, looking out the windshield, waiting.

"You're right. I'm used to getting what I want through fear and intimidation. It just doesn't work with you." He leaned closer, lowering his voice. "So what do you want?"

I turned my head toward him, narrowing my eyes. "You're serious."

"As a heart attack."

I shook my head. "You don't have a stinkin' thing that I want."

"Are you sure about that?" He watched me again, his eyes twinkling with the promise that he knew something I didn't.

I remembered our phone call the day before. "That's the second time you've said that. What are you getting at?"

"You want Deveraux's safety."

My temper erupted. "You're threatening *him* now? *Will you never learn?*"

"Not me. Someone else."

My head felt fuzzy. "Who?" I managed to say.

"I'm not sure yet. But I think his fate is tied to mine. So tell me your vision."

"Why do you think Mason's safety has anything to do with you?"

"Call it a hunch, but I got where I am by following hunches."

Mason was in danger. I tried to get myself under control so I could find out more. "Honestly, there's not a lot I can tell you about the vision. You and Jed were in your office. He said Rogers was turning, and you said he needed to be taught a lesson."

He stroked his chin with the tip of his finger. "Rogers, huh? That's not a huge surprise. I knew he was on the fence."

"What's that mean, anyway?"

"He's decided to side with someone else instead of giving his allegiance to me. The question is to who?"

I shook my head. "I don't know. It wasn't in the vision."

"Then force one of me now. Focus on what you saw, and maybe you can find out more."

Groaning, I grabbed his hand and squeezed, focusing on my memory of the vision. The same images repeated themselves, and it ended exactly where it had ended before.

"That's it?" Skeeter asked, getting angry.

"Don't shoot the messenger, Skeeter," I said, irritated.

"Try something else."

Instead of focusing on the previous vision, I concentrated on Rogers and who he was siding with . . . and got the same exact vision I'd experienced the first two times.

"Try it again," he huffed out.

"I'm not a Magic Eight-Ball. You can't keep making me have visions until you get something you like."

"Then what am I supposed to do?"

"Hey, here's an idea: Find out from Rogers himself."

He considered this for a moment. "Yeah, you're right."

"Now who's threatening Mason?"

"I told you I don't know. But as soon as I find out, I'll let you know."

"You mean like how you hustled to get my money back after I gave you information about the bank robbers?"

"The deal was that I got your money back. I lived up to my end."

Maybe so, but he hadn't exactly been in a hurry. I needed more reassurance than his vague response. What proof had he offered me that some unknown force was out to get Mason? How did I know I wasn't being duped? "I want you to promise to leave Mason alone too."

"What?"

"Stop messin' with him."

He laughed. "That's it?"

"No, it's just a start. You have to promise me you won't hurt him." Then I added while ticking off my demands with my fingers, "And you can't get anyone else to do it either. And you have to look into who might be after Mason and take care of it."

"You're serious."

I gave him a grim smile. "As a heart attack."

"That's all you want?" he asked, shaking his head. "Don't you want money?"

"Mason is worth all the money in the world to me and more. I don't want a dime. Only his guaranteed safety. You have to tell me the minute you know something about who's after him."

"Hell, I already told you I would." He waved his hand as though I'd asked him to do the simplest task. "Why are we going over this again?"

"You have to promise."

His amusement fell away. "You know I'm not a man of my word, Lady."

My eyes bore into his. "But you are, Skeeter. You just haven't admitted it to yourself yet."

Uncertainty flickered in his eyes. "I won't touch a hair on his head." When I started to protest, he added, sounding angry, "And I won't let anyone else do it, including whoever is out to get him, too. You're right. I'd rather this arrangement be based on mutual need. That way you'll be more inclined to help and not withhold information from me."

"Fine."

I'd just made yet another deal with the devil.

I reached for the door handle again. "I've gotta go."

He flicked his hand, still brooding. "Go."

101

When I climbed out, Jed was leaning against the hood of the car. He turned to me with raised eyebrows. "He might be a little cranky," I volunteered.

He nodded and moved for his car door while I crossed the lot to my truck. I left first, heading for the landscaping office while pondering what I'd done. Would Skeeter renege on our deal since I hadn't been able to give him the information he wanted? For some bizarre reason, I trusted him. It wasn't a safe bet. At all. Yet, like him, I'd learned to go with my gut.

Bruce Wayne was bent over his computer when I walked into the office. He looked up with a grimace.

I briefly considered telling him about my meeting with Skeeter, but decided the less he knew the better. "What's givin' you such a long face?"

"I've been sitting here all morning, and I don't think I'm smart enough to figure out this computer stuff."

"The landscaping program or the computer itself?"

He threw up his hands. "Any of it."

I gnawed on my lip for a moment. "I'm not sure I'm the one to teach you. I barely know how to use one myself. We need someone to teach us."

The doorbell jingled, and Neely Kate walked in. I swung my gaze toward her, realizing she might be the answer to my prayers.

"What?" she asked when she noticed the way I was looking at her.

"Have you ever taught anyone how to use computers?" I knew she was good with them. She used them all the time to search the Internet for ideas about decorating her baby's room and recipes . . . Maybe asking her for help wasn't such a good idea after all.

She shrugged. "I taught my eighty-six-year-old great-grandma how to shop on eBay."

I gave Bruce Wayne a conspiratorial look before turning back to face her. "How do you feel about tutoring me and Bruce Wayne?"

She looked confused. "Sure, but not now, right? I want to run out to Tabitha's before my lunch break is over."

I glanced up at the clock on the wall. "Neely Kate, it's barely eleven-thirty. You yourself said your cousin's best friend doesn't get up until noon."

"I know. But it's going to take us a bit to get where we're going."

"And where's that?"

"Big Thief Hollow."

"Big Thief Hollow," Bruce Wayne said, narrowing his eyes. "Ain't that where—"

Neely Kate grabbed my arm and started to drag me toward the door. "Good thing you haven't even taken your coat off yet. We need to get going." She opened the door and kept tugging. "See you later, Bruce Wayne."

As she continued to drag me down the sidewalk, I wondered if I would have been better off hanging out with Skeeter.

Chapter Ten

W hat's going on, Neely Kate?" I asked as I climbed in the truck.

"Nothing. I just want to get goin' is all. On account of it will take a good thirty minutes to get there, and I need to get back before my boss figures out I took an extra-long lunch."

I put the keys in the ignition and turned over the engine. "Try again. Why did Bruce Wayne act like that when you said the name Big Thief Hollow?"

She shrugged. "There's a bunch of meth- and pot-heads down there."

"So why did you drag me away when he started to say something?"

"Because Joe did a big bust of Big Thief Hollow last week. He ain't wastin' any time lettin' people know he's in charge."

I shook my head in confusion. "I thought the sheriff was in charge."

"Not really. Not since the whole department got cleaned out. The sheriff has kind of lost his umph, so he's been lettin' Joe call all the shots. At least for the time being."

"So what's the big secret?" I asked as I drove out of the square. "Why try to keep that from me?"

"Because Joe's got guys still watching the place from time to time. I wasn't sure you'd still go if you knew that."

I thought about it for a moment, trying to decide if it was a reason for us to stay away. "We're not doing anything illegal. We're just asking Dolly Parton's best friend if she knows anything, right?"

"Yeah."

I sat up straighter as I headed down Highway 82. "And besides, your aunt filed a missing persons report, and if the sheriff won't do anything about it, how can anyone in the department fault us for doing the job they refuse to do?"

Neely Kate looked indignant. "Yeah, that's right."

I just as quickly lost my bravado. "Now tell me why it's a bad idea to go there."

"There's no reason," she insisted, turning to me to plead her case. "We're not buying meth or pot, although I have to wonder how much there's even left to buy after the sheriff's department burned their pot fields."

"I thought Daniel Crocker was the big pot dealer in Fenton County."

"He *was* until he got arrested. Then his business took a tumble, so other people filled the gaps."

"Huh." I couldn't help but wonder if the person in charge of Big Thief Hollow was the person Skeeter's guy was supporting.

Neely Kate studied me with her microscope lens vision. When she studied something that closely, she was practically a mind reader. This time was no exception. "What does *huh* mean?"

I kept my eyes on the road, trying to play it cool. "It's just that I've learned so much since Momma was killed last May. Who knew this whole criminal underworld mess existed right under my nose?"

"Speaking of the criminal underworld . . ."

I tried to suppress a groan. How was I going to keep my morning with Skeeter from her? I knew she wouldn't approve, and I didn't want to lie to her. Instead, the heaven above was looking out for me, and Neely Kate's phone started to play "Wildflower."

She released a frustrated grunt and answered, "What's goin' on?" Her face puckered in disapproval. "Granny, I told you not to raise a ruckus last night."

I cast an inquisitive look at her. I'd only met her grandma once—at Neely Kate's wedding—and she was quite a handful.

"Well, you can't blame him for wanting you to pay for the damage to the doggone raccoon, Granny. It's been hanging in that lodge for twenty years." She paused and rolled her eyes. "No! Do not have Reggie go shoot a raccoon to replace it! Let me talk to him, and I'll see what I can do." She paused. "No, I'm not bringing you Big Bill's hot wings tonight. I don't have time to sit in the Fenton County General Hospital for hours after you claim the indigestion has given you a heart attack. One of these days you're really gonna have one, and the ambulance drivers are gonna be sorry that they stop for ice cream at the Burger Shack every time they answer one of your calls."

Neely Kate sighed as she hung up. "She's gonna be the death of me."

"I take it there was trouble at bingo last night."

"You have no idea. I'm not sure when she'll ever be allowed back. You might just get out of your promise." She turned to me with a grin. "No wonder I like you so much. You're just like my granny."

I laughed. "I'm gonna take that as a compliment." I cast a glance at her. "So what's the deal with you and Tabitha?"

She tried to look innocent. "Nothing."

"It can't be nothing if she won't even talk to you."

"I'm just takin' precautions is all."

"Huh."

She quickly changed the subject, talking about some new recipes she'd found the night before. "Ronnie refuses to eat them." She crossed her arms in a huff.

I wanted to tell her that I understood why, but I didn't have the heart. "Well . . . it does take a more refined palate than most people around here have."

She waved her hand. "And that's exactly why I want Mason to try my food. He lived up in Little Rock. He's more continental than Fenton County folk."

"You know who you should try?" I said, trying to keep a straight face. "Joe. He lived up in Little Rock for years. He even went to law school there." I gave a half-shrug. "I bet he'd love it." As soon as the words were out of my mouth, I kind of regretted it. Joe showed every intention of staying in Fenton County, and Neely Kate was bound to run into him. She still held a grudge against him for walking out on me back in September. I should have been encouraging her to mend fences with him rather than stirring up more trouble.

"Yeah . . ."

When Neely Kate realized we were close to Big Thief Hollow, she started coaching me on what to say. "Tell her that you know Dolly Parton from school and you're looking for her because you want help planning your class reunion."

"Maybe I'll just wing it. Especially since I thought Dolly Parton was younger than us."

"So? You have one of those timeless faces."

"I'm not sure if that's a good thing or a bad one."

"Oh definitely good," she assured me, patting my arm. "You use a great moisturizer."

"Okaaay . . . Anything else?"

"Find out the last time she talked to her, along with anything else that will help us find her now."

"Got it."

She gave me directions to a group of duplexes set off a county road. A beat-up car sat in front of the pale blue eyesore on the end; a tree made from blue wine bottles was the only landscaping in the grass-spotted yard. The other duplexes, painted in varying shades of pastel, looked just as neglected. A handful of cars were parked in various driveways.

"Pull in behind the Buick," Neely Kate said.

I did as she instructed and put the truck in park, turning off the engine. "Are you sure she's here?"

"That's her car right there." She shrunk down in the seat. "I think it'll be better if I wait here in the truck."

I opened the door and looked over my shoulder. "Okay."

I walked onto the front porch and rang the doorbell. After visiting Billy Jack the day before, I half expected to hear a pack of yipping dogs, but was met with blissful silence instead. After ten seconds, I rang the bell again, getting antsy.

A guy in his twenties opened the door, wearing a stained T-shirt and a pair of boxer shorts. He had a serious case of bed head, his dark blond hair going every which direction. "What the hell do you want?"

I took a step back. "I'm looking for Tabitha."

He yawned and lost some of his irritation. "I thought you was one of them Baptists trying to save me again. I keep tellin' 'em that the best way they can save me is to bring a cold six-pack, but they don't seem to get the hint."

I almost laughed, but he was dead serious. "Those Baptists never are any fun."

He leaned into the door frame, scratching his crotch. "You got that right."

I tried to look away. "About Tabitha . . ."

"Oh yeah." His hand left his nether-region, and he started scratching his cheek. "She's down at the community center."

"Oh." I tried not to cringe as I thought about where his hand had just been. "And where is that?"

"Head down to Orchard, take a right, and it's a quarter of a mile down."

"Thanks."

I turned to leave, and he called after me. "If you don't know where the community center is, how do you know Tabitha?"

"Uh . . . I'm friends with Dolly Parton."

"The singer?" he asked, his eyes flying open. "No *shit?*"

I could have corrected him, but decided not to bother. "You have a good day."

I hopped in the truck and started to back up, shaking my head at the sight of Neely Kate still crouched down in the passenger seat.

"Well?" she asked, lifting her head to look over the dashboard. Tabitha's gentleman friend had already shut the front door.

"She wasn't there."

"Who were you talkin' to? I heard you talkin'."

"I was talking to the half-naked guy who answered her front door, but he didn't know a thing about Dolly. I thought you said she and Tabitha are best friends? How is it that he doesn't know about his girlfriend's best friend?"

Neely Kate's face scrunched in disgust. "Everybody knows that Tabitha sleeps around."

Apparently not everybody. "She's at the community center. He seemed surprised that I didn't know where it was. Why's that?"

"Everyone around here knows it as the commune. It's *the* place to buy drugs and moonshine."

"And it got busted? Should we be *going* there then?"

"Why not? It got busted last week. It should be fine now."

She had a point.

There were several cars in the parking lot of a building that looked like a converted church. I pulled into a spot and turned to Neely Kate. "Are you really gonna hide in the seat again?" I asked in disbelief when I saw that she was hunched down again.

"Yes. I am."

Sighing, I climbed out of the truck, leaving the engine running. Before I shut the door, I looked down at her. "What's she look like?"

"Look for long dark hair, big brown eyes. Tight clothes. That'll be her."

"Okay . . ."

I couldn't imagine what Tabitha might be doing at the community center, but I discovered as soon as I walked through the door. A group of older women were in the middle of a large room that looked a lot like a school cafeteria. There was a stage at one end, and round tables were shoved against the two side walls. Racks of folding chairs were stored opposite the stage. Middle Eastern music blared, and the gray-haired women were wearing scarves with bells hanging off them, gyrating their hips to the tempo. A beautiful young woman stood in front of them, wearing a crop top and booty shorts, shaking her hips in circles.

"Come on, Maybelline," the young woman said, looking over her shoulder. "Shake them hips so Harvey'll want to grab 'em and get busy."

Most of the women giggled, but a few looked horrified.

The song ended, and the young woman turned around. "Great lesson, ladies! See y'all next week!"

The instructor walked over to a duffel bag on top of one of the round tables and looked me up and down. "Were you here for the belly dance lesson? Because you're about fifty years too young."

"No, actually . . . I'm looking for Tabitha. Is that you?"

She stood up, looking wary. "Maybe, maybe not."

Maybe she didn't want to admit she was Tabitha, but every other female in the room looked close to retirement age.

When I didn't say anything, a panicked look filled her eyes. "I meant to show up for that twelve-step meeting last week, but look—" she swung an arm toward the women who were in the process of removing their scarves, "I'm here teaching these geriatrics just like I promised my probation officer."

I shook my head. "No. It's nothing like that. I need to ask you about Dolly Parton."

Her eyes widened. "What about her?"

"Do you know where she is?"

She crossed her arms and looked down her nose at me. "And who's askin'?"

"I'm sorry." I took a step closer. "I'm Rose. I'm a friend of Dolly's, and I haven't seen her in days. I know you're her best friend, so I figured you'd know how she's doin'."

She still eyed me with suspicion. "How do you know her?"

"Uh . . ." I panicked, forgetting Neely Kate's coaching. "We work together." Oh crappy doodles. I didn't even know where she worked.

Her arms dropped, and she looked less defensive. "At Gems?"

Gems? Billy Jack said she'd run off with the bartender from where she worked. Gems had to be a bar or a restaurant. "Yeah, that's right."

A slight smile lifted her lips. "Why didn't you say so?" She looked me over, shaking her head. "I have to say that you don't look the type. But then, Mud's one for the unusual."

I had no idea what she was talking about, but at least she was still talking. "She hasn't shown up for work in a few days. And neither has the bartender she's been seeing. Do you happen to know where she is? Her momma's worried."

She shook her head with a frown. "I told her not to take a job there. Gems is nothing but trouble."

"Why's that?" I asked.

"Everyone knows that Mud is up to no good. It might pay better than the other place, but it's not worth the risk."

"What's he up to?"

She looked at me like I was a crazy person. "You're the one workin' there. You tell *me*."

Oh, yeah.

"So you don't know where she's run off to?"

"I don't know what she's up to half the time anymore. Not since her bitch of a cousin's wedding. If anyone knows what Dolly's up to, that woman would know." Disgust covered her face. "Neely Kate River."

What on earth had happened to make her hate Neely Kate so much? And she knew Neely Kate was married, but she'd called her by her maiden name and not her married name— Colson. Based on the timing, the fight had to be related to Neely Kate's wedding. Maybe Tabitha was upset she hadn't been asked to be one of Neely Kate's many bridesmaids, since nearly half the county had been in the wedding.

"Her boyfriend, Billy Jack, said she took off with a bartender from Gems."

"Oh, really?" she asked, getting excited. "Which one?"

Panic set in. "Cute. Brown hair."

A sly grin spread across her face. "Good for her. I told her that weasel Billy Jack was foolin' around on her." She laughed. "I heard from a girl at the club that Dolly busted his ginormous flat screen a couple of weeks ago."

Huh. Billy Jack had told us she'd busted it just a few days ago, right before the bartender picked her up. "Okay, thank you." I handed her one of my business cards. "If you hear or think of anything, could you let me know? Like I said, her momma's really worried."

She looked it over. "This says you own a landscaping business, but you said you work at Gems. Which is it?"

"Uh . . ." I hadn't even considered that. "Both. Do you have any idea how much business a landscaping company gets in December?"

She gave me a blank stare.

"None, that's how much it gets. Christmas is coming, and I need to buy presents."

Tabitha seemed to accept my answer and stuffed my card into her bag. "I hear you there, girl. We're all desperate in our own way."

One of the older women walked up and asked, "Tabitha, you said that hip gyration could be used in sexual intercourse. What about with an inflatable pump? Won't it break it?"

My eyes flew open. "I gotta get going. Thanks, Tabitha."

She snickered and turned to answer the woman as I hurried out the door.

At least I knew what our next steps should be. Neely Kate and I needed to go to Gems to see if the bartender was really missing and if anyone there knew what was going on. In fact, I couldn't believe that Neely Kate hadn't thought of that first.

I had made it out to the parking lot and was walking toward my truck when Neely Kate sat up in the passenger's seat.

"You've got to be kiddin' me!" Tabitha shouted from behind me, rushing past me. "You get out of that truck, you lyin' whore!"

I stopped, watching in horror as Tabitha wrenched open the door and started to pull Neely Kate out of the truck.

"I'm not the lyin' whore!" Neely Kate yelled as she stumbled to get her footing. "You are, you back-stabbing witch! You tried to steal my husband!"

"Me?" Tabitha screeched, lunging for Neely Kate's hair. "He was mine to start with!"

"Let go of me!"

I finally got my wits about me and rushed forward to save my friend. "Tabitha! Have you lost your mind? Let go!"

But Tabitha was holding on tight, pulling Neely Kate's hair with all her strength as Neely Kate grappled for her hands. I started searching the parking lot, looking for something to use to stop Tabitha. A crowd of older women had formed around us, and they looked on in shock and horror. One of the women had a mostly full water bottle. I grabbed it from her hand and twisted off the cap. Rushing toward the two women, I started sloshing the water on Tabitha, who began to shriek as she let go of Neely Kate's hair.

Tabitha turned her murderous gaze on me, and I gave her one last slosh for good measure before tossing the bottle on the pavement, and took off running. But Tabitha had longer legs and tackled me, dropping me hard into the grass. "I'm gonna kill you!"

I rolled to my side as she grabbed my throat, her eyes wide and crazy, and I suddenly wondered what crime she had committed to earn her probation. Oh, crap.

"You let go of my best friend!" Neely Kate screamed, wrapping her arms around Tabitha's chest and pulling. Tabitha lost her balance and fell to her side, her legs still pinning my waist to the ground.

The two women were shouting at each other while I tried to get out from underneath the both of them.

Suddenly a woman's voice shouted with authority, "Move out of the way. Get out of the way." The older women surrounding us let through a redheaded woman in a sheriff's uniform. Deputy Hoffstetter, the sheriff deputy who had insulted Muffy in my own front yard, looked down at the lot of us with disgust, her eyes going wider when her gaze landed on me. "You all stop that nonsense right now. You're under arrest."

Chapter Eleven

If Deputy Hoffstetter thought her command was going to stop Tabitha, she had another thing coming. The crazed woman had managed to grab poor Neely Kate's hair again. The deputy had pulled out her taser and was about to go to town with it when one of the older women followed my lead and dumped the contents of her mug on Tabitha. Unfortunately, it was a mug full of steaming, hot coffee.

Tabitha started screeching as she jumped up, ready to go after the poor blue-haired Good Samaritan. Instead, Deputy Hoffstetter jumped on top of her, wrestling her to her stomach and slapping a handcuff on one of her wrists.

I managed to crawl away from the pile, rolling over to sit on my bottom as I watched the deputy fasten the other handcuff on the wild brunette. Climbing to my feet, I started to help Neely Kate up. When I saw the tears in her eyes, I panicked as I realized that Tabitha had knocked my *pregnant* friend to the ground.

I held up my hands. "Don't get up. We have to make sure the baby's okay. I'm going to call an ambulance."

"The only person you should be calling is your attorney," the deputy said. "Like I said, the three of you are under arrest."

Everyone started shouting at once. The older women were taking sides—some backing up Tabitha, the others taking Neely Kate's side after hearing she was pregnant.

Taking advantage of the mayhem, I quickly pulled out my phone and hit call. "Mason," I said the moment he answered the phone. "I'm in trouble."

"Are you okay?" he asked, sounding panicked.

"Yes . . . no. I don't know. Deputy Hoffstetter's about to arrest me and Neely Kate."

"Why? What happened?"

"We got attacked by Neely Kate's cousin's friend. She knocked Neely Kate to the ground, Mason. I'm worried about the baby, but the deputy won't listen."

"Where are you?" he asked, anger in his voice. But I knew his anger wasn't directed at me.

"Big Thief Hollow. At the community center."

"I'll be right there, but in the meantime, don't talk to the deputy. Tell her you're waiting for you attorney. Hang on, sweetheart. I'm coming."

"Thank you."

Before I could say anything else, the deputy pushed through the crowd and snatched my phone. She didn't look amused. "No calls." She shook her head. "Why am I not surprised you'd think you could flout the rules?"

I suspected the deputy recognized me from the other night, but we didn't know each other personally. Why would she make an assumption like that? "You told me I could call my lawyer," I said as she spun me around and put a handcuff on my wrist.

"You're gonna need one."

"Is that really necessary?" I asked.

"If I had my way, you'd be barricaded in a county jail cell," she said, fastening the other cuff.

I tried to look over my shoulder at her to see if she was joking, but I was fairly sure she wasn't.

She sat me on the ground next to Neely Kate, who was also cuffed. We watched the deputy haul Tabitha to her feet and stuff her in the back of a patrol car.

"Are you okay? Do you think the baby's okay?" I asked her, consumed with worry.

"I think so," she said, her voice quivering. "But I don't know if my hair will survive the attack, and I'm fairly sure my pride won't."

"I called Mason. He's on his way, and he's furious." She gave me a worried look. "Not at us. Don't worry." I turned toward her. "But what on earth just happened, Neely Kate? Why does Tabitha hate you so?"

Her eyes hardened as she stared at the woman screaming in the back of the sheriff car. "She tried to steal Ronnie."

"*What?*"

"Of course she has another version. In any case, I knew she'd never talk to me, which is why I sent you. What did you find out?"

The deputy was coming toward us.

I tilted my head toward the approaching law enforcement officer and whispered, "Mason said not to talk to her. To tell her we're waiting for our attorney."

"Okay," Neely Kate said, tears in her voice.

I wished my hands were free so I could hug her. Instead, I leaned the side of my head against hers. "Mason's gonna take care of this for us."

The deputy put her hands on her hips and gave me her best withering glare. "What do you ladies have to tell me about what happened here?"

I lifted my chin, trying to look dignified. "I'm waitin' for my attorney to show up."

"Your *attorney?*"

I didn't respond. I knew she'd heard me.

"Did you ever stop to think that the Assistant DA has better things to do other than drop everything and run to Timbuktu to save you every five minutes?"

I didn't answer, though perhaps she had a point.

"And what about you?" Deputy Hoffstetter asked Neely Kate. "What's your story?"

Neely Kate squinted up at her. "I think I'm gonna wait for my attorney as well."

The deputy shook her head in disgust. "I bet you are. The two of you are like peas in a pod."

That surprised me. What did she know about us? Or was she just talking about this particular incident?

Ten minutes later, Tabitha was still screaming that she was gonna kill us, making me thankful she was sitting in the back of the sheriff cruiser. The darts of hate Deputy Hoffstetter kept shooting at us made me wonder if she was thinking about putting us in the back with her, hoping for a cage match. Another sheriff car pulled up and Joe got out, the irritation on his face clear even from across the parking lot. I wasn't sure whether to be happy he was there or not.

He stopped and talked to Deputy Hoffstetter, and from the look on her face, there was a whole lot of unhappiness going on around here. Then Joe marched over to the two of us and squatted next to Neely Kate, reaching behind her to unlock her handcuffs. "I've got an ambulance on the way," he said to her, sounding concerned. "Are you hurt? Is the baby okay?"

She rubbed her wrists. "I have a doozy of a headache from where she tried to rip my hair out of my head, but I think the baby's fine." But her unusually subdued voice gave her away as she got to her feet.

Joe grabbed her elbow and helped her up. "Why don't you call the doctor while we wait for the ambulance?"

"I don't have my phone. It's in the truck."

He pulled his phone out and pressed a couple of buttons before he handed it to her. "You go to the Henryetta Family Clinic. Right? Hilary says she's seen you there. I have them on speed dial."

Hilary talked about Neely Kate to Joe? I wasn't sure what to think about that. I didn't want that woman even thinking about my friend, let alone talking about her.

She took the phone and moved a couple of feet away while Joe looked down at me, his expression vacillating between amusement and irritation.

"Are you going to take these cuffs off or not?"

He grinned. "I think we should leave them on. They give you a dangerous look."

"You've seen me in cuffs before, Joe Simmons. Back when you planted a gun in my shed and ran off my dog. Take them off."

He chuckled and knelt beside me.

"How'd you know we were here, anyway?"

"Mason. He's on his way, but he knows that Abbie Lee has no love lost for you, and he was worried she'd take it out on Neely Kate. He figured I could get here first."

"Abbie Lee?"

He grimaced. "Deputy Hoffstetter." He finished removing the cuffs and helped me to my feet.

"This wasn't my fault, Joe."

"It never is." He didn't sound as amused this time.

An ambulance pulled into the parking lot with its lights flashing, but no sirens, thank goodness. Two men got out, looking around. Deputy Hoffstetter pointed toward us, her mouth pinched.

Neely Kate walked back and handed Joe his phone, her expression much more relaxed. "My doctor says as long as I feel okay, there's no need to worry unless I start to cramp or bleed. He said it's a good thing I'm not very far along."

Joe didn't look convinced. "The ambulance is already here. I'd feel better if you went to the hospital."

She shook her head. "Dr. Miller said there wasn't any need to go in."

The two paramedics sauntered up to us. One was tall and skinny, and the other was shorter and stockier with a trimmed beard. The taller man had a spot of what looked to be chocolate on his chin.

"Hey, Neely Kate," the shorter guy said, scanning the crowd. "Where's your grandma?"

"It's not her grandmother, you fool," Joe said, irritated. "It's Neely Kate herself who needs the ambulance."

Neely Kate shook her head, pointing to his chin. "Really, Tiny? You stopped at the Burger Shack *again?*"

He swiped his chin with a thumb, looked at it and licked. "We heard your name and thought it was your granny, so we stopped off for sundaes first." Tiny looked her up and down. "You look fine. What's wrong with ya?"

"I am fine. It was a mistake."

Joe's eyes narrowed. "Let me get this straight. You received an emergency call, and you stopped for *ice cream?*"

The shorter medic shrugged. "Like we said, we heard Neely Kate's name and assumed it was her grandma's heartburn again." He turned his attention to my friend. "If you don't need us, we're gonna get going." He looked at his watch. "If we can make it to the Wild Chicken before two, we can still get some fried pickles."

She gave him a blank stare for a second before she said, "Yeah. Go get your pickles."

Joe shook his head as he watched them leave. "I'll look into that, Neely Kate."

She shrugged. "In all fairness, my granny cries wolf all the time. I've warned her that it's gonna reach up and tweak her in the hiney."

"There's no excuse. You could have been gravely injured."

"I wasn't." She shrugged again. "But thanks."

"And speaking of bad behavior, there seems to be a lot of it going on today."

I was sure Joe was going to start making all kinds of accusations against me, but to my surprise he kept his gaze on Neely Kate.

"I apologize for the deputy's behavior," Joe said, looking her in the eye. "A few witnesses have told her that they saw Ms. Stone open the truck door and pull you out. That *she* attacked you and you were merely trying to get away." Joe scowled, shooting an angry glare at the deputy. "Add in the fact that both of you and several witnesses told her about your pregnancy, and she failed to see to your safety, and . . . well, let's just say this matter will be addressed."

Neely Kate didn't seem to know how to handle a Joe who was looking out for her safety. She was too used to being angry with him.

Joe turned his attention to me. "The real question is, what did you say to set her off?"

"Me?" I shouted. "Why do you assume it's *me?*"

"Isn't it always? I have a group of older women who all corroborate that you came into the community center to talk to one Ms. Tabitha Stone, the suspect who allegedly attacked Neely Kate. Do you deny it?"

And here I thought he was actually being nice for a change. "I'm not saying another word until my attorney gets here."

"You can't use the man who's gonna file charges against you as your personal defense attorney."

"Who says I need one?" I lifted my eyebrows. "I thought you said the witnesses said we were completely innocent."

"The witnesses said *Neely Kate* was completely innocent. You, Rose Gardner, rarely are."

Neely Kate snorted.

I gave him an indignant look. "I'm waitin' for Mason."

Mason arrived five minutes later. As soon as he got out of the car, his gaze scanned the growing crowd until it landed on me.

Joe was talking to a group of older women, but he watched as Mason made a beeline toward me and Neely Kate. As soon as he reached me, Mason pulled me into a tight hug and looked over his shoulder at my friend. "Are you girls okay? Neely Kate?"

"I'm fine, Mason," Neely Kate said. "Really. I've called the doctor, and he says not to worry as long as I don't notice any problems. Thanks for sending Joe."

"I was worried. I know the deputy is ambivalent toward Rose—"

I broke away and put my hands on my hips. "Joe pretty much said the same thing. Why does she hate me? I've never even met the woman before she showed up at our house the other night."

Mason turned sheepish. "She knows . . . your dating history."

"What does that mean?"

"She knows you dated Joe and then started dating me a month or so later. I've been told that she thinks you're a badge bunny."

"A *what?*"

He looked embarrassed. "She thinks you're fixated on law enforcement officers."

I shook my head. "That doesn't make any sense. You're not a law enforcement officer."

He shrugged, his cheeks beginning to go pink. "But I am *in* law enforcement. I file the charges."

I knew him well enough to know he was keeping something from me. "There's more. What aren't you sayin'?"

"Some of the other deputies have told me that she thinks you fabricate or set up situations to get yourself into trouble so the police will be called."

"That's the most ridiculous thing I've ever heard!" Neely Kate shouted. "Is she *crazy?*"

The deputy turned to stare at my friend, and I grabbed Neely Kate's arm. "It's okay."

"No, it's not!"

It wasn't, but I was used to people thinking the worst of me. So why did it still hurt so much? "Who else thinks that?"

"No one, Rose." Mason pulled me into another hug. "No one that I know of."

"Would you tell me?"

"Yes. I would." He kissed my forehead and pulled back.

"Oh, my stars and garters," Neely Kate exclaimed, putting her hands on her hips and narrowing her eyes. "She's jealous!"

"What?" I asked, glancing up at Mason. His cringe confirmed it.

"He *was* the second most eligible bachelor in Fenton County," Neely Kate said, "before *you* took him off the market. It's not too much of a stretch to figure out that Abbie Lee Hoffstetter wants your boyfriend."

Mason looked like he wanted to crawl into a hole. "I'm gonna get Joe over here so you two can give your statements, okay?"

"Yeah."

He lifted my chin, searching my eyes. "Are you okay? Really?"

I took a second to answer. "Yes, but I need you to know that this wasn't my fault, Mason."

Surprise flickered in his eyes. "I know that. I never doubted you, Rose."

"Thank you."

He gave me a gentle kiss and left me with Neely Kate. A few moments later, he and Joe walked back together. They didn't exactly look comfortable standing so close to each other, but at least they weren't about to start a brawl of their own.

Joe studied Neely Kate and me for several seconds, then turned to me. "Ms. Stone says you were asking about Dolly Parton Parker."

"I was."

"You don't know either of these women. What are you up to?"

My chest filled with indignation. "You very well know that Dolly is Neely Kate's cousin. I asked you about her just yesterday. We're trying to find her."

"So what are you doing down here at a place that was busted for meth distribution just a week ago?"

"I came here to ask Tabitha if she knew where Dolly was. I went to her house first and her . . . boyfriend told me she was here. Since all y'all won't look for her, and Neely Kate's got a bad feeling about her disappearance, we figured someone had to check it out."

"And did Ms. Stone tell you where she was?"

"No, she didn't know. Which is another reason why y'all need to be looking for her."

"The fact that she's missing doesn't mean she's in trouble." Joe grunted in frustration. "You have to take her history into consideration. She's run off before. Neely Kate having a feeling that something isn't right doesn't mean I can take deputies off cases with real evidence to go on a wild goose chase."

I started to protest, but Joe held up his hands. "There are only so many deputies, Rose. Our resources are limited."

I glared at him. "Yet Deputy Hoffstetter has time to stalk me."

He sighed. "She wasn't stalking you. She was doing a drive-by of the community center. I told you that we had a big bust here last week."

I scowled. His explanation sounded plausible, but I wasn't sure if I bought it. "Mason?" I asked, turning to him.

"I'm sorry, Rose. I'm going to have to side with Joe on this one. Dolly's run off before, and the sheriff's department has its hands full with other, more pressing cases." He glanced at Joe. "If she doesn't turn up in a few more days, maybe you can reconsider."

Joe gave a brisk nod. "Let me know if she hasn't turned up by Friday afternoon, and I'll see if I can spare someone."

I could see their point, even if I didn't like it. Friday afternoon was two days away.

"I've got to get back to the office," Joe said, glancing at the crowd before turning to look at me. "Rose, I'd tell you to stay out of trouble, but that would be wasted breath." Then he walked off before I could respond.

Mason looked like he wanted to go after Joe and throttle him.

"Mason, I'm going to keep looking for my cousin," Neely Kate said defiantly.

He nodded, his anger fading. "There's nothing wrong with you looking for her. Just try to steer clear of people who have a personal vendetta against either one of you, okay?" He grinned. "And I thought everyone liked you, Neely Kate."

Neely Kate crossed her arms over her chest. "She tried to steal my husband days before my wedding. Ronnie dated her in high school. She hates me because Ronnie chose me."

Mason's grin widened. "And that confirms what I already knew: Ronnie is an intelligent man."

"I know, right?" Neely Kate beamed. "But that's why I had Rose talk to her. I figured Tabitha wouldn't tell me a thing."

Mason put his arm around my waist and tugged me to his side. "I know you didn't do anything wrong, but I feel the need to reiterate that if you continue to pursue this matter, you shouldn't put yourselves into dangerous situations."

Neely Kate nodded solemnly. "We'll steer clear of crazy ex-cons in the future."

What *had* Tabitha done that made her an ex-con?

"I have to get back to work," he said, leaning over to give me a kiss. "Check in with me today so I know you're safe, okay?"

I looked up into his face, feeling so lucky that this man was mine. "I love you, Mason."

He pulled me flush against him and gave me a toe-curling kiss, right there in front of everyone. Then he lifted his head with a grin. "I'm counting on that."

"Deputy Abbie Lee is fuming right now," Neely Kate laughed.

I didn't even look at her; I just watched Mason walk back to his car, still in a daze. Neely Kate looped her arm through mine. "Come on, love bird. We've got work to do."

Chapter Twelve

We got back in my truck and I turned to her. "Tabitha really doesn't know where Dolly Parton is. Apparently she hasn't talked to her much since your wedding."

"Dolly picked me over Tabitha?" she asked in surprise. "She didn't tell me."

"It sounds like it. But she told me something that doesn't mesh with what Billy Jack told us. He said Dolly broke his TV on the way out the door, but Tabitha said she heard from a friend that Dolly had broken it a couple of weeks ago."

"Why would he lie? What's he hiding?"

"I don't know, but Tabitha said your cousin was working somewhere new. A place called Gems."

Neely Kate tapped a finger to her cheek. "I knew she'd started working there, but I'd hoped she'd come to her senses and quit. I suppose we should go there next."

"Sounds like it, but don't you need to go back to work?"

Neely Kate shrugged. "I think maybe I can sneak away for another hour or so before Stella the Hun realizes I've gone." She forced a smile. "So let's go to Gems."

"There's only one problem: I've never heard of it. Do you know where it is?"

"It's down Highway 79, outside of Holler Creek."

I pulled out of the parking lot and headed straight for Holler Creek. "Tabitha mentioned that Gems wasn't a good place to work. Something about her boss, Mud, being up to no good. Do you know what that's about?"

"No," she said, looking out the window, deep in thought. "But I'm not surprised. It's a new place and maybe a little shady."

It *was* southern Fenton County. "Do you think it's safe?"

"Yeah." She waved her hand. "I think it's fine."

Neely Kate's phone went off, filling the truck cab with her ringtone. The cringe on her face when she glanced at the screen was at odds with the happy song still filling the car. "It's the courthouse." She pressed the screen and held the phone to her ear. "Hello?"

The shouting from the other end was almost loud enough for me to hear each and every word.

Holding the phone away from her ear, Neely Kate said, "I had to run an errand. I told—"

There was more shouting and then nothing.

"What happened?" I asked as she lowered the phone.

"The good news is I don't have to worry about getting back to work. I just got fired."

"Neely Kate. I'm so sorry." I reached over to grab her hand. "Maybe I should take you home. The whole day has been pretty traumatic."

Her mouth tilted up into a grim smile. "Rose, you and I both know how much I hate that job. Let the old Nazi have it."

Despite her words to the contrary, I knew Neely Kate was upset at the prospect of being unemployed. "Maybe Joe can tell her about why you were late if she—"

"It's okay, Rose. I'll be happier without that job."

I had no doubts about that, but she wasn't the only person it concerned. "What will Ronnie say?"

She smiled even though her eyes brimmed with tears. "That's just it. Ronnie won't care. He's been bugging me to quit for months."

"Well, see there? You hated your job, and Ronnie wanted you to quit. It's a win/win situation."

"But I wanted to decorate the nursery for little Ronnie Jr. I want to get him new furniture, not ugly hand-me-down stuff from my cousins."

"You still can. Maybe you can get another job. A temporary one until you have the baby."

"Who's gonna hire a pregnant woman?"

My grip on the steering wheel tightened. "I'm pretty sure it's against the law to discriminate like that."

"We're living in Fenton County, Arkansas. Do you really think most employers here actually *care* about the law?"

Neely Kate had a point. "Violet's going to need help in the nursery. Maybe you can work part-time there."

She released a short laugh. "*Me* and Violet working together? Did Tabitha shake something loose in your head when she knocked you down?"

"No, but my side sure hurts." I turned to her with a grin.

She was quiet for a moment. "Thanks for having my back in that mess."

My smile dropped, and I glanced into her eyes for a second before turning back to the road. "Always, Neely Kate."

She wiped a tear from her cheek and a mischievous grin spread across her face. "I'm glad to hear *that*."

"Why do I already regret saying that?"

She laughed. "Because you're a smart woman, Rose Gardner."

I asked Neely Kate to tell me about some of the nursery ideas she'd found on the Internet, assuring her that everything would work out and she'd be able to decorate Ronnie Jr.'s room however she pleased once she had confirmation he was a boy.

"You could just have a vision and tell me now," she said. "It would save me an awful lot of aggravation."

I pressed my lips together. "You know how I feel about that."

She released an exaggerated sigh. "I guess it's for the best. I've always wanted to be a chef, and after I confirm Ronnie Jr.'s a boy, I'll be too busy decorating to cook anymore."

I squinted. "Since when have you wanted to be a chef?"

She gave me a half-shrug.

I suddenly wondered if I was being played.

Before I could confront her, we drove into the tiny town of Holler Creek, which consisted of a shabby gas station/convenience store, a café, a used bookstore, and a post office.

"Where's Gems?"

"I think it's just outside of city limits. A lot of towns don't like to be associated with establishments like that."

"You mean bars?"

Neely Kate pointed straight ahead. "Turn there on County Road 135."

We drove about a half-mile before a big clearing appeared to the left. "She works at the race track?" I asked, confused. They'd put a dirt track in a few years before, but I was pretty sure they only raced once or twice a week.

"No, I think it's on the other side," Neely Kate said, sounding unusually cheerful.

We drove past the track, and my breath stuck in my chest. Up ahead was a tall neon sign that read, "Topless," accompanied by the silhouette of a girl. The name Gems was painted on the side of the building. I hit the brakes and stopped in the middle of the road. "Oh, no."

"You said you'd help me."

"Neely Kate!" I pointed to the sign. "There are naked women in that building!"

"Not naked." She looked up and pointed to the sign on the pole. "It says topless. There's a difference."

"Do I even want to know how you know that?"

"Because Dolly Parton worked at the Bunny Ranch before taking a job here a month ago."

"So she's an *experienced* stripper?"

"Hey, don't knock it. The pay's good if you find the right place." She grinned. "Maybe I could make some extra money here."

"Have you plum lost your mind?" I turned to her, my eyes wide.

A car horn behind me blared, making me nearly jump out of my skin.

"You're in the middle of the road. At least pull into the parking lot."

"Then it will look like we're actually goin' in there."

"We *are* goin' in there. Pull into the lot."

Grumbling, I pulled off of the road, and into the long line of parking spaces.

"It's not that bad, Rose. Really."

I slammed the gear into park. "You've actually *been here before?*"

"No, but I visited Dolly when she worked at the Bunny Ranch."

"You really expect me to go in there." I pointed to the front door. "Into that building filled with naked women?"

"I thought we'd already established that they aren't naked. They just take turns being topless and dancing around a pole."

"*They're pole dancers?*"

"Of course, they're pole dancers! What other kind of dancers would they be?"

"I don't know," I semi-shouted, shaking my head. "You know . . . the kind that just dance around and take off their clothes." I couldn't believe I was actually *having* this conversation.

"They haven't stripped like that for years." Neely Kate stated the fact like I was an idiot.

"I'm sorry. I was sick the day they covered the evolution of stripping in history class."

Neely Kate started to laugh. "What on earth do you think's gonna happen in there?"

"I don't know." I cast a wary glance toward the red front door.

"The sheriff's department knows all about this place, which means it has all its permits and everything, or you can bet your backside that Deputy Abbie Lee Hoffstetter would shut it down just like that." She snapped her fingers, making me jump.

"Can women even go in there?"

"Sure. And there's probably a bouncer at the door right now and maybe security. If somebody bothers us, the staff won't put up with it. Not that anyone will bother us. They're here to see the dancers."

"I'm not sure this is a good idea."

"You were the one who said we needed to go by Gems and ask about the bartender. Hopefully we'll get some information we can use and leave."

She was right. It was the logical place to look. We weren't doing anything illegal, and Neely Kate seemed to think it was safe. "Will anyone be dancing in there?"

Neely Kate looked at the scattered cars in the parking lot. "Probably." She opened her door. "Look, I can do this on my own. Just wait here, and I'll be back in a few minutes."

I watched her walk across the parking lot, waging an inner war. We'd go in and out. Easy cheesy. But what was Mason gonna say if he found out?

It took me no more than two seconds to figure out what he would say. He knew we were looking for Dolly, and I'd promised to stay out of danger. He'd want me to stay in the truck . . . but Neely Kate was my friend, and I didn't want her to go in there alone.

"Neely Kate! Wait up." I climbed out of the driver's side and hurried toward her. "I'm coming."

She hugged my arm. "Thank you."

"But I'm leaving at the first sign of trouble."

"Fair enough."

She led me to the front door and stopped. "Let me do most of the talkin', okay?"

"Fine by me." She'd proven herself to be a great interrogator in the past, and she'd know what questions to ask in this situation.

"Okay, then follow my lead." She opened the door and strutted in, stopping in front of the bouncer.

He eyed us both up and down.

A grin spread across Neely Kate's face. "We're here to apply for the job."

Job? I tried to keep my shock from showing—not that the guy at the door was paying any attention to me.

He waved to the doorway at the opening of the short entryway. "Mud's who you need to talk to, and he's in the back. Just have a seat at a table, and someone will come out and find you for your interview."

"Thanks," Neely Kate said, strutting through the opening with a swagger she didn't normally possess.

I followed her, trying not to freak out over the fact I was not only about to walk into a strip club, but I was there for an *interview*.

We entered a bigger, dimly lit room. A bunch of mostly empty tables and chairs were arranged around a long stage against the back wall. A pole was at its center. A couple of guys sat in chairs by the front, drinking beers as they watched the girl dance on stage. Only I wouldn't call it dancing, and she wasn't dressed in anything I would have expected. She had on a black bra with silver spikes all over the cups, paired with a G-string that barely filled the gap in her crack and rode high on her hips. A band of fabric was wrapped around her hips, and her bare buttocks hung out, but it was what she was doing with the pole that grabbed hold of my attention and wouldn't let go.

I stopped in my tracks, staring as she grabbed the pole behind her with her hands and started gyrating her hips.

Neely Kate captured my arm and tugged me over to a table. "Don't look so shocked. They'll never buy that we're here for a job." She looked me up and down, then pushed me into a chair. "Then again, maybe they'll like it."

"What's that supposed to mean?"

"Dolly likes to play the innocent act. But that only works for a few months before regulars figure it out. That's part of the reason she switched to here. Plus, Mud promised her more customers for lap dances."

My eyes just about fell out of my head. "Lap dances?"

"That's how you make the real money. You dance on the stage to give them a taste, and then they pay you for a lap dance."

The girl on stage had hooked her leg around the pole and was spinning around—upside down, no less. I couldn't stop staring, even though all I wanted to do was look away. "Tabitha said Mud would like me. That he liked the unusual girls. What's that mean?"

She studied me for a moment. "I have no idea."

"Is Tabitha a stripper too?"

"An exotic dancer," she corrected. "And yes. She got Dolly the job at the Bunny Ranch."

A redneck-looking guy wearing jeans and cowboy boots came out of the back door and headed straight for our table. "Are you the girls who are here for an interview?"

"Yes, we are!" Neely Kate replied just a little too eagerly, even for the man sent to fetch us.

The cowboy led us down a long hallway and stopped in front of a door with a sign that said, simply enough, Office. "He's waiting for ya."

"What are you waiting for?" a gruff male voice called out from inside. "Get in here."

Neely Kate walked into the room and looked him square in the eye. "I'm here about a job."

She was still partially blocking the entrance to the room, so I leaned forward to glance over her shoulder. A middle-aged man with a cigarette hanging out of his mouth was sitting at a desk covered in papers. The small office was covered in old paneling. It felt familiar, but I couldn't quite place it. I certainly knew I'd never been here before.

The man eyed Neely Kate up and down, and then his gaze landed on my face. "Did you bring yer friend to hold yer hand, or is she here about a job too?"

Neely Kate stepped to the side so I was more visible. "She's applying too."

He glanced down at his desk and scratched his crotch. I took the opportunity to elbow Neely Kate in the side, and I was impressed when she barely flinched. All the abuse she'd taken from her cousins had toughened her up.

"There is a job opening, ladies, but only one."

"That's okay," I volunteered. "She needs it more than I do."

"Is that so?" he asked, giving Neely Kate more attention than I liked. He shrugged, then motioned for us to come into the room.

There was only one extra chair, and I didn't plan on staying long enough to use it. I only hoped the fact that Neely Kate didn't take it meant she wasn't planning to stay either.

"I can only give you four nights a week, and only one of 'em's a weekend. Otherwise the other girls'll be squallin'."

He paused, and Neely Kate said, "Okay."

"You pay the house thirty-five dollars for every shift, and then give ten percent of the money you earn in tips to the D.J. and the bartender to be split."

"Tips?" I asked.

Mud's eyes bugged out, and the cigarette dangling out of his mouth nearly fell out. "I take it you never danced before."

I was pretty sure he wouldn't count me dancing for the first time last June in the Henryetta splash park with my niece. "Uh . . . no."

He shook his head and turned to Neely Kate. "What about you?"

"Sure." She shrugged, tossing her hair over her shoulder. "Down in Shreveport. I had to move back home to take care of my momma."

Seeming to accept her answer, he turned to me, looking at me like I was an idiot. "Tips is what the dancers get when the customers tuck money in their G-strings." He pantomimed to reinforce his words. My face flushed, and he laughed. "But most of the money is made from lap dances. The house rule is that it's twenty bucks a dance."

"Okay," Neely Kate said. "I heard one of the other dancers quit."

"More like didn't show up," he grumbled. "You plan on sticking around?"

"I need a job, Mr. . . ?"

"Just call me Mud."

She shifted her weight. "I really need the job, Mud."

"You can start tomorrow night, but first I gotta see you dance. We're a classy joint, and we gotta keep up our standards."

The brown stain on the wall in the hallway screamed of class and sophistication. But I still couldn't shake the fact that this place felt familiar, which creeped me out even more.

"Okay," Neely Kate said without hesitation, and I fought to hide my horrified shock.

"You prepared to dance today?"

"Of course."

His gaze returned to me, and his eyes roamed my body. "I'd like to see you dance too. You never know when there's gonna be another opening." He had to have an active imagination; I was wearing jeans and boots and a heavy brown wool coat over an oversized sweater.

My mouth dropped open, and I started to protest, but Neely Kate's eyebrows lifted so high in warning she gave herself a temporary facelift.

He waved to the door, already givin' his attention to the papers on his desk. "Show your dance to the girls and Roy. If you're any good, I'll watch. Roy will meet you in the hall and show you where to change."

Neely Kate practically shoved me into the hall.

"Shut the door!" Mud shouted after us, and Neely Kate closed it.

I turned on her like a barracuda. "Are you out of your ever-loving mind?"

She covered my mouth with one hand. "Shh!"

I swatted her hand off and whispered, "We can't do this! It's not right!"

Her lips pressed tight. "There's nothing illegal about dancing. I told you that this place has all their permits in line and everything."

My tactic obviously wasn't working. "Neely Kate. You can't strip! What will Ronnie say? Not to mention the fact that you're pregnant! You just started getting your morning sickness under control. All that twirling around is bound to stir things up."

"Rose, calm down. We're not strippin'."

"You're about to audition! *We're* about to audition!" I shook my head in horror. There was no way I could spin on that pole, let alone strip while doing it.

"I'm just borrowing more time."

"You're sure gonna need it. You got nothing out of Mud. You didn't even try."

"He's not just gonna give us answers, Rose."

I shook my head in confusion. "Then what are we doin' here? Why do we have to pretend we want to work here?"

The boss must have contacted Roy somehow, because the cowboy who'd led us back into the hallway had reappeared and was moving toward us. We were running out of time.

She released a heavy sigh. "Trust me."

The thought of getting up on that stage and taking off my clothes scared the bejiggers out of me. There was no way in tarnation I would do it. "I'm gonna be honest, Neely Kate. You're making it awfully hard right now."

"I know, but I have a plan."

Lordy, I hoped so.

Chapter Thirteen

D id you bring something to dance in?" Roy asked, walking past us and leading us through a door.

"No," Neely Kate said. "We plum forgot."

He ushered us into a big room filled with tables, the length of one wall lined by a mirror. He pointed to a laundry basket of clothes. "You can wear your own bra and panties, then put some layers from the basket on over them. After Sparkle comes off, you're up next."

Neely Kate's face froze. "What?"

"I said you're up next."

She blinked and pulled out her best indignant attitude. "I was told this was an audition."

"It is. *On stage*. Our afternoon crowd is pathetic at best. If you suck, no harm, no foul."

He walked out of the room, and I shook my head, my eyes wide with horror.

Neely Kate took a step toward me. "Now Rose, calm down."

"*Calm down?*" I took a step back. "This is crazy even for us."

She took my hands. "Okay. We'll tell them you don't want to do it. It'll be fine."

"You're actually gonna do it?"

She cocked her head. "I *know* how to dance on a pole, Rose."

"What?"

"Dolly Parton taught me back when she was at the Bunny Ranch. She had a pole in her momma's garage she used to practice on. It's really good exercise, you know."

My mouth opened, but no words came out.

She pulled her cotton shirt over her head, revealing a pink with white polka dot bra.

"Neely Kate! *What are you doing?*"

She gave me a condescending glare as she unbuttoned her pants and started to slide them over her hips. "Hell's bells, Rose. I've worn less than this at the Henryetta pool. Calm down."

"How can I calm down when my best friend is about to strip on stage?"

"I'm not gonna take off my bra. I'll go out there, swing around the pole some, and then they'll boo me off stage when I don't show them the goods."

"Then why do it at all?"

"When Sparkle comes back here, you can quiz her about Dolly Parton and the bartender."

The song streaming in from the bar area came to an end.

"Can you do that?" she asked.

What in the world was happening?

"Rose," she hissed, moving closer and grabbing my shoulders. "Can you do that?"

I nodded. "Yes. Just be careful."

She laughed. "Nothing dangerous is happening here. In fact, if I didn't know it would give Ronnie a conniption, I'd take off my bra to show 'em what I've got." She laughed from my shock. "What? I'm gonna be whippin' my boobs out to breastfeed soon enough. What's the difference?"

She had a point.

A girl with jet-black hair came through a door. The color of her hair was a sharp contrast to her pale skin, but more noticeable was the fact that she was topless and wearing the tiniest pair of red underwear I'd ever seen.

I felt my face getting hot.

Her hard gaze landed on the two of us, roaming over Neely Kate's girl-next-door underwear. "Roy says you're both auditioning. That ain't gonna cut it around here."

Neely Kate put a hand on her hip. "I wasn't prepared to audition today. I keep the racy stuff for the stage, so this'll have to do for now. But all I have are these boots for shoes." She lifted a leg to show the stripper her three-inch heeled black patent leather boots.

"Those'll work for this afternoon," Sparkle said, then her gaze returned to me. "Why aren't you ready?"

Neely Kate lifted her shoulder with a graceful shrug, her blonde hair tumbling down her arm. "She can't bring herself to do it. She's a little shy even though Dolly Parton told us this was a great place to work."

"Dolly Parton?" Sparkle asked as she reached for a bra on the table.

"You probably know her as Sapphire."

"Oh." Her eyes widened with recognition, but then she scowled. "That girl ran off with Nikko and left us high and dry. We're short-handed right when our business is picking up. I can't complain too much, since the money's damn good, but you can only do so many lap dances in a day, you know?"

I really had no idea, and the thought made my face even hotter.

She leaned close to me. "Your thighs start to give out," she stage whispered.

"Why is business picking up?" Neely Kate asked.

"'Cause Mud's got a master plan to take all the business from the Bunny Ranch."

"Why's he trying to take all their business?" I asked.

"Because of who owns it."

"Something Bad" by Miranda Lambert and Carrie Underwood started playing in the bar.

Sparkle slipped her arms through the bra straps and pointed a thumb toward the stage. "That's your cue, sugar. You better get goin'."

Neely Kate flashed me a grin. She sure didn't look very nervous. If it were me, I'd be on the verge of throwing up. "Wish me luck."

She didn't look like she needed it. "Break a leg."

Neely Kate disappeared between the curtain, and I was tempted to go over and watch. I sure was curious to see what she could do on a pole. But I knew she'd kill me if I didn't get something out of Sparkle.

"So you chickened out?" Sparkle asked, fastening the back of her bra strap.

"I wouldn't say that . . . I'm having second thoughts."

She walked past me and picked up a pair of four-inch platform heels. "Everyone feels that way the first time. It's kinda scary shaking your ta-tas in front of pervs."

Apparently, everyone except for Neely Kate felt that way.

"But if you find the gumption to do try it, it does get easier." She studied me for a minute. "Do you really want to work here?'

"I . . . uh . . ."

"You already know that one of our bartenders ran off with Sapphire last week. Well, the rest of us girls have been filling in." She sat on the edge of the table and slipped on her shoes. "Mud sent a couple of guys out to Nikko's place at Sugar

Branch, but he mustn't have been there because he never came back."

Finally. Useful information. Neely Kate wasn't dancing for nothing.

"We might be able to work something out for you, you know. Most places usually hire guys to tend bar, but you could fill in for a bit and see if you want to give dancing a go. Wear something low-cut, and the guys'll tip you really well."

"She's just trying to get out of sharing ten percent of her own tips," a woman said from behind me. I jumped, not having heard her approach. "Don't let her fool you."

When I turned to look at the newcomer, I saw a pretty girl in her twenties with shiny dark brown hair cut into a short bob. She was topless and wearing a purple thong with a five-inch band of black spandex around her hips that looked like it was meant to be some kind of skirt. She held a black bra in her hand.

Sparkle gave a haughty laugh. "So? We both know you don't like sharing yours either, Crystal. If we have a girl tending bar, the guys will tip her, and we can keep the share we usually have to fork over. It's a win-win for all of us."

Crystal laughed. "You're gonna have to convince Mud. But it might not be so hard. Roy says Mud has a thing for ya." She directed this last comment to me. Then she brushed past me, her naked breast grazing my arm as she turned to face me again. She was taller than me and with her towering heels, her naked breasts were nearly eye level. Where on earth was I supposed to look?

Wait . . . "Mud has a thing for *me?*"

"Yep, Mud likes 'em fresh off the farm, if you know what I mean."

"But he hardly paid attention to me!"

"He must have paid enough attention to see your pretty little blush." Her fingers brushed my cheek. "Mud has a thing for defiling virgins."

"But I'm not a virgin," I blurted out.

"Even better," Crystal purred.

"Stop messin' with her, Crystal."

Crystal dropped her hand and walked over to a table, sorting through a pile of clothes. "Come on, Sparkle. We ain't had any fun since Nikko left, and Mud's all worked up over the owner showing up on Friday night. That boy was fine to look at, and he knew how to party after we got off."

"Who has time to party after shaking your ass in guys' faces all night long?"

"So he and Sapphire were dating?" I asked.

"Dating." Sparkle giggled. "That's so cute."

Crystal's eyes narrowed. "How do you know Sapphire?"

"We went to high school together. She told me what a great place this was, so when my friend and I realized she took off, we decided to see if one of us could get her job."

"Huh." Crystal grunted, but she seemed to buy my story, so I decided to press on. "Yeah, I was really surprised to hear she ran off with him. She and her boyfriend, Billy Jack, seemed serious."

"They weren't sleeping together," Sparkle said. "That's the weird part. Nikko and Crystal had a thing goin', and Sapphire only ever talked about her boyfriend. It doesn't make sense that they ran off."

"When was the last time you saw them?" I asked. "Were they flirting a lot?"

"The last time I saw them was last Friday night. And if they were hot for each other, they hid it pretty good. They acted like they couldn't stand each other," Sparkle said, shooting a sympathetic glance back at Crystal. "Sapphire and

Nikko closed up together and neither one of them showed up for their shift on Saturday."

Groans and a bit of shouting came from behind the curtain, and Neely Kate burst through still fully clothed—or as fully clothed as she had been when she went on stage. Her pale face had a guilty look on it.

Both dancers looked up in surprise.

"What are you doing? Your song's not over, and your bra's still on!" Sparkle said in disgust. "Get back out there."

Neely Kate shook her head, placing a hand on her stomach. "Trust me, no one wants to see me back out there."

"What are you talking about?" Crystal asked.

Roy burst through the dressing room door, his face contorted in anger. "Get out!"

Neely Kate snatched up her shirt and pants. "Don't worry. I'm goin'."

"Do you want one of us to go out there?" Crystal pointed her thumb toward me. "Daisy here ain't goin' on."

"Daisy?" I asked.

Crystal pinched my cheek with a grin. "You're as fresh as a daisy straight off the farm."

"No one's going out on stage until one of y'all cleans up the mess," Roy snapped.

Oh, no. "What happened?" I asked.

Clutching her clothes against her chest, Neely Kate grabbed my arm and pulled me to the back door. "I'll tell you later."

"Think about my proposition, Daisy!" Sparkle yelled after us as I stumbled over a pile of clothes. "We can still use you!"

Neely Kate pushed the door open, dropped my arm and took off running to the truck in her bra and underwear.

"Neely Kate! Slow down!" I shouted, running after her.

"Trust me. We don't want to slow down." She didn't stop until she'd opened the passenger door to the truck.

The back door flew open, and Roy stood in the entrance, shouting.

Neely Kate locked her seat belt. "Rose! Go!"

She didn't have to tell me twice. I jerked the truck into reverse and sent gravel flying as I backed out into the parking lot. A bit of it hit Roy in the head, and he fell to the pavement like a ton of bricks.

"Oh, no!" I shouted, trying to see if he was getting up in the side mirror. "Did I kill him?"

"Don't worry. If you did, it was self-defense," she said, pulling her shirt over her head.

"What happened?" I cast a glance toward her. "I have a pretty good idea, but some perverted part of me wants to hear the details."

"Well . . . I strutted out there like nobody's business, shaking my butt and grabbing the pole and all. Just like Dolly Parton showed me. Then I saw Mr. Turner, my second grade Sunday School teacher, sitting in a chair with some girl's hoochie in his face. But I figured it was none of my never mind, you know? My job was to spin on that pole. So I hooked my leg around and started spinning, and then I climbed up and hung upside down. Dolly had showed me a couple of spins like that, although for the life of me, I have no idea why guys think a girl in a bikini hanging from a pole is sexy."

I could see her point. "So why did Roy get so upset?"

"All that spinning was making me dizzy and my stomach a tad bit upset. So I got off the pole and started just dancing, hoping things would settle down. But I caught Mr. Turner's eye, and he pushed the hoochie girl away and walked to the edge of the stage. Then he proceeded to stick a one-dollar bill under the edge of my panties." She turned to look at me. "A *one-dollar* bill. Can you believe it?"

I shook my head. "No. You're worth at least five."

"I know, right?" she asked, indignant, then gave a tiny shake of her head. "Anyway, that just ticked me off. He was leering at me, saying 'take it off,' and all I could think about was sitting in the cold Sunday School classroom with Mr. Turner making us memorize Bible verses. Well, something just riled up inside me, and I gave Mr. Turner a tongue lashing, asking him if Mrs. Turner knew he had someone else's hoochie in his face. And if that wasn't bad enough, I said he was cheating his former Sunday School student with his cheap ass ways."

"You didn't!"

"He just stood there, his eyes buggin' out of his head, looking like I'd just shot him." She gave me an ornery grin. "And then I threw up on him."

My mouth dropped in horror. She'd thrown up on someone *again?*

She shrugged, her grin spreading. "Needless to say, I don't think I got the job."

We broke out into laughter, and when we settled down I told her everything I'd found out, including the way the office felt really familiar.

"Oh!" she exclaimed, excited. "Maybe you were there in a previous life." She lifted her eyebrows as she leaned close. "I've been studying up on those. Most people suppress all the memories of their previous lives, but maybe one of yours is popping through."

"That might be true except that place couldn't have been built more than twenty years ago, and I just turned twenty-five last month. It was built when I was a kid."

"Hmm . . ." She tapped her chin. "I guess you have a point. Do you think your momma or daddy ever took you there?"

"To a *strip joint?*"

She waved her hand. "It wasn't always a strip joint. It used to be a Chick-a-Dilly."

I shook my head. "I'm sure I've never been there. It must remind me of something else."

"Don't worry. You got lots of other information we can use," she said. "I think we need to go to Sugar Branch and try to find Nikko. It can't be too hard to find him there. Sugar Branch is a two-stoplight town, and Nikko's not a common name. Unless it was a stage name."

"It's worth a try," I said. "Although I'm not sure what we're gonna find out. Mud sent men to find him, and they came back empty-handed, although it's mighty suspicious that Mud sent men after him at all. My old boss never came looking for me when I didn't show up for work, and she actually planned to kill me."

Neely Kate lifted her rump and pulled her pants up. "But Billy Jack said Nikko picked her up from the trailer a few days ago. That would make it around Sunday night. If that's true, why didn't they go to work on Saturday?"

I shook my head. "Maybe it was a generic 'couple of days' and he really meant Friday. Even so, Sparkle said Dolly Parton was definitely at the club on Friday night. If Nikko picked her up on Friday rather than on Saturday, maybe he was just giving her a ride to work?"

"Sure, but they could have still run away together after their shift. They worked late hours at the club, and Crystal said they both closed that night, which happens at around three in the morning."

"The fact remains that they were last seen at the club on Friday. Something must have happened. But what? Tabitha said Mud was up to no good. And the other dancers said Nikko and Dolly didn't get along too well, so either they're really good actors, or it's unlikely they would run away together. What if they saw something they shouldn't have and they either took off or someone did something to them?" I asked, feeling bad for how I'd phrased that last part.

Neely Kate nodded, looking worried. "I think you're right."

"We need to tell Joe what we know. Maybe it's enough to get the sheriff's department to do something."

"I doubt it, but it's worth a try." She pulled her cell phone out of her purse. "I'll give him a call. He's gonna flip his lid when he finds out you were there."

"It's none of his business what I do."

She snorted. "Like that's gonna stop him." A few seconds later she was telling him everything we'd discovered, only she left my name out of it, and she didn't mention we'd visited the club. She only gave him the information we'd found. As the conversation went on, she got angrier and angrier.

"I tell you that I think my cousin probably saw something illegal, and you refuse to do anything about it?" she demanded.

I heard snatches of Joe's voice through the phone. ". . . Neely Kate . . . you don't know that . . . not enough . . . Friday afternoon . . ."

"When you can actually plan to perform your sheriff's responsibilities, Joe Simmons, you let me know." She hung up the phone and jammed it into her purse.

"That didn't sound like it went well."

"What's it gonna take for them to get involved?"

"You heard Mason. They're stretched thin right now, and she's run off before. Maybe Joe thinks you're exaggerating the evidence because you're worried. I guess when you step back, it looks like they worked a shift together and ran off."

"We have to find her, Rose."

"We will." I squeezed her hand. "I think I know what will make you feel better. Do you want some ice cream?"

"Does a bear poop in the woods?"

"I guess that's a yes. But one slight problem. Mason asked me to stay away from the Burger Shack."

"But it has the best soft serve ice cream in town." She pursed her lips.

"I know, but after my vision of Eric, I promised Mason I wouldn't go there."

"Well, where are we gonna go?"

"The Emporium is a coffee shop now. I heard it serves ice cream. How about we go there?"

"Is it any good?" she pouted.

"It's ice cream. Of course it's good." I cast her a pleading look. "Neely Kate, Mason specifically asked me to stay away from the Burger Shack, and I think he's right. What if I have another vision? What if it gets me into trouble?"

She sighed. "I know. You're right. I'm sorry. Turns out getting tackled, being snatched nearly bald, auditioning for a pole dancing job, and then throwing up on your old Sunday School teacher makes you cranky."

I grinned. "I think you're entitled. Not to mention you lost not one, but *two* jobs today."

She snorted. "I'm really on a roll."

"Are you going to tell Ronnie?"

She gave me a mock exasperated look. "He's bound to notice when I don't go to work tomorrow."

"You know that's not the part I'm talking about. Or maybe you shouldn't mention that your stripping job didn't turn out so great."

"Hey! The dancing was great. Baby Ronnie Jr. just didn't approve."

"That baby's a genius already."

I parked the truck in front of the Emporium, which was located a couple of blocks north of the town square. The business had possessed the same name for years, but the owners were continually changing what it actually was. Previously it had been a drugstore and a bookstore, and it had also enjoyed a very brief run as a yoga studio.

"Are you sure it's open?" Neely Kate asked as we walked to the door. "This parking lot is like a ghost town."

"See," I pointed to an old rusty car in the parking lot with its bumper partially hanging off. "There's someone here."

"Are you sure it's not there as a decoration?"

If it was, they sure could use some help from RBW Landscaping, but when I opened the door, a scruffy-looking guy was sitting at a table for two, nursing a paper cup. "Look over there," I whispered over my shoulder. "There's a customer."

"Are you sure that's not a homeless man drinking a cup of coffee?"

I scowled. "He's not a homeless man. Everybody knows the Baptist church finds vagrants like a metal detector finds coins. They scoop them up and take them to their center."

"Concentration camp," she muttered.

I shot her an exasperated stare. She was really in a humdinger of a mood this afternoon, but I guessed she deserved to wallow for a while. I saw another car pull into the parking lot and pointed to it. "Look there. Another customer. You do what you want, but we're already here, so I'm getting something."

Leaving her in the middle of the shop, I moved to the counter and studied the menu board on the wall, feeling a sudden urge for coffee. "I'd like a decaf mocha," I told the older woman behind the counter.

"Do you want whipped cream?" she asked.

"Uh, yeah."

"I'm not sure if we have any whipped cream," she mumbled, lowering the glasses perched on her nose. "I'll have to check with Fred." Then she walked into a back room.

"I don't need whipped cream!" I called after her, but I figured she didn't hear me since she kept going.

I realized that Neely Kate wasn't standing next to me, so I spun around to see if she was going to order something. Which was when I saw who was walking through the open door.

"Why hello, Rose," Hilary said in a syrupy sweet voice. "You look *lovely* today."

While I wasn't in my stained jeans and work coat, I knew I didn't look exceptional. But at least I was wearing makeup and my hair wasn't in its usual ponytail. I figured I must not look too bad if the manager of an exotic dance club had taken such a shine to me. But Hilary was standing there in a cream-colored skirt and jacket with a pale blue silk blouse underneath. She looked like she'd just walked out of a fashion magazine. I had no doubt that she'd intended her "compliment" as an insult.

The sight of her lit a fire in my belly, and her two-faced behavior only stoked it. I wanted to tell this woman off. She'd purposely trapped Joe and used a poor innocent baby to do it. She was lower than pond scum, but whether I liked it or not, she was going to be the mother of Joe's baby—a poor defenseless baby that was going to need all the help it could get. If I was going to be Joe's friend, I needed to put a stop to this continued animosity between Hilary and me. "Thank you," I forced myself to say. "You're looking really good considering your . . . condition. How are you feeling?"

Her forced smile grew bigger. "Isn't that a sweet thing for you to say? I've had some queasiness off and on, but I've felt well for the most part. Which is surprising when you think about what a rabble-rouser Joe is. You'd think his baby would be stirring up trouble right from the start."

I nodded. "Well, that's good." I wanted to point out that her baby was already stirring up trouble, but I didn't want to open that can of worms.

We stood in awkward silence for a few seconds. I wasn't sure what else to say to her. I couldn't stand there and pretend I wanted to talk to her. This new civility tactic was going to take some getting used to.

For once, Neely Kate seemed to be at a loss for words. She'd stood there right along, gaping in silence like she'd just undergone a lobotomy. But then she'd had a pretty rough day.

I grabbed her arm and pulled her toward the counter. "Come on, Neely Kate. Let's get Ronnie Jr. his ice cream."

She let me drag her several steps forward while she kept her eyes fixed on Joe's ex-girlfriend.

"You're looking much better, Neely Kate," Hilary said, following us. "I know that you had a bad run with morning sickness."

Neely Kate stiffened, and I leaned into her ear. "Try to be nice."

"Why?" she growled.

If Hilary heard us, she did a good job of ignoring it. "When's your due date?"

Neely Kate took a defensive stance as if they were about to duel. "July 1st."

"Oh, my goodness." Hilary placed her hand on her chest. "Mine's a week later. July 8th. Wouldn't it be amazing if we had our babies on the same day?"

"What?" Neely Kate gasped.

Hilary ignored her less than enthusiastic response. "Just think about it . . . our babies are gonna grow up together!"

"So you're planning on staying in Henryetta?" I asked.

"I've rented a house a couple of blocks from here. It's quite charming. I think the owner is going to let me buy it." Her right eyelid twitched, and her eyes hardened. "I'm not going anywhere."

To heck with it. I'd give civility a shot some other day.

I put my hands on my hips. "Why in tarnation do you think I care if you live here or not?"

Her grin tightened. "I just want you to know where things stand between me and Joe."

"I don't give a flying fig how things stand between you and Joe." My voice rose higher. "I'm livin' with Mason Deveraux. Why would *I* care?"

"Just in case you get an urge to see if the grass is greener in my backyard." She took a step closer. "I'm warning you—I won't put up with any trespassing."

"You are unbelievable!" Neely Kate shouted. "Who the hell do you think you *are?*"

The woman behind the counter, who had reappeared, looked worried. "Can you please keep it down? There are other customers here."

I shot a quick glance to the homeless-looking guy at the table ten feet from us. He was gripping his take-out cup of coffee so tightly the cardboard was denting. Judging from the expression on his face, he was definitely enjoying the show.

"Neely Kate, darling. You should calm down. You're in a delicate condition," Hilary said, her voice smooth as honey.

"I've faced a hell of a lot worse than you today, you lizard-tongued monster!" Neely Kate shouted, bobbing her head. "I can take you any day of the week."

I grabbed her arm. "Neely Kate. Let it go. She's not worth it."

She shrugged me off. "No, Rose! She thinks she can get away with whatever she wants, and she does because no one ever stands up to her." Neely Kate moved closer to Hilary until they were about a foot apart. She had to tilt her head back to look the taller woman in the eye. "You don't scare me, Hilary Wilder. There's absolutely nothing you can do to me or Rose, so don't even try."

Hilary's eyes glittered with anger, and her gaze turned to me. "Are you sure about that, Rose?"

The blood rushed from my head.

She knew.

Neely Kate stepped between the two of us. "What are you talking about?"

How did she know about J.R.'s blackmail? Did Joe tell her?

An evil grin lifted the corners of Hilary's mouth. "Ask Rose."

"I'm not asking Rose. I'm asking *you*."

Hilary's grin faded. "Don't pick a fight with me, Neely Kate. I am one person you don't want to tangle with." She gave us a final distasteful look before glancing at the woman behind the counter. "These women are verbally accosting me. If this is your usual clientele, I think I'll do business elsewhere."

The older woman's eyes widened in panic. "You two need to leave."

"What?" Neely Kate screeched.

"You're shouting and disrupting the customers. You need to leave."

"No!" Neely Kate shouted. "She's the one who came in here, riling things up. We were here first."

An older man stepped out from the back room, a phone pressed to his ear. "No need to make them leave, Opal. I called the police, and Officer Ernie is on his way."

I tugged on her arm. "Neely Kate, we need to go. *Now.*"

"No!" She turned to me, her eyes blazing. "It's not right, Rose! If we leave, we're lettin' her win. *Again.*"

She had a point, but I had no doubt that the Henryetta police would be here in a matter of minutes. The gloating look on Hilary's face was almost enough to make me stand in solidarity with my friend, but I was a firm believer in picking your battles. Plus, if Hilary knew about J.R.'s blackmail material, I didn't want to provoke her.

I grabbed Neely Kate's shoulders. "Don't think of it as letting her win the war. Think of it as letting her win the skirmish."

"Listen to your friend, Neely Kate," Hilary said, pretending to look at her nails.

The look in Neely Kate's eyes was murderous.

Grabbing her hand, I dragged her toward the door as sirens sounded in the distance. "Neely Kate, you can't hit a pregnant woman. Let's go. *Now.*"

She stopped resisting me and allowed me to shove her into the truck. After I got in and pulled out of the parking lot, Neely Kate turned to me in dismay. "But I didn't get my ice cream!"

"It's okay," I said. "I'll drop you off at the Burger Shack. But first we need to find Joe."

"What on earth for?"

"To keep us out of jail," I said, cringing at the sight of the flashing lights pulling into the parking lot we'd just left.

Chapter Fourteen

I grabbed my phone. "Joe," I said as soon as he answered.

"Rose," he groaned. "I can't spare the manpower to be chasin' after Neely Kate's cousin."

"This is something else."

He groaned again. "What on earth did you and Neely Kate do now?"

His attitude ticked me off. "It wasn't our fault, Joe Simmons! You need to teach your girlfriend some manners."

"My girlfriend?" A second passed before he groaned yet again. He was really on a roll. "She's not my girlfriend. We are *not* together."

"I'd love to discuss the current status of your relationship, but I'll look it up later on Facebook and see if your relationship status says 'it's complicated.' Right now I need you to get your baby momma to call Officer Ernie off Neely Kate."

"What happened?" I heard the alarm in his voice.

I told him everything . . . well, everything except for the fact that she'd insinuated she knew J.R.'s secret.

"You girls lie low for a bit, and I'll take care of it."

"Thank you."

I parked in the lot next to the Burger Shack and let Neely Kate run in for her ice cream, and then I took her to Maeve's and texted Joe to let him know where we were. I knocked on her front door, wondering how she'd feel about the two of us showing up on her doorstep, but Mason's mother was thrilled.

"I thought we'd drop by and check on you," I said, feeling a tiny bit guilty that I hadn't done so sooner. "I hope we're not interrupting anything."

She ushered us inside. "Don't be silly. You're always welcome here!"

Maeve gave Neely Kate a quick tour, and I was impressed by how put together everything already looked. "I can't believe you've practically finished unpacking," I said.

"It's a small house, and I'm not one to sit idle."

I knew that from all the time she'd spent cooking and cleaning at my house.

"I was about to make a cake if you girls want to come sit with me."

We helped her make a red velvet cake and dinner too. I texted Mason to tell him we were eating at his mother's house. I worried about leaving Muffy all alone, but I didn't want to venture out onto the Henryetta streets until Joe gave us the all-clear. The last thing Neely Kate and I needed was another almost-arrest.

We were in the middle of frosting the cake when there was a knock at the front door. Maeve excused herself to answer it, and I was surprised to hear Joe's voice.

"I'm sorry to bother you, Mrs. Deveraux, but Rose told me that she and Neely Kate were hiding from the law here."

My breath stuck in my throat. I hadn't considered that Joe and Maeve had only met for the first time a few weeks ago. Since I knew the encounter had been painful for both of them, I had no idea what to expect.

I breathed a sigh of relief when Maeve laughed. "They're both here, but I didn't realize I was harboring fugitives. Come on in."

Maeve entered the kitchen with an ornery grin, Joe trailing behind her.

"Did you arrest your girlfriend, Joe?" Neely Kate asked, pointing her cake spatula at him.

"Nobody's getting arrested," he grumbled, "but everything's taken care of."

"When's she goin' back to Little Rock where she belongs?" Neely Kate asked with a frown.

"You know very well that she's not goin' anywhere," I said, trying to take the pressure off Joe.

Neely Kate put her hand on her hip. "Can't you evict her from the county or something?"

A tiny grin lifted his mouth. "Don't you think I would have done it already if I could?"

"Hmm," she grunted.

Joe took a step toward the door. "Well, I just wanted to let you girls know that you're safe to roam the streets of Fenton County . . . or as safe as you two are capable of being."

"Thanks." I gave him a soft smile.

"Joe," Maeve piped up. "Would you like a piece of cake before you go?"

He shook his head, eyeing the cake on the stand. "Thanks, but I need to get back to work."

"Well, how about one for the road?" she asked. "You can take it with you and eat it later."

He grinned at her. "It's hard to turn down a piece of homemade cake."

"You wait right there," Maeve said, pulling a small white plate from the cabinet. She cut a generous slice of the red velvet cake and put in on the plate, covering it with plastic wrap before handing it to him. "You enjoy that now."

"Thank you." He nodded, his eyes glistening.

I couldn't help but wonder if I was missing something.

"I'm gonna get out of you girls' hair," he said, heading for the front door.

"Let me walk you out." I cast a quick glance toward Maeve, hoping she wasn't upset with me, but she and Neely Kate had already started to wash the dishes.

I went out the front door and stopped on the front step, Joe following behind me. He swung the squeaky front door back and forth before shutting it and turning to me.

"If this is about Neely Kate's cousin or Hilary—"

"Does Hilary know about J.R.'s blackmail information?"

His eyebrows lifted. "What?" He shook his head. "No. I never told her. I swear."

"I think she knows."

"Why do you say that?"

I told him about our encounter, and he took a deep breath, rubbing his hand across his forehead. "She may not know anything."

"But there's a chance J.R. told her, right?" I asked.

"Yes."

I already knew, but his acknowledgment stole my breath away. "Will she tell anyone else?"

His face paled. "I don't know."

"Do you think she's going to use this to try to get you to marry her?"

"Maybe."

I stepped off the porch and began to pace in the yard.

"I'll talk to her and see what she knows."

"What if she's bluffing?" I stopped and looked up at him. "I don't think I reacted to her statement, so at least I didn't confirm anything. She knows your father wanted to split us up, and she knows how much you wanted to be with me. It doesn't take a genius to figure out your father threatened you with something. Maybe she's fishing for information."

"Yeah, you're right." He paused. "Does Neely Kate know?"

I wrapped my arms around my chest, the cold wind biting through my sweater. "No. The fewer people who know, the better. But Mason does."

He nodded, then gave me a soft smile. "That explains why she's still so mad at me."

"I'm sorry."

"No. It's for the best. I'm glad you have her for a friend."

"Me too." We stared at each other for several seconds. "I'm going inside. I just wanted you to know." I walked past him toward the front porch, but he reached out and grabbed my arm.

"Rose, don't tell Mason."

My mouth fell open. "What?"

"Don't tell him that Hilary might know."

I shook my head. "No, I'm not keeping this from him."

"Then just give me a few days, okay? Let me figure out what she knows." He swallowed and leveled his gaze on mine. "No sense worrying him if it's nothing."

I squinted up at him. "Since when did you care about Mason?"

He hesitated. "He's under a lot of stress at work right now. There's some fallout from his boss over that Black Friday bust."

I scrutinized him to see if I could catch him in a lie. "He hasn't mentioned it to me."

"He probably doesn't want to worry you."

"Is his job in trouble?"

"Honestly? I don't know."

Anger burned in my chest. "You're just trying to stir up trouble between us."

"I'm not, Rose. I swear. And while there's no love lost between Mason and me, I'd rather work with *him* than the actual DA."

"I don't want to keep this from him. It's too important."

"I know. Just give me until next week."

"No." I steeled my back. "I'll give you until the weekend."

He started to protest, then stopped. "Okay."

I turned around and started up the porch steps.

"Rose."

I looked over my shoulder at him.

"Tread carefully around Hilary. I'd truly kick her out of town if I had the authority, but I don't. Try not to rile her up."

His words rekindled my anger. "I'm done hiding from the world, Joe Simmons."

"And I wouldn't have it any other way. But until this is sorted out, try to avoid her if you can."

"That shouldn't be too hard," I said sarcastically. "Why don't you tell her the same thing?"

I walked back into the house, worried that Maeve would be upset that I'd stayed outside for so long with Joe. But she seemed more concerned about the leak under her kitchen sink.

"The inspection showed some issues, but I got the house for such a steal we didn't make the owner fix them." She put a large plastic bowl under the pipes. "This should take care of it for now."

"That won't work for long," I said.

She sighed, and I reached down to help her up. "But it'll keep the floor dry for the time being. I'll just have to remember to keep emptying the bowl."

"I thought the realtor said he was going to give you the names of some repairmen."

"He did, but none of them seem to be in a hurry to run over for nickel-and-dime repairs."

We finished putting the meatloaf together, making a double batch so Neely Kate could take one home to bake for her and Ronnie. I was impressed, though not surprised, that Maeve had already gone grocery shopping and picked up all the essentials.

Neely Kate looked beat, so I offered to drop her and her meatloaf off at her car so she could get home to put it in the oven. Maeve cut another couple of generous slices of cake and put them on a plate for my friend to take with her.

"I'm gonna get as huge as a whale if I keep hanging out with you, Maeve," Neely Kate joked as she put her coat on. Then she winked. "I'm sure Ronnie won't mind."

"You're welcome here anytime," the older woman said with a warm smile, looking pleased as punch. She'd only been in her house for a couple of days, but it was already obvious the move had been a good decision.

As soon as we got in my car, Neely Kate started grilling me. "I hope you gave Joe an earful about Hilary."

"Neely Kate, he doesn't want her here any more than we do. He says he's really done with her, and I think he means it this time."

"Hmm." She pressed her lips together.

I cast a glance at her, wondering if I should come clean about J.R.'s fabricated evidence, but there was no telling what she'd do. I couldn't risk it.

I pulled into an empty space several spots from her car. "Are you worried about telling Ronnie that you got fired?"

She shook her head with a grin. "Nope. I've decided it's a blessing in disguise. You're right, I've hated that place all along."

"Then do you want to go to Sugar Branch tomorrow and look for Nikko?"

She threw her arms around me. "Thank you. I wasn't sure if you'd still want to help me after what happened today."

"Hey." I gave her a squeeze and leaned back to look at her. "We have to find Dolly Parton, don't we? It's the next place to look."

"Do you want me to come by your office? If you'd like, I can get an accounting program set up on your computers before we go."

"Really?"

She shrugged and opened her door. "Sure. Turns out I have loads of time now."

"See you in the morning, Neely Kate. Take it easy tonight, okay?"

"I'll give it a try." She shut the door and waved. I watched her walk to her car, deciding I had just enough time to run home and get Muffy before Mason showed up for dinner.

My phone rang as I pulled out of the parking space, and I cringed when I saw who was calling.

"Skeeter, you haven't bothered me for two weeks, so why do you keep calling me now?"

"I need you to come read someone."

"Skeeter!"

"It'll just take a minute, and he'll never know it's you. We'll put a hood on him."

A hood? "Who is it?"

"You don't need to know that."

"Are you holding him hostage?"

"No."

"Then how are you gonna explain the hood to him?"

"He thinks it's something kinky."

I gritted my teeth. "I am not—"

He laughed. "Relax, Lady. I've got it covered."

What was gonna be uncovered was what had me worried, but I didn't say anything. If I continued down this path, it was going to end badly. There was no doubt about it.

"I think this guy has information about who's after Deveraux."

For all I knew, he was making it up just to push my buttons. And damnation and hellfire if it wasn't working. "I am not looking at naked people. I've seen enough topless women today to last me a lifetime."

"What's that supposed mean?"

"Never you mind. The fact is, I'm about to have dinner with Mason and his mother."

"You and your damn dinners."

I lifted my chin. "I wouldn't expect someone like you to understand."

"Well, your dinner's postponed. Mr. Assistant DA's about to go into a meeting, so he'll be late. You have time."

My shoulders knotted with tension. "How do you know that?"

"Lady, I make it my business to know things. But if you want to make sure he doesn't notice, you need to come now."

I grunted my frustration. "Where?"

He laughed. "Go north on 82 and turn onto County Road 36. Go two miles and turn off into the lot of the old feed store. Jed will meet you there."

"Fine," I huffed. "I'll head there now. But I can't be seen."

"Don't worry. It's like I said, *I* don't want you to be seen."

I hung up on his laughter and called Maeve. "I'm gonna be a little late. I have an errand to run."

"Take your time, dear," she said. "Mason called right after you left and said he was going to be late himself. An unplanned meeting with his boss came up."

Well, crappy doodles. Skeeter was right. Mason was meeting with the DA. That rarely happened. I couldn't help wondering if there was some truth to what Joe had told me too.

I pulled into the empty parking lot of the feed store, wondering once again how I'd gotten into this predicament. To be safe, I drove around the back of the building and found Skeeter's sedan idling there.

I parked as Jed got out of the car and walked over, opening my door. "Skeeter wants me to take you to the place we're going."

"I can't drive there?"

He shook his head. "He doesn't want your truck there. I'll drive you."

That made sense, and I was grateful for the secrecy, but I didn't like the idea of being at their mercy.

Jed sensed my hesitation. "You're perfectly safe, Lady. I guarantee it." He looked me in the eyes as he said it, with an earnestness I wouldn't have expected from one of Skeeter's men.

I got out of the truck. "Okay."

He opened the back door to the sedan, and I started to get in, but he stopped me. "I have to blindfold you first."

"*What?*"

He pulled out a black handkerchief from his coat pocket. "It's for our protection as well as yours. If you confess what you've been doing to the Assistant DA, you won't be able to show him where you've been."

I stared at the cloth in his hand. It made perfect sense, but it made me nervous nonetheless.

He leaned closer. "Rose, I swear to you that I'll keep you safe."

I narrowed my eyes in suspicion. "Why would you do that?"

"Because you saved Skeeter's life."

"So you're doing it out of loyalty to Skeeter?"

"He took a chance on me when no one else would. He's like a brother to me. You didn't have to help him, but you did."

"It wasn't altruistic, Jed. I did it to get my money back." As soon as the words tumbled out, I wondered if I should have admitted that.

He chuckled. "I don't believe that for one minute. You could have let him get killed, no skin off your nose. But you didn't." He gave me a grin. "I'll look out for you."

I took a deep breath and glanced down at the handkerchief one more time before looking up into his face. "Okay."

"Turn around."

I faced the car as he put the folded fabric over my eyes and gently knotted it in the back, trying not to catch my hair. He took my arm and helped me into the backseat.

When I heard his car door shut, I asked, "Will it take long to get there?"

"Skeeter said to tell you not to worry. That you'll get back in time for your dinner."

I couldn't hold back my snort. "Of course he did."

"I'm gonna turn up the music pretty loud. Skeeter doesn't want you to know where you are from the sounds."

"This feels an awful lot like a kidnapping. How do you know I won't just rip off this blindfold?"

He laughed. "Because I'm pretty sure *you* don't want to know where you are."

He had a point.

Loud country music filled the car, and four songs played before Jed turned the music down.

"Can I take my blindfold off now?"

"No, I'm gonna lead you in."

Jed got out, and then I heard the back door open. He guided me out of the car and took my elbow, coaching me on where to walk and telling me when we came to a step. My heels echoed off wood slats under my feet as we moved along, but after a few moments, Jed pulled me to a halt.

"Lady," Skeeter said. "Thanks for coming."

I raised my hand to the side of my head. "Can I take this off yet?"

"I'd prefer for you to keep it on until we go inside."

I lowered my hand.

"I'd like you to talk as little as possible once we're in there. I'd prefer for him to not even know you're there."

"You know I'm gonna blurt something out about the vision I have. I can't stop that."

"I know, but we'll keep the talking in his room to a minimum, and even if he hears you, he won't be able to see you."

"You were serious about the hood."

"Yes."

"I really don't want to see anything kinky, Skeeter."

He laughed. "You won't. He's drugged, so he won't remember much. He'll wake up next to a blonde with big tits and think he partied too much. He'll get pissed because he won't remember screwing her."

I took a deep breath. "Okay."

He led me through a door, and I entered a room that smelled like mildew and pine.

"You can take your blindfold off now," he whispered next to my ear.

I tugged it off and blinked as I took in the living room covered in paneling and green shag carpet. It looked like a house straight out of the 1970s.

Skeeter motioned to the dark hall, and I followed him to the last door. He opened it and stepped inside, giving me enough room to walk past him.

A guy lay on the bed, dressed in a white T-shirt and green plaid boxer shorts. His legs and torso were pale, but he had a fading tan on his arms that ended at his biceps. He wasn't obese, but he had a bit of flab on him. He was on his back with his arms all akilter over his head. A pillowcase with a kitten pattern on it covered his head, making it hard for me to guess his age. I knew he wasn't a teenager, but he didn't look too old either.

I leaned close to Skeeter, suddenly realizing he smelled really good. Maybe it was because the rest of the place smelled like dirty socks original to the 1970s decor. "Can he breathe with that thing on his head?" I whispered.

"Yes. We'll take it off after you're done. It's for your protection."

And yours, but I kept that to myself. At the moment, it didn't matter why he wanted to hide me—it just mattered that he did.

I moved closer to the bed, not sure if I wanted to sit on it. It hadn't been made after its last use, and the man was sprawled over the rumpled sheets and blankets. I decided to squat at the side, and I reached over and grabbed the man's hand, which currently lay on his pillow.

The man promptly rolled toward me, blindly reaching out for me and grabbing a handful of my hair.

"Mmm, baby," he moaned. "I love your hair."

My eyes flew open in alarm, but Jed freed my strands in an instant, all while I still held onto the guy's hand. I looked up at Jed and mouthed, "Thank you."

He nodded with a tight smile and stepped away from the bed.

I looked up at Skeeter and whispered, "What do you want me to look for?"

He squatted down next to me. "Let's start with whatever you see, and then we can discuss whether you need to narrow it down."

I nodded and closed my eyes, concentrating on the unconscious man. The vision came seconds later with a strong force. I was in a living room I didn't recognize, looking at a man I didn't know.

"That's not how he wants it done," I said in a deep male voice. "I'm supposed to get his schedule and turn it over. That's it."

"Well, things change. This is how it's going to go down now."

The vision ended, and I was thrust back into the bedroom with more force than usual. I fell backward on my butt, saying, "You're gonna do it differently than he wants it done."

Skeeter lifted me to my feet. I wobbled and almost collapsed. Sensing my weakness, Skeeter wrapped an arm around my waist and held me up. "What did you see?"

I shook my head, feeling drugged. "I don't know," I whispered. "It doesn't make sense."

"Tell me, and I'll see if it makes sense to me."

After I told him about my short vision, he shook his head. "Schedule? What schedule?"

"I don't know."

"It's worthless."

I wasn't so sure. I'd now had two visions that had left me with a bad feeling, both of which were seemingly ambiguous. What did it mean? "Then what do you want me to look for?"

"I want to know who he's selling me out to."

I took a deep breath. "Okay."

I squatted next to the bed again and held the man's hand again, focusing on Skeeter's question. The next vision took longer. This time I was in a room lit by a bunch of fluorescent lights in a dropped office ceiling. I sat with a group of men around a dark wood conference table. Skeeter was at the opposite end, his face contorted with fury.

"Somebody tipped off Rodriguez, and nobody's leaving here until I figure out who it was."

The room was deadly quiet as I hid a phone under the table and wrote a quick text. *He knows.*

My eyes flew open. "Someone tipped off Rodriguez, and you're gonna text someone."

I glanced up at Skeeter, whose eyes had turned murderous. "So there *is* a traitor." He pointed to the man in the bed. "Is it him?"

I stood and whispered. "I don't know, but he hid his phone under the table and texted *He knows* to someone." I shook my head in confusion. "I think you were in a conference room. A bunch of you were sitting around a table."

"Anything else?"

"You said you weren't going to let anyone leave until you figured out who'd tipped him off. And I think it was night time."

"Did you recognize anyone else who was there?"

I closed my eyes, trying to recall more details. "Jed and Merv were with you. I didn't recognize anyone else."

He was silent for a moment. "Okay, we're done here." He led me out to the living room with Jed following behind us. Skeeter picked up the handkerchief and lifted it, but I stopped him before he could put it around my eyes.

"Wait. I need to ask you something."

A grin teased his lips. "Okay."

"Do you know the strippers at the Bunny Ranch?"

Skeeter burst out laughing. "What?"

I'd been thinking about it all afternoon. Mud wanted to put the Bunny Ranch out of business because of who owned it. Skeeter already admitted there were unsavory characters determined to bring him down. Skeeter had his hands in all kinds of endeavors, and he seemed like the kind of guy who wouldn't bat an eye about associating himself with a strip club. In fact, he probably found his dates there. "You own it, don't you?"

He looked amused. "I do."

"There was a girl who worked there. Dolly Parton. Do you remember her?"

He shook his head. "Was that her stage name?"

"No. But she goes by Sapphire at Gems."

His eyes narrowed. "*Gems?* They're trying to put me out of business."

That squared with what Sparkle had told me. "What are they doin'?"

"They didn't need to do much more than open their doors. There's not enough business to support two clubs. There's hardly enough to cover one."

"So why would they have opened up in the first place?"

"Good question." He looked like he knew something he wasn't sharing. Not that it was any of my business. He grinned. "You lookin' for a job? I've got another way to put you on the payroll without you resorting to dancing on men's laps."

I shuddered. "Gross. No. I'm not lookin' for a job. I have my own business, thank you very much."

He chuckled. "Then why are you asking about a girl from my club?"

"She's my friend's cousin."

He leaned his shoulder into the wall and crossed his arms. "You don't say."

"She's missing. She worked a shift on Friday night, and no one has seen her or the bartender since then."

"Tell your ex-boyfriend and have him look into it."

"He won't do anything. She's taken off before, and he thinks that's what's goin' on this time."

"But you don't?"

"Well . . . at first I didn't. I was just helping out because my friend insisted. But then we went to Gems—"

He held up his hands, his eyebrows shooting up. "You went to Gems?"

"We had to ask around to see if anyone knew what had happened to Dolly Parton."

"And?"

"And I walked away with a job offer and the information that she and the bartender disappeared after they closed together on Friday night. Oh, and that Mud sent men to Nikko's house to look for him."

He stood up. "Mud sent guys after the *bartender*?"

"Yeah, I thought it sounded suspicious too. Someone from your club told me that Mud's up to no good. I think Dolly and Nikko saw something they shouldn't have and took off. Mud knows they saw it, and that's why he sent guys after them . . . unless it's all a front and he did something to them."

Skeeter rubbed his stubbly chin. "This is good, Lady. Given how much he's hurt my business, I've been trying to get some intel on him for weeks. This is my first real lead."

I shot him a condescending look. "You're *welcome*."

He laughed and moved closer to me. "So this job offer . . . did you dance for Mud?"

I took a step back. "No! And that wasn't the offer."

"Then what was?"

"Bartending."

He laughed again. "The gateway job to dancing."

"I didn't take it."

"Good." His voice was hard. "If you need a job, you'll come work for me."

"So you can't help me with Dolly?"

"I didn't say that. I'm just as curious about where she is as you are."

"Only because of what she might have seen?"

His eyes pierced mine. "I'm not a charity, Rose, so don't sound so surprised. But let's just say that tracking her down could be mutually beneficial."

I steeled my shoulders. "Like our arrangement."

"They're your terms, Lady."

He was right. I couldn't let myself forget it.

Chapter Fifteen

I was back at Maeve's house before Mason showed up, but I'd chewed up too much time with Skeeter to stop home and get Muffy. I was thankful Maeve didn't ask any questions about where I'd been. When Mason showed up about fifteen minutes after me, he was subdued, but he loosened up as we ate.

The three of us sat at Maeve's kitchen table, and I couldn't stop thinking about how blessed I was to finally have the family I'd always wanted. I insisted on staying and helping clean up the kitchen, and I gave Maeve a long hug before we left.

Both of our vehicles were parked at Maeve's, but we decided to leave Mason's car and drive my truck home. He offered to drive.

"Is everything okay, Mason?" I asked after a couple of minutes of silence passed between us. I turned sideways in my seat to study him.

He flashed me a guarded smile. "Why do you ask?"

"Because you had an unexpected meeting with your boss, and you were quiet as a church mouse throughout dinner."

"I've got a lot of pressure on me at work. Nothing to worry about."

"Don't do that," I said. "Don't dismiss your feelings because they're related to work. Tell me what's goin' on. Why did he want to talk to you?"

Mason took a deep breath. "He'd heard about an investigation I'm working on, and he wanted to know more about it. I told him what I could, but I got a dressing down."

"Does this have anything to do with J.R. Simmons?" I'd wanted to ask him since I first heard of his troubles at work, but hadn't been sure how to broach it.

"No." His voice was hard.

"I'm sorry." I unfastened my seatbelt and slid into the middle seat, re-buckling and leaning into his side.

He glanced at me and kissed my temple before wrapping his arm around my shoulders, pulling me closer. "What worries me is *how* he found out. Only a handful of people know."

"What are you investigating?"

He hesitated for several seconds. "I can't talk about it, sweetheart. Official business."

"How can it be official business if your boss doesn't approve?"

He turned down our hidden drive, the headlights bouncing off the front porch. "You're going to have to trust me."

He was hiding something important from me, but I was hardly in a position to demand answers, and the last thing I wanted to do was add to his stress. Still, I had to ask my question again, especially after my encounter with Hilary that afternoon. "You're sure this doesn't have anything to do with J.R.?"

I was worried he'd be offended that I hadn't accepted his first answer, but he sighed, then answered, sounding tired. "No, Rose. I'd tell you if it did. Okay?"

"Okay." It wasn't really. Something big was up, but without knowing what it was, I had no idea how to console him.

Mason parked in front the house and kissed me, wrapping his arms around my back to pull me closer. I tangled my hands in his hair as his hands slid under my sweater.

"I love you, Rose," he murmured against my lips.

I tried to tug his coat off and whacked my hand. "This steering wheel's in my way," I said, reaching to unbuckle his seatbelt. "Let's go inside."

"Gladly." But first he kissed me again, his mouth and hands driving me crazy.

He opened the door and helped me out, then pushed me back against the truck, kissing me senseless.

Suddenly he lifted his head and turned his face toward the front porch. "Something's wrong with Muffy."

He was right. I was used to her barking when we came home, but this time she sounded much more urgent and panicked than usual. I'd been too wrapped up in Mason to notice.

The light of a lamp shone through the living room window, giving the first floor a warm, homey glow—a sharp contrast to Muffy's alarmed cries. I knew she hated being left at home all day, and I felt guilty that I hadn't come home to get her before we ate dinner at Maeve's. But unless her separation anxiety had leaped to new levels, something was seriously wrong.

Mason ran up the steps, and I followed him, but as soon as he realized I was behind him, he spun around, his face hard. "Rose, go back to the truck."

"Not if something's wrong with Muffy!"

"Then please just stay at the bottom of the steps."

"What if someone broke in? I need to get her. She's clearly upset!"

"Rose, *please*," he pleaded as he unlocked the front door and pushed it open. I waited for my little dog to run out to me like she usually did, but her barking only grew more desperate.

I started up the steps, but Mason turned to face me, pointing at my feet. "*Wait there*." Then he went inside, leaving the front door open.

The fact that I couldn't think of a single time he'd ever issued me an order was what kept me in place.

Several seconds later, Muffy's barks turned to high-pitched whines, and it took everything in me to not run inside to see what was wrong with her. I was in tears when Mason walked out the door with Muffy in his arms. He hugged her close as he stroked her head.

"Why was she upset?"

"She was shut in the hall closet."

"What?" I asked in dismay.

His body was rigid, and he looked furious. "Someone broke in through the back door. They must have locked her up."

My poor little dog was nearly hysterical. I started to cry. "How long was she in there?"

His gaze softened as he handed her to me. "I don't know, but she's safe now. Her front paws are a little raw from scratching at the door, but I think she's okay. I'm going to call Joe and ask him to check this out."

I wanted to ask him why he was calling Joe personally, but he'd already stepped away and pulled out his phone. Their conversation was short and he spoke low enough that I only heard bits and snatches. ". . . break-in . . . I'm not sure . . . she's fine . . ."

When he hung up the phone, he turned to me. "Joe's on his way. He'll be here in a few minutes. Why don't you let Muffy do her business, and then get into the truck, okay?"

"What are *you* gonna do?"

"I'm going back inside to look around."

"Is it safe?"

"I'm sure whoever did this is long gone."

"Then why are you telling me to get in the truck?" Mason was still hiding something.

"Because I want to make sure you're safe on the off chance they're still here."

"That's crap, Mason! You should wait for Joe."

He ignored me, turning his attention to Muffy. She still whined in my arms, and Mason rubbed under her ears. "It's okay, girl. Your momma's got you."

"Why did you call Joe and not just 911?"

His hard face was back. "Because I trust Joe to handle this the right way."

"Did you call him because you think this has something to do with J.R.?"

His face hardened even further. "We won't know anything until Joe gets here." He headed for the door. "Stay out here."

I wanted to protest, but Muffy was squirming in my arms, so I set her down in the yard. She continued to whimper while she did her business, then hung close to my leg, so I squatted and rubbed the back of her head while watching for Mason's silhouette in the windows.

The more likely reason behind the break-in was *me*. Did this have anything to do with my shenanigans with Neely Kate earlier in the day? Had I done this to Muffy? Or maybe Eric at the Burger Shack thought I knew something after my strange behavior the day before. Of course, it could have something to do with Skeeter. He'd told me that someone was after Mason. He'd also told me about Mason's meeting with his boss before Maeve did. Anger and betrayal rose up inside me at the very thought. But it didn't make sense . . . Unless I was deluded, he was trying to earn my trust, and besides, what could he possibly want from me other than my "gift"? Anyway, Skeeter Malcolm was smart, so if he'd wanted to break into my house, he wouldn't have been this obvious about it.

Mason emerged from the house as headlights appeared on the driveway. He walked down the steps toward me.

"You're supposed to be in the truck," he said without recrimination.

"It didn't feel right with you inside and all."

He tried to give me a reassuring look as the sheriff car parked on the other side of my truck.

"Mason, I'm sorry."

"Why are you saying you're sorry?"

"This is probably my fault." One way or the other, it always was.

He pulled me close. "This isn't your fault, Rose," he murmured against my hair. "You're safe, and Muffy seems to have calmed down. That's all that matters."

Joe walked up to Mason and me, all business. He'd changed out of his uniform and was dressed in jeans and a leather coat. I expected Muffy to bolt for him, but she seemed too scared to leave my side, so I picked her up and cuddled her. If Joe noticed the fact that she didn't run to him, he didn't comment—instead he honed in on Mason.

Joe started to say something, but Mason interrupted him. "Rose only knows there was a break-in."

"What's that supposed to mean?" I asked.

They ignored me, Joe's face hard. "I want to look around."

Mason nodded. "I haven't touched anything. Come on in, and I'll show you." Mason looked up at me. "Rose, stay outside."

I put Muffy down, then put my hands on my hips. "No! You tell me what's going on."

Mason moved over to me and grabbed my upper arms. "Sweetheart, I really need you to stay outside with Muffy. Once Joe—who, as you know, is trained to go over these things—says it's clear, then you can come in. Okay?"

I wanted to know what they were hiding, but I figured it would be better to press them for information after they'd looked around. "Okay."

Relief washed over his face, but he still seemed really worried. "Thank you."

I glanced up at him, wondering what was inside that was spooking him so, but I let him leave with Joe, who appeared to be getting angrier by the second.

They disappeared into the house, letting the front door gape open. I kept expecting the upstairs lights to turn on, but they never did. That was odd. If we'd been burgled, wouldn't they look upstairs?

About five minutes later, both men emerged through the front door, and Joe started to yell. He waved his hands around and gave Mason a shove. To my surprise, Mason didn't try to fight back.

I was up the porch steps faster than a lightning bolt. "Joe McAllister! You get your hands off my boyfriend!"

Joe took several steps back, his chest heaving as he jabbed a finger at Mason. "I told you this was a bad idea!"

Mason didn't say a word.

"What's going on?" Fear lodged in my throat. "What's inside my house? Who broke in and why?"

Neither one of them answered me.

"I have a right to know! Who did I upset this time?"

Mason's eyes flew open. "Rose, no one's upset with you. It was me."

I blinked. "What are you talking about?"

"Whoever broke in went to my office and broke a lock on the desk drawer."

That meant they were after something Mason had been working on at home. "Did they steal some of your work papers?"

He shook his head, but he looked worried. "No. I can't figure out what they were after. There's a file in there that might have been of interest, but it wasn't taken."

"Get a damned safe, Mason!" Joe shouted.

I spun around to face Joe. "Why are you yelling at him?"

"Because he's putting your life in danger! He's bringing his work home, and now people are breaking into your house, Rose."

"Oh."

Mason released a heavy breath. "I think you should spend the night at Violet's house."

"And where do you plan on staying?"

"Here."

"Then I'm not goin' anywhere."

"Rose," he pleaded with me.

"You said they were here looking for something—just in your office—and it doesn't look like they took anything." I flung my arms out from my side. "So they're done. They're not coming back."

"We don't know that."

"And we don't know if the groundhog is gonna see his shadow on Groundhog Day, yet we're still gettin' out of bed."

He shook his head.

I clenched my fists. "I'm stayin'."

Joe cursed under his breath. "You are the most hardheaded woman I ever met."

I gave him a tight smile. "Thank you."

He brushed past me and started down the steps. "I'll send someone out to dust for prints, and I'll also set up a protective detail to sit out here at night to protect Rose."

Fury burned my gut. "You should be settin' that up because the Assistant District Attorney's home was broken into, not because it happened to be Rose Gardner's house."

To my surprise, Joe seemed properly chastised as he turned around to face me. "You're right. I'm sorry." He looked up at Mason. "Get a safe. And a damned alarm system."

We watched Joe drive away, and I gave Mason a hug. "Are you okay?"

"He's right. I'm putting you in danger by bringing my work home."

I shook my head. "You do that so we can spend more time together. This was a random occurrence."

"That's just it . . . I don't think it was."

"Does it have something to do with whatever the DA doesn't want you working on?"

"I don't think so. Only a handful of people know about it."

"So I'm going to ask you again: does this have to do with J.R.?"

He rubbed his mouth. "The file I've been putting together on him is still there."

"Then we'll do what Joe suggested. You just get a safe, and we'll put in an alarm system."

He shook his head. "I'm not sure that's enough."

"Mason, stop. If you don't want to bring your work home, I'll just start hanging out at your office at night. And I'll bring

Muffy to stink up the place." I gave him a teasing grin. "I just have to figure out how to sneak her through security."

He smiled and kissed the top of my head. "I love you."

"I love you too, so enough of that nonsense."

We went inside and waited for the sheriff deputy, and I couldn't help thinking that whatever Mason and Joe were hiding reeked of J.R. Simmons, despite Mason's instance otherwise.

Chapter Sixteen

Apparently, the Fenton County Sheriff Department took a break-in at the county ADA's house more seriously than the Henryetta Police Department took a break-in at Rose Gardner's house. The deputies spent a lot of time dusting for prints and looking for evidence, but nothing conclusive was found. But I did hear them murmur that they'd found something in the drawer that they'd determined didn't belong to Mason—a pocket knife that had been used to pry open the drawer.

Mason kept trying to get me to take Muffy to Violet's or his mom's house, but I was sufficiently freaked out over his safety that I couldn't bear to leave him.

The deputies did a sweep of the second floor and declared it untouched, allowing me to take Muffy upstairs instead of waiting outside in the cold. Mason followed them around like a shadow, and while they checked out the living room, dining room, and kitchen—paying particular attention to the back door, which had been busted open—they spent the majority of their time in Mason's office.

I sat on the steps for a while with Muffy on my lap, studying Mason as he stood to the side and watched the deputies work.

My phone buzzed in my pocket, and I pulled it out, expecting to see Neely Kate's number. I sucked in my breath when I saw SM instead.

I set Muffy down and walked upstairs to my room—my little dog trailing behind me—and answered. "Did you find something out about Dolly Parton?"

"No, I heard about your incident."

How had he heard already? But it had probably been on a police scanner. "Do you know who did this?"

"No. But I don't like it."

"Well, thanks for your concern."

"Oh, I'm not concerned for your boyfriend. I think whoever broke into your house was looking for dirt on me . . . maybe hoping to pin the break-in on me too."

"*What?*" I shook my head.

"Did they find anything there?"

"You're asking me to feed you information about evidence, Skeeter."

"I'm goin' to ask you one more time: Did they find any evidence there?" He paused a second. "Like a pocket knife?"

"How'd you know?" I asked before I could stop myself.

"Because I'm missing my pocket knife and my prints are all over it. It was my grandfather's, and I carry it with me all the time. I noticed it missing two days ago. Someone close to me must have stolen it and planted it in your boyfriend's office."

"How do I know you didn't break in and leave it here?"

"I'm gonna pretend the woman who accused me of being intelligent this morning isn't asking me if I left important evidence at a crime scene."

Crappy doodles, he was right. When I'd been attacked back in July, Mason had convinced Joe that Skeeter hadn't been behind the attack, that he wouldn't be sloppy. You couldn't get much sloppier than this.

"I need you to have a vision of Deveraux and tell me what you see."

"No."

"You work for *me*, Lady." His words were harsh.

"If I force a vision of Mason, it would be for *him*, not you," I said hatefully.

"Fine, justify it however you like. I just want to know what you see." Then he hung up.

Could Skeeter be right? Was the break-in really about him?

I knew Mason was investigating Skeeter. Did he have information that an enemy of Skeeter's would want? What could it possibly be?

What a mess.

By the time the deputies left shortly before midnight, Mason was a bundle of nerves. He sat at the kitchen table, drumming his fingers on the surface as he stared out the back windows.

"I can make you a cup of chamomile tea," I said, rubbing his shoulders. "It might help you relax."

"Sure," he murmured, then looked around. "How's Muffy? Is she still upset?"

"No, she's asleep on our bed."

"Good." He closed his eyes. "Rose, I'm so sorry."

I leaned my butt on the table next to him. "Why are you saying you're sorry?"

"They could have really hurt Muffy, and it was my fault."

"But they didn't," I said. "She's okay." I pushed on his chair, and he scooted it back, making room for me to sit sideways on his lap. "Look at all the times Muffy's survived break-ins at my house. She's a fighter."

He looked into my eyes as he lifted his hand to my cheek. "I figured that out when we were running in the woods. She's a special dog, and she's important to you. If I were ever the cause of her or you getting hurt, I don't—"

I grabbed both of his cheeks and lowered my lips to his, kissing him gently. "We're both fine."

"I don't want to put you in danger. Maybe we should go away somewhere."

I leaned back and gaped at him. "What?"

"I'll take you to Italy as an early Christmas present. We can leave Saturday."

I shook my head, suddenly scared. "You're serious."

His jaw tightened. "Yes."

I stood up. "You can't just take off. You have a job. You just got into trouble over something tonight. What's your boss gonna say if you just take off without notice?"

"I don't care."

"What about *my* job? I'm setting up the landscaping office."

"You told me yourself that you won't have much to do besides busy work until the first of the year. Who knows when you'll be able to leave after you reopen? Now's the perfect time."

"Mason, I need to know what you're not telling me."

He stood, moving in front of me and pulling me into his arms. "Nothing, I'm just spooked. Someone broke into our house and nearly hurt your dog. I want to keep you safe." He kissed me, his mouth insistent, and tightened his arms around my back. "I've done nothing but work since we've been together, and this break-in has made me realize I'm wasting precious time that I could be spending with you." He turned me around and rested my bottom on the kitchen table. "If something happened to you . . ." His mouth found mine again, his lips and tongue desperate and insistent. He grabbed the bottom of my sweater, breaking our kiss so he could pull it over my head.

As I fumbled with the buttons on his shirt, his mouth returned to mine, his hands moving behind my back to unfasten my bra. He slid the straps over my shoulders and down my arms. I spread his shirt apart and let my bra fall to the floor. Spreading my palms over his bare chest, I looked up into his eyes. I gave him a saucy grin as I reached down and began to unfasten his belt.

He kissed me again as I worked on unfastening his pants, then he kicked off his shoes and stepped out of his pants and boxers so that he was standing in front of me in nothing but his opened dress shirt.

His hands slid down my sides, then up to cup my breasts. His mouth lowered to one of them, and I grabbed the back of his head as I arched my back to give him better access.

He pushed me back so I was lying on the table, then reached for the button on my jeans as I lifted my hips so he could pull them off with my panties.

He stood between my open legs, his eyes roaming over my body as I lay on our kitchen table, feeling naughty. Good girls didn't have sex on their kitchen tables, but I didn't want to be a good girl with Mason. "You make me feel very wicked," I confessed.

A fire flickered in his eyes. "And do you like feeling wicked?"

"Yes," I exhaled, watching his reaction.

He leaned over me, his mouth finding one breast while his hand fondled the other. Then his mouth trailed down my abdomen and lowered between my legs. He hooked my leg over his shoulder, and I closed my eyes and gasped, overwhelmed with what his mouth and hands were doing.

Doing this on the kitchen table was so wrong, but that only excited me more. It didn't take long before I needed more.

"Mason."

But he continued to work wonders with his mouth.

"Mason, *please*."

"What do you want, Rose?"

"You. I want *you*. Now."

He slid up my body, his face hovering over mine, his eyes burning with intensity. "Don't you know that you already have me? I'm hopelessly and unceasingly yours." Then he entered me, and I clung to him as we showed each other how desperate we were for each other.

Afterward, Mason rolled onto his side, bringing me with him so that I faced him, my leg slung over his hip. His hand stroked my cheek as he searched my eyes.

I grinned. "The next time your momma comes over for dinner, we're gonna have to eat in the dining room, because I'm not sure I can sit at this table with her without blushing."

He grinned, looking wicked. I loved the contrast of good Mason, who wore dress shirts and ties in the office, and naughty Mason, who made me want to do things I'd never considered.

His fingertips stroked my shoulder in lazy circles. "I mean it, Rose, I want you to go away with me. I'll grab my laptop right now and book two tickets for Saturday. Where do you want to go? Rome? Venice? Tuscany? We can visit all of them. Hell, we can move there."

I pulled back. "Where is this coming from?"

"I already told you."

He had, and while I believed him, I knew there was more to it. "I can't go to Italy. I don't have a passport."

He slid his finger up and down my arm. "Then we'll go somewhere else. Somewhere far away from here."

"We don't have to go away to spend time together, Mason. We can do it right here."

"I could spend time with you in a cave and be perfectly content. But you deserve so much more than that, Rose, and I want to give it to you." He propped himself up on an elbow, brushing the hair off my neck and lowering his mouth to my collar bone. He worked his way up until he abruptly stopped, lifting his head. "Why are there bruises on your neck?"

"Tabitha."

"*What?*"

"There's a big bad world out there, Mason Deveraux, and try as you might, you can't keep me safe from all of it."

Tears filled his eyes. "But I'll die trying if I have to."

I cupped his cheek in my hand. "That's enough talk about dying. Tonight is all about *living*."

He tugged me against him, kissing me with a ferocity I didn't expect. Then we did things on that kitchen table and a couple of chairs that made it clear that it would be Easter before Mason's mother could come close to the kitchen.

Chapter Seventeen

The next morning, Mason still wanted to go away, but I finally convinced him that neither of us could just pick up and leave. He had his job, and I had promised Neely Kate I'd help her find Dolly Parton. And true, there wasn't much going on with the business, but I didn't feel right about leaving Bruce Wayne to deal with anything that might pop up. He might be my partner, but I needed to pull my weight.

We ate breakfast together, and Mason was quieter than usual, but I knew he was still spooked about the break-in.

"I'm going to see if I can get an alarm system put in today. Until then, I don't want you here without me."

I buttered a slice of toast. "Don't you think you're overreacting?"

"*No.*"

I put my knife down on my plate. "Mason, do you *really* think they're coming back? They either found what they were looking for or they didn't. They only searched the office, which means they didn't expect to find it anywhere else. They're not coming back."

"I know you're helping Neely Kate today, but try to be more careful than usual."

"I will." I took a bite of my toast, looking down at Muffy, who sat on the floor next to me, waiting for scraps. "I can't bear to leave Muffy alone today, but I don't want to take her on the road with me either."

"What do you want to do?"

"Maybe I could see if Violet will watch her," I said.

"Isn't Violet planning to be at the nursery for the next few days?"

"Ugh. You're right." I ran my hand through my hair. "I forgot. I could ask Bruce Wayne, but he's looking at a lawnmower and an edger this afternoon. He got a lead on an estate sale."

"I'm sure Mom wouldn't mind watching her. We're going by her house to get my car so it wouldn't be out of the way."

"Are you sure? I really don't want to impose on her."

"Mom loves that little dog, and I suspect she wouldn't mind the company. I'll ask her if you'd like." He shot me a grin. "She's not afraid to tell me no, so you'll know she really doesn't mind when she says yes."

Maeve was thrilled at the idea of having Muffy spend the day with her, and I was relieved to know my little dog was in good hands. Muffy was excited to see Maeve, whom she greeted with lots of kisses, and Mason walked me out to my truck once she was settled.

"I mean it, Rose, please don't place yourself in danger today."

I grinned at him, wrapping my arms around his neck and pressing my chest to his. "How many times do I have to tell you I'll be careful?"

"As many times as it takes for me to believe you."

"Ha. Ha," I teased.

He pulled me closer and gave me a long kiss. "If you change your mind about running off somewhere, I'm just a phone call away. As soon as I finish something up on Friday night, I can take you away. For as long as you want."

My smile fell. "How much trouble are you in, Mason?"

He studied me for several seconds. "I'm not sure yet. Maybe a lot."

My breath caught in my chest. "What kind of trouble? Are you gonna lose your job?"

He hesitated before answering, his face grave. "Maybe." He sighed. "Rose, I'd tell you more about it if I could."

I tried to figure out how upset he was over that. The night before, he'd insisted he needed to spend more time with me. Was he trying to convince himself he'd be okay with losing his job, or had he really meant it?

I winked. "How good are you at digging?"

He laughed. "Are you suggesting that I should be looking for ditch-digging jobs?"

I cocked my head and gave him an ornery grin. "It just so happens I know this landscaping company that might need some manual laborers this spring."

He grinned. "You don't say. Do you know anything about the owner?"

I lifted my mouth close to his. "I hear she can be very demanding. And she might make you work without a shirt."

"Sounds intriguing," he teased. "Do you know how I can get an interview?"

I kissed him, and his arm tightened around me. "If you play your cards right, I might be able to get you one."

He chuckled and shook his head. "For your sake, I hope you don't need to hire me. I inherited my mother's black thumb."

"Everyone is trainable."

He released a long laugh. "Why do I have the feeling you might be referring to getting me to lower the toilet seat rather than digging up shrubbery?"

"Hope springs eternal, Mason Deveraux." I swatted his bottom. "Now get to work."

He kissed me again and stepped back a few paces. "You're not even my employer yet, and you're already bossing me around. I think I should just give up now and obey your commands."

"I *knew* you were a smart man."

He started to get in his car and turned back to look at me. "I'm making a run out to the sheriff's office before I head to the courthouse, just so you don't wonder why I'm not heading downtown."

"Is this about the break-in?"

He paused. "Yeah."

"Okay. Good luck when you get to work." No matter what he claimed, I knew he didn't want to lose his job. Not after he lost his job in Little Rock.

Bruce Wayne wasn't in the office when I got there, and the space seemed lonely without him. I decided to focus on getting our finances in order, which meant purchasing and downloading an accounting program like Neely Kate had suggested. Once that was taken care of, I started to enter in all our information.

An hour later, Neely Kate walked through the door as I was cussing out my computer.

"Whoa, if I didn't know better, I'd think you'd been hanging out with my cousins," she said as she walked up behind me and studied the screen. "What on earth are you doin'?"

I threw my hands into the air. "Trying to put information into an accounting program."

"Did you link it to your bank account?"

I gave her a blank stare.

She picked up a receipt and read it. "What category are you putting this equipment rental under?"

"*Other*?"

She groaned as she tossed the receipt onto my desk. "You're making a mess of it."

"I have no idea what I'm doin'."

She chuckled. "That's pretty obvious. You should have waited for me."

"So how'd it go last night?" I asked.

Neely Kate rolled Bruce Wayne's chair closer to mine and sat down. "Fine. I talked to Roger at the bingo hall, and he's gonna let Granny pay off the damage to the raccoon."

I still wasn't clear on what had happened, but I also wasn't sure I wanted to be. "I was talking about Ronnie and your job situation."

"Oh, that." She sat back in her chair. "He was fine with it."

"Well, that's good."

"I told you he wanted me to quit. I think he got tired of hearing me complain." She leaned her elbow on the arm of the chair. "Now I'll have more time to cook."

"Oh." *Crappy doodles.*

I stared at her for a couple of seconds. Should I come clean and tell her that her food was disgusting? I didn't want to hurt her, but I wasn't sure my stomach could handle any more *gourmet* delicacies. But maybe there was another way. "You know, Neely Kate, now that you have all this free time, you could use it to decorate Ronnie Jr.'s room."

Her mouth puckered. "It'll be another three months before I have my first ultrasound."

"Maybe not . . ." My voice rose on the end with a playful tone.

She grabbed my hand, her eyes wide with excitement. "Are you serious?"

Was I? What if I saw something bad? I couldn't bear the thought of blurting out something awful to her. Saving my gastrointestinal tract wouldn't be worth it. Nevertheless, I'd opened this can of worms, and I couldn't turn back now. "Neely Kate," I said, turning serious. "Think about this. Are you sure you don't want to wait until the ultrasound? You can have a party to celebrate when you find out. You know, like making one of those cakes with a blue or pink center to surprise everyone with the news. You won't get that if we find out now."

She didn't answer, still holding my hand.

"And what about Ronnie? Doesn't he want to be with you when he sees Ronnie Jr.'s . . ." I cringed, "you know . . . *part* on the ultrasound screen?"

She shook her head. "He doesn't care about that. The doctor's office makes him squeamish."

I told a deep breath, then whispered, "What if I see something bad, Neely Kate? Have you thought of that?"

Tears filled her eyes. "Yes. That's why I'm so desperate for you to try. My granny read in her tea leaves that I'm gonna lose the baby."

I gasped. "Why didn't you tell me?" I squeezed her hand. "You know she gets almost everything wrong. You can't believe that."

"She's seen it more than once, Rose." Her bottom lip quivered. "I couldn't tell anyone, not even Ronnie. I was superstitious enough to think it might come true if I said it out loud."

I lifted my chin. "Then I'm going to have a vision to prove her wrong, okay?"

She sniffed and nodded, fear filling her eyes before determination replaced it. "Okay. One way or the other, let's find out."

Butterflies swarmed my stomach as I closed my eyes, concentrating on Neely Kate's pregnancy. What if by some freak of nature her grandmother was right?

Several seconds later I was standing in a small store filled with baby clothes, standing next to . . . well, *me*. I grabbed a blue sleeper embroidered with "My daddy is a mechanic. What super power does your daddy have?" off a rack of clothes and held it to my chest. "What do you think, Rose?"

Vision-me was looking through a stack of baby clothes on a display table. I was wearing my black and cream tweed coat and a cream-colored knit hat. Lots of people were walking past the store's big picture windows while jazzy Christmas music played overhead. Vision-me glanced up, shaking my head. "I think you're crazy, but if you really want to do it, we can."

"And what about the sleeper?"

I laughed. "Ronnie will love it."

The vision faded, and my eyes flew open. "You're shopping for baby clothes, and you want to do something crazy."

Her red nails painted with little Christmas trees dug into my hand. "Baby clothes?"

I nodded, and she breathed a sigh of relief.

"Tell me what you saw." After I relayed the vision to her, she asked, "Where were we?"

"Definitely not Henryetta, but the store was playing Christmas music." I lifted my eyebrows, anticipating her next question. "And I have no idea what you wanted to do."

"Hmm . . ." she said, sounding happy. I realized my dream hadn't been that far into the future, but Neely Kate seemed content, so I wasn't going to press the issue. Instead, I looked at the computer screen in front of me and resisted a groan of frustration. "You know," I said, giving her a pleading look. "Since you have nothing but time on your hands, maybe you could help me with this. I was going to pay a bookkeeper to get us set up anyway, so I'll just hire you, and you can earn money to decorate Ronnie Jr.'s nursery."

"Oh, my stars and garters!" she shouted, throwing her arms around my neck. "We can work together! How amazing is that?"

"Something Bad" by Miranda Lambert and Carrie Underwood started playing, muffled from the inside of Neely Kate's purse.

My eyebrows rose. "You changed your ringtone? To the song you danced to?"

She gave me an ornery grin as she dug in her purse. "It seemed appropriate after yesterday. In more ways than one."

She dug it out and answered. "Hello?" Her forehead quickly furrowed. "Why can't you tell me on the phone?" She let out an exasperated groan. "Fine. I'll meet you, but this better be worth my time, Billy Jack."

"Billy Jack?" I asked as she hung up.

"He says he knows something about Dolly Parton that he couldn't tell us before. He wants to meet us at the Blue Plate Diner down on Highway 82, on the other side of Pickle Junction."

"What if it's a trap?" I cringed. "He wasn't very happy with us when we parted."

"Billy Jack'll hold a grudge, all right, but he sounded really spooked." She paused and searched my eyes. "I think he knows something."

"Okay," I said, "let's meet him. What time?"

"Eleven-thirty."

"That's less than half an hour from now." I stood up and grabbed my coat. "Let's get going. I'll tell you about my night on the way."

She glared at me. "If you're talking about someone breaking into your house yesterday, I already know."

I was bound to pay for that.

We got in my truck and headed southwest while I told her everything about my evening—minus my visit with Skeeter. I knew she wouldn't understand, and I wasn't up for a lecture. The less she knew about Skeeter, the better.

Thankfully, Neely Kate wasn't one to hold a grudge. "So you think Mason's gonna lose his job?" she asked after I told her about his strange behavior.

"I don't know, but something's definitely going on with him."

"You know," she said, more reserved than usual. "I think you might be right."

This was one instance I wished I wasn't. Was there something *she* wasn't telling me?

Twenty-five minutes later, we were pulling in front of the diner, the side lot full of big tractor-trailers.

"Truckers like to eat here," Neely Kate said as she opened the door. "Billy Jack said he'd find us inside. Come on. I'm starving."

The hostess seated us at a table by the window, and the waitress came by to take our orders.

I glanced out the window. "Is Billy Jack running on West Coast time or something? Because he's fifteen minutes late."

"I don't know," she said. "He insisted he'd be here. He said he'd find us." The waitress dropped off a basket of rolls, and Neely Kate practically pounced on it. "Besides, it's not like coming to this place was hardly a waste. They have the best dinner rolls this side of the Mississippi."

Our food came, and by the time we'd finished eating, Billy Jack was still a no-show.

"What do you want to do?" I asked.

"Let's go check out Nikko's place. Then maybe we can swing by Billy Jack's on the way back to town."

"Sounds good."

It took us twenty minutes to get to Sugar Branch. I drove into the small downtown and turned to look at my best friend. "How do we go about finding Nikko once we get there? Do you have any idea where he lives?"

"Nope. But we need to find the local hair salon."

"Now doesn't seem like a good time for a haircut, Neely Kate."

She grinned. "*Everybody* knows the best place to get gossip is the hair salon or the barbershop."

"Oh." Seeing as how I hadn't spent much time in hair salons, I supposed I wouldn't know.

After we drove through the commercial center of the small town—a bunch of small businesses including a gas station—we turned on a side street and found the Cut and Curl. I considered it a good sign that there were a couple of cars in the parking lot.

Neely Kate reached for the door handle as soon as I parked the truck. "Come on."

We entered the four-sink salon and found two hairdressers working on clients, one of them an older woman getting her already poufy hair teased, and the other a younger woman with a head covered in tin foil strips.

"Howdy," the hairdresser working on the older woman said as she picked up a can of hairspray. "What can we do for ya?"

"Hi." Neely Kate put her hand on her hip. "I'm lookin' for Nikko. Do any of y'all know where I might find him?"

The younger woman in the chair sat up straighter, lifting her chin with a bit of attitude. "And who's askin'?"

"I used to work with him," Neely Kate said. "Back before he started at Gems. He never came by to pick up his last paycheck, so I figured I'd drop it off for him."

The woman squinted at Neely Kate, suspicious. "Doesn't his check have his address on it?"

Neely Kate dropped her arm to her side and took a step closer, lowering her voice. "It's kind of an under-the-table payment . . . if you know what I mean."

"Oh." The young woman's defenses fell, her disappointment replacing bravado. "Nikko said he was gonna stop that nonsense after he got arrested this summer. He stopped working at that garage north of Henryetta and everything."

Neely Kate hesitated, so I jumped in. "As far as we know, he did. This is from when he was still at Weston's." I added the last part purely as a guess, figuring the more we seemed to know, the better. "That's probably why he never came back to pick it up. Because he wanted out."

Tears filled her eyes. "I told him that Daniel Crocker was no good, but does he listen to his sister? Hell no. He thinks he's smarter because he's eleven months older, but he's dumber than a stump if you ask me. Otherwise why would he be missing now?"

"What happened to him?" Neely Kate asked, pretending not to know.

"I don't know," the woman said. "The last time I saw him was on Friday evening. He was about to go to work at that Gems place and . . . well, he never came home. He'd told me that he suspected something was goin' on there, and I told him to quit, but he never listens to me." She sniffled, and her hairdresser handed her a tissue.

"Do you think he got into some kind of trouble?"

"I know he did, but what am I gonna do?" she asked, wiping tears from her cheeks. "He's not exactly friendly with the sheriff's department, if you know what I mean, so I don't feel like I can call them."

I moved closer to the woman and sat in the empty chair next to her. "We'll help you look for him," I said. "He disappeared with a woman named Dolly Parton Parker, do you know her?"

Her back stiffened. "How do you know that?"

I pointed over my shoulder at Neely Kate. "Because Dolly's her cousin, and she disappeared too. The same night and place as Nikko. We're trying to find her."

The young woman's eyes glazed over. "That's so weird that you have Nikko's last paycheck and your cousin disappeared with him."

If Nikko's sister was the brighter of the two of them, Nikko was in grave trouble.

Neely Kate shot me an exasperated glance before she said, "I know, *right?*"

"I'm always sayin' it's a small, small world." The young woman looked over her shoulder at her hairdresser. "Ain't I saying that, Nancy?"

Nancy released a low whistle. "You sure are, Alaina."

"Do you have any idea what was goin' on at Gems?" I asked.

Alaina shook her head. "I don't know. But I know it was illegal. Nikko got mixed up with Crocker's guys this summer. Then when Crocker broke out of jail and went cuckoo, Nikko quit and said he was done. But times are tough, you know?"

"I know," I said.

"He kept trying to find an honest job, but the bills were piling up. Then he found out that Gems needed a bartender." She shook her head. "I told him not to take it, but he was desperate. He was gonna lose his trailer, and he swore that Mud promised him the business was on the up and up even though it was a strip club."

"But it wasn't on the up and up? What did he say?"

"Nothing specific, just that he knew something was going on. There were weekly meetings on Friday nights, but if he knew why, he didn't say. He did tell me that Mud was taking orders from someone else."

"Who?"

"The owner. Mud's just the manager."

"So who's the owner?"

She shook her head. "I don't know."

"Do you know if your brother was dating Dolly Parton? She went by Sapphire at the club?"

She shook her head, emphatic. "No. He had a thing for another girl at the club, Becky. I think she goes by Crystal there."

"Is there anything else you can think of that might help?"

"No. Nothing. Nikko never told me nothing about workin' for Crocker. The only reason I know as much as I do is because he got drunk one night and told me. The next day he seemed real sorry and told me to forget it."

I glanced at Neely Kate, and she looked worried. We had more information, but it wouldn't get us very far.

"Do you think we could look around his trailer with you? We know Mud sent some guys over to Nikko's place. We're trying to figure out what he was looking for," I said. "I know you don't know us, but maybe there's something there that will help us find your brother and Dolly Parton."

She studied us for several seconds. "Yeah. Sure. I'll take you there after I get done here. It shouldn't be much longer, should it?" She looked up at the hairdresser.

"Yeah, you've got about five minutes left with the foils. Then I'll wash it and cut it. Say twenty-five minutes?"

"Does he live around here?" Neely Kate asked.

"Yeah, just outside of town."

"Say, is there any place around here to get donuts?" Neely Kate asked.

Judging from the silence that descended on the room, everyone was confused by her question.

Neely Kate shrugged. "We've got twenty-five minutes to kill, and Ronnie Jr. wants donuts."

Nancy, the hairdresser, came to her senses first. "The closest place to get donuts is the gas station on County Road 22, but I gotta warn you, they're not very fresh."

"You probably passed it when you came into town," said the older woman who was getting her hair fluffed to resemble a lion's mane.

"Thanks," Neely Kate said. "We'll be back."

I followed Neely Kate out to the truck. "We just ate lunch. Are we really getting donuts?"

"Sure we are. Ronnie Jr. likes the jelly-filled kind. Plus, this'll give us a chance to go over all the facts we've gathered."

"Well, let's hope they have what he wants." I laughed. At least she wasn't craving spicy Buffalo wings again.

The only donuts the Feed and Fuel had were dried-out glazed donuts and hard long johns. Neely Kate settled on a package of powdered sugar donuts instead, along with a bottle of milk. We sat in the parked truck, looking out the windshield at the cars passing by on the county road.

"So the last people to see Dolly Parton and Nikko were at the club on Friday night—or rather early Saturday morning," I said. "But neither one has been seen since."

"That's nothing new," Neely Kate groaned. "I feel like we've beaten that dead horse to death."

"But something's bothering me."

"What?"

"Billy Jack said that Nikko came and picked Dolly up from his house. Why would Nikko do that? It doesn't sound like they were friends, and Alaina said her brother was running late. He wouldn't have had time to run to Pickle Junction to pick her up before heading to Gems."

"But why would Billy Jack have lied?" Neely Kate asked. "What happened at Gems doesn't seem to have anything to do with them."

"I don't know, but I don't believe him. It's really suspicious."

"Maybe that's why he wanted to talk to me." Neely Kate's words were mumbled around a big bite of one of the donuts. "Maybe he lied and feels guilty."

"I wouldn't be surprised. Between the thing with the TV and his claim that he saw Dolly Parton and Nikko after Friday, his story is suspect," I said.

"Yeah, it's not adding up. We really do need to track him down and talk to him."

"Maybe we should tell Joe."

She snorted. "You remember what he said. He's not gonna listen to a thing we have to say until tomorrow. And then he'll *try* to find someone to investigate her disappearance. And it's not like Billy Jack is gonna volunteer any information to the sheriff's department. We need to find him ourselves."

Unfortunately, I suspected she was right.

"I've felt uneasy about this whole situation from the start. But I always thought I'd find her shacked up with someone. I haven't given much thought to findin' her in . . . in a bad state."

"I don't think she's dead, Neely Kate, if that's what you're thinking. I bet she's hiding with Nikko for some reason. Mud obviously thinks the same thing. Otherwise why would he have sent men to Nikko's house?"

Tears filled Neely Kate's eyes. "Maybe they were looking for something they thought Nikko had. He told his sister he was getting out of trouble, but what if he just said that to get her off his back? Maybe he stole something from them."

I took her hands in mine. "Maybe. We definitely need to check out his trailer."

"Don't you think Mud's guys would have found what they were looking for if it was in there?"

"Maybe not." I shrugged. "Maybe Nikko hid it good enough that they couldn't find it." I gave her a hopeful smile. "His sister might know where it is. Or maybe she can help us figure out where Nikko and Dolly are hiding."

"Thank you for helping me."

"Of course." I gave her a hug. "We're best friends. If you need my help, I'm there for you. No questions asked."

We drove back to the salon, where Nancy was finishing up Alaina's hair.

"You actually came back," Alaina said, her tone not quite as friendly as before.

"We said we would," Neely Kate said.

"How do I know you really have a cousin who's missing? How do I know you're not working for Mud?"

Neely Kate pointed to me. "Does she look like the kind of girl who'd work at Gems?"

Alaina scrutinized me for several seconds. "No, I guess not."

Part of me wanted to protest, but then I reminded myself that that was a good thing.

"We're trying to find my cousin. I swear it. If we can just look at Nikko's house to look for any clues, it might help. Both of us."

When Alaina didn't look entirely convinced, Neely Kate dug out her phone and started scrolling on her screen. "Look." She moved closer to her and showed her the screen. "This is Dolly Parton. She's my cousin, and I'm scared to death something awful has happened to her." Neely Kate's voice broke. "So I'm beggin' you, *please* help us."

Alaina looked up at Neely Kate and nodded. "Okay, but if I find out you're lyin', I'm gonna snatch you bald."

What was it with women wanting to rip out Neely Kate's hair? But she took it in stride and lifted her chin. "Well, just in case you screw up my intentions, it's a good thing I have a lot of hair. Now let's go."

Chapter Eighteen

Nikko owned a tiny mobile home on the side of a county road. There was an astounding assortment of them, spanning from nice trailers with potted plants to absolutely trashy ones.

Alaina pulled off the road in front of a faded white and loam-green trailer, and I pulled in next to her. As she unlocked the front door, Alaina looked over her shoulder at us. "Nikko gave me a key, but I haven't been in here since last week."

"Okay," I said. That meant we had no idea what we'd find.

Alaina pushed the door open, and we followed her into the dark living room. All the curtains were drawn, so it took a few seconds for my eyes to adjust, but the stench of something rotten hit me first.

"Oh, my stars and garters!" Neely Kate gushed, looking at the mess. "They've totally ransacked the place!"

There were clothes strewn everywhere—on the floor and covering the sofa and recliner. Along with the laundry were empty beer and pop cans, discarded chip bags and cracker boxes.

"*This?*" Alaina asked in surprise. "This is how Nikko lives. That boy never did learn to pick up after himself." She leaned over and picked up a T-shirt, took a whiff and cringed, then tossed it in a chair.

Neely Kate put a hand to her chest. "Oh."

"What exactly are you lookin' for?" Alaina asked, stepping over a pair of jeans.

Neely Kate glanced over at me, her eyes wide. We had no idea what we were looking for, and the fact that the place was totally trashed didn't help.

"We were hoping to figure out what Mud's guys were looking for," I sighed as I walked past her into the kitchen. The trash was overflowing, and the smell was worse near the container.

"Honestly, we're grasping at straws," Neely Kate added. "Can you look around with us and tell us if anything looks out of place?"

"Sure," Alaina said.

I was curious how she was gonna figure that out, but we followed her as she made her way down the hall, and I noticed the back door was cracked. I pushed it open and saw the doorframe was bent and splintered.

"Has it always looked like this?" I asked. After seeing the state of the living room and kitchen, I wouldn't put it past Nikko to have broken the back door in if he'd misplaced his key.

"No," Alaina said, her voice tight.

"Then Mud's guys must have broken in when they came to look for them," Neely Kate said.

Alaina continued into the bedroom. The bed was unmade, and the whole room smelled musty. Drawers were partially open, and clothing hung over the sides. A pile of clothes filled the open closet.

"This is Nikko's room."

"This is hopeless," Neely Kate whispered in my ear. "How can we tell if they looked for anything, let alone found it?"

I had to admit she was probably right. "Did Nikko have places where he hid things? Like if he didn't want anyone to find them?"

"No," Alaina said. "He didn't have anything worth hiding."

"Well, thanks," Neely Kate said, disappointment heavy in her words. She headed down the hall with Alaina, but I looked around the room, trying to figure out where Nikko might have hidden something.

On closer inspection, I realized the top mattress had been shifted. Nikko might be a slob, but I couldn't imagine anyone willingly sleeping on a crooked mattress.

I took two steps and stopped.

Mud's men had been searching this space for something other than Nikko.

I wasn't sure how skinny he was, but there was no way he could hide under the mattress or even under the bed for that matter. The box springs were on a frame that was barely six inches off the floor.

"Neely Kate!"

She was back in the doorway in seconds. "Did you find something?"

"I don't know." I showed her the mattress and told her my theory. "This confirms they were looking for something."

"I think you're right," she said. "But what on earth were they looking for?"

Alaina had followed Neely Kate and stood behind her.

"Alaina," I said. "What did Nikko do for Crocker?"

She shook her head, her eyes getting hard. "He never worked for that looney tune. My brother's smarter than that."

"Okay," I drawled. "What did he do for Crocker's *men?* I know his car parts ring was pretty well done by the summer." Which meant all that was left were some drugs and fencing stolen goods.

She grimaced, and I could tell she didn't want to tell me.

"I'm not gonna judge him," I said in a soft voice. "I know two people who worked for Crocker—a guy I work with and my ex-boyfriend. And I don't hold it against them. They both got out. Just like Nikko."

Neely Kate shot me a look of surprise, but didn't correct me. Technically Bruce Wayne and I did work together. And Joe *had* worked for Crocker. He just happened to be undercover for the state police at the time.

"Nikko told me they had expanded their drug business into meth. Nikko helped deliver it." An angry look filled her eyes. "But he wasn't a dealer, so don't you be thinking that."

I held up my hands. "I don't doubt you."

Tears filled her eyes. "He's really done it this time, hasn't he?"

I gave her a sympathetic look. "I don't know." I paused. "You said Nikko and the sheriff's department didn't get along. Did they know about his association with Crocker? Or was it something else?"

She started to cringe, then stopped herself. "Nikko's always liked to stir up a little trouble. But nothing really bad," she insisted. "Just some cow-tipping and TPing the high school principal's front yard. Mischief."

Neely Kate shifted her weight. "What about Mud?" she said. "I mean maybe Nikko really did try to go the straight and narrow and thought his job at Gems was really a bartending job. But what if Mud found out he worked for Crocker's guys? Maybe he wanted information on how the whole racket was run."

Alaina shook her head. "That's crazy."

I wasn't so sure Neely Kate was far off from the truth. "Alaina, you said someone besides Mud runs Gems, right?"

"Yes, but I don't know who."

According to Skeeter, the person who'd opened the place did it to try and put him out of business. "There's not enough clientele to support two strip clubs. So why would the owner of Gems open it? Why go to all the trouble?" I asked.

Both women looked at me with blank expressions.

"They came here looking for something. I bet they think Nikko had something from his time with Crocker's guys, something that might help them take down Skeeter Malcolm. He's the new king of Fenton County, and he got there by acquiring Crocker's business. There's a bunch of people who are unhappy about that, and I wouldn't be surprised if some of them were trying to take him down."

Neely Kate's eyes pinned me with a steely gaze. I was gonna catch hell when we left.

Alaina shook her head in confusion. "I don't know how that helps us."

"I don't know yet either, but can you think of any hiding places Nikko might have?"

"No." She sounded disappointed.

"Well, if you think of something, will you let us know?" Neely Kate asked.

"Sure."

We looked around for another ten minutes, turning up nothing. Digging through Nikko's filth made me feel guilty for bothering Mason about leaving his dirty socks on the side of the bed. After the break-in last night, I had the sudden urge to talk to him.

We went outside, and Neely Kate and I walked around, looking for anything that seemed out of the ordinary. Not that either one of us had a clue of what to look for. We were woefully out of our league.

When we reached the front of the trailer, Neely Kate talked to Alaina, who'd trailed silently after us, while I climbed in the truck and sent Skeeter a text.

I need to talk to you. Text me.

Neely Kate got back into the truck and shot me a glare. "You have some explaining to do."

I tried to look innocent as I started the truck and pulled onto the county road. "What are you talking about?"

"All that Skeeter nonsense. How do you know about that?"

I tried to look irritated. "You know I was at the auction."

"That's not what I'm talking about, and you know it."

"What?" I looked at her.

My cell phone rang just then, and I wanted nothing more than to throttle Skeeter. I'd told him to text me. Now how was I going to explain talking to him to Neely Kate? In my haste, I reached for my phone more quickly than usual, and Neely Kate sensed I was trying to hide the call from her and snatched it from me.

"Neely Kate!" I shouted, reaching for the phone.

"What are you hiding from me, Rose?" she said, looking at the phone. "It's Joe."

Chapter Nineteen

Neely Kate looked up in surprise. "Why are you hiding a call from Joe?"

"I'm not," I said, snatching the phone from her. "I didn't know it was him."

Why *was* he calling?

"Hey, Joe?" I answered.

"Rose, are you driving?"

I cast a weird glance to Neely Kate. "Yeah, why?"

"I want you to pull over."

My heart started racing. "Why?"

"Rose, darlin', just do it. Please."

"Okay," I said breathlessly, panicking over what Joe needed to tell me. It had to be bad if he wanted me to pull over to the side of the road.

"What is it?" Neely Kate asked.

"I don't know." I pulled the truck onto the shoulder as I tried to catch my breath. "Okay, I'm pulled over. What is it?"

"Mason's been in a car accident."

"*Oh, God.* Is he okay?"

"They've taken him to the hospital. He hit his head pretty good, so they want to do a CT scan."

"What happened?"

"He'd just left the sheriff's department and was on his way back to the courthouse. He ran off the road and hit a pole."

I shook my head. "But he's such a careful driver. How did it happen?"

"I don't know. We're investigating the accident now."

"Why isn't *he* calling me? Oh, no." A new wave of panic hit me. "Is he hurt really bad?"

"Rose, calm down," he said in a low, soothing voice. "I spoke with him after the accident, and while he was dazed for a bit, he seems better now. He cut his forehead and there was a lot of blood, so I'm sure he needs stitches. I think they just wanted to be safe."

Something didn't feel right. "I'm on my way," I said, my voice breaking.

"Rose, just stop and take a deep breath. Wait a few seconds to let this sink in, okay?"

"Okay." Tears burned my eyes. "Do you think he's going to be okay?"

Joe chuckled. "Mason Deveraux's too hard-headed to let a light pole seriously injure him."

I laughed through my tears. "Yeah, you're right."

"I'm sorry to be the one telling this to you, and I didn't want you to hear it from someone else."

"Thank you."

"Is Neely Kate with you? Maybe she should drive."

I took a deep breath. "No. I'm fine. I'll be at the hospital soon."

"Rose." He hesitated. "Call me if you need anything, okay? I'm here for you."

"Thank you."

I hung up and turned to Neely Kate.

Her eyes were wide with fright. "Is Mason okay?"

I nodded. "Joe thinks so. He was in a car accident, though, and he hit his head. Joe said he needs stitches, and they're going to do a CT scan to make sure nothing's wrong."

"Do you want me to drive?"

I took a deep breath, feeling calmer as I slowly let it out. Joe assured me that Mason was fine. My feeling of foreboding was just an overreaction. "No, I'm okay. I'm sorry we can't try to find Billy Jack, but I have to see Mason."

"Rose." She leaned over and rubbed my arm. "Mason comes first right now. It's okay."

Neely Kate talked to me all the way to the hospital. I was glad she was there to keep me company, because my mind was racing with all kinds of worst-case scenarios, despite Joe's insistence that Mason was okay. If he was okay, why hadn't he called me himself? What if Joe had pretended Mason was in better shape than he was because he was worried I'd have my own accident on the way to the hospital? Neely Kate could tell I was a bundle of nerves by the time we got to the hospital twenty minutes later.

"You know that Mason's too bullheaded to let anything bad happen to him, right? His run-in with Daniel Crocker proved that to be true."

I nodded, but tears stung my eyes. Something was really wrong. An ache filled the back of my head, reminding me of the feeling I'd gotten with two of my recent visions. What did *that* mean?

As soon as I parked, I raced through the emergency room entrance up to the counter. "I'm here to see Mason Deveraux."

The receptionist, a woman who appeared to be in her forties or fifties, looked up at me with mild interest. "Are you family?"

"I'm his girlfriend."

Her gaze returned to her computer. "Then you'll have to wait in the waiting room," she said, sounding bored.

I splayed my hands on the chest-high counter and leaned forward. "And if we were married? Would I have to wait then?"

"No," she said as though I'd asked the stupidest question in the world.

"Can you at least tell me if he's okay?" My voice rose in frustration.

"We only give that information to family members." She glanced up at me with disdain, then said, "But you're welcome to sit in the waiting room."

I wasn't about to take no for answer. "Will you at least tell him I'm here? He's been a patient here before, and I sat with him in his exam room. Just a couple of months ago."

She shook her head, looking irritated. "Sorry. I can't relay messages from the waiting room to patients. You'll just have to stay where you are."

I walked away from the counter and pulled out my phone, dialing Mason's cell phone. My anxiety grew when it went straight to voice mail. I considered calling Maeve, but I didn't know if anyone had informed her yet. I didn't want to scare her, since I didn't know anything other than what Joe had told me.

I stared into Neely Kate's face, pulling back my shoulders. "I'm not gonna wait. I'm goin' back there."

She gave me a slight nod, a determined glint in her eyes. "Don't worry. We'll get you in to see him. Just wait until the receptionist is distracted enough, then run back there."

"What are you gonna do?"

She laughed. "Create a distraction." She started moaning and grabbing her stomach. "Oh, I feel like I have the flu."

There were about twenty people gathered in the waiting room, and a few looked up at her.

She coughed several times, spinning around in a circle, spreading her "germs." "*Hypothetically*, if I had just gotten back from Africa a few days ago, and I *might* have been on a bus with some people who were throwing up blood, what do you suppose they had?" she asked, wide-eyed and innocent.

A couple of people jumped out of their seats in panic.

"Ebola!" one of the men shouted, pointing at her.

The waiting room became deafening as people screamed and scrambled to grab their things.

The receptionist stood up, looking over the counter. "What's going on in there?"

"She has Ebola!" an elderly woman shouted.

The whole room was soon in an uproar, and the receptionist started for the door to the reception area.

"Someone call security!" a man shouted.

Neely Kate leaned close to me. "When that receptionist gets out here, you make a beeline for the back."

"Thank you," I murmured. Neely Kate was bound to get into a lot of trouble for this, but she was grinning ear to ear.

The receptionist waddled next to Neely Kate, clearly irritated. "What is the meaning of this?"

I edged back to the door, slipping through the opening. I would have made a clean getaway except a woman pointed at me and shouted, "She was with the girl who has Ebola! She must have it too!"

I knew I didn't have much time, so I hurried down the hall to the first exam room. I peeked through the window in the door and saw a little boy with his mother.

The receptionist burst through the doors, flinging them open so hard they bounced off the walls. "You can't be back here!"

I looked into the second room and found it empty, then quickly moved on to the next room. "I'm sorry, but I have to see Mason."

She was shorter than me, but she had to outweigh me by a good seventy pounds. Still, she was faster than I'd expected. "You are in a lot of trouble. Security is on their way."

I moved to the next window. An older couple looked up at me with alarm, not that I could blame them. Shouting was still streaming in from the waiting room, and now some crazed woman was playing Peeping Tom.

The receptionist had quickly gained ground and was several feet away. My desperation grew. I wasn't leaving until I saw Mason with my own eyes.

"Mason!" I called out. But what if he was in a coma hooked up to wires and IVs? He wouldn't be able to hear me, let alone find me.

"Miss," she hissed, her fingers digging into my arm as she caught up with me. "This is a hospital filled with sick people. You are being disrespectful by shouting like that."

"I don't want to make trouble, really. I just have to see him, then I'll leave. Please!" I shouted.

I put up a good fight, but she started tugging me back up the hall.

Just then a door at the end of the hall opened, and Mason appeared in the opening. "*Rose?*"

The sight of him upset me instead of giving me relief. A nasty cut about two inches long ran across his forehead, and the left side of his face was covered in dried blood. The front of his shirt had a large bloodstain on it, and his face was paler than usual. "*Mason!*" I jerked hard and broke loose, running down the hall toward him.

"Hey, it's okay." He pulled me into a hug, and I clung to him, even though the thought registered that this was all wrong. I was supposed to be the one comforting *him*.

"You're covered in blood." My voice broke.

"I'm okay."

The receptionist grabbed my arm. "You are leaving *now*."

Mason's grip on me tightened. "She's staying."

"Mr. Deveraux, she and her friend have disrupted the entire waiting room in a stunt to get her back here without permission. We can't reward bad behavior."

"Neely Kate, I presume?" I heard the dry amusement in his voice.

The woman crossed her arms over her ample bosom. "It's not amusing, Mr. Deveraux. That young woman has convinced half the waiting room that she has Ebola."

His eyebrows lifted as he looked down at me. "She told everyone she had *Ebola?*"

"No." I tried to look innocent. "She only asked a hypothetical question."

I could see he was trying to decide if he actually wanted to know more.

"I asked the receptionist nicely, Mason, I swear. But she wouldn't let me back here, and she wouldn't tell you I was here. I was scared to death. I knew you were getting a CT scan of your head, and I kept envisioning you in a coma. I couldn't just sit out there and wait."

He gave me a soft smile. "It's okay. I'm sorry you were so scared."

"She has to come with me, Mr. Deveraux."

Mason stepped between us. "And I said she's staying." When the woman still glared at him, he gave her his no-nonsense look. "Or I can leave with her."

She huffed out a loud breath. "I'm filing a report."

"You go ahead and do that," Mason said, sounding angry. "And I'll file one too."

"I'm sorry," I said as he ushered me into the room and shut the door behind us. "I didn't mean to cause so much trouble. But I had to see you or at least know you were okay."

"No." He grimaced as he sat on the edge of the bed and grabbed my hand, tugging me to sit next to him. "This is all my fault for not calling you in the first place. How did you know I was here?"

"Joe."

A scowl covered his face, then he grimaced in pain.

I turned to look at the gash on his forehead.

"Honestly, Rose, it looks worse than it actually is. Head wounds tend to bleed a lot, and I have a nasty cut."

"I can see that. Do you really need to get a CT scan?"

He frowned. "Joe talks too much."

"Well, is it true?"

"Yes, but I'm sure it's an overreaction. I lost consciousness for a short bit, probably less than a minute, and my pupils were a little dilated. While I've assured them I'm fine, they're still insisting that I get my head checked out."

"You should be lying down, Mason."

"Rose, I'm fine. I've lost a little blood. I have a killer headache, and my side hurts some. Otherwise, I'm perfectly okay."

"You are not fine. Why haven't they given you stitches yet?"

"They said they were going to wait until after my CT scan."

I hopped off the table and pulled several paper towels out of the holder and held them under running water. "What happened?"

"A car passed me, then stopped abruptly, but mine didn't slow down when I stepped on the brakes. So I ran off the road to avoid rear-ending the car. I tried to miss the pole, but when I swerved, the tires hung up on some gravel. I clipped it with the left front end."

"Your brakes didn't work?"

"They must have gone out."

I walked over to the exam table and set most of the paper towels down, then started wiping his cheek with the one still in my hand. "And your head?"

"The air bag went off, but I still hit the door." He reached up and grabbed my hand. "You don't have to do that, Rose. The nursing staff will do it."

"I have to do *something*."

He leaned over and gave me a kiss. "I know."

I looked away, focusing on wiping off the blood. "So, why *didn't* you call me?" I tried not to sound accusatory, but it was hard to hide my hurt feelings.

He hesitated. "I'm so sorry, Rose. I should have. But I lost my phone in the accident, not to mention I knew what I looked like. I didn't want to scare you."

I tossed the bloody paper towel into the trash and picked up another wet one. "Well, you scared me worse. I imagined all kinds of terrible things."

"I know, and I'm sorry. What can I do to make it up to you?"

I gave him a stern look. "Promise to call me immediately if you're ever in an accident again."

A soft smile lit up his face. "Okay. I promise."

"Have you called your mother?"

"Not yet. For the same reason."

"You need to call her, Mason," I said as I continued to scrub.

"I will. After I'm released. Our family has given her enough to worry about."

I scowled, but I understood his reasoning. How many times had I avoided calling Violet after all of my scrapes?

He was silent for several seconds while I continued to scrub. "With the break-in last night and then our shenanigans later, I never got a chance to ask you how your investigation into Neely Kate's cousin's disappearance is going."

"Slow. We found out some things, and Neely Kate told Joe, but he said it still wasn't enough to do anything. At this point, I'm counting on his promise to have someone start looking for her tomorrow if we haven't found her or if she hasn't turned up."

"Well, that's something, right?" he asked. "What did you find?"

"She got a job not too long ago at a new club—"

The doors swung open, and a man wearing scrubs entered pushing a wheelchair. "Time for your CT scan, Mr. Deveraux."

He gave me an apologetic grimace. "I'm sorry. Will you fill me in when I get back?"

"Of course. I think I better check on Neely Kate and make sure they haven't stuck her in quarantine."

"Good idea. She might be in some trouble. She really should have thought of some other distraction." He climbed into the wheelchair, and the orderly pushed him into the hall, with me at his side.

I stopped with them at the elevator. "I'll be here when you get back."

"Let me know if Neely Kate needs help."

"Okay."

I watched him get on the elevator, then went into the waiting room, where Neely Kate was talking to a hospital security guard. The waiting room was still in chaos, but it was much calmer than when I'd made my flight.

"Is Mason okay?" Neely Kate asked as she saw me approach.

I nodded. "They just took him to radiology for a scan. Joe was right. He's going to need stitches. But otherwise, I think he's okay."

One of the security guards snapped his fingers in Neely Kate's face. "Hello, I'm talking to you."

"*Excuse me?*" She shot him a condescending look. "You did not just snap your fingers in my face."

"Getting a statement out of you is like squeezing glue out of a dried-up bottle."

"Well maybe if you weren't so rude, I'd be more willing to cooperate."

"You caused a panic!" He raised his voice, then looked around to see if anyone had noticed before continuing in a calmer manner. "I think we should call the Henryetta Police Department to take you in for questioning, ma'am."

"*Ma'am?*" Neely Kate screeched. "Do I look like a *ma'am* to you?"

His face lost all expression.

A man with dark brown hair walked over. He appeared to be in his thirties and was dressed in a button-down shirt and loosened tie. "Excuse me, Officer, I'm sorry to interrupt, but I observed the entire incident, and I'm not sure you have sufficient evidence to press charges."

The security guard looked confused. "What?"

"I think you're trying to invoke the *Schenck* case, and I assure you, that case has no precedence in this matter."

Neely Kate was at a loss for words, and the security guy scratched his forehead, equally at sea. "Huh?"

"Miss . . ." The man's blue eyes twinkled as he turned to Neely Kate. "I'm sorry, but I don't know your name."

"Neely Kate," she fumbled out. "Neely Kate Colson."

He turned back to the security guard. "Miss Colson did not announce to the room that she *had* Ebola. She merely asked what someone might have if they presented certain Ebola-like symptoms. To truly be comparable to the *Schenck* case, she would have had to tell everyone that she herself or someone else in the room had contracted the disease. Thus, you have no grounds to have her arrested. Any charges filed would never stand up in court."

The security guard looked irritated. "And how do you know all this?"

The man broke into a wide smile and held out a hand. "Carter Hale, attorney at law."

The guard studied the man's hand and gave it a light shake before dropping it as though the attorney himself might have Ebola.

"I guess you're right," he grumbled. "But we'll be watching out for you," he told Neely Kate.

"Well, I hope you're watching in about seven months when I come here to have my baby. Ronnie Jr.'s sure to make an entrance just like his momma."

The guard didn't look happy. "Thanks for the warning." He walked over to talk to the rest of the people in the waiting room, who had crowded together on the other side, and assured them it was a false alarm.

Neely Kate turned to the attorney. "Thank you for calling me Miss and not ma'am, Mr. Hale." She shuddered dramatically, then winked. "And thanks for helping me get out of that mess."

"Honestly, I'm not sure why I did it," he said. "Your announcement scared the hell out of me too, you know."

Neely Kate cringed. "Sorry. I was trying to create a distraction, and it was the first thing that came to mind. I didn't have much time to prepare."

"Well, good job on creating a disturbance. I'll be sure to seek you out should I ever decide to create a flash mob."

"Thanks for helping me. For once we didn't have to rope in Rose's boyfriend or ex-boyfriend."

He grinned mischievously. "And who might they be?"

I cringed. The last thing I needed was someone else in town thinking I was a "badge bunny." "It doesn't matter. Thanks for your help, Mr. Hale."

"Please, call me Carter." He held his hand out toward me.

"I'm Rose. Rose Gardner."

"Nice to meet you, Rose Gardner." I wasn't sure I liked the recognition in his eyes when I shook his hand. At least he didn't add that he'd heard a lot about me, even though I was sure it was true.

He leaned closer to us and stage-whispered, "I lied."

"What?" Neely Kate asked.

"I think they could have convicted you in a court of law."

Neely Kate put her hand on her hip. "Then why'd you help me?"

He laughed and held out his hands. "I'm a defense attorney. It's in my blood, I guess. I just can't help myself."

Neely Kate gave him her best stare-down, and he didn't flinch. Crappy doodles, he was good.

I turned to Neely Kate. "I'm not sure how long I'll be here." I purposely avoided using Mason's name. "Do you want me to take you back to your car?"

"You don't have to leave, Rose. I can find another way to the town square."

"The town square, you say?" Carter asked, looking amused. "I'm headed that way to my office now. I can give you a lift."

Neely Kate put her hands on her hips and gave him a sassy look. "What are you even doin' here, anyway?" she asked. "Are you ambulance chasin'?"

"Neely Kate!" I gasped.

He chuckled before reaching into his back pocket and pulling out a business card. "Here's proof that I am who I say I am." He pointed to the card. "You'll notice right away that it says *defense attorney* and not *ambulance chaser*."

"Oh, I *know* who you are," Neely Kate said. "I've heard all about you."

He laughed. "Is that so?"

"I'm married, *Mr. Hale*."

"It's only a ride to the courthouse. I've saved you from these fumbling fools who call themselves security officers. Surely I don't plan to ravage you in broad daylight on the way to the courthouse." He winked. "I'd save that for after dark."

Neely Kate tried to look horrified, but it was easy to see she was amused. "Well, as long as you don't take six hours to get to the courthouse, we should be good."

"I do know a long way . . ." he teased.

I pulled Neely Kate to the side. "Are you sure? I don't know how long Mason's gonna be getting his CT scan. I'll have plenty of time to take you back." I shifted my eyes toward Carter Hale who stood three feet away with his arms crossed, looking like he'd caught the world by its tail. "He looks too cocky."

"I know all about Carter Hale's exploits," she said with a grin. "Even if I were single, I wouldn't be stupid enough to get caught up in his web of lies. He's a love 'em and leave 'em kind of guy, and god love 'im, he's soon to run out of women in Fenton County." She laughed. "I'm safe, but if it makes you feel better, I'll text you when he drops me off."

"Good. But don't be thinking about going to find Billy Jack without me, okay? He's bound to still be ticked off at us. We should go together."

She gave me a hug. "If you need me for anything, call me. And keep me updated on Mason."

"Okay."

She walked out the door, with Carter following behind her. He tried to put his hand on the small of her back, and she shoved it off as though it were a white-hot poker. I almost felt sorry for him.

Almost.

Chapter Twenty

I went back to Mason's room to wait for him, the receptionist shooting me a hateful glare as I passed. A short while later, Neely Kate texted me to say she'd made it to her car, safe and undefiled. I wasn't used to sitting around, so I started thinking about Dolly Parton again, trying to piece together the clues we'd found about her disappearance and Nikko's, but we were still missing too much information.

After a half hour Mason still hadn't returned, and I started to worry, but the door opened several seconds later, and the orderly pushed Mason back into the room. He'd changed clothes and was now wearing a blue hospital gown. And he didn't look happy about it.

"Is everything okay?" I asked, getting to my feet.

"They refused to tell me anything," Mason complained. "But I feel fine. It's a waste of time."

The orderly tried to help Mason out of the chair and onto the bed. Mason grabbed the opening in the back of his gown and shot the orderly a frown. "I have a cut on my forehead and a pounding headache. I'm not a damned invalid."

I laughed and gave the poor hospital worker a sympathetic look as I said to Mason, "You *do* seem to be feeling fine."

The orderly hurried for the door, and Mason called after him, "Would you please send a doctor in here to stitch up my head so I can get the hell out of here?"

The poor guy mumbled something unintelligible and left the room.

"You really should be nicer to them, Mr. Cranky Pants," I said, moving next to him.

His face broke into an ornery grin. "You mean like shouting something about Ebola in a crowded waiting room?"

"For the record, Neely Kate regrets that. Especially after hospital security threatened to call in the cops."

He sat up. "Does she need help?"

"No, an attorney was sitting in the waiting room, and he got her out of it."

His back stiffened. "Which attorney?"

"Carter Hale. Do you know him?"

His mouth pursed. "Oh, I know him all right. What was he doing here?"

I paused. "You know, he never told us. He heard Neely Kate talking to a security guard and cited some court case to get her off the hook. Neely Kate knew of Carter and accused him of sitting in the waiting room to chase ambulances."

He laughed. "I wish I could have seen that."

"Is he that bad? He took Neely Kate back to her car by my office. Maybe I should have taken her instead."

"No, he'll be harmless to her. If anything, she's liable to chew him up and spit him out."

The door opened, and a doctor entered the room.

"It's about time," Mason muttered.

"You need to be patient, Mason," I said in a low voice. "What happened to your usual patience?"

"It's nonexistent when it comes to hospitals."

The doctor introduced himself and said, "You're not the first man to be eager to escape this place, and you won't be the last. Let's see what we can do to get you on your way." He put on a pair of gloves before he poked and prodded.

Mason grimaced a few times but kept silent.

"You have two choices," the doctor said. "I can stitch it, and there will be a slight scar, or we can get a plastic surgeon in here to work on it. There's no guarantee it won't scar with him, but it will probably scar less." The doctor grabbed a mirror and handed it to him. "Why don't you have a look at the position of the gash before you decide?"

Mason examined the wound, which was diagonal across the left side of his forehead. "I'm fine with a slight scar. You can stitch it."

"It will give you roguish look," I teased.

The doctor chuckled as he began to work. When he finished, Mason was eager to go. "Can I get dressed now?"

The doctor stopped in the doorway. "We're waiting for the CT scan results. It should only be about another half hour or so."

After the door closed, I moved close to him, examining the doctor's work. I counted five stitches. "What on earth are you so eager to get back to?"

"Nothing," he said a little too defensively, hopping off the table. "But after my last stay, I can't stand being in the hospital. The sooner I get out of here, the better."

I studied him for a second. He was keeping something from me. "It sounds like you still have a bit of time to kill." I glanced at the clock. "It's after two o'clock, and you have to be starving. How about I go to the cafeteria and get you something to eat?"

"You don't have to do that."

"I know. Just let me take care of you. You take care of me all the time."

He grinned. "Okay."

I went to the cafeteria to pick up a couple of sandwiches and chips, and by the time I got back, the doctor was back in the room talking to Mason.

"You have a mild concussion, but I don't think it's something to be overly concerned about. Just have someone keep an eye on you to make sure you're alert and that you're not slurring your speech or that your eyes are unevenly dilated."

"I can do that," I said. "I'll be with him."

The doctor nodded. "Sounds good. I'll go get your discharge paperwork started."

I handed Mason a sandwich after the doctor left, and my head got fuzzy.

Suddenly I was in a dark hotel room. The door burst open, and the sound of gunshots filled the room. Pain and pressure exploded in my chest.

I gasped as Mason's face came back into focus. "Someone's going to shoot you."

Mason's eyes widened. "*What?*"

My head ached, and I felt like I was going to be sick. "I just had a vision. Someone's going to shoot you." My legs began to shake, and he grabbed my hand and set me down on the gurney.

"Okay, sweetheart," he said. "Start from the beginning."

I told him everything I'd seen, my voice breaking. When I finished, he didn't look all that surprised.

"Mason, why is someone trying to kill you?"

The door opened before he had the chance to answer. I expected it to be one of the hospital staff, but Joe stood in the opening instead, wearing his sheriff's uniform. He nodded to me, then turned his attention to Mason, his eyes hardening. "How are you doing?"

"Rose had a vision."

Joe's eyebrows lifted. "Why do I think it wasn't about what you're having for dinner?"

"Mason was shot," I said.

"Tell me."

I told him everything, my head still hurting. "There's something else," I said. "Remember the vision I had at the Burger Shack? The one that made me feel bad afterward? That's how I feel now."

"What do you think it means?" Mason asked.

I took a deep breath. "I think that vision had something to do with someone trying to kill Mason too."

"Remind me of what you saw in that earlier one," Joe said.

"Eric was sitting in the front seat of a car next to a guy. The guy asked, 'Are you ready?'"

"That's it?" Joe asked.

"Do you remember anything about the car?" Mason asked.

My shoulders tensed. "I don't know."

He took my hand. "Yes, you do. Close your eyes and think about it."

"It was two days ago, Mason. I might not remember anything."

"You won't know unless you try," Joe said.

He was right. "Okay." I closed my eyes and concentrated, and was gratified when the image I'd seen started to fill my vision. "It was an old car. It had a big dashboard and a long front hood. Kind of like Miss Mildred's Cadillac."

"What color was it?" Mason asked.

"Light blue."

Mason glanced up at Joe. "The car that swerved in front of me before I crashed fits that description."

Joe grimaced. "Well, I guess that makes sense. Your accident wasn't so accidental."

My breath caught. "What does that mean?"

"The brake lines were almost entirely cut through. It's like the person designed it so that Mason would drive for a while before they went out. It wouldn't take much use to get them to give way completely."

"Like braking to avoid an accident?" Mason asked, his voice hard.

Joe's mouth pursed. "Yeah."

Skeeter was right. Someone *was* trying to kill Mason. The blood rushed from my head, and I sat in the chair next to the bed.

"What do you remember about the car in front of you?" Joe asked.

"Like I said, it was an older car. Pale blue, maybe a Buick. It braked hard as soon as it was in front of me. I passed out, but I wasn't alone when I came to." He paused. "Did you find my phone?"

Joe shook his head and crossed his arms. "At the scene you said there was a guy in the passenger seat next to you, but you couldn't remember much about him. Has anything else come to you?"

Mason sighed, looking exhausted. "Yeah, I was pretty out of it. It's still a little fuzzy, but parts are coming back. He was fumbling around on the floorboard, but he took off when a woman approached the driver's side door. He had shaggy dark brown hair and was wearing an army jacket." Mason closed his eyes. "I don't remember much about his face besides that he was clean-shaven."

"Anything else?"

Mason glanced up at Joe, hesitating. "I got a pretty good knock to the head, so I can't be sure I saw this part correctly. It came to me while I was having my CT scan."

"Why don't you tell me what you remember, and let me deduce if it was something you hallucinated?"

Mason shot a look to me, then back to Joe. "I'm fairly certain he had a gun."

"Do you think he intended to use it?"

"Yes."

Joe exhaled and ran his hand through his hair. "So Plan A was to run you off the road in the hope the crash would kill you, making your death look like an accident. Which was incredibly stupid," Joe grunted. "You're the ADA. They were overlooking the fact that we'd do a thorough investigation. Unlike the Henryetta Police and Rose's—" Joe stopped as he realized what he was saying.

"Unlike how the Henryetta Police handled Dora's accident," I finished, feeling light-headed. My birth mother had died as the result of a car accident. The Henryetta police hadn't put much effort into an investigation, despite speculation her brakes had been cut.

Joe nodded, not looking happy about it.

"What was Plan B?" I asked. "You said Plan A was to have him die in an accident."

Joe hesitated, uncrossing his arms. "The gun. He was going to shoot him."

"So that's why he was in the car with Mason?" I asked, trying not to freak out. We were discussing Mason's attempted murder as though we were talking about the chance of rain at a church picnic. "So what was he looking for on the floorboards?"

"Mason's phone."

"Why would he want Mason's phone?"

Neither man answered.

"They didn't finish the job. So they're going to try again, which is what I just saw in my vision," I said.

"Rose," Mason said, determination in his eyes. "I could use a cup of coffee. Could you get me one?"

"No." I shook my head, glaring up at him. "I'm not going anywhere."

"Rose . . ."

"Does this have to do with the break-in at the farm last night?"

Joe hesitated before answering, "Possibly."

"What were they looking for? Who's doing this?"

"Rose," Joe said, apologetically. "It's official business. It would be easier for all of us if you took a short walk."

"*No.* It's official business that could get Mason killed. I have a right to know."

"I'm sorry." His eyes softened. "Not this time, you don't."

I stood, so furious I could spit. I turned to Joe. "Did your father do this?"

His eyes widened. "What?"

"Did your father try to have Mason killed?"

His face lost all expression.

"Mason was gathering information on your father to stop him from hurting me. Did J.R. find out and try to stop him?"

Joe's body stiffened. "My father isn't this sloppy. If he wanted Mason dead, he'd be dead already."

I put my hands on my hips, anger singing through my blood. "*That's* reassuring."

Fury lit up Joe's eyes. "This is official Fenton County business, *Ms. Gardner,* and despite your delusions of being a super sleuth, you are *not* on the Fenton County payroll." He pointed to the door and yelled, "Now go."

"That's *enough*, Simmons," Mason barked.

I stepped closer to Joe, clenching my fists at my side. "I'm not giving up, Joe."

Joe stood his ground. "No, you never do."

I stomped out the door and into the hallway, pacing outside the door and straining to hear what they were talking about. It didn't take a minute before they started arguing.

". . . knew this was a possibility!" Joe shouted.

Mason said something I didn't understand, followed by Joe's low voice.

"What about Rose?" Mason's voice boomed. "How can you be so short-sighted?"

Their voices were too low to understand. What were they talking about?

Soon after there was more shouting, this time from Joe. "I'm the chief deputy sheriff! Let me do my damned job!"

I tried to hear more, but their voices lowered again. My cell phone vibrated in my pocket, and I pulled it out, surprised to see it was Skeeter. "I told you to text me." I moved farther down the hall, keeping my eye on Mason's door.

"This is too important to leave to a text. Meet me in the hospital chapel."

I shook my head, glancing around. "*What?* How do you know I'm at the hospital?"

"I know someone tried to kill Deveraux and that he's at the hospital. It makes sense that you'd be here."

"How did you know someone tried to kill him?"

"I make it my business to know everything in this county."

"Or maybe you know because you were the one to do it. You admitted that he's trying to bring you down. It makes sense that you would try to get rid of him," I said hatefully.

"I'm going to pretend you didn't say that," he growled. "And I'm going to presume you want to find out who *did*. If I'm right, meet me in the chapel in fifteen minutes." Then he hung up.

I stuffed my phone back in my pocket and tried to catch my breath. Did Skeeter really know who had tried to kill Mason? Could I trust him?

In the end, what choice did I have? If I even had the slightest chance of helping Mason, I'd do it.

Mason's door opened a few minutes later. Joe's face appeared, and he didn't look happy. I wasn't sure if that was a good sign or a bad one.

I walked into the room and glanced back and forth between the two men. Mason looked furious, and Joe wasn't much happier.

"What's goin' on?" I asked.

Both men were quiet before Joe cleared his throat. "The pocket knife found in the office at your farm was covered in Skeeter Malcolm's fingerprints. But Malcolm's alibi checks out, and frankly, I can't believe he'd be that sloppy. I'm not ruling him out, but it's a bit too tidy."

I was surprised by how relieved I felt.

"I'm sending someone to pick up Eric Davidson at the Burger Shack for questioning, but your vision leads me to believe he's taking orders from someone else. Until we figure out who that is, we can only presume he will try again. Which is why I think it's best if Mason stays in the hospital for another day or so."

Mason released a grunt.

"They're going to try again, Joe!" I fought to control my panic.

"I know. You're sure you saw a motel room and not a hospital room, right?"

"Yeah."

"Then all the more reason to keep him here." Joe shifted his weight. "We'll say he's being kept for observation after his accident. He can work in his hospital room—a controlled environment that most sane people wouldn't try to breach. And if some insane person tries it, we'll have an officer on guard."

"Are you sure that's enough?"

"Yes," Joe said, sounding official. "And I think it would be best if you didn't stay at the farm tonight. In case the person responsible for this doesn't realize Mason's not there."

I spun around to look at Joe. "You really don't have any idea who's behind this?"

"I've got a couple of hunches, and I've put several of my best deputies on the case. We will find out who's responsible and bring him or her to justice."

"Rose," Mason said. "Everything's going to be okay."

I nodded, my nerves still jittery from my phone call with Skeeter and seeing Mason sitting on the gurney. Suddenly, this was all too real. My anger was burning off, leaving fear in its wake.

Mason turned to Joe. "Since I'm stuck here, can you get a deputy to pick up some work for me? I can call my secretary and have her gather some files." He rubbed his temple. "My laptop was in the bag in the car."

"Your car was towed to the sheriff's lot. But a deputy pulled your bag out and took it to the station. I'll have him bring it to you."

"Thanks."

Joe shifted his weight. "I'm going to go out into the hall and start making arrangements. In the meantime, Mason, stay in this room until we can get another one set up for you."

Mason gave him a grim smile. "I'll be here."

After Joe left the room, I rushed over to Mason, wrapping my arms around his neck. "I'm so scared."

He leaned back and stared into my eyes. "I'll be fine. The sheriff's department isn't the Henryetta Police Department. I'll be protected, and they'll find out who's responsible."

"Okay."

"Joe's right. You can't stay at the farm. Muffy's still with Mom. Why don't you stay with her tonight? I'll call and tell her what's going on. Joe's said he'll make sure the Henryetta police do some drive-bys."

"You and I both know that never does any good."

"I know." He looked worried.

I needed to reassure him, not confirm how inept the HPD was. "We'll be fine. We have Muffy the watch dog, and I'll call Joe if I see anything suspicious."

That didn't make him look any less worried.

"Do you want anything from home?" I asked. "I need to pick up some things for myself. I can get you some clothes and toiletries while I'm there."

He gave me a warm smile. "Thanks. That would be great."

I buried my face into his neck, pressing my chest to his. What if something happened to him?

"I'm going to be fine, Rose."

"Maybe I should stay here with you tonight."

"No. You'll be safer at Mom's than with me. If this person tries something, it's liable to be in the middle of the night. Joe's going to make a press statement that I've been in an accident and am being held for observation. The suspect will know where to find me, and with any luck at all, they'll catch him or her."

I leaned back, my eyes narrowing. "You mean you're bait."

"It's a good plan, Rose."

Maybe so, but I didn't like it.

"If you're going home to pick some things up, do it now, okay? I don't want you there after dark. In fact, maybe Joe should send a deputy with you."

I wanted to argue with him, but I didn't want to cause him any more stress. "I'll ask Joe what he thinks."

Relief covered his face. "Thank you."

I cupped a hand around his cheek and stared into his eyes. "I love you, Mason. Please be careful."

He smiled and wrapped an arm around my back, pulling me closer. "I'm not going anywhere." Then he kissed me.

When I stepped away breathless a minute later, I flashed him a grin. "What is the hospital's policy on conjugal visits?"

He laughed. "Maybe we'll discuss it later."

I walked into the hallway, surprised to see Joe finishing a phone call. I checked the clock on the wall. I still had five minutes before I was supposed to meet Skeeter.

Joe was about to make another call, but he glanced up and turned his attention to me. "Where are you staying tonight?"

"Maeve's," I said as I stopped in front of him.

He nodded. "That's good. I'll have a deputy watching the house. I think you two will be fine, but I'd rather make sure you're safe."

I blinked in surprise. "A deputy? What about the Henryetta police?"

His face hardened. "I'm overstepping their jurisdiction on this since it's the Fenton County ADA. They could put up a fight, but I suspect they'll be too lazy to do so."

"I'm going out to the farm to get a few things. Mason thinks a deputy should go with me."

"That's probably a good idea. I'll have one meet you out there and make sure the house is clear before you go in."

"Okay, but I need to go run an errand first."

"How about an hour then?"

"Sounds good."

"I'll have someone meet you there at four o'clock. Okay?"

"Thanks."

I started down the hallway. "Rose," he called after me. "Stay out of trouble."

If he only knew who I was about to meet.

Chapter Twenty-One

The chapel was empty when I pushed the door open, and I worried that I was late. But I sat in the second row and looked up at the stained glass window behind the tiny pulpit, figuring a moment of prayer was probably a good idea about now.

I was partway through concocting my list of promises of what I'd do to keep Mason safe when the door opened behind me, and the thud of footsteps filled the space.

Skeeter slid into the pew behind me over a few feet away. He leaned forward, draping his forearms over the back of the pew. "Good to see you could make it," he said quietly.

I kept my eyes forward. "You knew what to say to get me here. What do you know?"

"Not as much as I'd like, but enough to know your boyfriend's in deep shit."

"You said you knew who did it," I huffed.

"*No . . .* I said meet me here if you wanted to know who did it."

"I'm sick and tired of the games, Skeeter Malcolm." I started to get up, but he reached over and placed a hand on my shoulder, pushing me back down.

"Do you want to find the guy or not?"

"You know I do."

"Then sit down and listen."

I pushed my back into the seat, crossing my arms. "Go on."

"Someone wants to kill the ADA and pin it on me. That's why they planted my knife in his office."

"Don't say that so callously." I looked over my shoulder to glare at him. "You're talking about my boyfriend!"

His eyes hardened. "I'm only stating the facts, Lady. I want to find who's behind this and stop them."

I turned back to look at the stained glass window. "So what do you want from me?"

"There's a meeting tonight. I want you to come as the Lady in Black."

"*What?*"

"Your presence will do two things. One, it's a display of power on my part. No one knows your real purpose in working with me, and like you suggested a few weeks ago, they think you're an investor."

I was well aware of that theory from Mason.

"And two, this meeting will be filled with the men who pose the biggest threat to my position in the Fenton County underworld. If anyone is trying to overthrow me, they'll be in that room tonight."

"And you want me to have a vision."

"Yes."

"What happens if I announce to the whole room that one of those men is trying to kill Mason? Who's going to protect me?"

"Jed." His voice was hard. "He'll protect you with his life if necessary, but hopefully we'll figure out a way around it."

I wanted to say no. As far as I could tell, the whole Lady in Black business was finally dying down at the courthouse. Her reappearance was bound to stir things up again. But if there was the slightest chance I could find out who was trying to kill Mason and Skeeter could stop them, no wasn't an option.

"So what do you want me to do?"

"Meet Jed at eight-thirty at the same feed store where you met him last time. He'll bring you to the pool hall, and we'll fill you in on the rest when you get there."

"Okay." I turned to look at him. "I need to ask you about something else."

His hard expression fell away and he looked amused. "You can ask, but I might not answer."

"It's about Gems."

He grinned. "Have you changed your mind about dancing? Because I'll tell you again that I can offer you something better."

"No," I said in disgust. "I want to know who owns it."

He sat back in the pew and spread his arms out along the back. "Well if that isn't the million-dollar question."

"So you don't know?"

He tilted his head and smirked at me. "I didn't say that."

"If you knew, you'd tell me."

He shifted to the side. "It changed hands a couple of months ago to a corporation, but it's unclear who the actual owner is."

"Do you think whoever it is could be trying to take over Crocker's drug empire?"

His arms dropped to his side, and he leaned forward. "I took over Crocker's drug empire."

I turned to face him. "Nikko, the bartender who disappeared at Gems—he used to work for Crocker. Running drugs. But he quit and couldn't find a job until Mud hired him."

He watched me closely. "Go on. I'm listening."

"I told you that I had a feeling that he and Dolly Parton saw something and ran off to hide."

"Do you have any proof of that?"

"No, but I do know Mud sent men to Nikko's trailer to find him."

He scowled. "You told me that already."

"I was in his trailer this morning, though, and I don't think the men there were just looking for Nikko. The way they'd moved things around implied they were looking for something else."

"So?"

"Skeeter." I turned all the way around, getting on my knees to face him. "What if he wants Nikko's information about Crocker's business? You already said the owner of Gems wants to put you out of business. What if this is just one more way to put you out of business?"

His eyes turned murderous, and I knew if that anger was directed at me, I'd be terrified.

"Is there some way to figure out who owns it?"

"We've traced it to a farmer in Louisiana, but there's no way he's the real owner."

I shook my head in confusion. "Why not?"

"Identity theft. Someone stole his identity and is using it to remain anonymous."

"And you really have no idea who?"

His anger returned. "I've already told you I didn't."

"Do you think that the person who's responsible could also be trying to kill Mason and pin it on you?"

"I don't know. Maybe. It could be any number of guys. Three come to mind, and all three will be at the pool hall tonight. Jed will fill you in on who they are when he picks you up." Skeeter stood. "We shouldn't be seen leaving together.

I'll slip out through the back door, and you can wait a few minutes and go out the main entrance."

I didn't answer, but he didn't wait. He headed for the exit without looking back.

As I waited my several minutes, I made a mental list of things I needed to get at the house, adding a few things I hadn't planned to ever need again: a black dress, shoes, and the veiled hat.

The Lady in Black was back.

Chapter Twenty-Two

I left the chapel and stayed with Mason until it was time to leave for the farmhouse, but I was terrible company. My vision about Mason kept repeating in my head, making me anxious, and thoughts of my impending date with Skeeter only made it worse. Mason kept trying to reassure me, but the only thing that would set me at ease would be to find out who was behind this and make sure he or she was stopped.

When I pulled up to the farmhouse an hour later, a sheriff's car was already parked outside in the drive. Deputy Miller climbed out and I gave him a warm smile as I greeted him at the bottom of the stairs.

"Deputy Miller. I'm glad you're the one meeting me."

He chuckled. "Anyone in particular you trying to avoid?"

I grimaced. "Deputy Hoffstetter."

His grin spread. "Aww . . . yeah, she has a thing for Mr. Deveraux. She's none too happy he's living with you. She thinks you're—"

"Yeah," I scowled. "I know what she thinks."

He snickered. "I need to check out the house before you go in. Why don't you wait out here, and I'll tell you when it's safe."

"Okay." I handed him the keys to the front door and paced the yard in front of the porch until he returned. "It's clear."

Deputy Miller waited in the living room while I went upstairs and packed our things into two bags. My Lady in Black clothes and accessories were buried in a box in our bedroom closet. Neely Kate had loaned me a few things as a costume for my Thanksgiving Day escapade and then told me to keep them, figuring she wouldn't fit into the shoes or dress once her feet swelled and she started gaining pregnancy weight. Neither of us could risk wearing the hat casually, as it had become the hallmark of the Lady in Black.

I gave Deputy Miller a few leftover cookies to take with him before he followed me back to the hospital. While I found his presence comforting at the moment, how was I going to ditch him later to meet Jed? He was supposed to follow me back to Maeve's house to stand watch for the night.

By the time I got back, Mason had been moved to his new room on the second floor. He was sitting in a chair with a laptop, wearing a pair of blue scrubs.

"I brought your clothes, but you look good in scrubs," I teased as I entered the room.

He set the computer on the bed and stood. "Did you have any trouble out at the farm?"

"No."

"I talked to Mom, and she's got the guest room ready for you." He gave me a kiss. "The three of you will be safe with Deputy Miller watching you."

"Three?" I asked.

He grinned. "Muffy, although I think she could take the deputy's place as your guard."

"True enough." I pulled him over to the side of the bed and sat down. "Mason, I want you to tell me the truth."

His smile fell. "About what?"

"Does this have anything to do with J.R. Simmons?"

He studied me for a few seconds. "No, I think Joe is right. If his father wanted me dead, it would have been done."

I started to protest.

"Rose. It's not him. That's not how he works. Killing someone would be too easy. J.R. Simmons is more interested in giving people prolonged suffering. Something like this wouldn't satisfy his quest for vengeance."

"Did the deputies find out anything from Eric?"

Worry flickered in Mason's eyes. "No," he said, his voice quiet. "They found him dead in his car. It was parked in the garage of his home. Carbon monoxide poisoning."

My stomach dropped. "He killed himself?"

Mason put his hands on my arms to steady me. "Joe's not sure. It could have been set up that way to make sure he didn't talk."

"So Joe's no closer to finding out who's responsible than he was before?"

"No."

I stayed with Mason a little while longer until he insisted I go to his mother's, since it was getting dark. I didn't want to leave him, but the truth was I could do Mason more good as the Lady in Black.

I wrapped my hands around his neck and pressed our foreheads together, careful of his stitches. "Please be careful, Mason."

"I'm here under guard," he said, his palm pressed to my cheek. "I'm more worried about you and Mom, but knowing there will be a deputy parked outside Mom's house to keep an eye on things makes me feel better."

I only hoped they wouldn't be watching too closely. "I wish you had your phone so I could call and check on you."

"I think someone's going to bring me a loaner until I can get a new one. I'll let you know when I find out the number. In the meantime, be careful."

"I plan on it."

Deputy Miller followed me from the hospital to Maeve's house. He parked across the street and waved as I walked to the front porch. Maeve had obviously been waiting for me, because she opened the front door immediately, looking more worn than usual. "Did you see him? Is he okay?" she asked as I shut the door behind me.

Muffy jumped up on my legs, excited to see me. I picked her up and hugged her close.

"He's fine, I promise. He has a few stitches on his forehead and a headache," I said, giving Maeve a reassuring smile, even as I was trying to convince myself I was telling the truth. "You know how stubborn he is. He's not going to let something as mundane as faulty brakes do much damage." Since Joe wasn't telling the public about the attempt on Mason's life, they'd decided it was best to keep it from Maeve as well. Mason told her that the house was being watched because of our break-in the night before. "They're only keeping him as a precaution. Just to be safe."

Her mouth tipped up into a small grin. "You're right."

"You look exhausted. Why don't you sit down, and I'll figure out something for dinner? I promise that I really do know how to cook."

She let me lead her to one of the chairs at the kitchen table. "I already made a chicken casserole. It should be ready to come out of the oven."

"Well, I definitely know how to use a pair of potholders," I teased. I pulled the casserole out and set the pan on a trivet on the kitchen table. Glancing down at her, I noticed she was wiping her eyes. I squatted in front of her and grabbed her hands. "Maeve, he's going to be okay."

Her chin trembled. "He's all I have left, Rose."

"And he's going to be fine," I insisted. "Joe will make sure of it."

I realized that I'd slipped and implied that there might be more going on than a concussion, but she didn't seem to notice. In fact, for some reason, my statement calmed her. She took a deep breath. "Yes. You're right."

"Besides, you're *not* alone. You have me and Muffy."

She smiled through her tears. "And I'm grateful for that. More than you know."

She was quiet throughout dinner, and when I pressed her to make sure she was okay, she said she had a migraine and was going to go to bed early. I'd been worried about concocting an explanation for my meeting with Jed, but while it was a blessing in disguise, I was still worried about her.

My next obstacle was getting past the deputy, which was actually easier than expected. An alley ran behind Maeve's house, with the detached garage opening onto it. Deputy Miller seemed more worried about the cars turning into the alley than the ones leaving it. After I dressed, I carried my hat and shoes in one hand and tiptoed into the kitchen to snag Maeve's car keys off the counter. In case she woke up, I left her a short note saying I couldn't sleep but would be back soon. With any luck at all, she'd never read it and neither she nor Deputy Miller would be any the wiser about my evening with criminals.

At eight-thirty, I parked Maeve's car behind the feed store, my stomach a bundle of nerves. This was equivalent to a suicide mission. I tried to assure myself that I was too valuable to Skeeter for him to let something happen to me, but I couldn't be one hundred percent sure of that.

Jed was waiting in the sedan when I parked. I pinned my hat into place as he got out and opened my car door. He reached for my hand to help me out.

"Jed, you don't have to do that."

"When you're dressed like this, you're the Lady in Black, and in Skeeter's eyes that's the same as royalty."

Now I was really worried about my personal safety. In revolutions, royalty was often the first to get beheaded.

Jed helped me into the back of the car and took off toward Henryetta. After he pulled onto the county road, he glanced in the rearview mirror. "No one would ever guess who you really are. That dress alone is completely different than anything you usually wear. If anything, the guys will all be staring at your chest."

I instinctively reached for the base of my throat. He wasn't wrong. The plunging neckline was lower than anything I'd ever worn before, and what little cleavage I had was in full view. I wasn't wearing Neely Kate's dress—the one I'd worn to the auction. I doubted most men would remember, but in case they did, I needed to portray a woman with class and money. And that meant I couldn't be an outfit repeater. I'd bought this dress a week after Thanksgiving, telling myself I'd wear it for Mason on a date some night, but if I were honest with myself now, I wasn't sure I could ever wear it in public and show my face.

Thinking of Mason made me anxious. What if this was all for nothing? My chest tightened, and I suddenly needed to hear his voice. I checked my phone one more time to see if I'd missed a text or call from his new number. Nothing.

I looked out the window at the trees lining the county road, surprised Jed hadn't blindfolded me. "Do you know what I'll being doing tonight?"

"When we get there, I'm supposed to drop you off at the front door. I'll text Skeeter to let him know so he can meet you at the entrance. Skeeter wants you to say as little as possible. I'll walk in and act like your bodyguard."

"Who's watching Skeeter?" I couldn't imagine that he would leave himself unprotected.

"Merv and another guy. Cal."

"Oh." I paused. "I thought you were Skeeter's right-hand man. Why'd he switch things up?"

"Skeeter usually has a list of priorities for each meeting or event he attends—the order in which we protect things in case something goes down. With our line of business, we need a contingency plan. At the auction it was him, his money, then you."

I pursed my lips in irritation. It was nice to know his money ranked higher than I did, although not entirely surprising. "So what's his priority list tonight?"

Jed paused and looked into the rearview mirror before answering. "You. Then Skeeter."

I gasped. "*Me?*"

He nodded. "The men don't understand it, and there were some protests earlier when Skeeter gave us our instructions."

"Why would he put me first?"

Jed hesitated and swallowed. "Skeeter's never been a here-and-now kind of guy. He's a lot more far-sighted than most people realize. Skeeter waited a year for Daniel Crocker to self-destruct, and he was ready to make his move once it happened. He was the one who suggested that Bull hold an auction to sell the business. He also created issues that *may* have made Bull want to sell the business."

None of that came as a surprise to me. "That still doesn't explain why he'd put me as top priority tonight."

"You're an investment, Lady. Especially after the last few days, he sees the potential you have for him and his business. He's going to protect that at all costs."

While I should have been reassured, I didn't like the implications. Any hope of ever cutting our ties to him had gone the way of the wooly mammoth.

"But my boyfriend is the Fenton County Assistant DA. How can he trust me? How can *you* trust me? How do you know I won't run off and tell him or Joe Simmons everything?"

"Skeeter can read people. It's kind of a gift. He can usually tell who's going be loyal or not, and he rarely gets it wrong. After the auction, he pegged you as loyal. Very loyal." He paused. "Merv and I didn't agree with him. Merv is still suspicious of you, but I've become a believer."

I shook my head. "But Skeeter barely knows me."

He grinned. "There are all kinds of gifts in this world, Lady. You can see the future. Skeeter can judge people. It shouldn't be all that surprising, especially for you."

I supposed he was right. "But sometimes he gets it wrong?"

"Just like you can change what you see in your visions, sometimes people change, although most people don't ever *really* change, so it's rarer. But the possibility's there, so he's always reevaluating everyone." His eyes turned serious. "That is not public knowledge, so you can't tell anyone, and I mean *anyone*. Not even your best friend, Neely Kate."

A shiver ran down my spine. "How do you know about Neely Kate?"

"I told you that Merv and I didn't agree with Skeeter's evaluation of you at first. So I've watched you."

I was starting to have second thoughts about Jed. "You've been *stalking* me?"

"I had to make sure you weren't a threat," he said unapologetically.

I crossed my arms, suddenly creeped out.

"My job is to protect Skeeter. At all costs. After the auction, I knew he'd call you again. It was only a matter of time. I had to check you out for myself to make sure you wouldn't betray him." He gave me a sheepish grin. "But if Skeeter ever found out . . ."

I shook my head, and against my better judgment I said, "He won't hear it from me. But if you're worried about him finding out, why are you telling me at all?"

"Because I can judge people too. Nothing like Skeeter, his is a true gift, but I know people. You have a good heart, Rose Gardner. You are loyal to your friends and the people who help you. If you give Skeeter a chance, he can help you far more than you know."

I released a breath. "While I thank you for your compliment—really I do—I have no intention of getting mixed up in Skeeter's underworld any more than I already am." I lifted my chin. "And I'm not stupid. I know that any gift from Skeeter comes with a whole assortment of tangled strings. Not that he'd have anything I want."

Jed's face turned serious. "Don't be so sure about that. He's trying to save your boyfriend."

"He's trying to save himself. Saving Mason just happens to be part of the deal."

Jed remained silent.

I shifted in my seat, my anxiety returning as we entered Henryetta. "So I'm still not sure what I'm doing tonight."

"After you arrive, Skeeter will start his meeting. At some point he'll have you read the men, one by one, but it won't be until he gives you the go-ahead."

"I'm supposed to walk around and have visions of everyone there? Because that won't look suspicious . . ."

"Skeeter's trying to set up a way that it will work. Which is why he'll give you the signal when it's time for you to start. The three guys he's most worried about are Seth Moore, Bear Stevens, and Neil Winn." He turned a corner to avoid driving downtown. "Moore runs a pawnshop up by Sweet Briar."

I cringed. "Given who I know, do you really think I should be hearing this?" I could only imagine what illegal activities Seth Moore was up to with his pawnshop. "Maybe the less I know, the better."

Jed's mouth pursed. "This situation is far from ideal, but Skeeter's determined to make it work. He only wants you to know the barest of facts, but hopefully it will be enough to help you find what you need. It won't do anyone any good if you're searching blind."

I had to admit he had a point. "What do I need to know about the other two?"

"Stevens owns a marina on Fenton Lake, and Winn . . . we'll file everything else about him in your 'the less you know, the better' folder."

I decided to take him at his word. "Do you think the guy who's trying to kill Mason will even be here?"

"There's a really good chance," Jed said, "at least if it's the same guy who owns Gems. The bar may be owned by a small corporation, but the odds are five to one that the owner or one of his higher-ups will be in that meeting tonight."

"And what happens if the guy figures out that I know what he's doing?"

"We'll deal with that possibility if it presents itself." Jed looked in the mirror again. "Don't forget you are priority number one tonight. Just trust Skeeter and follow his lead."

Trust Skeeter. There was an oxymoron if I'd ever heard one. But for some reason, I believed that I could. I supposed it helped that I didn't have much of a choice.

We drove the rest of the way in silence, without even music from the radio. As we pulled into the parking lot, I looked around. We were in the lot of an old tire recycling plant. "This isn't Skeeter's pool hall."

"He couldn't have the meeting there around all of his customers, and it would have looked suspicious if he'd closed the place early. So he's having it here."

"But this place isn't abandoned."

"No. He owns it."

Skeeter owned Robison Tire Recycling. That was news. It was common knowledge that it was owned by a corporation based in Texarkana. I suddenly wondered what other things I didn't know about Skeeter.

"But that's also on the do-not-share list," Jed said with a grin.

"Maybe I should be taking notes," I mumbled.

Jed texted Skeeter, then drove around to the back of the plant. Several cars were parked in the lot, and Jed pulled up next to the back entrance, parking parallel to the building. "Wait here."

Within a few seconds, Skeeter emerged from the back entrance. He was dressed differently than he had been earlier. Tonight he had on a tight-fitting black T-shirt and dark jeans, along with a pair of boots. His dark beard was trimmed closely, so he only had a bit of scruff. He looked intimidating, which I supposed was his intention, but strangely enough, I found his appearance reassuring. Hopefully anyone inside that building would be worried about pissing off the man opening my car door.

"Lady," Skeeter said formally as he helped me out of the car.

My stomach was a tangled mass of nerves. "Skeeter."

"Everyone's here. I want you come inside and sit next to me."

"Okay."

We walked down a long hallway, my four-inch heels clacking on the concrete floor.

He leaned in close to my ear. "You look stunning tonight."

I waited for him to try to grope me, but he kept his hands to himself. "I'm still the outside business partner, Skeeter, not your current romantic entanglement. Don't forget it." I knew if he made any kind of advance on me in that room full of adversaries, I wouldn't be able to smack his hand away. I had to set him straight before we went inside. "You'll come off stronger if it doesn't look like I'm only here because I'm sleeping with you."

Stopping in front of a door, he grinned, his eyes lighting up with mischief. "And more's the pity. But you're right. Purely business it is." His playfulness faded. "Are you ready?"

"I'm scared." I wasn't sure why I admitted it to him, but then again, I'd never applied for this position. I wasn't trying to prove I was brave or worthy of it.

He took my hand and held tight, leaning closer to look through my veil. I could feel his breath on my face. "Nothing will happen to you tonight. Your safety and identity will be protected. I give you my word." He paused. "And you know how I feel about giving my word."

I took a deep breath and nodded, his sincerity sinking in. "Thank you."

He tipped his head in acknowledgment and let go of my hand as Jed made his way down the hall toward us. "Showtime."

He pushed the door open and entered the room, and I followed him inside. "Gentlemen, the Lady in Black has joined us."

Over a dozen men sat in chairs around a large conference table. A dozen pairs of eyes landed on me, and my face grew hot under the scrutiny. Then I realized they were staring at my chest, and my cheeks got even hotter. I expected a few lewd comments—the men in this room didn't look refined or gentlemanly—but they kept their thoughts to themselves.

"Lady, if you care to sit here," Skeeter motioned to a chair by the head of the table.

Jed pulled it out, and after I sat, he scooted it in and took the empty seat on my left. Skeeter stood at the head of the table. The silence in the room was eerie.

"Gentlemen, now that Lady has arrived, we can begin our meeting."

A guy with a bushy beard and beady eyes leaned his arm on the table and glared at Skeeter. "I still don't get why she's here."

Skeeter returned his stare. "She's here because I asked her to be here."

"But what's she do?" he pressed, leaning into the table more. "I've never seen or heard of her before the auction. What if she's responsible for the bust?"

I felt Jed tense beside me, although his outward appearance was attentive but disinterested.

Skeeter planted his palms on the table, leaned over, and gave the man an intimidating glare. "Maybe we should look into the real cause of the bust. Where's your paper with the code on it, Bear?"

A guilty look flooded the big man's face.

Skeeter stood, a commanding presence with his six-foot frame and solid body. I'd never realized how muscular he was, but the shirt hid nothing. I was sure that was for effect too. "I know for a fact that several unauthorized papers with the code were in circulation before the auction. The sheriff's department got hold of one of them. Jeff Dimler's not in charge anymore, boys, and you best not forget it."

I shouldn't have been surprised that Skeeter knew that Joe was the one who was really in charge, but it felt surreal to hear him talking about my ex that way.

"I trust Lady, and each one of you knows that I don't trust hardly anyone. If you have a problem with her being here, let me know right now." Skeeter scanned the group, but everyone remained silent. "Good, then let's get started."

He sat in his chair at the head of the table, and the next half hour was filled with Skeeter asking the men to report on various aspects of his business. Drugs, theft, gun-running, moonshine—Skeeter ran an empire of more illegal activities than I wanted to know about. I resisted the urge to squirm in my seat. What in the world was I doing here? I was helping the very man Mason and Joe were justifiably trying to bring down. But I reminded myself I was here to find out who had tried to kill Mason. If I had to wade through filth, I would.

Skeeter finally sat back in his seat. "Does everyone understand their assignments for the next two weeks?" When no one answered, he nodded. "Good. Now I invite you all into the next room to celebrate a successful transition."

The men stood and headed for the door, obviously knowing where they were going.

Skeeter offered me his hand, and I stood. Several of the men in the room watched us.

"I'm pleased with the progress of the transition, Mr. Malcolm." I needed to act like I had a purpose for being here outside of Skeeter's say-so.

His back was to the men and his eyes sparkled with playfulness. "Thank you, Lady. Your support has been instrumental. I know you have a drive ahead of you, but I insist you join us in the next room to celebrate."

"Thank you." I was glad he wasn't upset that I'd broken the no-speaking rule, but was nervous about the next phase of the evening. Clearly, this was when my true purpose for being here would come into play.

Skeeter leaned into Jed and whispered in a growl, "You stay within inches of her until she leaves with you. If she goes to the restroom, you go in with her and hold the damn stall door closed. Got it?"

Jed nodded, his face solemn.

Skeeter moved back and motioned to the door. "After you."

The men who were still in the room stepped back and watched me leave the room with Skeeter and Jed on my heels. We emerged into what appeared to be a large rec room with a small kitchen and bar at one end, sofas and chairs scattered around, and a pool table and air hockey table in the middle.

Skeeter led me to the bar, which was covered with an assortment of alcohol bottles. "Let me get you a drink, Lady." He grabbed a bottle from under the counter and poured it in a glass full of ice before handing it to me.

I almost mentioned that I didn't drink anything but wine, but it didn't seem like a good time to bring it up. He poured himself a drink from the same bottle before returning it to the cabinet and shutting the door. Then he raised his glass toward me, his face serious. "To a profitable partnership."

I clinked my glass with his, hoping our definition of profitable was the same thing. When I took a sip of the light brown liquid, I prepared myself for the dreaded burn, but it went down easily. It wasn't alcohol. It was diluted tea.

Skeeter winked, then leaned toward my ear. "We need to keep our senses about us while the others lose theirs. If you need another drink, Jed will see to it that you get a refill. And never let your drink out of your sight."

"Okay."

"Do whatever you have to do to see what you need to see tonight. But remember that I have to keeping working with these men, and you *will* make future appearances."

I had no idea what that meant. "Okay." I tried to ignore his pronouncement about my continued presence in his life.

Skeeter held his hands out at his sides, his glass still in his hand. "Gentlemen, the bar is open."

As he walked over to a small group of the men, I scanned the room in dismay. I had no idea what I was doing.

Jed, who had followed close behind me, whispered in my ear, "What do you want to do?"

"I don't know. Give me a moment."

The more I thought about Skeeter's cryptic words, the more I realized what they meant. He thought I was going to lure these men with my exposed cleavage, lead them on, have a vision, and then send them away before anything could happen, using Jed to make them leave if necessary. Based on the outright leers and stares I was receiving, I knew it would work in the short term—if I could bring myself to pull it off. But in the end, I'd look like a slut, and I'd never gain their respect, which was what I'd tried to do from the moment I climbed out of Skeeter's car at that auction.

"I need a quiet place to talk to them."

"Okay," Jed said without hesitation. "Here or somewhere else?"

If I took them somewhere else, it could be misconstrued, but I didn't like the thought having multiple visions here, in full view of everyone. "I'd like to remain in public view, but with enough privacy for no one else to hear what's being said." I pointed to a seating area in the dim back corner of the room. "That would work if we can keep the others away."

"We can arrange it."

"I want to meet with them one by one, but I want to do it as the Lady in Black, Skeeter's business partner. Maybe they can be introduced and I can talk to them for a minute or so and then have a vision. It's how they'll react after my visions that worries me."

"If we wait another hour or so, we can start with the ones who are drunk already and work our way up from there. If they're drunk, we can play it off somehow."

I nodded. I hated to be here longer than need be, but it was a great idea. "Okay."

Jed motioned to a guy who hurried toward us. "Tell Skeeter that Lady would like him to formally introduce her to the men in an hour or so, one by one, starting with the ones who are the most drunk. In the meantime, I'm going to keep them away from her."

The man made his way through the crowd and leaned into Skeeter. Several seconds later, Skeeter turned his gaze to me with a slight smile before returning his attention to the man across from him.

"That was smart," Jed said behind me.

I shrugged, wondering how in the world I was going to spend the next hour. "It gives me authority and Skeeter as well. I worry about looking like I've usurped him, though. I don't want anyone to think I'm the one with the real power."

"I think you can pull it off as an equal pairing."

For the next hour and ten minutes, I watched the men in the room, trying to figure out which one might have tried to kill Mason. The men lounged around, playing pool, drinking and talking. "It looks like Skeeter holds regular meetings here," I whispered to Jed. "The fact that he owns this place has to be the best-kept secret in Fenton County, given the fact so many people clearly know about it."

Jed leaned close. "Over in the corner, the guy with the beard is Bear Stevens."

I studied the burly-looking bearded guy who'd spoken out at the meeting. It was easy to see how he'd earned his nickname. The guy he was talking to caught my attention. Though he was pretty average looking, his eyes were cold and hard. He looked like the kind of man who would do anything to put Skeeter out of business. Including kill Mason.

"Who's he with?" I asked.

"Rich Lowry. He's a sadistic bastard. He wouldn't think twice about screwing you while he was trying to kill you. Hell, he'd probably get off on it. Stay as far away from him as possible if Skeeter and I aren't with you."

"Could he be the one we're looking for?"

"He's a two-bit player. Any money he gets, he loses on bets. He might be gunning for Skeeter's position, but he can't afford it. We'll follow Skeeter's lead when it comes to him."

I was bored out my mind, and my stomach was a mess from worrying, so when Skeeter made his way toward me, I was equally thankful and alarmed.

"Okay, Lady," he whispered in my ear. "Let's catch a would-be killer."

Chapter Twenty-Three

Skeeter took the empty glass from my hand and gave it to Jed. "Go refill Lady's drink."

Jed nodded and headed for the bar.

"You have the men all abuzz. The fact that Jed's been angling his deadly stare at them has both kept them away and kept them intrigued. Some are drunk enough that they'll come on pretty strong when they're alone with you."

"I can handle it."

"I'd prefer you let Jed handle it. It shows more authority that way."

"Don't they wonder why your guy is watching over me?"

He grinned. "Yeah, but it's another thing to keep them on their toes."

I watched Jed open the cabinet and pull out the bottle Skeeter had used.

"You don't trust Jed?" He chuckled.

"You told me not to let my glass out of my sight. I'm only following your wise advice."

"Wise?" He laughed. "You make me sound old."

"How old are you, Skeeter Malcolm?"

"I'll be thirty-nine in January. Why are you asking?"

I gave a half-shrug. In some ways he seemed both older and younger. "Just curious."

"I'm not too old to give you the best night of your life."

"You wish." I shot him a glare, not that he could see it through my veil. "You're old enough to know that it's time to stop sleepin' with every loose woman in the county."

"Are you suggesting I settle for one woman?" He laughed. "And accept a life of boredom? That would be like eating toast for breakfast every morning for the rest of my life."

I shook my head in disgust. "And that right there shows that while you might be thirty-nine years old, you're as stupid as a stump. Maybe you should be looking for pancakes and bacon for breakfast instead of settling for toast."

Skeeter's smug grin wavered as Jed returned and handed me my glass.

"I'm ready to do this. Let's get started."

Skeeter's eyes darkened. "There's been a change of plans. Instead of just having a vision, I want you to ask them general questions about their involvement in the business—see if you can get anything out of them that might be helpful to me. Save the vision for last."

I shook my head, starting to panic. "No, I can't do that."

"Look at me." His eyes narrowed. "You *can,* and you *will.*"

I took a deep breath and tried to see a positive side to this tactic. If I could question them, maybe I could get some answers of my own. "Okay."

His mouth tipped up into an appreciative grin. "Jed will be there listening to everything. Go through the first door to the left of this room."

"We were going to use the corner," Jed said. "So we can keep it in the public eye. For Lady's reputation."

Skeeter considered the suggestion. "No, use the office. You'll be in there to dispel any lies that might pop up. I think you'll get more from them if you talk to them in a separate room."

Jed nodded.

My hands began to tremble as the insanity of the situation hit me full on. I was about to question hardened criminals.

"I'll send them in to see you, so when one guy leaves, wait until the next comes in."

"Okay," Jed said.

Skeeter leaned close, peering through my veil. "You can do this. Now go find out who's responsible."

Jed led me into the office and flipped on the light. I expected a utilitarian space, but the room was larger than I'd expected. A large wooden desk sat toward the back wall with a luxurious leather office chair behind it. The back wall was a solid bookcase filled with books.

In the corner opposite the door was a leather sofa with two leather chairs in front of it. A table topped with an unlit lamp was tucked next to the couch.

"Is this Skeeter's *real* office?"

"The pool hall office is just a front. The guys in the other room had to prove themselves trustworthy to be here."

"That can't be too true since Skeeter has me questioning them. I thought you said Skeeter could read people's characters?"

"And I also say they could change, although it's rare. But some will change if there's a powerful enough incentive. Like greed."

I suspected a lot of people would change for greed.

"The first guy will be in here soon. Where do you want to do this?" Jed asked.

I stood in the center of the room, spinning around to take it all in. "If I sit at the desk, I'll show more authority, but I'll have to get up to force a vision." I turned to study the sitting area. "If I sit there, they might want to sit next to me and . . . be more inclined to talk." My voice trailed off. I knew why some of them might want to sit by me.

"I think the sofa area is a good idea."

"But let's turn on the lamp and turn off the overhead light. So it's more . . . comfortable."

"Good idea."

I nodded and sat on the sofa close to the table, setting my glass on a coaster. "Is it gonna be that bad?" I asked.

"With most of them? No. And I suspect Skeeter will send the easy ones first to get you warmed up."

My nerves kicked in. There were eleven men in the other room, so this could very well go on all night. But I didn't have time to dwell on it.

Jed opened the door, and the first man walked in. He paused in the doorway, but Jed said, "Come on in, Seth. As Skeeter probably told you, Lady would like to meet you. Lady, this is Seth Moore."

So much for starting with the easy ones. Mr. Moore was on the questionable list.

Seth moved toward me, his eyes moving from the empty chairs to the sofa. I'd chosen where to sit strategically. If the guy I was questioning sat next to me on the sofa, it would be easier to reach over, grab his hand, and have a vision. But it also meant he would probably be more forward. It was a double-edged sword.

He sat on the cushion next to me.

Jed shut the door and took a seat in the chair opposite of where I sat.

"Seth, thank you for meeting with me." I clasped my hands in my lap, hoping my trembling didn't show. "I'm a very hands-on investor, and I think it's important for me to get to know the men who work closely with Mr. Malcolm." I crossed my legs and leaned toward him. "And perhaps you'd like to know more about me too."

His eyes were glued to my cleavage. "Yeah . . ."

"I've been studying everyone since I walked into the conference room, and I can tell that you are a man who will be instrumental to Mr. Malcolm. Tell me about your position in the organization." I cast a quick glance at Jed, and he tipped his head slightly with a tiny smile.

The alcohol on his breath loosened his tongue. Seth spent several minutes telling me how important he was to Skeeter, which had something to do with fencing stolen goods in his pawnshop.

"I'd love to know about your prior experience. An enterprising man such as yourself has surely worked his way up the ladder."

He filled me in on his petty thefts and burglaries, none of which was useful information.

"I have a question," Seth said, leaning toward me.

Jed's jaw tightened.

"I'm listening."

"Why do you always wear a veil?"

I should have expected that. Reaching my hand to my chest, I said, "I was in an accident that left me with a terrible scar. I'm embarrassed to be seen with it, so I cover it with a veil."

"I'm sure you're beautiful without it." He reached over and put his hand on mine.

Jed shifted in his seat as though he was ready to pounce, but I grabbed Seth's hand and held it between both of my own.

"Can I read your aura?"

"What?" he mumbled, his eyes on my chest again. It was easy to see which part of me he found most beautiful.

"I know it sounds new-agey, but I read auras. You're such an interesting man, and I'd love to read you."

He leered at me. I suspected the fact that I was still holding his hand gave him courage. "I'd love for you to read me."

"Thank you." I lowered my voice. "You sit still. I'll be quiet for a bit while I concentrate, and then I'll blurt out some nonsense before I tell you about your aura. Don't worry—it's all part of the process."

"Okay."

I cast a glance at Jed, who seemed tense. I could hardly blame him. Who knew what would pop out of my mouth and what this man would do afterward? Jed was in a terrible position of both having to protect me and maintain damage control.

"Then let's get started." I closed my eyes, wondering what to focus on. If I tried to find out if he was connected to Mason's attempted murder, what would I see if he *wasn't* involved? I supposed it was worth a try. I concentrated on his connection to Mason's murder and the inky blackness gave way to a gray haze. I squinted, concentrating harder until a fuzzy image appeared.

I was sitting in lawn chair, holding a beer in my hand. A man sat in the chair next to me with a beer of his own.

"You gonna mow the lawn?" a woman screeched behind me.

I took a guzzle from the can. "Quit your naggin', woman."

"You hear about Billy Jack?" the guy asked.

I shook my head. "Nothing good can come from that."

Suddenly a woman with baby on one hip stood in front of me, her hand on her other hip. "Get your worthless ass up and mow. Now."

"You don't want to mow the grass," I blurted out.

"What?" Seth asked, sounding confused.

My heart raced. Did Billy Jack have anything to do with the attack on Mason? But Seth was waiting for an answer. "I told you I'd talk nonsense at first. You're such a complicated man, I'm having trouble honing in on your aura. Let me try one more time."

"Okay." He slid closer to me so that his thigh touched mine, giving him a better view of my chest. Pervert.

I closed my eyes again, still holding his hand between both of mine. I considered holding both of his hands, since he was close enough for his other hand to fondle me, but I figured Jed had me covered. This time I focused on whether Seth had betrayed Skeeter and if so, who he was working with. But when the room faded, I saw the same gray nothingness I'd experienced before the start of my previous vision. I felt stuck in the haze, and I was starting to panic when I thought of something else I was sure I'd see—what Seth was going to have for lunch tomorrow. Instantly an image of his hand holding a hot dog topped with sauerkraut popped into my head.

The vision faded, and I said, "You're going to have a hot dog for lunch tomorrow."

"That's weird," Seth said. "I was just thinking about hot dogs tonight."

"That's quite a coincidence," I said, a dull ache starting in my forehead.

"So what color did you see?"

"Oh." I dropped his hand and scooted back toward the arm of the sofa. What had Neely Kate told me about auras? "Your aura is a light greenish-blue. It means you're loyal to Skeeter . . . a loyalty that will be rewarded."

He gave me a leer and slid closer, reaching for my hand again. "I'd like to prove my loyalty to you."

But before he could finish his sentence, Jed grabbed his arm and pulled him to his feet. "Skeeter would prefer for you to save your loyalty for him."

Panic washed over Seth's face. "But she works for him. I'm loyal to 'em both."

Jed pulled him to the door. "She works *with* Skeeter, not *for*, and you best not forget that."

"I didn't mean nothing by it. I swear."

"I know, Seth. I won't mention it to Skeeter, but for the record, he considers her *his*, if you know what I mean."

"Sorry, I didn't mean—"

Jed opened the door and pushed Seth out before closing it without another word to the man. "Did you have two visions?" he asked me.

I nodded. "One to see if he was part of the plot to kill Mason and the other to see if he was going to betray Skeeter."

He chuckled. "And you saw a hot dog?"

"No. I saw absolutely nothing the second time around, just gray haze. I kind of got stuck in it, so I decided to think about what he's going to have for lunch tomorrow."

"What about the lawn mowing?"

"I think his wife was nagging him to mow the lawn, but some guy next to him asked if he knew about what happened to Billy Jack."

"Who?"

"Neely Kate's cousin's boyfriend."

"The girl who's missing?"

"Yeah. He sound familiar?"

He pressed his lips together and shook his head. "Nope, don't know him."

Billy Jack could have something to do with whoever was after Mason. Was Dolly's disappearance related to it too? Maybe she and Nikko had uncovered the plot?

I'd have to puzzle it out later. Another man was about to walk through the door. "Are there any questions I didn't ask that I should have?"

"Nope, you're a natural."

I wished I felt like one. I spent the next twenty minutes interviewing the next three men. I'd forced two visions with each, and none of them were involved in either Mason's attack or the betrayal of Skeeter. Instead, I found out what all three of them were getting for Christmas—the question I asked in a panic when I got stuck in the gray haze after asking about Mason—and I knew what they would have for lunch the next day. By the time the last of them left, my head was pounding.

I pressed my hand to my temple. "Can I get a glass of water? And maybe some ibuprofen?"

Jed picked up my glass. "Does your head hurt? How often have you done this sort of thing?"

"I've never had this many visions in such a short time period, let alone forced ones."

"Maybe you should just have one vision each for the rest of these guys." He went into the bathroom that was connected to the room and came back with a glass of water and two tablets. He handed them to me, worry in his eyes.

I swallowed the tablets and put my glass on the table. "I need to figure out how to combine the questions. Maybe I'll try it with the next guy. How many are left?"

"Seven."

My stomach rolled at the thought. "One at a time, right?"

"You can stop any time you need to."

I shook my head and instantly regretted it. "I can't. I'll be fine. I was too nervous to eat much for dinner. I'm sure that hasn't helped."

Jed studied me as a knock came at the door. He walked over to peek through the peephole, then turned to me. "Good thing you took that medicine."

He opened the door and the suspicious bearded guy from the meeting barreled in. Bear Stevens. He didn't look the least bit happy to there. "This is a fucking waste of my time," he said without any preliminaries.

My back stiffened, and I struggled to keep my breath even. I'd known I'd face resistance from some of them, but I still wasn't prepared for his reaction. I suspected I'd see something with him, and I had no idea how he'd react when I did.

"Bear, have a seat," Jed said, motioning toward me.

All four of the previous men had sat on the sofa beside me, but Bear sat in the chair that Jed had occupied. I wasn't surprised, but I knew it would be tricky to find an excuse to touch him . . . one that wouldn't put me in personal danger.

"Thank you for sparing a few moments of your time, Bear," I said, crossing my legs and placing my hands on my knees. Thankfully, my voice didn't betray my fear. "What do you do for Skeeter?"

Jed sat in the chair diagonally across from me, and Bear turned his attention to him rather than looking at me. "Why do you want me to waste my time telling this bitch what I do for Skeeter?"

Jed gripped the arms of the chair, his knuckles turning white. "You will treat Lady with respect."

"Lady," the burly man sneered. "What kind of name is that?"

"If you feel like comparing names, Mr. *Bear*," I said calmly, surprised at the authority I mustered, "then let's compare what our given names are. Would you like to start first?"

His face turned red.

"No, I didn't think so. You chose Bear for a reason, right? You want to put out a specific image." I paused for effect. "I chose the name *Lady* for the same reason, Mr. Bear, so please don't forget it."

Bear looked furious and close to walking out the door.

"I have partnered with Mr. Malcolm, but it's risky for me, both financially and personally. So I insisted on meeting the highly respected members of his organization."

He snorted. "Then why did you talk to Seth?"

I uncrossed my legs and sat back in the seat. "Every parent has favorites, Bear, even if he or she insists otherwise. The parent needs each child to feel just as loved as the others, even if it's not true."

He gave me a sarcastic grin. "So which am I? The child who's being lied to or lied for?"

I had to be careful with this man. He definitely wasn't Seth Moore. To fight my growing anxiety, I stood up and moved to the cabinet from which Jed had pulled the glass. "You're a smart man. I think you can figure it out."

He laughed as I took out two glasses, picked up a decanter, and poured amber liquid into each glass. "I'm a businesswoman, Bear, and while I don't micro-manage my partners, I do like to be assured they are making wise choices." I picked up the glasses and handed one to him, thanking those business books I'd read once again.

He took a sip of his drink, then grinned at me.

"I hear that you're important to Mr. Malcolm's operation, so I'm curious about you," I said.

"What exactly would you like to know?"

I took a sip of the alcohol and was grateful it didn't burn as it slid down my throat. I sat on the arm of the sofa and studied him for several seconds. "I want to know how ambitious you are."

He downed the rest of his glass and slammed it onto the corner table next to him, then burst out laughing.

I continued to stare at him, although I realized he couldn't see me through the veil. My heart beat against my chest.

"Now that there is an interesting question." He shoved the empty glass toward Jed. "Jed, get me a refill."

Jed's eyes hardened as he glanced at me.

I gave him a slight nod. "You haven't answered me, Bear."

He waited for Jed to hand him his glass. He took a sip and grinned. "You realize it's a no-win question."

"Is it?" I asked. "I can understand how you might see it that way, but I would hazard to guess that ambition is what has gotten you to where you are today. Skeeter wouldn't find you nearly as valuable if you weren't ambitious."

He grinned again and took another sip.

"No," I said, standing. I placed my glass on the corner table and slipped behind him, resting my hand on his shoulder. I needed to have the visions and get him out of here. "The real question is your loyalty."

Bear stood, grabbing my hand and holding onto it. "And where does *your* loyalty lie, Lady?"

Jed tensed, but remained in his seat.

I kept my rising panic at bay. "It lies with Skeeter, of course."

"Then why do you hide behind this veil?" His free hand lifted toward my face, and I grabbed it.

"Bear, do you have secrets? Something you want to keep hidden from the world?" I laughed, but it was a humorless sound. "Of course you do. Everyone does. Mine is surface deep. Would you like me to start prying to find out what you're hiding? Because I assure you that it would be fun to start digging around. Maybe I won't have to dig very deep. Maybe you haven't hidden it very well at all."

His hands dropped. "What do you want?"

"I want to know where your loyalty lies."

"Do you really have to ask?"

"Yes." I moved over to the desk and leaned my butt against the edge, grateful when he followed me. He sat in the chair in front of me. I put my arms onto the desk behind me to prop myself up.

"And if I said my loyalty lies with you?"

I pulled myself up so I was sitting on the desk. "I wouldn't believe you."

"And if I said Skeeter?"

"Then I'd argue that you've taken an awfully long time to admit it." I paused.

He stood and moved in front of me. "I want to see your face."

"Then tell me your deep dark secret, and I'll show you mine."

Jed stood but hung back by the chairs.

Bear glanced over his shoulder at him before returning his gaze to me. "Why is Jed here as your bodyguard?"

"Maybe I need one with you."

He laughed.

I wasn't going to get anything out of him, and the longer he stayed in here, the more dangerous our interview was becoming. I was glad I'd decided to try both questions at the same time when I forced a vision, because there was no way Bear would let me do this twice.

I reached for his hand and traced the lines on his palm with my fingers. "You have very big hands, Bear."

"I can show you what I can do with them if you'd like," he said in a low voice.

I concentrated on whether he was behind Mason's attempted murder and if he was betraying Skeeter.

A vision slammed me hard, and I was plunged into a dark room.

"Is this going down or not?" Bear asked.

I could barely make out the man in front of me. He stood in front of a window, his back to me. "I told you it was."

"I didn't sign on for murder. I need extra for this."

"You're getting what you want. What are you griping about?"

"It's a bigger risk if I get caught."

"Great reward comes with great risk."

Then I was back in Skeeter's office, clutching Bear's hand in a death grip. Bear was trying to pry my hand off, while Jed was trying to pull him off me.

"You're gonna kill someone," I said.

"You're damn right!" Bear shouted. "I'm gonna kill you if you don't let go of my hand."

I dropped my hold as though he were on fire.

"You're one crazy-ass bitch!" He lifted his now freed hand as if to hit me, but Jed stepped between us, his chest heaving.

"Get the hell out of here right now, Bear." I heard the threat behind his words even though he didn't raise his voice.

"Gladly!"

He stormed out of the room, and Jed shut the door behind him and locked it. I could hear Bear raising a ruckus in the other room.

A sharp pain throbbed in my temples, and I leaned forward, clutching my head.

"Are you okay?"

I wanted to say I was fine, but I figured the fact that I was seeing two of Jed wasn't a good sign. "Give me a minute."

"What did you see?"

"A man wanted him to kill someone. Bear was reluctant, and he said he wanted more money. The other guy told him that he was already getting what he wanted, but Bear said it was too risky. The man said great reward comes with great risk, and that was it."

"Did you know who the other man was?"

"No. His back was to me." The pain in my head was getting worse. "I think I have to throw up." I ran into the bathroom and lifted the veil in time to lose my meager dinner in the toilet.

Jed followed me in, holding my glass. "I'm going to go talk to Skeeter, but as far as I'm concerned, you're done."

I shook my head, bringing a fresh wave of nausea. "We're not done yet. I still need to read Neil Winn."

"There's no way in hell you can handle him like this." He dumped out the whiskey and filled it with water from the faucet.

"Just give me a few minutes."

He set the glass on the counter. "You have until I get back from talking with Skeeter."

"Skeeter said not to leave me alone."

"I'll lock you in."

The thought should have scared me. Jed was locking me in a windowless room, in essence holding me hostage, but all I felt was relief. When had I reached this place of trusting criminals so blindly?

But I didn't have the energy to think about it. I barely had the energy to lift my head off the toilet seat. Thank God it had been clean. Who would have thought Skeeter knew how to aim?

I closed my eyes and only opened them again when I heard Jed and Skeeter's voices in the office.

"We have to get her out of here," Jed said.

"I agree, but she has to walk out on her own, or this was all for nothing," Skeeter said, moving toward me.

"I can walk," I said, trying to lift my head.

"You can't even stand," Skeeter said, squatting beside me. I expected him to be angry with me for not finishing with all of the readings, but his voice was surprisingly gentle.

"I can, just help me up."

Skeeter put an arm around my back and lifted me to my feet.

I wobbled in my heels. "See? I'm standing."

"You look like you're drunk, but there's no way you drank enough of my twenty-five-year-old whiskey to get that way." I heard his irritation.

"Sorry."

"Jed told me what you saw with Bear. It was worth the information."

I took a deep breath. "If you give me a few minutes, I can try to talk to Neil Winn."

Skeeter shook his head. "As much as I want you to do that, we just can't risk it."

I walked over to the sink. Skeeter stood behind me, his tanned face a sharp contrast to my pale one. "But I want to try—"

"No," both men said.

I grabbed the glass off the counter and rinsed out my mouth. "Then I've failed."

"How can you say that?" Skeeter asked, staring at my reflection in the mirror. "Bear's the one. We know that thanks to you."

"How do you know there aren't others in on this with him? We don't know who was giving him orders. That's the person who's in charge or at least higher up than Bear. We need to find him."

Skeeter put his hands on my shoulders, searching my face in the reflection. "And I will, Rose. You did your part, now I'm going to do mine. We know Bear is involved now, so we'll follow him everywhere he goes."

"But how do you know the person following him isn't one of the guys who's in on it too?"

"I'll use one of the guys you've already read." Skeeter's tone left no room for argument. "You look like you're feeling well enough to walk. What do you think?"

"Do I smell like barf?" I could only imagine what that would do for my image.

He grinned and bent his face into my neck, his mouth and nose less than an inch from my skin. He breathed in, then out, his breath warm on my skin. "You smell good."

I elbowed him in the stomach.

He gasped and stepped back, laughing as he clutched his gut. "What the hell was that for?"

"For messing around. It's never gonna happen with me, Skeeter, so let it go."

He backed out of the bathroom, his hands raised. "You can't blame a guy for trying."

I lowered my veil and studied myself in the mirror. With the veil down, I looked no worse for wear. "If I'm leaving, then let's go."

"Let me leave the room first," Skeeter said, "then follow me. Lady, can you say something about having to leave due to an emergency? Then Jed will take you to the car."

"I can do it."

I followed Skeeter into the room full of men. I noticed Bear wasn't in the room and neither was Neil Winn. Did that mean Neil was the other man in my vision?

Skeeter stopped in the middle and plastered on his cocky grin. "Gentlemen, I know you were all looking forward to meeting Lady tonight, but unfortunately, she's been called away." He turned to me.

"Yes," I said, fighting a fresh round of nausea. "Something has come up with one of my warehouses, and I have to get back to address it. But thank you to those I met. I look forward to meeting the rest of you when I return." Even if I had no intention of voluntarily returning.

Jed gave me a tiny push on my back, and I headed for the door to the hallway. We moved down the hall toward the exit, Jed in a bigger hurry than I thought necessary, but I wasn't about to argue.

The car wasn't in front of the building where Jed had dropped me off. He silently pointed it out to me across the lot, but when we reached it, Neil Winn stepped out of the shadows of a truck, a twisted grin on his face.

"Lady, you aren't leaving already, are you? We haven't had a chance to chat."

"She's been called away for an emergency," Jed said, stepping between us. "You can talk to her the next time she's in town."

"I don't think so." Neil lifted a handgun and pointed it at Jed's chest. "I think we'll talk now."

The fear coursing through my blood added to my nausea. Neil Winn looked prepared to use the weapon in his hand, and

Jed looked prepared to call him on it. "Jed, it's a long drive back to Louisiana. I think I can spare a few minutes for Mr. Winn."

"You know my name?" Neil asked.

"Of course. I know all of Skeeter's top men." I moved next to Jed, my heart racing. "But I'm not gonna say a word to you unless you get rid of that gun."

Neil hesitated. "Fine, but I want to talk without Skeeter's boy listening. He steps away, and I'll put the gun away."

Jed shook his head and said in disgust, "There's no way in hell—"

I put my hand on Jed's arm. "Jed, I'll do it."

"*No.*"

Neil took a step closer, aiming his gun at me now. "I'll shoot her, Jed. I know how important she is to Skeeter. Do you want to risk that?"

"Skeeter's gonna kill you, Winn. You know that, right? You hurt a hair on her head, you're a dead man."

"I'm only gonna hurt her if *you don't back away.*"

Jed searched my face, not that he could see it through the veil. I felt like crap and wanted nothing more than to lie down and sleep for the next day and a half, but I couldn't let Jed get hurt, and I couldn't pass up the opportunity to find out if Neil was the guy in Bear's vision.

I lifted my chin, trying to reason through this. "Jed only backs up enough so that he can't overhear you. He's not leaving."

Neil laughed. "Fine. But if you act like you're gonna do something stupid, Jed, I'm gonna kill her *and* you."

"Jed, go," I forced out, trying not to shake with fear.

Jed leaned closer and lowered his voice. "You don't have to do this."

"We both know I do," I whispered, still keeping an eye on Neil.

Jed turned his head slightly so his mouth couldn't be seen. "I have my own gun, and if I think he's about to hurt you, I won't hesitate to kill him."

I nodded.

Jed lifted his hands as if in surrender. "I'm stepping away."

"About damn time," Neil muttered as Jed continued to walk backward. He stopped in the middle of the parking lot and dropped his hands to his sides.

"He's far enough," I said. "Put away the gun."

He stuffed it into the waistband of his jeans. I had the fleeting hope that he'd accidently shoot his foot or an appendage even closer to the gun tip and undoubtedly more cherished, and I didn't even feel bad about it.

"What do you want?'

"I want to know why you're so damned special to Skeeter."

"You had to send Jed away for that?" I snorted. "I'm special because Skeeter says I am. His reasons are none of your damned business."

"You just popped out of nowhere at that auction. He wasn't supposed to win it, you know." He moved closer and wobbled. He let out a huff, and I was engulfed in a cloud of alcohol.

He was drunk. I wasn't sure if that was a good thing or a bad one.

"So I hear. A group of amateurs robbed a bunch of places and gathered the money to outbid Skeeter. Only they didn't."

"They got interrupted." He stood in front of me. "What do you know about that?"

"I know the sheriff showed up. As for the rest? I only know what Skeeter told me." I looked up into Neil's cold eyes. "What do you know about Gems? Are you the owner?"

He laughed. "No."

"Do you know who is?"

His grin turned evil. "No. I wish I did. I'd offer to help him."

"Why do you hate Skeeter?"

He shook his head. "That's none of your damn business."

I felt like I was talking in circles. He was never going to voluntarily give me the answers I wanted. Which meant I needed to have a vision, despite the fact that I was risking my life to do it. He was drunk and had a gun he wouldn't hesitate to use.

I grabbed Neil's arm and concentrated on his connection to Mason and Skeeter.

My peripheral vision faded, and a vision hit me hard, making me stagger back into the side of the car. The night faded to someplace sunny, then a stabbing pain filled my head.

Everything went black.

Chapter Twenty-Four

When I opened my eyes, I was in the backseat of a moving car. I experienced a moment of confusion before remembering the last few moments before I'd passed out. Jed's voice was the only thing that pulled me out of a panic.

"We're almost to the feed store."

"Jed?" I asked, trying to sit up, but the pounding in my head kept me down.

He glanced back over the seat. "How are you feeling?"

"Like someone smashed a sledge hammer into my skull. What happened?"

"You were talking to Winn, and then you grabbed his hand. You had a vision, didn't you?"

"I tried. Why do you sound so mad?" I asked, grabbing hold of the seat back in front of me.

"Skeeter told you no more visions tonight. You disobeyed him."

"Skeeter's not the boss of me. I saw an opportunity, and I went for it."

"You insisted I leave you alone with that maniac. Are you crazy?"

"I needed to talk to him, Jed. I had to do it. You could still see me." What was it with all the bossy men in my life?

"Besides, I think he would have shot you if it had gone down differently."

"You're lucky he didn't shoot *you*."

"So what happened after I passed out?"

"He pried off your death grip, then took off running. I picked you up off the hood of the car, threw you into the backseat, and called Skeeter."

"How long was I out?"

"About fifteen minutes."

That didn't sound good.

Jed pulled into the parking lot, and I dug out my keys and reached for the door.

"Where do you think you're going?" Jed asked.

"Home." I jiggled the handle, but the door wouldn't open. "Let me out, Jed."

"Not until Skeeter gets here."

"No, I need to go now."

"What's your hurry?"

I let go of the door and slumped back in the seat in exhaustion. What was my hurry? Mason was locked up in a hospital room, and I still had to figure out how to sneak back into Maeve's house.

"Skeeter is only minutes behind us."

What did it matter? I leaned my head back on the seat and unpinned my hat, laying it on the seat next to me as I blinked to stop the tears that were blurring my vision. Everything I'd done tonight suddenly became overwhelming. I just wanted to go home and crawl into bed with Mason, Muffy plastered up against me. Only Mason was locked away, and I couldn't even talk to him.

The car door opened a couple of minutes later, but I didn't sit up.

"Lady?" Skeeter asked, sounding worried as he slid in next to me and shut the door.

"My name is *Rose*." I lifted my head, but it took tremendous effort, like I'd been drugged and every movement was delayed.

"Why did you talk to Winn?"

"Maybe because the gun he pointed at me was pretty convincing."

Jed must have described that part of the situation to him in some detail, because he didn't seem surprised. He just said, "What did he tell you?"

"He wanted to know why you were so interested in me. Somehow he figured out that there was a connection between me and the guys who tried to outbid you."

"What did you say?"

"I asked him what his connection was to Gems."

Confusion flickered in Skeeter's eyes. "Why would you ask him that?"

"It was a hunch. He denied being the owner, but when I asked him if he knew who it was, he said he wished he did so he could help him. Then I tried to have a vision and passed out."

"So you risked your life for *nothing*," he growled.

"*Not* for nothing. I think he helped the guys who tried to take you down at the auction. I'm pretty sure he was the guy in Bear's vision. And he admitted that he hates you. That's *something*."

His jaw clenched. "So they're both trying to overthrow me."

"And kill Mason?"

"Yes, if they murdered the ADA and pinned the blame on me, I'd be out of the picture. They could take over without

293

anyone in their way." His eyes narrowed. "It's a helluva plan. And it almost worked."

"What's their connection to Gems?"

Skeeter shook his head. "There isn't one."

"But you said Gems was trying to put you out of business. It's connected."

"No. Neither Stevens nor Winn have anything to do with Gems."

"You can't be sure."

"I am. Trust me. I've already checked."

"But what about Dolly and Nikko?"

"It doesn't have anything to do with this."

"But—"

"Gems is small fry, Rose. It's the least of my worries. Go home, get some sleep, and I'll check in with you in the morning."

"I'm still looking into it."

"*Leave it.*" His words were hard, and if he'd used that tone with me weeks ago, I would have been scared.

What I did wasn't Skeeter Malcolm's business, but I knew when to pick my battles. "Then you have to promise to tell me whatever you find out about Bear and Neil."

He didn't answer.

"Skeeter, you trust me to share everything that I find out. I have to be able to feel the same way."

He was silent for several seconds, studying the headrest in front of him. Finally he said, "Okay. If I think anything is helpful to you I'll share it, but you don't want me to share *everything*. Trust me on that."

"You're right about that." I reached for the door handle. "Can I go now?"

"Yeah." He sounded distracted.

I opened the door, and he put his hand on my arm. "Jed told me how you handled all of those interviews. I'm impressed."

I shook my head, and pain shot through every part of my skull. "I did what I had to do to save Mason."

"It was more solid information than I've gotten in weeks. Thank you."

I turned to look at him, guessing that *thank you* were two words he rarely strung together. "Coming from you, that means a lot. I appreciate everything you're doing to help me save Mason. I know it would be easier for you if he . . ." My voice trailed off, and I swallowed the lump in my throat. "Thank you."

"Go home," he said gruffly.

With any luck at all, Mason would be able to come home tomorrow.

Getting back to Maeve's was tricky. There was a new deputy parked out in front of Maeve's house, so I left her car around the block and snuck through the shadowy alley to the back door. I made sure to grab my note on the way to my room.

My headache was so bad I was sure I'd never get to sleep, but as soon as my head hit the pillow, I was out like a light.

When I woke up the next morning, the sun was shining through the blinds on the window, and Muffy was snuggled against me, snoring lightly. I sat up, and my stomach felt queasy, like I was suffering from a hangover. A vision hangover. At least I knew the consequences of forcing so many visions in a short period of time. I grabbed my phone to check the time and discovered I'd slept until nine-thirty. I also found two texts and three missed calls.

One message was from SM. *Call me* was all it said. The second was from a number I didn't recognize that read: *This is my temporary number. Call me when you get a chance. Mason.* Two of my missed calls were from them too.

I called Skeeter first, worried he'd send Jed if I didn't answer right away. He picked up on the first ring.

"Why haven't you called me?" he grunted, sounding pissed.

"I just woke up, and my phone was on silent."

"How are you feeling this morning?"

"Better." I rubbed my temple. "Is Mason safe now?"

"He's safe. They've been contained."

"Even Neil Winn? Didn't he run off?"

He hesitated. "Jed took care of him personally." I didn't want to think too closely on what he meant by that, but at least I probably didn't have to worry about Mason anymore.

"Tell Jed thank you. For everything."

"If you need anything, and I mean *anything*, you call. Do you hear me?" he asked, his voice gruff.

"Yeah . . ." I said, not used to his protectiveness. I wasn't sure I liked it. "Thanks."

I called Mason next, and was relieved to hear his voice. "How much longer do you have to stay there?" I asked.

"I don't know. Joe's supposed to stop by in a bit so we can discuss it."

"I'm going to get ready, and then I'll come by to see you."

"Okay."

The third missed call was from Neely Kate.

"How's Mason?" she asked when I called her.

I realized I hadn't checked in with her or Bruce Wayne at all the previous afternoon. She didn't know Mason's "accident" had truly been a murder attempt. "He's better."

"What time do you want to go look for Billy Jack?"

I realized I'd never solved that piece of the puzzle. Where did Billy Jack fit into the mix with Mason and/or Skeeter? What had Seth's friend meant when he said it was too bad about Billy Jack? "I overslept. I'm going to go check on Mason at the hospital, then we can go."

"Oh my stars and garters! I thought he just needed stitches in his head!" she said, alarmed. "Is he all right? Why didn't you call me? You must be a nervous wreck!"

I scrunched my eyes shut. "No, he's okay. Really. And I'm okay. I'll tell you about it in a bit. How about I pick you up after I see Mason?"

"Okay . . ."

"I'll explain everything. I promise."

Maeve was in the kitchen, kneading dough on her table when I wandered out.

"Are you making homemade bread?" I asked as my stomach growled.

She laughed. "Yes, but it sounds like you need something to eat sooner. There's a coffee cake on the counter and a fresh pot of coffee."

I picked up a cake knife next to the plate and started slicing. "You're spoiling me, Maeve."

"You must be hungry after being gone so late last night."

I hesitated, then continued cutting. "Why do you say that?"

"My car is the next block over."

"I . . ."

She stopped kneading and turned around to face me. "I'm not sure what you were up to, and I'm not going to ask. But I suspect it had something to do with Mason. Am I correct?"

I studied her face for a couple of seconds.

"Something's goin' on that Mason doesn't want me to know about. Am I right?"

I could lie to her, but I didn't want to. "Yeah."

"Just be careful, Rose. Mason would be devastated if you got hurt doing something to help him."

"I know." I gave her a grim smile. "Are you going to tell him?"

"If he specifically asks if you went out last night, I won't lie to him, but otherwise I'll keep it to myself."

"Thank you." I paused. "For what it's worth. I think he's safe now."

Relief filled her eyes. "*Thank you.*"

After I got ready, she offered to watch Muffy while I went to see Mason and help Neely Kate. But she looked a bit nervous.

"I know Violet will be working over at the nursery today," she said. "What would you think about me going to help her?"

My eyes widened. "Oh."

"If you're not comfortable with it, I completely understand. I know you two aren't getting along right now."

"We're working on it," I said, "but I think it's a great idea. Violet needs the help, and even if I wasn't busy today . . . I just can't."

"I know, Rose. Give it time."

Violet and I were going to need more than time.

Once I got to the hospital, I had to get through two guards to get into Mason's room. He was on the phone and pacing when I walked up to him. He looked over at me, and a grin tugged at his lips. "I have to go," he said, then hung up, sliding his phone into the front pocket of his jeans. "You're a sight for sore eyes."

He pulled me into a hug and kissed me, showing me how much he'd missed me.

"We need to get you home," I murmured against his lips. "Soon."

"I like the sound of that. We'll have to wait and hear what Joe's found out."

Stupid me. I hadn't stopped to consider that I couldn't tell Joe or Mason what I'd found out with Skeeter last night. "Does he have any leads?"

"Last time I talked to him, no."

I tried to hide my disappointment. I had to figure out a way for Joe to discover what I already knew—who'd been out to get Mason.

"What do you have planned today?" he asked.

"Neely Kate and I are going to try to track down Dolly's ex-boyfriend so we can talk to him again."

"I don't—"

The door opened, and Mason tensed, putting himself between me and the door—the first time he'd shown how seriously he was taking this situation.

"Relax," Joe said. "It's just me."

"Did you find something?" I asked, stepping around Mason.

Joe's gaze landed on me. "No," he admitted with a sigh. "But we've got a few leads."

Crappy doodles. I really needed to figure out how to tell them.

"That's something," Mason said.

"Well, there's something else . . ." Joe didn't look too happy to admit it. "We're going to move you to a safe house."

"Where?" I asked.

Joe gave me a grim smile. "It wouldn't be a safe house if I told you, now would it?"

"Can I go with him?"

"No," both men said.

Their answer didn't surprise me. "How long will he be in hiding?"

"Until I know the threat's eliminated." Joe took a couple of steps into the room. "Rose, I need you to say goodbye to Mason and take off."

"Why?"

"We have some official matters to discuss."

I hesitated, and Mason's eyes found mine. "It's okay, Rose."

I nodded. I knew he was probably safe now. Skeeter would take care of the threat against him, if he hadn't already, but I was still nervous. I had a hunch that Gems and Dolly Parton's disappearance were connected to Mason somehow. I just couldn't put it together.

"One more thing, Rose," Joe said. "Until we know the threat is gone, you're going to have a deputy shadow."

If I was actually in danger, I would have been relieved. Instead, I had a feeling this was going to be a huge hindrance. "Shouldn't you have all your deputies working on Mason's case?"

"Assigning you a deputy *is* working on Mason's case."

"Is it Deputy Miller?"

He grinned. "The deputy's waiting outside the door for you."

Mason turned to Joe. "Can you give us a moment?"

Joe mumbled something under his breath and left the room.

Mason tugged me flush against him, wrapping an arm around my back and looking into my eyes. "Rose, it's not safe to go traipsing around Fenton County right now. I know you're hanging out with Neely Kate today, so why don't you two do something low key? Maybe you could go get pedicures, my treat."

"I'll be fine. Just come home soon, okay?"

His smile fell. "I'm not sure when I'll get to talk to you again. I won't be able to make any calls."

"Oh." I wasn't sure why I was surprised. "But—"

He lowered his mouth to mine and kissed me until I was breathless. When he finally pulled away, he said, "Don't forget me while I'm gone."

"Not likely." I gave him one last kiss. "Be safe."

"You too."

I opened the door and found Joe leaning his shoulder against the wall.

"Ready?" he asked.

"Yeah."

His grin was back. "Deputy Hoffstetter is ready to escort you."

"Deputy *Hoffstetter?*" I asked in dismay. "She hates me!"

His grin turned ornery. "Maybe so, but she'll watch you like a hawk hopin' to catch you doing something you shouldn't be doin'. I can't think of anyone more determined to watch your every move."

That's precisely what had me worried.

Chapter Twenty-Five

Deputy Abbie Lee Hoffstetter was waiting for me at the end of the hall. Her red hair was pulled back into a bun, and her hands were on her hips. She eyed me like I was a three-day-old tuna sandwich on rye.

"Well, well, well, *Ms.* Gardner," she said. She took a step toward me and stood with her feet shoulder-width apart. "You and I get to spend some quality time together." Her eyes narrowed. "Thanks for that."

I stopped in front of her and tilted my head. "I don't know why you have a bee in your bonnet about me, but I don't have time to sort it out. I have pressing issues to attend to."

"Like stirring up trouble? Chief Deputy Simmons doesn't have time to run after you, and Mr. Deveraux's currently incapacitated. Thanks to your previous bad choices, I get to babysit."

"Look, you obviously don't want to spend time with me, and I don't need you, so why don't we part ways and go about our own business? Individually."

"Not likely." Her eyes squinted to slits. "The chief deputy has assigned me this job, and as much as I detest it, I'm going to show him what a great deputy I am."

This was never gonna work. "Okay. If you insist on tagging along, let's go."

"Tagging along?" she sneered. "There's no tagging along. I'm taking you into protective custody."

"*What?*"

"Chief Deputy Simmons didn't mention that part?"

There was no way I was going anywhere with this woman. I made a dash past her and hurried down the hall, the deputy on my heels.

"Stop!"

I ran down the stairs and made a bolt for the exit. Deputy Hoffstetter caught up with me as I was opening my car door.

"You're gonna wish you hadn't done that," she said, out of breath.

"Am I under arrest?" I asked. "Because unless I'm under arrest, I think I can go wherever I want."

She grunted, her lips curling. "My job is to protect you. You're not making that easy."

"Mason should be your priority, not me. I don't need protection."

She smirked at me. "And how do you know that?"

Oh, crappy doodles. "Just a gut feeling. Now I've gotta go." I climbed inside my car and locked the door as she pulled on the handle.

"Open the door! Where are you going?"

I started the car and backed up.

"Stop that car!" she shouted, jumping in front of it to block my path.

Now what was I gonna do?

She grinned. "That's right. You're not going anywhere."

I glanced in the rearview mirror. She was wrong about that. I threw the car in reverse and drove backward. The deputy ran after me, but I found another exit and backed up past it before putting the car in drive and turning out of the parking lot.

I dug my phone out of my purse. "Neely Kate? I need you to meet me somewhere."

"Okay, where?"

I took a deep breath. "I don't know . . . Um . . . how about the parking lot of Jonah's church?"

"But I thought Jonah was out of town until Saturday. Isn't he doin' that special holiday themed televangelist Jeopardy taping?"

"He is. That's not why I'm meeting you there. I'm kind of running from the law again."

"*What?*"

I looked into the rearview mirror to see if the deputy was following me. "I'll explain when I see you."

"That's what you said this morning."

"So now I have more to tell you. Can you meet me really soon? And we need to take your car so she won't track me."

"Who?"

"Deputy Hoffstetter."

I got to the parking lot before Neely Kate, not that I was surprised. The hospital was five minutes from the church, and Neely Kate was a good twenty minutes away. I used the opportunity to call Bruce Wayne.

"Hey, Rose," he said, sounding cheerful. "Good news! Mason's call lit a fire under our penny-pinching landlord, and the fuse box is getting fixed today. What are you up to?"

"If you're at the office, you might want to be prepared for what's about to show up on our doorstep."

"What's that mean?"

"It means a deputy's probably gonna come by lookin' for me."

"What did you do?"

"Nothing. Not this time. I swear it. Someone's trying to kill Mason, and Joe's assigned a deputy to watch out for me. Only Deputy Hoffstetter thinks that means protective custody."

"Whoa, whoa," he said. "What do you mean someone is trying to kill Mason?"

I filled him in on what I knew from Joe, keeping the Skeeter part to myself, but in the last month or so, Bruce Wayne had gotten really good at reading between the lines. "How does Skeeter Malcolm play into this?"

"What are you talking about?"

"I'd heard rumors that the Lady in Black was spotted last night, but I didn't want to believe it."

I groaned. "Bruce Wayne . . ."

"You're supposed to let me help you, Rose." The hurt in his voice was like a stab in the chest.

"It's too dangerous for you, Bruce Wayne. You're on probation. You can't get mixed up in this."

"We're *partners*, Rose. The only reason you're tangled up with him is because I was stupid enough to set up that meeting. You need to let me help you."

"I'm done with him."

"The hell you are."

"I'm done with him for today, then."

"Rose." His voice was heavy with disappointment.

"He said he could help me find out who was trying to kill Mason. How could I pass that up?"

"How about letting Joe take care of it?"

"Because, officially, Joe's no closer to finding the culprits, while I found two of them last night."

"Did you tell Joe?"

"No." I swallowed. "They were Skeeter's men. They wanted to pin it on Skeeter, so he'd go to jail, and they could take over. He took care of it."

"Are you sure about that?"

"You think Skeeter's men are going to betray him and walk free?"

"That's not what I'm talking about, Rose."

"Then what?"

"How do you know Skeeter's not behind it all and duping you into thinking he's helping?"

"I had visions, Bruce Wayne."

"Did you have any visions that specifically told you Skeeter wasn't behind the attempt on Mason's life?"

I scowled. Of course, I knew there was a chance Bruce Wayne was right, but my gut instinct, which I'd learned to rely on, told me it wasn't true. "No, I guess not."

Bruce Wayne was silent for a moment. "Skeeter's bad news, Rose. Stay away from him."

"I told you. I have no plans to see him again."

"If he calls you, don't answer."

Neely Kate's car pulled into the parking lot. "Neely Kate's here, so I have to go. I just wanted to warn you about Deputy Hoffstetter."

"If you need me, *call*."

I was getting all kinds of offers for help today. "Thanks, Bruce Wayne."

Neely Kate stopped her car next to mine. I started to get out, but she shook her head and climbed out from behind the wheel. "We can't use my car, Rose. I barely made it here. Something's wrong with it."

I suppressed a groan. "Okay, we'll make this work. Surely she won't think to look for me at Billy Jack's."

"Why does Joe have her trailing you anyway? Does he not want us to visit Billy Jack?"

"No. Someone tried to kill Mason yesterday." I repeated what I'd told Bruce Wayne as I drove down side streets in an attempt to avoid Deputy Hoffstetter.

"Then what are you doing runnin' around?" she asked. "I know you don't want to spend all day cooped up with that cranky woman, but this isn't worth risking your life for, Rose. If someone's after Mason, they might be after you, too."

"Calm down. I'm safe."

"You don't know that."

"I do." Mostly. I couldn't escape the nagging feeling there was more to this.

"What were you *really* doing?" she asked in her Neely-Kate-snooping voice.

I stopped at an intersection and turned around to face her. "Honestly, Neely Kate. The less you know, the better."

She stared at me for three full seconds. "You've been running around with Skeeter Malcolm again." Her face was expressionless.

I didn't answer.

Her eyes rolled as she threw up her hands. "You have!"

"Skeeter's been set up to make the sheriff's department think that he's trying to kill Mason, but he's not."

She grabbed my hand and held tight, giving me a sympathetic look. "Oh, honey. Of course Skeeter says he's not. He wants you to keep helpin' him."

I knew both she and Bruce Wayne believed it, but I just couldn't. I pulled my hand from hers. "No, Neely Kate. He was being set up so he'd lose his crown as king of the underworld. There are a lot of people who are unhappy with how the auction got busted just after Skeeter won. Two of his men thought they could take out Skeeter and Mason all at the same time."

"And you really believe that?"

"Yes, Neely Kate. I *do*. I had visions to back it up."

She was silent for a moment. "Did you tell Joe?"

"No. I'm trying to figure out how to do that."

"Okay. We'll figure something out. Do you want to hide out somewhere so we can avoid getting caught by your deputy?"

"No." I shook my head. "Billy Jack's somehow involved in the plot to kill Mason. I just don't know how, which means the threat might still exist. Skeeter doesn't believe it, and he wants me to let it drop. But I can't." I turned toward her.

"Do you think it has anything to do with Billy Jack wanting to see me yesterday?"

"I don't know," I said. "Maybe. Maybe he knew someone was doing something to Mason's car."

"Did you tell Joe *that*?"

"Tell him what? I had a vision in Skeeter's clubhouse, and I saw some guy talking about Billy Jack when I tried to have a vision about Mason's attempted murder."

"Yeah," she sighed. "You're right. Anything else I need to know?"

I shrugged. "Maeve's helping Violet unpack inventory at the nursery today."

"Wow. I didn't see that one coming."

"I know."

We made it to Pickle Junction without getting spotted by any Fenton County deputies, and I turned down Billy Jack's gravel drive, my stomach knotting into a ball. "We need some kind of plan."

"I suggest we just show up at his doorstep and ask him why he called and then didn't show."

I stopped the truck where I'd parked last time and glanced over at Neely Kate. "Maybe you should stay in the truck."

"Why?"

"What if he's still mad, Neely Kate? I don't want you getting hurt."

"He called *me* yesterday, Rose. I'm going."

We got out of the truck and walked toward the trailer.

"His car's here," Neely Kate said, pointing to an old muscle car.

"It wasn't here last time."

"He probably had it parked in the garage behind his trailer the other day. He doesn't like to leave it out if he thinks it's gonna rain or snow," she said, walking over to the black vehicle. "Hey . . . there's a chance of snow tonight. I can't believe he'd just leave it out like that." Neely Kate peeked inside the passenger window. "The keys are in the ignition." She stood up. "There's no way he'd do that. Something's up."

"Let's see if he's home," I said, the hair standing up on the back of my neck.

"Yeah . . ."

We walked up to the front door, and Billy Jack's dogs started barking frantically. Neely Kate rapped on the front door, and we waited for a good ten seconds before Neely Kate knocked harder. The door creaked and opened, leaving a small gap.

"Oh, crap. That's not good," Neely Kate said, turning around to look at me. "He's totally paranoid. He'd never leave his door unlocked and open."

"Maybe we should call Joe," I said.

"Do you think he'd come? What are we going to tell him? That Billy Jack's car is here and he's not home?"

"I don't know. Maybe."

"Joe doesn't care about Dolly Parton." Neely Kate sucked in her bottom lip as she concentrated. Then she turned back to the door. "Billy Jack!" she called out. "Billy Jack! Are you home?"

The dogs went crazy barking, and Neely Kate pushed the door open wider. The Chihuahuas rushed out, and one attached itself to my leg.

"Again?" I muttered, shaking it off.

Neely Kate took a step over the threshold. "Billy Jack?"

"Neely Kate!" I hissed. "What do you think you're doing? Billy Jack's gonna kill you if he catches you in his trailer."

She grinned. "Then we better not get caught."

Oh crap.

I had no choice but to follow her. She stood in the center of the tiny living room, looking around.

"Something's not right, Neely Kate," I said after a moment, a shiver running down my back.

"I know."

But we'd come this far, so there was no turning back now. "Let's just look around to see if we can find something tying him to Mason."

"Like a journal entry that says, 'Dear Diary, I'm gonna kill the Assistant District Attorney today'?" Neely Kate asked sarcastically.

"Very funny." Only it wasn't. Hearing her say the words terrified me. "I don't know. Just keep an open mind. Maybe we can find out something that will help us with Dolly Parton too."

"Okay."

"You look out here, and I'll check the bedroom." I took off down the dark hall and pushed open a door to reveal a guest room that was surprisingly tidy, considering the state of the front part of the trailer. I left it and passed the bathroom before pushing open the door to what I guessed to be the master bedroom. Feet planted in the doorway, I stared inside with disbelief.

Billy Jack lay in his bed, fully clothed, with a bloody hole in his forehead, his hand gripped in a fist.

"Neely Kate . . ." I called out to her.

"Just a minute. I think I found something. Nope . . . nope, I didn't."

"Neely Kate," I said more insistently, still staring at Billy Jack's face. His eyes were wide open.

"I just found Billy Jack's porn stash. Disgusting."

"*Neely Kate!*" I yelled.

"What?"

"I found Billy Jack."

"What?" She was behind me within seconds. "Oh my God! Is he . . . ?"

"Dead? Yeah. We have to get out of here." I spun around and pushed Neely Kate toward the living room as I dug out my cell phone.

"Who are you callin'?" she asked.

"Joe. He's bound to listen now." He didn't answer, and it went to voice mail. I immediately called him back, and he answered after the first ring, sounding irritated. "Are you calling to complain about Abbie Lee?"

"No. I'm calling because Billy Jack's dead."

"Billy Jack?" he asked in confusion. "Who's Billy Jack?"

"Dolly Parton's boyfriend."

"My condolences."

"Joe! Listen to me! We just found him in his bed with a bullet hole in his forehead."

"*What?* Where's Abbie Lee?"

I cringed. This wasn't going to go well. "I lost her somehow. And Neely Kate and I went back to talk to Dolly's boyfriend."

"How'd you get in the house?"

"The door was open."

"Uh-huh."

I sighed. "Believe me or not, you need to send someone out here."

"If you're still inside that house, get out and wait in the truck. What's the address?"

I rattled off the address Neely Kate gave me as we walked to the front porch.

"You stay put," Joe said. "Someone's on the way."

Neely Kate's face was pale, and she looked like she was going to pass out. "I've never seen a murdered body before."

I didn't want to stop and think about how many I'd seen.

"Why was his hand in a fist like that?"

I shook my head. "I don't know. It looked like he was holding something."

Her eyes widened. "We have to find out what it was."

I released a sigh. She was right. "You sit here on the steps and wait for me." I was surprised she didn't argue, but she just sank down on the steps while I turned around and headed back inside.

I was scared to death as I crept up on Billy Jack's body, especially because I felt like his dark, cold eyes were staring up at me. I kneeled on the mattress next to him and leaned over and tried to see what was in his hand. I wasn't stupid enough to pry it out—it was evidence—but maybe I could get a look at it. It was a business card. I gasped when I realized what business it was for.

Gems. That couldn't be good. I tried to read the other print on the card, but it was crumpled in Billy Jack's fist.

I hurried to the front door and gulped big lungfuls of air.

"Could you see it?" Neely Kate asked. I was thankful her face had more color.

"It was a business card. For Gems."

"What does that mean?"

"I don't know, but the fact that he's holding it in a literal death grip has to mean something." I grabbed Neely Kate's arm and tugged. "Come on. Let's get you out of the cold."

I made sure she got into the truck, then walked around to the driver's side, catching a glimpse of cardboard on the backseat. "Dolly Parton's box. We plum forgot about it."

I opened the back door and lifted the lid off the box.

"What are you looking for?"

"Something to tie this together." I started riffling through the mess, finding clothes, some makeup, a toothbrush, and a book. Stuck to the paperback romance novel was a post-it note with a phone number.

I gasped and looked up into Neely Kate's face.

"What did you find?"

"This." I held up the paper.

"A phone number. Should we call it?"

"We don't have to," I said, feeling nauseated. "I know who it belongs to."

"Who?"

"Mason."

Chapter Twenty-Six

H is office number?"

"No. His cell phone."

"What was Dolly Parton doing with Mason's cell phone number?"

I sank back into the seat, tears burning my eyes. "I don't know."

"There has to be a good reason."

I shook my head. "What could it be?"

"Dolly was arrested this summer. Maybe she plea bargained, and Mason gave her his number."

I looked up at her in disbelief. "His *cell phone?*"

"I don't know," she said quietly. "I'm sorry."

I dug my phone out of my pocket.

"Who are you calling? Mason?"

I stopped. Something wasn't adding up. I knew Mason wouldn't give his number out to a criminal—not that Dolly Parton *was* a criminal—and I'd mentioned her name to him without sensing any surprise or recognition on his part. It hadn't fazed him at all to know Neely Kate and I were looking for her. "No. Not Mason." I pulled up my contacts on my phone, and Skeeter answered right away.

"What do you know about Billy Jack Peters?"

"Well, well, an undemanded call from you. We're making progress," he said with a teasing tone.

"Cut the crap, Skeeter. I just found Billy Jack dead in his bed. What do you know about that?"

Neely Kate gasped at the mention of Skeeter's name.

"What are you doing in Billy Jack's bed?" He sounded sinister.

"Ew . . ." I cringed in disgust. "Don't insult me. I wasn't *in* his bed—well other than when I kneeled on it to look at something in his hand."

"At what?" He didn't sound any happier.

"A business card. For Gems."

"I told you to stay away from Gems. And you didn't answer my question: what are you doing at Billy Jack's?"

"First, you didn't tell me to stay away from Gems, only that it's not part of the plot to kill Mason, and second, you asked what I was doing in Billy Jack's bed, not in his house."

"Answer me," he growled.

"We're still trying to find Dolly and Nikko, not that it's any of your business."

"What you do now *is* my business."

I wasn't having this argument right now. "Do you know how he's connected to Gems?"

"Since I wasn't clear enough the first few times I said it, stay away from Gems."

"Why? What's going on at Gems?"

"*Stay away from Gems.*"

"But what about Dolly Parton?"

"She ran off, Rose. Leave it at that." Then he hung up.

The hell with that. I got into the driver's seat and started the engine.

"What are you doing?" Neely Kate asked. "Joe said to stay here."

"And wait for Deputy Hoffstetter? I don't think so." I turned the truck around and headed for the highway.

"Where are we going?"

I fought back my anger. "To Gems."

"I thought Skeeter just told you to stay away."

I turned to her in surprise.

"What? He wasn't exactly whispering. I heard him." She paused. "Why on earth did you call Skeeter instead of Joe, anyway?"

"Because Skeeter seems to be the one with the answers, or at least the only one willing to share them."

"It's a bad idea, Rose, relying on him. You don't even know if he's telling the truth."

And she wasn't telling me anything I didn't already know.

"Why didn't you tell him about Dolly having Mason's phone number?"

"He doesn't need to know everything."

"So why didn't you tell Joe?"

"I don't know yet."

"Do you think Mason has done something wrong?"

I shook my head. *Mason?* I would believe it of anyone else before I believed it of him. "We don't even know if he gave it to her. What if someone else did? Also, he *did* have his phone stolen yesterday."

"You've had Dolly's box in your truck for three days, Rose."

"I know." I looked up the temporary number Mason had given me that morning, but when I called him, the phone went straight to an automated message. Tears welled in my eyes, and I fought back a sob. "He wanted to run off, Neely Kate."

"Who? *Mason?*"

"After the break-in. He was really upset, and he begged me to run off with him on Saturday—tomorrow. He wanted to go somewhere far away, and he seemed desperate to go."

Neely Kate put her hand on my arm. "I'm sure there's a rational explanation." But I heard a hitch in her voice.

"You know something." When she didn't answer, I started to freak out. "What do you know that you're not telling me?"

"Rose . . . let's go get some lunch and figure out what to do next." She paused. "And I'll tell you what little I do know."

I nodded, fighting my tears. Whatever Neely Kate knew had to be bad if she wouldn't tell me now. "Okay."

I drove to the diner we'd eaten at the day before and parked my truck behind a big rig so it couldn't be seen from the highway. Joe was gonna be ticked that we took off, but I'd rather deal with his wrath than be chained to the devil, who in this case happened to be Deputy Hoffstetter.

"What do you know?" I asked after we'd given the waitress our order.

She grimaced. "Some things are better left unknown, Rose. Especially when it's only bits and pieces."

"You said you'd tell me."

"Okay." She reached across the table and took my hand. "I was up by Mason's office one day a week ago—I thought you were there with him for lunch, so I dropped in to say hi. His secretary wasn't at her desk, so I was outside his door when I heard him . . ." Her voice trailed off, and she sounded unsure.

"Heard him doing what?"

She released a heavy breath. "I wasn't sure what I heard, Rose. I think he was on the phone because he was talking and no one was talking back. Something about money and meeting on a Friday night."

I shook my head. "That doesn't make any sense, Neely Kate."

"I agree, it didn't make any sense, but then on Monday I heard Joe talking to the DA. He mentioned Mason's name, and I heard something about bribes."

My heart skipped a beat. "You can't seriously suggest Mason is taking bribes."

"I didn't think that's what it meant at the time, but now . . . I don't know, Rose. I have no idea what's going on. But consider this: Mason said he wanted to leave tomorrow because he had something he needed to do tonight. And the owner of Gems is supposed to be showing up at the club tonight. Dolly Parton had Mason's cell phone number, and now she's missing."

I couldn't believe that Mason would knowingly do something bad.

"Has he done anything else to suggest he's in trouble?"

Tears burned my eyes. "Mason had a meeting with his boss on Wednesday, and that never happens. Skeeter even knew about it and said it was rare. Then Mason told me he thought he might lose his job."

"Rose, it doesn't look good."

"Neely Kate," I begged. "This is Mason we're talking about. *Mason.* He's one of the good guys."

She shook her head. "I don't know. I agree. It doesn't make any sense."

"What about Billy Jack? Where does he fit into this? He lied to us the last time we spoke to him."

"Yeah. You're right."

The waitress brought our food out, and we were silent for several minutes.

"Gems is the common denominator. It connects them all," I said. "Skeeter—even if he swears against it—Billy Jack, Dolly Parton . . . Mason. What's going on there?"

"I don't know."

"I'm going there tonight."

"Rose! Are you crazy? We need to tell Joe and let him handle it."

"If I tell Joe, he might arrest Mason and throw him in jail." I shook my head. "No. If Mason is really going to be at Gems, I have to be there to stop him."

"This is the craziest stunt we've ever pulled. How are we going to explain being there?"

"Not we. *Me.* You can't go back in there after your audition fiasco."

She held up her hands. "*No way.* You're not going in there alone, especially on a Friday night. You could barely handle it last time. Tonight it will be packed with men."

"I have to, Neely Kate, and I have the perfect in. My job offer."

"You're going to *dance*?"

"Shoot, no! Crystal said something about bartending."

"Do you even know how to make drinks?"

"No, but I'm sure I can download an app on my phone telling me how to make them."

"Do you have to be topless?"

"No, she said I could wear something low-cut."

She shook her head. "You never wear low-cut shirts."

I shot her a glare. "I wore a low-cut dress last night, thank you very much."

"When you were with Skeeter dressed as the Lady in Black. You can't hide your face under a veil if you work a shift at Gems. You'll be lucky if you make it through the night hiding your boobs."

"I'll do whatever I have to do for one night if it helps me save Mason. I have to talk sense into him, and I won't be able to get ahold of him beforehand because Joe put him into protective custody."

Neely Kate's mouth twisted to the side. "So Mason's caught up in *two* messes—the Gems thing *and* someone's trying to kill him. You can't ignore that Skeeter's probably tied to it too. He keeps insisting that you stay away from there."

Could I be fooled by Skeeter? He had promised to help protect Mason, but I knew he'd do whatever he had to do to advance his business. And he'd made no secret of the fact that he considered me a valuable asset. He might hide things from me on purpose for fear of how I'd react. Plus, Neely Kate was right. I couldn't ignore how adamant he'd been about getting me to stay away from Gems. As I stared into my best friend's worried face, there was one thing I was certain of: I couldn't trust anyone except Neely Kate.

She released a heavy sigh. "So you think you're just gonna show up and get a job? Then what? What's your plan?"

I frowned. "I don't know."

She shook her head. "I can't believe I'm helping you." Her mouth pursed. "After we finish lunch, we'll run by there, and you can tell them you want the job. Now we just need to figure out how I'm gonna get in."

I shook my head. "There's no way you can go back in there after what happened at your audition. They'll toss you out on your hiney."

She scowled but didn't answer. She knew I was right.

My phone rang, and I looked at the number on the screen and groaned. "It's Joe."

"You might as well answer it and get it over with," she muttered, dipping a fry in ketchup.

I cringed as I answered, prepared for yelling. Instead Joe asked in a low voice, "Where the hell are you?"

"Around."

"But not around the property of a murdered man, where I specifically asked you to stay." He paused. "It wasn't a bossy request, Rose. It was an official one. You were at a murder scene. I need your statement."

"And I'll give it to you . . . over the phone. I'm not letting that redheaded witch anywhere near me."

"What's Hilary got to do with this?" he asked in confusion.

"Not Hilary. Deputy Hoffstetter."

I could swear I heard him snort. "It's for your own protection, Rose."

I took a breath, hoping I didn't give myself away. "Did you move Mason? I tried to call the temporary number he gave me, and he's not answering."

He hesitated. "Yeah, we moved him."

"Have you figured out who tried to kill him?" I still hadn't figured out a way to tell Joe what I knew about the murder attempt, and now there was even more to tell. But now I considered holding off. If Joe kept Mason in protective custody, maybe Mason wouldn't be able to go to Gems tonight.

"I'm working on it, Rose." He sounded exhausted.

"I wasn't accusing you of anything, Joe. I know you're doing the best you can, and I appreciate it more than you know. I'm just really worried about him. I need to know that he's okay."

"I understand. And he is. I promise."

"Can I see him?" I asked. "Or at least talk to him?"

"It's safer if he doesn't contact anyone."

"Joe, I'm not anyone. *Please*. I really need to talk to him about something important."

"Then tell me what it is, and I'll pass it on to him."

I considered telling Joe about Dolly Parton having Mason's number, but I couldn't. While he wouldn't allow anyone to harm Mason, there was nothing to keep him from tossing Mason in jail if he found any evidence indicating wrongdoing on his part. "I can't."

"If you change your mind, tell Deputy Hoffstetter, and she'll pass it along."

"I'm sure she will," I said dryly.

"I've gotta go, Rose, but Deputy Hoffstetter's gonna call, and you're going to give her a statement. If you don't, I'll toss you into jail for obstruction of justice. And Mason's not going to be around to get you out."

"When you put it that way, fine." I had bigger things to worry about. Like applying for a job.

Chapter Twenty-Seven

There were only a few cars in the Gems lot when I parked the truck. Neely Kate had been coaching me the whole way there. "Okay, remember everything I told you and just go in and act confident. If you look nervous, they'll chew you up and spit you out. Tell them you've decided you want to try the bartending job and then wing it from there."

"Okay."

I got out of the truck and wiped my sweaty palms on my jeans. When I walked through the door, there wasn't a bouncer at the entrance like there had been last time. In fact, there weren't any customers either, just two girls on the stage dressed in booty shorts and tank tops.

"We're not open yet," one of the girls said. "We open at three on Fridays."

"Actually," I said, twisting my hands together in front of me until I realized what I was doing and stopped. "I was here about a job. When I was here the other day, Crystal mentioned the possibility that I could work as a bartender."

The first girl shook her head, her long dark brown ponytail shaking with it. "Mud doesn't hire girls to bartend."

"Wait," the other said, hopping down from the stage. "You were with the girl who barfed on that guy."

"Maybe . . ."

"Daisy!" she said, pulling me into a hug. "We wanted to call you, but we didn't get your number or anything. Mud said he definitely wanted to hire you."

"He did?" the girl on stage and I said at the same time.

She gave me a grin. "I bet you don't remember me. I'm Sparkle."

"Oh," I said in surprise. "You look different."

"With my shirt on?" she laughed.

A blush rose to my cheeks. "Well . . . yeah. But mostly your face. You're not wearing any makeup now." She'd been slathered in it before.

"Now I see why Mud wants her," the other woman said.

Why, did Mud have thing for women who blushed? Did he like to embarrass them? "So the job's still available?"

"Yeah, if you want it. Mud's in the back."

I took a deep breath, wondering if I should have worn something with a lower neckline. But I hadn't worn one last time, and he was apparently still interested.

I knocked on his partially open office door. "Mr. Mud?"

"Come in," he barked.

I pushed the door open and walked in, once again feeling that strange sensation of déjà vu, but I couldn't figure it out now any more than I'd been able to on my last visit. I stopped in the center of the room, and Mud looked up from his paperwork, a smile spreading across his face. "Ah, it's my mystery girl."

I didn't say anything, but he stood and started to walk around me. "Crystal said you were interested in dancing, but you're too shy. She suggested that I hire you as our bartender. I don't usually waste the girls by sticking them behind the bar, but I'm willing to give it a shot."

This was turning out better than I'd hoped, but I didn't want to come across as too eager. "What does it pay?"

"Tips, but I want to keep this one off the books. You'll get cash at the end of the night. You good with that?"

I nodded. "Yeah."

"Good. You'll start tonight."

That was a relief. "Okay."

"Since you're not dancing, you should wear a short, low-cut dress or short-shorts with a tight, low-cut T-shirt."

I was sensing a theme. As much skin as possible. "Okay. What time should I be here?"

"Around seven. That will give you enough time to learn the ropes before we get really busy."

"Thank you, Mr. Mud."

He sat down in his chair. "Just Mud," he reminded me. "And you need a name. The girls were calling you Daisy, but it doesn't fit in with the gem theme." He studied me for a moment. "How about Ruby?"

I was prepared for something stupid—after all, Skeeter had named me Lady—so I didn't have to fake my smile. "I like it."

"Wear something red to go with your name."

"Okay."

I headed back into the big room, where Sparkle was back on the stage with the other girl, who was hanging on the pole and spinning. I watched her for a moment from the back of the room, amazed that she was able to hold herself up by hooking the back of her knee around the pole even though she was spinning.

"Hey, Daisy!" Sparkle called out. "What'd he say?"

I moved closer to the stage, still watching the girl. "I got the job," I said with a grin. "Only now I'm Ruby."

"Well, welcome to Gems, Ruby," Sparkle said.

The other girl didn't look so pleased.

"When do you start?"

"Tonight. I'm supposed to be here at seven."

"You'll make good tips because it's Friday night," Sparkle said.

"I'm surprised he's having her start tonight with everything else goin' on," the other girl said in a low voice.

"Diamond," she hissed.

Was she talking about the owner showing up? I wanted to ask why tonight was so significant, but decided to play ignorant. For now. "Mud told me to wear shorts or a short dress. Which is better?"

"That's tricky," Sparkle said as the other girl climbed down from the pole. "Because you're not planning on taking anything off."

"Just go with shorts," Diamond said, sounding bored. She squatted on the stage in front of me, spreading her legs wide. "How good are you at keeping your mouth shut?"

My breath caught in my throat, and I tried to look away from her crotch as I forced out, "I'm not a gossip, and I'm loyal. I may be naïve, but I know things go on in places like this that shouldn't be repeated outside these walls."

She grinned, but it didn't make her look any friendlier. "Then you'll fit in just fine. Welcome to Gems." Then she stood and walked backstage, her booty swinging as she walked.

"Oh," Sparkle said, sounding excited. "You've already made points with Diamond. You're one step ahead of the game."

"What does that mean?"

"Diamond's sleeping with the owner."

"Oh."

"Yeah, she's nervous because he's coming tonight for some special meeting. He likes things to run just so, and the thought of a new person working tonight has her on edge."

"But isn't Mud in charge?"

"Yeah, but Diamond always pays for it if things don't go well."

I went out the front door, worried that Diamond was going to have to get a loan to pay for all the things that would probably go wrong tonight.

I expected Neely Kate to be happier about my new job, but she sulked instead. "You can't do this without me. Maybe I can wear a wig and go in disguise."

"You think you're going in there *alone?*" I shook my head. "I'll be working."

"Then I'll sit in the parking lot in case you need me."

I agreed to her plan. It would be comforting to know she was close by.

"I know what you need," I said. "Let's get you some ice cream. I think it's safe for me to go back to the Burger Shack again since Eric . . ."

"Took a long nap in his car?"

"That seems strange, don't you think?" I asked. "For him to show up dead just when the sheriff deputies go to question him?"

She shrugged. "Not so strange. He probably knew he was in a heap of trouble for what he did before that auction, and he was too chicken to face it. It happens all the time."

"Maybe . . . but the bottom line is that we can get ice cream at your favorite place."

"What about Deputy Hoffstetter? Aren't you hiding out from her?"

"She hasn't called yet, but how about I call her so we can deliver our statements? Then I can tell her to come pick me up in Tahoe Junction."

"Tahoe Junction is over twenty miles north."

I grinned. "I know."

"You're more wicked than I thought, Rose Gardner," she teased.

"Since I'm working at Gems tonight, maybe that's a good thing."

Abbie Lee Hoffstetter was fit to be tied when I called her, and my ears burned from the heap of insults she flung at me. "When I find you, I'm going to make you pay for making me look bad in front of the chief deputy."

"That's not exactly making me want to cooperate, Deputy Hoffstetter."

"I'm a law enforcement official. Trust me. I'll find you. You don't need to tell me where you are."

Not if I could help it. "I called to give you my statement. Do you want it or not?"

"You're damn straight I do. Then when we're done, I'm coming for you."

It didn't take long for me to give my statement, and then Neely Kate took the phone and gave hers. When she was finishing, I said loud enough for the deputy to hear, "You're sure the Chick-a-Dilly in Tahoe Junction is just around the corner?"

Neely Kate gave me an evil grin. "Rose! Shhhh!!!" Then she told the deputy goodbye. "That should keep her busy for a while."

"Let's just hope it's long enough."

We got Neely Kate's ice cream and headed to her house. I needed clothes for my shift at Gems, and Neely Kate insisted she had something for me to wear. I certainly didn't have the wardrobe to supply my uniform, and I couldn't risk a shopping trip. When we got to her house, I parked the truck in her garage so Deputy Hoffstetter wouldn't see it from the road in case she drove by.

"What are you going to say to Ronnie about being gone tonight?"

"It's poker night. He's not even coming home after work. He'll never know I'm gone."

Neely Kate offered to make us one of her gourmet dinners before we left for Gems, but I knew my nervous stomach couldn't handle it. Instead, I suggested I make some buttered noodles.

After we ate, I got ready. Neely Kate curled my hair, but I drew the line when it came to my makeup. It was bad enough I was wearing short-shorts and a show-every-curve red tank top, in December no less. I wasn't about to put on enough eye makeup to help me look like a hooker.

"You have to play the part, Rose."

"No," I insisted. "I only have to play the part of a *bartender*, and only until I find Mason and figure out what he's doin' and stop him."

"You don't even know if he's gonna show," she said. "How long are you gonna stay in there if he doesn't? And if he does show, what are you gonna do then?"

"I don't know. One way or the other I'm gonna get some kind of answers before I leave that strip club. Honestly, I hope he doesn't show, either because Joe's got him locked up somewhere, or because this was all a big misunderstanding. But just in case it's not, I'm going."

She gave me a hug and squeezed me tight. "I understand. If it was Ronnie, I'd do exactly the same thing."

"And if it was Ronnie, I'd help you too."

We left around six-thirty, and just on the other side of Henryetta, I realized I'd been driving all over creation and my truck needed gas. When I told Neely Kate I had to stop, she was relieved.

"Who knows how long I'll be sitting in the truck waiting for you? I'll run in and get some snacks and go to the bathroom while you're pumping the gas."

After I parked at the gas station, I inserted my debit card into the pump, my bare legs freezing in the cold wind. As I watched Neely Kate go into the convenience store, it struck me again that I had no idea what I was getting myself into . . . and I wasn't talking about the stripping. Something was going on at Gems, and the only person who knew I was going to be there was Neely Kate. And while Neely Kate was resourceful, I wasn't sure she'd be able to get me out of trouble if trouble came my way.

Before I could change my mind, I grabbed my phone out of my pocket and called Skeeter.

"Twice in one day. You must really miss me."

"I got that part-time job I was telling you about. I start tonight."

He paused and lowered his voice, a hint of controlled anger in his voice. "At my competition?"

I realized there must be someone close by him that he didn't want to know what he was talking about. "I heard the owner's going to show up later."

"You don't say." He was quiet for a moment, and then I heard traffic sounds in the background. "I thought I told you to stay away."

"This whole thing started with my search for Dolly Parton, and I still haven't found her."

He paused for a second. "Why are you really doing this?"

"I have my reasons."

He was quiet for so long that I wondered if he'd hung up on me, but he finally said, "Do you think you can handle it?"

I breathed a sigh of relief. "My friend's going to be hanging around."

"The two of you girls?" He sounded unimpressed.

"Hey, girl power. Don't knock it."

"Don't forget your friend disappeared while working there. There's no reason for you to go at all," he said. "I could just send Jed and Merv to check it out."

"What if someone recognizes them? Then we might not get anything at all. Besides, I can force a vision if I need to get more information."

"But what if someone recognizes *you?* I'd rather Jed get nabbed than you."

"No," I said, glancing at the building, thankful Neely Kate was still inside. The less anyone knew about Mason's possible involvement, the better. "I'm doing this."

He was silent for several seconds. "You've proven yourself resourceful on several occasions," he said, not necessarily sounding happy about it. "You're determined to do this, aren't you?"

"Yes."

"When are you supposed to show up?"

"At seven. In fifteen minutes."

"Check in with me by ten. If I haven't heard from you, I'm sending Jed to check on you."

Oddly enough, I found that reassuring.

Chapter Twenty-Eight

I had no idea that so many men in Fenton County were obsessed with breasts. But then again, Joe had told me that there were twenty-five thousand residents in the county—if half were male, I supposed thirty men was still a low percentage.

I'd been behind the bar for nearly two hours, and while I wasn't topless, I still got plenty of men checking out my chest. It was a good thing I wore Neely Kate's pushup bra to give them something to look at.

For the most part, the men sat at tables, staring at the stage. The girls took turns dancing on the pole, stripping off their multiple layers of underwear until all that was left was a tiny G-string.

Some of the men noticed me behind the bar and came to the counter to get drinks instead of letting the girls who were walking around get them. Most of them ordered beer, but some of them ordered drinks I'd never heard of, let alone knew how to make. My plan to use an app on my phone didn't pan out. The first time I pulled it out, I was told phones weren't allowed. When I asked the guy I was working with how to make a bourbon neat, he shot me an irritated scowl. "Figure it out yourself."

The bourbon was easy enough, but some of the other drinks were tougher. When I figured out that the men didn't care, I started creating my own concoctions.

A bearded man who looked to be in his forties sidled up to the bar. "Hey, sugar. Can you get me a drink, then come sit on my lap?"

I shot him a scowl. "I'll get you the drink. Someone else can sit on your lap." I got him his beer and watched him shuffle back to his table.

"You'll never make any money that way," Kip, the bartender who was working with me, said.

I tried not to look surprised. In addition to my drink recipe inquiries, I'd been asking leading questions during some of our lulls, and he'd been annoyingly tight-lipped.

"Some men might get off on you being cold, but most of them are here because they're lonely."

"You're kidding."

"Nope. Some guys will pay girls just to sit and talk to 'em. But the guys who go off to the little rooms are lookin' for more than that."

"What little rooms?"

He laughed. "You really don't know anything about this place, do you?"

"That's why I'm back here. I'm trying to learn."

He gave me a condescending grin. "Is that why you think you're back here?"

What did that mean?

He shook his head with a smirk, then leaned his mouth close to my ear. "You see how some of the girls are dancing on guys' laps?"

I'd spent most of my night trying not to notice. "Yeah."

"If a guy pays more, she'll take him to a VIP room."

"And what happens in those?"

"It depends on who's dancing and who's asking." He winked. "On Friday nights, from eleven until two a.m. or so, we see more action in those rooms than on any other night."

"Why?"

He leaned into my side and reached behind me to cup my butt cheek. "Smart girls don't ask questions here."

I elbowed him as hard as I could. He grabbed his side, doubling over. "I think smart girls do ask questions," I said. "Otherwise I wouldn't have known you should have paid me twenty dollars to do that."

He laughed. "Maybe there's hope for you yet. But for the record—" his eyebrows rose playfully, "I would have needed a whole lot more than that for twenty dollars."

I was never gonna let any man here get close enough for me to have to remember that piece of advice.

The crowd got bigger over the next hour, and I kept busy getting beers and making my bad mixed drinks. Amazingly enough, I'd started to get the hang of working behind the bar, even if my drinks seemed be getting worse as the night wore on.

The music changed, and a new dancer emerged on the stage. She wore a sequined, bedazzled red bra and a black wrap-around skirt. When she started her routine, it was apparent she was a real dancer. Her moves were fluid and graceful, yet inherently seductive. Every man in the room watched as she put her back to the pole, grabbed it overhead, and arched her pelvis out. I'd seen the other three girls working the place do it all night long. With them, it had looked gross and tasteless, but this dancer was classy—which seemed like an oxymoron in this place—and she was successfully seducing the room.

She spun her body under her arms and moved to the other side of the pole, unknotting the skirt's tie at her hips when she looked up, her long brown hair bouncing around her shoulders.

I'd seen her somewhere before. Where?

Kip leaned into my ear, raising his voice to be heard over the music. "Diamond brings the boys to the yard. And a few girls too."

Diamond? She looked nothing like the woman I'd seen on the stage that morning. While she hadn't looked girl-next-door, she hadn't looked like this siren currently entrancing a room full of men.

"That's why the boss likes her."

Then it hit me why I always experienced déjà vu in the office—Diamond was the woman from my vision in Billy Jack's trailer. They'd been in the office at Gems.

"Ruby, we're out of ice." Kip handed me a bucket. "There's an ice machine in the back. Go get some."

I took the container and headed into the back room, thankful that I had a legitimate excuse to have a private place to text Skeeter. I pulled my cell phone out of my back pocket and cringed when I saw the time on my phone: 10:03. I hoped Skeeter hadn't sent Jed, since Mason still hadn't shown up, and I still hadn't found out anything really useful. While I still wanted to find Dolly Parton, my top priority was Mason. I sent a quick text.

This is my first chance to text you. The owner will be here later. The bartender says lots of business takes place in VIP rooms between 11–2 on Friday nights.

I wasn't sure what he'd make of it, but I knew it couldn't be a coincidence that Dolly Parton and Nikko had disappeared on a Friday night. Had they seen or heard something in one of the private rooms? Maybe from the owner?

Skeeter texted back immediately. *Let me know when he's there. Jed's close on standby.*

"Where's that ice, Ruby?" Kip shouted.

I jumped and looked toward the door, wondering if he'd seen me on my phone, but all I could see was the back of the bar. "Coming!" I scooped the ice with one hand while texting Skeeter *Okay* with the other.

I sent Neely Kate a text next. *I'm okay. No need to worry.*

I'd nearly filled the bucket, and she still hadn't answered. She was parked in the dirt track lot behind the club. Had someone found her? But just as I was close to a full-blown panic, my phone vibrated with her response. *Okay. I fell asleep.*

I stuffed my phone in my front pocket and hefted the bucket up on my hip. When I carried it out front, Kip pointed to a bin where I could pour it. "Took you long enough."

"Sorry."

The cooler was already over half full, so when I finished pouring the ice in, it was overflowing.

"Why did we need more ice?" I asked. "We've mostly sold draft beer."

Kip's lips curled into a menacing grin, and he tapped my nose. "Remember what I said about smart girls asking questions. Are you a smart one or a stupid one?"

Fear slithered up my back and settled into the nape of my neck. "I'm not trying to be hard-headed, Kip. I just want to do a good job so Mud will be happy he hired me."

"Honey, you could screw up every order you take tonight, and Mud would be happy."

While that was probably supposed to be reassuring, it was anything but. I couldn't think of a single reason for the man's approval that didn't give me the creeps.

Diamond was still dancing, and I found myself mesmerized again. I dragged my eyes from her and worked on filling more beer orders. When I glanced up at the door, I saw two men talking to the bouncer. He pointed to a table in a dark corner by the door. The room was full of men, so it took a second to figure out why they'd grabbed my attention. Then I came up with two reasons.

First, they were the only men in the room who weren't paying attention to the woman on stage. And two, one of the guys was Rich Lowry, one of the men from Skeeter's meeting.

I couldn't think of a single reason why Skeeter would send Rich Lowry to check on me—from what Jed had told me, he was bad news on a silver platter. Which meant Rich was probably in cahoots with the owner of Gems. I had no idea if his being here had anything to do with Mason, but I planned to find out.

I hurried over to Kip. "I want to take those guys' orders." I pointed toward their table, but kept my hand below the counter.

His eyebrows rose. "Once you step around the counter, you become fair game, Ruby."

I took a deep breath. Would I get information from them if I served them drinks? I was bound to get more than if I kept hiding back here.

I gave a nervous shrug, and he laughed, shaking his head. "Go ahead."

One of the other girls was already working her way back to Rich's table. She shot me a dirty look when she realized where I was headed and that I was going to beat her. I was breathless by the time I reached the edge of the small table.

Both of the men stared up at me, and a grin stretched Rich's mouth. "You're new."

So *he* wasn't new. I put my hand on my hip and tried to give him a suggestive smile. It felt more awkward than sexy, but hopefully they wouldn't notice. "Tonight's my first night."

"You don't say?" the other guy said, scooting back in his seat and spreading his legs slightly. "I'd love to show you the ropes."

Disgusting. But I was scared to death. Jed had called Rich a sadistic bastard, and while I hoped the bouncers would keep him from hurting me, I couldn't be sure. What in the world was I doing? But it was too late to tuck tail and run. I'd already committed to this. I was good and stuck. I forced a laugh and let my hand drop from my hip to my side. "Let's get your drinks first."

Rich's dark eyes were glued to my chest. If his interest helped me get information, I'd send a personal thank you note to the creator of the pushup bra. Especially if his eyes were the only part of him that touched me. As though he sensed me watching him, his gaze lifted to my face.

I smiled slightly and tilted my head to the side. "That's on the menu for later. Right now it's just drinks, gentlemen." Where in creation had that come from?

His grin spread, and his gaze reminded me of a bobcat hunting its prey. "A scotch on the rocks."

"A beer," the other guy said, but my eyes were locked with Rich's. He was obviously the top dog at the table, and I wasn't about to waste time on the small fries.

I put my hand on my hip again, trying to hide the fact that it was shaking. "I'll be right back." I sounded way more confident than I felt, which had to be a good thing.

"And we'll be right here waiting," Rich said, his eyes on my booty as I walked away.

I went behind the counter, and Kip wandered over to me. "I watched you out there. You did good. I'll show you how to make his drink."

His about-face made me suspicious. "You've refused to help me with drinks again and again tonight. Why now? Why him?"

"He's special." He waggled his eyebrows. "And if you keep in good with him, you won't need to know how to bartend."

I didn't tell him that I didn't plan to make a habit out of this. Especially with Rich Lowry.

He grabbed a glass and scooped it into the ice bin, and I turned my back to him, facing the back wall as I grabbed a mug for the beer. Making sure Kip wasn't watching, I sent a text to Skeeter as quickly as I could.

Lowry's here.

I stuffed my phone back into my pocket and returned to the counter.

"You're a lot like Sapphire, a girl who worked here until last week." Kip watched me with an intense gaze that made me worry he'd seen my phone.

My heart jump-started into overdrive, but I tried to look confused. "How so?"

"She liked powerful men too. Most of the girls are afraid of 'em." He picked up a bottle of scotch and poured it into a glass full of ice. "This is why we needed more ice, by the way. Most of the high-rollers show up right around now."

"There're high rollers in Fenton County?" I asked in shock as I pulled the draft beer.

"They're not all from Fenton County. We get customers from Louisiana and the neighboring counties too."

Considering we were less than thirty minutes from the state line, that shouldn't have surprised me.

Kip handed me the two glasses. "Ask them if they want to put the drinks on their tab. Most men have to pay per drink, so it will show them *you* know they're special."

"Why are you helping me?"

"Keeping them happy is good for business. But Ruby," he leaned into my ear, "just remember: be careful when you play with fire, or you're liable to get burned."

"Thanks," I mumbled as I headed for their table. What kind of fire was I headed into?

I set their drinks on the table. "Would you gentlemen like to put these on a tab?"

"She thinks I'm a gentleman." Rich laughed, sending chills down my spine. "Yes, darlin', I *do* want to put it on my tab so I can save all my cash for you." He put a hundred-dollar bill on the table.

I fought my rising panic. He expected a lap dance, but there was no way I was gonna give it to him. Instead, I gave him a smile, hoping I didn't look as nervous as I felt. "That's too much."

He laughed again, turning to his friend. "She *is* new." Then they both laughed together.

A new group of men appeared in the door, and it was easy to see that they fit Kip's high-roller profile too. The bouncer sent them toward Rich's table. I started to walk toward them once they sat down, but Rich grabbed my wrist and jerked me back.

I looked down into his narrowed eyes. "I saw you first, sweetheart, and that makes you mine."

"The girls here dance for everyone," I forced out, trying not to show my fear.

"Not tonight." His fingers dug in tight, and I knew I wasn't getting loose until Rich was ready to let me go. I'd seen men grab other dancers throughout the night, and a bouncer always showed up in seconds to make sure the guy knew he couldn't touch a girl without her permission. But the bouncer turned his back after casting a glance at us.

So this was what it meant to play with fire. The rules didn't apply to these guys.

I leaned forward so my face was closer to his. "Sugar, a girl needs to pay the bills."

Rich nodded his head toward his friend, and the guy put two more hundreds on the table. "This cover it?"

"I'm new," I said, sounding breathless, to my chagrin. "I'm not sure what that means."

A wicked grin stretched across his face, and his free hand landed on my waist, slowly sliding down my hip. "It means you're mine for thirty minutes in a VIP room."

"I think I'll need at least another couple hundred," I said. "I bet I'm your first brand-new girl. That has to mean something."

I thought that would make him change his mind, but he seemed even more excited. "Okay. But first you dance for me here." He released my wrist but kept his hand on my butt.

Oh, crappy doodles.

Out of the corner of my eye, I saw a man with dark blond hair walk through the front door. Unlike all the other men who had entered the club, he waited next to the bouncer. Heart in my throat, I turned slightly, nearly gasping when I realized it was Mason.

"I see you've met Ruby," Mud said from behind me, and I wasn't sure whether I'd earned a reprieve, or if I was in even deeper trouble. I could only imagine what Mason would do if he knew what I was up to, and it wouldn't be good for either of us.

Rich's eyes remained on me, a smile tugging the corners of his lips. "Ruby and I were just getting acquainted."

"I knew you'd like her, but she'll have to wait until after business. He's here."

Rich's eyes turned dark. "Already?"

Mud tilted his head toward the door. "Yes." Then he walked toward his new guest.

Rich pulled me closer and lifted the hem of my tank top, running his rough hand over my stomach before looking up at my face. "Wait for me, Ruby. I'm looking forward to really getting to know you."

My breath stuck in my throat as I waited for Mason to storm over and possibly get us both killed. My only hope was twofold—one, that my back was to him and he wouldn't recognize me, and two, that this would the last place Mason would expect to see me.

I didn't say anything as Rich got to his feet, still staring into my face. For one horrified second I thought he was going to kiss me, but he bent his mouth to my ear.

"I'm looking forward to later."

I shivered from fear, but he laughed as he lifted his head. "McDonald, keep an eye on her."

"Got it," his friend said.

I watched Rich strut to the door that led to the office and the entrance to the girls' dressing room, trailing behind Mason and the club's manager.

I hurried back behind the bar, trying to gather my wits together, torn between running as far from this place as possible and figuring out a way to find out where the three of them went and what they were discussing.

"Lowry's comin' on strong," Kip said, "even for him. Mud was right."

I looked up at him, stuffing down my panic. "Right about what?"

"Rich likes a certain type of girl, and you fit the bill."

"What? Brown hair?"

He laughed. "Actually, yeah, that's part of it. Long brown hair, not too skinny but not too stacked either. But it's more than that. He likes 'em a little classy but not overly done up."

"Girl next door," I finished.

"Yeah."

"And he always gets what he wants, right?"

"*Anything* he wants. The sooner you accept that, the better off you'll be—financially and otherwise."

Now it made sense why Mud had been so interested in hiring me. "We got interrupted. He had to go meet someone. Why didn't his friend go with him?"

"His friend isn't important enough to meet the owner."

Mason was meeting the owner. That couldn't be good. "The owner?"

"They meet every Friday night, and then Lowry meets men in the VIP rooms later. But something different's going on tonight. That guy at the front door is new."

I shot a look of surprise up at him. I'd been peppering him with questions, forgetting his rule about smart girls. So what did it mean that he was actually answering me?

He shrugged, guessing the source of my confusion. "Lowry picked you. That means you're in. The way he's taken with you, he'll probably have you with him for some of his meetings."

"Did Sapphire sit in on some of his meetings?"

"Only the last night she was here. Lowry didn't like her as much as he seems to like you."

"Because she wasn't his usual type?" I asked.

"Plus, she was a little bit too eager to suit him. But the man has his needs, and he couldn't have Diamond because she belongs to the owner."

I hated the way he talked about us like we were property. But I had more pressing concerns than his misogynistic attitude.

I had to figure out how to get Mason out of here.

Chapter Twenty-Nine

I have to go to the bathroom," I said.

"Now?" Kip groaned.

"Yes."

He pointed to the door Mason had just disappeared through. "It's in that hallway. Hurry."

I circled the counter, and Rich's friend, McDonald, watched as I went through the door to the backstage area.

The second door on the left was marked "Ladies." I ducked inside the single bathroom and pulled out my phone. There was a text from Skeeter.

Get the hell out of there.

I wasn't going anywhere. Not yet.

I wasn't sure what to do, so I called my best friend. "He's here, Neely Kate."

"Mason?"

"Yeah." My voice broke as it finally sank in why he was here.

"Oh, honey. I'm so sorry."

"He's somewhere in the back with Mud, one of Skeeter's guys, and the owner. I don't know what to do."

"There's nothing *to* do. You can't stop him. Just walk out the back door and let's go home."

"I can't, Neely Kate. It's Mason!"

"Rose . . ."

"No! Something doesn't make sense. If the owner of Gems is meeting with Mason right now, and Mason is taking bribes from him, why were Skeeter's guys trying to kill him?"

"You saw visions of *Skeeter's* men. Isn't it obvious? Skeeter's behind it."

"No." I shook my head. "He promised me if I helped him that he wouldn't hurt Mason."

"Rose, he lied to you. Why does that surprise you? He's a hardened criminal."

I pressed my back against the door and closed my eyes.

There was a knock on the door behind me, and I jumped.

"I gotta take a leak!" one of the dancers shouted.

"Just a minute!" I called out to her.

"Rose," Neely Kate said. "I'm beggin' you. Come out and let me take you home."

Part of me said she was right. There was nothing I could do. This was what Mason had chosen. But I couldn't wrap my head around the why of it. I knew him. Mason would *never* take bribes. There was something going on here I didn't understand. What on earth would motivate Mason to throw everything away?

What if it somehow had to do with me?

"I'm not leavin' yet."

The phone vibrated almost immediately after I hung up. Skeeter. I declined the call and seconds later Skeeter sent a text.

You get your ass out of that building or Jed's busting in to get you.

I texted back. *I can't!*

Give me one good reason why not.

Mason's here.

There was nearly a ten-second pause. *You have fifteen minutes.*

Shit.

The dancer pounded on the door again. "Come *on!*"

I shoved my phone in my pocket and opened the door. One of the dancers I hadn't met yet was in the hallway, fuming.

"How long's it take to pee?"

"Sorry." I tried to sound sheepish.

She brushed my shoulder as she went into the bathroom.

I headed back to the bar, and McDonald watched my every move. When I got behind the counter, Kip looked pissed.

"Where the hell have you been?"

"I told you," I said, trying not to sound defensive. "I had to go to the bathroom."

"Well, you've been summoned, and now you're late."

"Summoned?" I squeaked out.

Kip pointed to McDonald. "He's requested you."

"Oh."

He leered at me as I walked over to his table.

"There you are, baby." He patted the chair next to him. "Why don't you keep me company?"

I gave him a tight smile. "I thought I was supposed to wait for your friend."

"He wants me to keep an eye on you, and I can't think of a better way."

"I can't be gone too long from behind the bar." I nodded my head to the side. "We're short-staffed and all."

His grin turned menacing. "Why don't you ask the last bartender how disobeying worked out for him?"

I froze and grew light-headed. It was obvious he was talking about Nikko. I had to calm down and think this through carefully. I forced a sweet smile. "I'm not disobeying, sugar. It's just that we're so busy tonight, and I figure your friend is going to be gone awhile."

He tilted his head to the side, putting a toothpick in the side of his mouth. "Maybe not so long."

"Oh?" I asked, trying to keep my tone light. "I would think an important man like him would need lots of time for business."

A smirk spread across his face as he half-shrugged. "Turns out things ain't what we thought they would be."

I sat down in the chair and leaned toward him, partially because my legs had begun to shake, and partially because I wanted to look way more friendly than I was feeling at the moment. Two people had disappeared only a week ago, probably for secrets they'd uncovered in this place. I didn't want to end up like them, but I had a feeling Mason was in serious trouble, and I wasn't about to leave him in a lurch. "You don't say?"

His eyes narrowed. "You seem awful interested in Lowry's business."

"I love powerful men, and I knew the moment you and your friend walked into the joint that you fit the bill. I'm eager to get him into the VIP room."

His eyes glittered. "Don't you worry." He reached over and trailed a finger down my cheek. "Rich needs to help his associate deal with some unpleasant baggage, then he'll be back for you."

Unpleasant baggage?

I stuffed down my panic. I had to find Mason, but first I had to think of some excuse to get away from the table. I noticed his beer was over half-empty. "Let me get you a refill, sugar," I said as I stood.

"Sounds good."

On the way back to the bar, I racked my brain for an excuse to head to the back area. As I grabbed a fresh mug and got McDonald's beer, my gaze drifted to the stage. One of the girls from earlier in the night was dancing, and there was no sign of Diamond.

"I want to dance," I blurted out to Kip.

"Really?" Kip asked in shock.

There was no way I was getting on that stage, but that was need-to-know information. And Kip didn't need to know. The dressing room was through the door to the back, so this could be my only shot. I turned to him and nodded. "Yeah."

"Do you even have any experience? It's Friday night, and the best girls work the stage."

My gaze drifted to McDonald. "I bet those two guys would love to see me dance." I glanced up at Kip and waited. The company policy seemed to be to keep them happy. I hoped it would work in my favor.

Kip studied me as though trying to figure out why I'd so drastically changed my mind in such a short period of time. Then he released his breath, his eyebrows lifted. "I'll need to clear it with Mud first, and he's in his meeting."

I couldn't afford to wait. "I don't have anything to wear. Can I go back and see if there's anything that will work?"

He laughed. "You'll have to get one of the other girls to share, and good luck with that." He looked around the room. "We've got a breather here, so why don't you take McDonald his beer and then run back there to check it out. But get your ass back here pronto. This lull won't last long."

"Okay." I took McDonald his beer and set it in front of him. When I started to turn around after grabbing his old glass, he wrapped his hand around my wrist.

"What's your hurry?"

"I have a special surprise for you." When he continued to hold on, I added, "On the stage."

He chuckled. "Be sure to wait for Lowry to get back. He's gonna wanna see."

I winked. "Don't worry. He'll be plenty surprised." I was sure Skeeter had a thing or two in store for Rich Lowry.

McDonald dropped his hold. "Then you best get going."

I dropped the mug off with the pile of empty glasses behind the bar.

"Five minutes, Ruby," Kip called after me as I hurried toward the backstage area.

Once I was behind the door, I stood in the hall and tried to figure out what to do next. Even if I found the room where Mason was, how would I get him out? Shoot, for all I knew, Mason wasn't the unnecessary baggage McDonald was talking about. But I couldn't take the chance. At the very least, I had to make sure he was safe.

The music from the bar filled the hallway, and I wondered how I was going to find him. I suspected he was in a room back here, but the music was so loud it was going to be difficult to eavesdrop.

I ignored the restrooms, and the dressing room seemed too unlikely to waste time on. Mud's office was at the end of the hall, but another short hallway intersected it. When I pressed my ear to the closed office door, I didn't hear voices. That left two doors—one to the left, which I presumed led outside, and another to the right. When I put my ear to that door, I heard the murmur of voices. I covered my left ear to drown out the music from the other room, closing my eyes to help my brain concentrate.

Mud's voice rose. "He knows too much."

"You're an employee here. Don't forget your place," a low male voice said, and the hairs on the back of my neck stood on end. I'd heard that voice before. I just couldn't place it.

"You can all blame each other later. Right now we have to figure out what to do with him," Lowry said.

"What the hell happened to our arrangement?" Mason asked. "I've lived up to my end of the bargain. I dropped the damned charges. Now you live up to yours. Where's the cash?"

My heart sank. Mason really *had* accepted a bribe. I'd hoped that this was all a misunderstanding, but he'd just admitted to it.

"That was before," the mystery man said. "Before I knew you were setting us up."

"What the hell are you talking about?" Mason asked, sounding indignant.

"Nikko." The room was silent before the man spoke again. "We know he was feeding you information."

"You're wrong."

"He told us, Deveraux!" I heard a loud bang, and I jumped. "It took us a few days to break him, but he sang like a canary."

I took a breath to calm down. Mason *was* in serious trouble. My heart hammered in my chest as I tugged my phone out of my pocket, my fingers shaky. I pulled up Joe's number and had just pressed send when someone grabbed my lower arm, his fingers digging painfully into my flesh.

I screeched in fright and lost my grip on the phone. Joe called out "Rose?" as it fell, but when it hit the tile floor, the screen shattered and went dark.

I looked up into the angry face of one of the bouncers. "What do you think you're doing?"

"I got lost," I blurted out. "I'm looking for the dressing room."

"Who were you calling?"

"No one. I was pullin' up MapQuest."

"To find the dressing room?" He squatted and picked up my phone, still holding my arm in a death grip.

I considered bolting, but his bulky frame blocked my escape. "I need to get back to the bar. Kip's gonna wonder where I am."

"You're not goin' anywhere." He tugged my arm with one hand while reaching for the doorknob with the other. "If you're so interested in what's goin' on in that room, how about we let you have a front-row seat."

"No, that's okay," I stammered, trying to pull free. "I don't want to bother them."

"No. I insist." He grinned and threw the door open, dragging me inside. "Look what I found snoopin' around outside the door."

Four people looked up from a small table, their eyes widening in surprise, but Mason easily looked the most startled. I knew and expected to see three of the men—Rich Lowry, Mud, and Mason—but the fourth face shocked me.

The missing veterinarian who'd master-minded the robberies to outbid Skeeter.

Mick Gentry.

Chapter Thirty

W ell, well, well," Mick said, leaning his elbows on the table. "What have we here?"

The bouncer released his grasp and gave me a tiny shove. I stumbled further into the small room, then froze, unsure of what to do. They were sitting at a rectangular table, taking up four of the eight chairs. Mick sat at the head of the table with Mud and Lowry on one side, Mason on the other.

"Who is she?" Mick asked.

Mud's face paled. "She's a new hire. She's taking Sapphire's place."

"Guess she takes *filling in* seriously, including hanging out in places where she doesn't belong."

Mason's hand, which was resting on the table, tightened into a fist, but I ignored him and kept my gaze on Mick.

Mick sat back in his chair. "What's your name, doll?"

I lifted my chin. "Daisy."

"Daisy what?"

"Daisy Miller."

"What are you doing snoopin' outside my door, Daisy Miller?"

"I wasn't snoopin', I swear. It's my first night, and I got lost."

The bouncer shook his head. "With your ear pressed against the door?"

I shrugged. "I tripped." I hoped I was convincing, but I was pretty sure it was gonna take a miracle to save me.

"What are you really doin' here?" Mick asked.

Mason shifted in his seat.

"I'm looking for Dolly Parton Parker."

"Who?"

"Sapphire."

He shrugged. "She's not here."

"Yeah, I figured that out." I took a step backward. "So I guess I'll be goin' then."

Mick shook his head. "No. You'll stay."

I couldn't panic. Mason and I weren't necessarily doomed. I'd called Joe, so he might show up to save us, but he had no idea that I was in trouble or even where I was. My best hope was Jed. Skeeter said he'd send him after fifteen minutes, but now I worried about Jed taking on all of the men in the club. But then again, Skeeter wasn't stupid and neither was Jed. Now that they knew Rich Lowry was present, I suspected they'd come prepared.

"What do you want to do?" Lowry asked.

"Take them both out back and deal with it."

I grimaced. "Look, I'm sorry for the misunderstanding—" I pointed my thumb to the now closed door "but Kip really needs me out front."

"Sorry, Daisy." Mick chuckled. "Your position is about to be terminated."

The full impact of his words sunk in. Mason pushed his chair back and stood, his back tense. Anger burned in his eyes as he looked from the other men to me, but Mud pulled out a gun and aimed it at him.

"Have a seat, Deveraux."

"Wait," I said, lifting my hands in surrender. "I can help you! Just don't shoot him."

Mick laughed. "How can *you* possibly help *me?*"

"Aren't you trying to get even with Skeeter and take his place? Isn't that what all of this is about?"

Mick's eyebrows lifted in surprise, but I had Mason's attention as well.

Mick leaned his elbow on the table. "Why would you think that?"

"I know things. Tell Mud to put his gun away, and I'll tell them to you."

Mick studied me for several seconds. "Deveraux, have a seat. Mud." He flicked his hand toward his manager, his eyes still on me. "Now go on."

Both of the other men followed his orders, neither of them looking happy about it.

I couldn't sell Skeeter out. I *wouldn't* sell Skeeter out. So what was I going to tell Mick? "Skeeter knows what you're up to, and he's not happy."

Mick laughed. "Since when does Skeeter confide in a *woman?*"

"I've heard things."

"What else have you heard?"

"Skeeter's planning to promote Bear Stevens." Telling him so was both a lie and a risk. But it was also an opportunity to see if Mick had been behind the attempts on Mason's life.

Mick's shoulders straightened. "Bear?" He grinned. "You don't say?"

"Bear's helping you, right?"

"And what makes you say that?"

"He's part of the plan to kill Mason, isn't he?"

Mick scooted forward in his seat and leaned his elbows on the table. "And how did little Daisy Miller get to be on a first-name basis with the Assistant District Attorney?"

Oh, crap. How was I going to explain that? "Every single girl in Fenton County knows about Mason Deveraux III."

"And how did you know someone tried to kill him? It wasn't in the news."

Oh crap. How was I going to explain that one? But wasn't the fact that Mick knew about it proof of his involvement?

"She's a badge bunny," Mason said.

My eyes flew wide open as I spun to face him.

He looked up at me with a convincing mixture of disgust and pity. "She hangs around the courthouse and the sheriff station. I knew she looked familiar, but now I realize where I've seen her. Hanging around outside my office. She must have overheard one of my conversations."

I put my hands on my hips and shot him a hateful glare. "That's an ugly way to put it, Mason Deveraux. I can't help it if you love me and just don't know it yet. If you'd just eaten that lemon pound cake with a lock of my hair baked into it, my love spell would have worked fine. You know, the cake I left on your office desk after you'd gone home that night? Did you find it?"

To me, Mason's non-response looked like an actor in a play who'd forgotten his lines. But I was fairly sure Mick would read it differently—interpreting his gape-eyed expression as horror.

I narrowed my eyes, deciding to up the ante. "And I smelled your office chair."

Mick shook his head as though he was trying to clear it. "*What?*"

Mason lifted his eyebrow. "You are batshit crazy if you think I'm ever gonna fall for you."

"You would," I said. "All you need to do is eat my lemon pound cake!"

"What is going on here?" Mick shouted. "Can we *focus?*"

"I am!" I insisted. "I don't think I could be any more focused on Mason Van de Camp Deveraux III if I tried." I gave Mason an exaggerated look of longing.

"Hey!" Lowry grunted. "What about me?"

I gave him a sympathetic look. "Don't worry, darlin'. Since Mr. Deveraux hasn't come to his senses yet, you can fill in until he does. What do you think about wearing a tie and shouting out legal terms while we're in the throes of passion?"

Lowry's eyes widened in shock.

"Enough!" Mick slammed his hand on the table, and I jumped. "Are you telling me that you don't really know anything useful?"

And here we were again. Where was Jed? "I know that Mr. Deveraux puts his shoes on left then right."

"What a creeper," Lowry muttered under his breath.

"Damn, Lowry." Mud shook his head. "You dodged a bullet with that nutcase."

"Who cares?" Mick growled. "Why would something like that matter at all, let alone in the situation at hand?"

"I'll tell you why!" I shrieked. "Puttin' on your shoes like that is backwards. Everyone else puts their shoes on right, then left." He gave me a confused stare. "It means I have to switch up the lemon pound cake love spell if I'm gonna make it work."

"Okay, Nutso Baker," Mick said with a cringe. "I'm gonna grant your wish. You're gonna get to spend plenty of quality time with the ADA. How does eternity sound?" He nodded to the bouncer. "Take them both to the shed and then take care of them."

"Wait!" I said. "Was I right? Were you the one trying to kill Mason?"

"So now you're Veronica Mars, trying to solve a case?"

"No," I snorted. "I just want to know if I was right. I have this thing about bein' right."

He rolled his eyes. "No, I had no reason to kill him. Not until tonight. It wasn't me." He flicked his hand.

The bouncer took a step forward and grabbed my arm again, his fingers twisting my skin. When I gasped, Mason jumped to his feet, his hands clenched into fists.

Mick laughed. "Settle down, Deveraux."

"Don't hurt her. She's obviously not part of this. Just let her go."

"No can do." Mick's voice lowered to a growl, and he nodded to the bouncer. "Take care of it. Lowry, you help them."

Lowry stood and strode over to me. "I want her."

"You can't have her, you idiot," Mick grunted. "She's a risk, and she's crazy town. Just take care of her."

Lowry jerked me free from the bouncer. "Then I'm at least going to take her out back first."

"I really don't want to go out back," I said, looking up at Lowry. "It's cold out there, and I'm not wearing a coat."

He leered at me. "You won't have to worry about bein' cold."

I cringed. Disgusting.

Mason had finally been pushed over the line. He lunged for Lowry, pulling him away from me. But Lowry and the bulky bouncer soon wrestled Mason into control.

"Deveraux," Mick said as though deep in thought. "If I didn't know any better, I'd guess that you actually care about Psycho Bitch here."

Mason's only answer was trying to jerk free from the bouncer's hold.

The sound of gunshots outside the door echoed through the room, and everyone froze for a half-second. If I could just get these guys to hold off shooting us, we had a chance at being saved.

Mick's eyes hardened. "Mud, go check it out." He pointed his gun at Mason. "How about you take a seat until we sort this out?"

Mason lowered himself into a chair, his hard eyes on the gun, but I saw him give a quick glance to my arm where Lowry was holding me.

"I'm takin' her out back," Lowry said.

"The hell you are," Mick said. "We're waiting here until we find out what's goin' on out there."

"We're business *partners*, Gentry. Despite what you think, you're not in charge. If I want to take her out back, I'll do it."

Mason's eyes shot to mine, and I could tell that he was thinking about doing something desperate to stop Lowry.

There were more muffled gunshots and yelling. The three men looked toward the door, and Mason took advantage of the distraction to jump out of his chair and grab Mick's arm. The gun clattered to the floor as Mason swung a punch at Mick's face. The bouncer jumped Mason and tried to pull him loose from Mick. Despite the bouncer having fifty pounds more muscle, Mason had determination on his side.

Lowry tugged me out of the way, and I watched in horror as the two men continued to attack Mason, who was holding his own while trying to get to the gun.

I jerked free of Lowry's hold with the intention of going after the gun myself, but he snagged my wrist. "Come on." Lowry opened the door and pulled me into the hallway.

Panicked, I tried to wrench myself free. Lowry's action distracted Mason, and the two men gained the advantage. They were about to beat Mason to a bloody pulp. "Mason!" I screamed and his head jerked up.

Mick took advantage of his distraction and brought the butt of a gun down on the back of Mason's head. He crumpled to the floor, unconscious.

"Mason!"

"Come *on*." Lowry dragged me to the back door, and I kicked and clawed, frantic to get free. The sound of fighting was a dull roar in the other room, and wisps of smoke floated under the door to the hall. The club was on fire.

Lowry got me to the back door, and I broke free for a half-second. I made a bolt toward the room where Mason was being kept, but Lowry snagged an arm around my waist and hauled my back into his chest.

"You're coming with *me*." He flung the back door open, and it banged into the exterior wall, bouncing back to hit Lowry's side. I grunted my frustration as I kicked his legs and clawed at his arms. Lowry's arm dug into my ribs as his hold tightened.

When the cold air hit my bare legs and arms, the reality of what was about to happen hit me hard. "*Let go of me!*"

"Do as the lady says, Lowry."

Lowry froze, and I stopped struggling, the man's voice flooding me with relief.

Skeeter Malcolm stood several feet away, holding a handgun that was aimed at Lowry and me.

Lowry hooked his arm around the front of my neck, putting me in a choke-hold. "Since when do you care about a piece of ass, Malcolm?"

"It's none of your damn business. Now let her go."

Lowry's hold on my neck tightened, and I fought to take a breath. "No. I don't think so. Go ahead and shoot her if you'd like."

"Hey!" I forced out through my limited air supply.

Skeeter's face was unreadable. I told myself to never play poker with him.

"Why's she so important to you?" Lowry asked. "She used to work at your club? You meet her at the pool hall?"

"It doesn't matter where I met her. All you need to know is that you better get your filthy hands off of her *now*."

"In the ten years I've known you, the only other woman you've shown any interest in is the Lady in Black," Lowry gasped, lifting his arm so my toes barely touched the ground. I fought to take a breath, and I was getting light-headed. "This is her, isn't it? Daisy's the Lady in Black?"

If Skeeter was surprised by Lowry's flight of logic or the fact that he'd called me Daisy, he didn't let on. He lifted his gun higher so it was eye level with Lowry behind me. "This is your last warning."

Lowry put a hand on the side of my head. "I'll snap her neck, Malcolm. Are you willing to put your precious 'Lady' at risk?"

"She won't be." His eyes narrowed, and the blast of his gun deafened my ear. Lowry's arm dropped, and I sucked in huge lungfuls of air. Lowry began to fall, and Skeeter pulled me to him.

"You okay?" he asked.

I started to shake and leaned into Skeeter as I stared at Lowry's body. He was lying at an awkward angle on the gravel parking lot, hole in his forehead. The realization that he'd almost killed me sank in—between that and the lack of oxygen, I felt close to passing out.

Skeeter grabbed my face and lifted it so his eyes pierced mine. *"Are you okay?"* His voice was menacing.

I nodded, still in shock.

He shrugged out of his coat and put it around my shoulders, then pulled out his phone. "I'll call Cal to pick us up."

"Wait!" I pulled loose. "Mason's in there, and he's unconscious."

Skeeter's face barely registered my comment. "I don't care."

"Skeeter, I'm not leaving him in there."

His jaw tensed. "You don't have a choice. I'm not letting you go back in there period, particularly not now that the building's burning."

"No! Stop! You promised to protect him."

"Not in this. I know he was here accepting a bribe. That makes our agreement null and void."

"You don't get to pick and choose what makes our agreement null and void! Since when did you become so high and mighty? Besides, he wasn't taking a bribe! He was there trying to take Mick Gentry down. Not that any of that matters! We had an *agreement*."

He glared at me. "I said no." He snatched my arm and started dragging me further from the building.

"You're no better than the rest of them in there."

"I never claimed I was." Skeeter's black sedan pulled around the side of the building and stopped next to us. He reached for the back door and opened it, giving me a little push. "Now get in the car."

I turned around and tried to bolt, but he pushed my head down as he shoved me in the car.

"Skeeter, *please!*"

"*No.*"

I started to cry. Even if I managed to get away from him, how was I going to get Mason out of the building? "I'll give you anything you want. I'll give you six months as the Lady in Black. No questions asked. *Please*."

He stopped shoving me, so I grabbed his arm and clung to it.

"Why would I save Deveraux's ass? That man would have me gunned down in a heartbeat."

"No, he wouldn't. He wants what he sees as justice, and that wouldn't include killing you. If you were in that building, *he'd* save *you*."

Skeeter snorted. "Not likely."

"He would." But when that didn't sway him, I said, "Then do it for me."

He studied my face, a hard look in his eyes. "Anything I want for six months."

"As the Lady in Black."

A wicked gleam filled his eyes. "You're more like me than them, you know."

I gasped. "What are you talking about?"

"You're right. Deveraux and Simmons each have their own code of ethics, but you and me . . ." He grinned, pulling me closer. "We realize there are a lot more gray areas than black and white."

I shook my head. I wasn't sure I liked what he was implying.

"I'll go find him, but you stay out here. If I catch you in there, I'm going to drag you out, throw you in the back of my car, and leave him to burn."

I had no doubt he meant it. "Okay."

His eyes searched mine. "Six months, Lady. You give me six months?"

"Yes."

"Where is he?"

"Go through the back door. He's in the room directly across."

He pulled out his phone and took several steps away from me to make a call, but he spoke so low I couldn't hear him. When he hung up, he pointed to his car. *"Wait there."* Then he strode to the back door and disappeared inside.

Cal got out of the car and cast a perplexed look in my direction, but otherwise ignored me as I paced back and forth, fighting off tears. A good minute passed, and there wasn't any sign of either of them as I began to hear sirens in the distance. Thick black smoke poured out of the vents in the roof, and my hysteria started to win out. But seconds later, the back door flung open, and three figures stumbled out. Two of the men were Skeeter and Jed, and they were dragging an unconscious Mason.

They continued to half-carry him away from the building and dropped him onto a strip of grass. I tumbled to my knees next to him and picked up his wrist, gasping with relief when his pulse thrummed against my fingertips.

I looked up at both men and forced out through my tears, "Thank you."

The sirens were closer, and Skeeter jerked on Jed's arm. "Let's go."

Jed hesitated, then climbed into the car after Skeeter. As they sped away, Mason started to cough.

"Mason?"

He looked up at me and sat up, releasing a groan and holding the side of his head as he pulled me to his chest. "Rose? Thank God." He lost his breath with a new round of coughing. "I was terrified he'd killed you. Are you okay?"

"I'm fine."

"What were you *doing* here?" I heard the anger in his voice, but he held me tight. "Joe told me he was putting you in protective custody."

"There was no way I was hanging around with the deputy from hell, so I escaped." Then I gushed out, "I found your cell phone number in Dolly Parton's box, and I couldn't figure out why she would have it, and Neely Kate confessed she heard a rumor that you were accepting a bribe and had a big meeting tonight, and then you said you wanted to take me away tomorrow . . . I thought you might be taking a bribe, Mason, although for the life of me, I couldn't figure out how you could be involved in such a thing. It didn't matter, Mason. I couldn't let you go through with such a thing." He gave me a blank look, and I worried his new head injury had addled his brain. "I was trying to stop you from taking a bribe. I tried to reach you all day."

"I wasn't taking a bribe, Rose. I was trying to get solid evidence on him to bring bribery charges against him."

"But Joe . . ."

"Joe knew all about it. I was supposed to meet the owner somewhere else, but one of his men brought me here. Joe's men were set up at the other place, and Mick's guy lost them. Only we didn't know the owner was Mick until I met him face to face tonight."

"So did someone really try to kill you? Or was that part of the cover story?"

"Yes, but my best guess is that it was Mick."

"He said it wasn't."

"Mick Gentry's a liar as well as a thief and a murderer."

"And he's missing again," Joe said, walking over to us. He glared down at me. "*What the hell are you doing here?*"

I cringed. "Looking for Dolly Parton."

"*At a strip club?*" he shouted.

I gave him a sheepish shrug. "It was the last place she was seen."

Mason climbed to his feet and pulled me up with him. "You're certain Gentry got away?"

"Unfortunately, I have two witnesses who saw him run out the front door. What happened?"

"Nikko. Gentry's men had him all along. They tortured him into admitting his arrangement with me. They killed him."

"Damn it." Joe put his hands on his hips and shook his head in disgust and disappointment.

"They'd just told me when one of the bouncers dragged Rose into the room. They planned to take us both out back, but a fight broke out in the other room. The manager and his goon knocked me out. That last thing I remember was hitting the floor as Lowry was pulling Rose to the back door." Mason glanced down at me. "How'd you get away from Lowry?" He looked over his shoulder, grimacing. "And is that him dead by the back door?"

Oh crap. I couldn't tell them about Skeeter's involvement. And how was I going to explain how I was wearing his coat? "I don't know. He dragged me outside, and some man confronted him. I plum passed out from fright, and when I came to, Rich Lowry was lying dead next to me."

Both men looked less than convinced by my story.

"How'd you know so much about Skeeter Malcolm's business?" Mason asked.

I swallowed, hoping I didn't look nervous. "I heard it workin' tonight. People'll tell bartenders anything."

Joe turned to Mason. "If you got knocked out, then how'd you get out here?" Joe asked.

"I don't know." He looked down at me. "Rose?"

"Uh . . . two guys carried you out and dropped you in the grass."

"Who were they?"

I shrugged. "I don't know."

"Good Samaritans?" Joe asked.

I almost laughed. Skeeter would hate being called a Good Samaritan.

"So Mick and his men killed Nikko. But what happened to Dolly Parton?" I asked.

"I think she's really in hiding," Mason said. "I think she saw something and took off, just like you suspected." He shook his head. "But I never put together the connection that Dolly worked here. I only knew of her as Sapphire, and then it was only hearing her name in passing from Nikko. You only mentioned that she worked in a bar."

"How did Dolly have your cell phone number?" I asked. "I found it in her box at Billy Jack's."

"Probably from Nikko. He approached me about a month ago, telling me they were going to bribe the DA to drop charges against one of their buddies. I didn't want him to use my official phone line in case my boss caught wind of it, so I gave him my cell. I've suspected the DA has been on the take for years. Joe and I are trying to build evidence against him. Only a handful of people knew."

"So who broke into our house?"

Both men remained silent, and Joe finally answered, "I don't know."

I studied Mason's face. "Did you get what you needed?"

"No. While I now have evidence they tried to bribe me, there's nothing pinning any previous transgressions to my boss. I can file charges against the men in that room for bribery, Nikko's murder, and our attempted murder, but my boss is still scot-free."

"Is it my fault?" I asked.

"No." Mason's face softened. "While I'm far from thrilled you're here, the truth is you helped save my life. That, and the brawl that broke out in the other room. They knew what I was doing from Nikko, which is why they told me to meet them at the bar in Big Thief Hollow to evade Joe. They knew he'd be there."

I looked around, suddenly remembering Neely Kate. I nearly panicked when I saw my truck and she wasn't inside. "Oh my word, where's Neely Kate?"

Joe shifted his weight. "She's fine—mad as a hornet, but fine. She was trying to get through the front door to get to you, but a deputy held her back. We should let her know you're okay."

We walked around the building to find her, and her face broke into relief when she saw us. "You scared me half to death!" she exclaimed, pulling me into a hug. "Don't ever do that again!"

Joe snorted. "Good luck with *that*."

"I heard that," I muttered.

"I intended you to," he said before he stomped off.

***

The next day, Dolly Parton, who'd been hiding at an old co-worker's house in Louisiana, finally resurfaced. She told Joe that Billy Jack had been helping Diamond and the owner of Gems. Dolly Parton had heard things at the club and was about to help Nikko deliver more information to Mason, hoping to get her latest solicitation charges dropped in the process. But Billy Jack caught wind and told Diamond, hoping for a payoff . . . and perhaps some good will from the pretty lady. Mick's men had captured Nikko that Friday night at Gems, but Dolly managed to take off in Nikko's car. Billy Jack must have experienced a change of heart when he called Neely Kate and arranged to meet with us, but someone had decided to stop him—in a permanent way—from leaking any information.

Skeeter swore up and down that the attempt on Mason's life had been carried out by his former associates, while Joe tied Eric Davidson to the crime via Mick. His theory was that Eric had tried to kill Mason after finding out he was setting them up. But Mason's phone hadn't been recovered, and I still had an unsettling feeling that the threat came from another source—Joe's father. Not that Joe or Mason would even consider it.

I just needed to find a way to prove it.

Chapter Thirty-One

On Sunday morning, I woke up snuggled next to Mason. He nuzzled my neck while his hands roamed my body under the covers.

"This is a pleasant way to wake up," I murmured drowsily.

"I thought so. I told you I was planning the entire day, and this is just the start," he said, rolling me over onto my back. "I have a couple of early Christmas gifts for you. Which do you want first?"

That woke me up. "I love presents."

He grinned. "I know. Almost as much as I do."

That was debatable, but I knew better than to tackle it with the former Pulaski Academy debate captain. "How can I choose which one I want if I don't have any clues?"

"They're both bigger than a bread basket."

I laughed, pulling his mouth to mine for a kiss. "You're the best present ever."

"That's a sad statement indeed," he teased, pulling my nightgown over my head. "I hope to rectify that. But later. Now you've distracted me," he murmured against my lips.

A half hour later, I lay next to him, half asleep again. "I don't ever want to get out of this bed."

"Not even for your presents?"

"It's not Christmas yet, Mason."

"And that's why I called them *early* Christmas gifts."

"Can I try to guess what they are?"

"You can try, but you'll never succeed."

"Will you tell me what you have planned for the day?"

"I thought we'd go to a Christmas tree farm and pick out a tree together."

My face broke out into a huge smile.

He grinned. "I take it you approve?"

"Yes. But we don't have any ornaments."

His smile wavered a bit. "You have two options. We can buy some at Wal-Mart, although those are probably pretty picked over by now. Or we can use the ornaments I found in the basement."

"Dora's?" I whispered.

He tucked a strand of hair behind my ear. "It's up to you, sweetheart. Whatever makes you happy."

"I already am, Mason."

"Then just imagine how happy you'll be after you get your presents."

"You keep talking about these presents, but I'm beginning to think they don't exist."

His face broke out into a mischievous grin. "Is that so?" He crawled over me and off the side of the bed, tossing the covers to the bottom of the mattress.

"It's cold!" I giggled.

He picked my nightgown up off the floor and handed it to me as he got my robe. When I put the robe on, he tied the belt, grinning. "I can think of some fun for this sash later."

"Mason." I flushed, and he laughed as he pulled me close and kissed me again.

"I don't think I can ever get enough of you, Rose. But I'd sure like to live a long, full life trying."

I grabbed fistfuls of his T-shirt and smiled up at him. "I like the sound of that."

"Present time."

He took my hand and led me downstairs and into the kitchen. "Surprise."

It took me a second to figure out what my present was. On the table, Mason had set out a rolling pin, cookie cutters, and a cookie sheet. I looked up at him.

His grin spread. "That's not all." He opened the refrigerator and pulled out a bowl covered in plastic wrap. "Sugar cookie dough."

"You made that? When?"

"Last night. After you went to bed." He set the bowl on the kitchen table and stood in front of me.

"But you don't cook."

His eyebrows lifted. "Or bake. But Mom gave me the recipe, along with some pointers. And I may have called her at midnight and woke her up in my panic because I didn't understand how to knead the cookie dough."

"You did that for me?" I asked, tears in my eyes.

"This was your dream, Rose. To decorate sugar cookies with your family. We're a family now. You, me, and Muffy. How could I not give it to you? I want to spend the rest of my life making sure you get all of your dreams."

I started to cry.

"Hey." He looked worried as he tipped my chin up to study my face. "Did I do something wrong?"

I shook my head. "No. You made everything perfect."

I kissed him, showing him how much I loved him, pushing him backward until the backs of his legs hit the edge of the table.

"I have to warn you, Ms. Gardner, that it's against the health code to have sex on the same surface you use to roll out your cookies, but now that I know that baking is so fun, I might have to become a pastry chef."

We spent two hours rolling out the dough and baking the cookies, making the frosting, and decorating our bounty. When we were done, Mason pulled my back to his chest, his arms wrapped around my stomach as we looked at the cookies. I laughed at Mason's, which were covered in globs of frosting. "You should definitely reconsider your new career path."

"You're just jealous of my savant-like talent."

"Yeah," I laughed as I spun around to kiss him. "That's it."

"You have another present," he said between my kisses.

"Later." I pushed him onto a chair and straddled his lap.

"It involves Neely Kate."

I lifted my head in surprise. "What?"

He laughed. "I knew that would get your attention."

"What is it?"

"It's in my pocket. Reach in and get it."

"That sounds naughty."

"I hadn't planned to give it to you this way, but your attempts to molest me caught me off guard."

I shifted and reached into his pocket, pulling out an envelope. "What is it?"

"This one is actually wrapped. You're supposed to unwrap it."

"It isn't wrapped," I teased. "It's in an envelope."

He grinned, obviously excited. "*Open it.*"

I gave him a kiss, grinning against his lips. "You're so bossy."

"Sometimes you like it that way," he said in a low voice that sent flutters through me.

Shaking my head, I opened the envelope. After I pulled out a paper and scanned the print, I looked up at him in shock. "Tickets to see *Wicked* in New Orleans?"

"I thought you and Neely Kate could use a few days away from Fenton County drama. You can drive down to New Orleans, see the play, eat beignets, Christmas shop, and just relax and have some girl time. I've booked you a room at a nice hotel. With room service even."

"Mason, I've never left Arkansas."

"I know, sweetheart." He gave me a soft smile and cupped my cheek. "Don't you think it's about time? You're ready."

"But without you?"

"You can do anything and everything you want. With or without me."

Fear rooted in my chest. "Are you going to leave me?"

His eyes flew open in surprise. "No! How can you think that? I have to go to Little Rock for a few days, and I didn't want you sitting here alone. So I checked with Ronnie to see if he was okay with Neely Kate going, and he thought it was a great idea too, especially since Neely Kate's not working right now. He's giving her the surprise today too." My phone started to ring with Neely Kate's ringtone, and he laughed. "We decided to give it to you girls at the same time, which is why I was so insistent you open it now."

I grabbed the back of his head and kissed him.

"Aren't you going to answer that?" he asked.

"It can wait."

His arms tightened around my back. And as he kissed me, I wondered what Mason was going to do in Little Rock. But I'd figure that out later.

I had some shenanigans to attend to first.

Thank you for reading *Thirty-Three and a Half Shenanigans*. Look for the next Rose Gardner Mystery in the spring of 2015, although Denise tends to spring surprise Rose novellas on her readers and often posts them on her website as free reads for newsletter subscribers.

For more information about the Rose Gardner Mystery series and Denise Grover Swank's other projects, check out DeniseGroverSwank.com

Also sign up for her mailing list to for current information and periodic free reads available only to her newsletter subscribers. http://denisegroverswank.com/mailing-list/

Acknowledgments

With every book I write, I thank God that I have Angela Polidoro to look over my mess and help me make it into something people want to read. She gets me and trusts that I can send her a big pile of poo in first round edits and send back something semi-wonderful for second line edits. I trust her with my stories and my characters, and that's huge.

Many thanks to Shannon Page and her exceptional copyediting. She helps put the extra polish on my words. Much gratitude to Cynthia L. Moyer for her wonderful proofreading, and to Carolina Valedez Miller, a new proofreader for this book. It definitely won't be her last project with me.

And many, many thanks to my amazing beta readers for this book—Rhonda Cowsert, Emily Pearson, and Anne Childon. Friends don't let friends look stupid in print. I swear we need T-shirts.

The character of Deputy Abbie Lee Hoffstetter was created by reader Tracy Burrows. The attorney Carter Hale was also semi-created by reader Devin Sauter. Reader Wendy Gitschier Eulinger won a contest for creating a character named Anna, but I decided to save her for Thirty-Four and a Half (??) and give her a larger role.

I am thankful every day for my children who tolerate my insane schedule and don't resent me for it. I try to carve time whenever and wherever I can for them. As long as they know that I love them to the moon and back, everything else is gravy.

And to my amazing and wonderful readers—my most sincere thank you. You encourage me to keep going, to keep telling my stories. I'm not shouting in the dark. You hear me.

About the Author

Denise Grover Swank was born in Kansas City, Missouri and lived in the area until she was nineteen. Then she became a nomadic gypsy, living in five cities, four states and ten houses over the course of ten years before she moved back to her roots. She speaks English and smattering of Spanish and Chinese which she learned through an intensive Nick Jr. immersion period. Her hobbies include witty Facebook comments (in own her mind) and dancing in her kitchen with her children. (Quite badly if you believe her offspring.) Hidden talents include the gift of justification and the ability to drink massive amounts of caffeine and still fall asleep within two minutes. Her lack of the sense of smell allows her to perform many unspeakable tasks. She has six children and hasn't lost her sanity. Or so she leads you to believe.

You can find out more about Denise and her other books at:
www.denisegroverswank.com
or email her at denisegroverswank@gmail.com

CPSIA information can be obtained
at www.ICGtesting.com
Printed in the USA
FSOW03n2246211016
26447FS